Praise for Lulu Taylor

'Pure indulgence and perfect reading
for a dull January evening'
Sun

'[This] engrossing romantic saga is a
hugely enjoyable, escapist treat'
Sunday Mirror

'Utterly compelling. A really excellent winter's story'
Lucy Diamond

'Taylor is at the top of the chick-lit tree with her
beautifully written, emotionally compelling stories,
and this is perfectly timed for Christmas'
Daily Mail

'Wonderfully written ... this indulgent read
is totally irresistible'
Closer

'A creepy story of obsession and deception.
Very chilling'
Irish Sunday Mirror

'A gripping psychological thriller'
Essentials Magazine

'This is a fantastic, all-consuming read'
Heat

'[A] gripping story'
Hello!

'The cold, snowy cover and winter setting make
this a great stocking filler for your mum or sister'
thelittlewildwoodkitchen.com

'The book is full of mystery and intrigue, successfully
keeping me guessing until the very end ... An evocative
read, full of dramatic secrets that will make the reader gasp'
www.novelicious.com

'A poignant, sophisticated and romantic love story'
www.handwrittengirl.com

THE
WINTER
SECRET

Lulu Taylor's first novel, *Heiresses*, was nominated for the RNA Reader's Choice award, and she has gone on to write many more well-received books. With *The Winter Children*, *The Snow Rose* and *Her Frozen Heart*, she became a *Sunday Times* top ten bestseller. After many years in London, she now lives in Dorset with her husband and two children.

www.lulutaylor.co.uk
@misslulutaylor

THE
WINTER
SECRET

Lulu Taylor

PAN BOOKS

First published 2018 by Pan Books
an imprint of Pan Macmillan
The Smithson, 6 Briset Street, London EC1M 5NR
Associated companies throughout the world
www.panmacmillan.com

ISBN 978-1-5098-4073-1

7 9 8

A CIP catalogue record for this book is available from the British Library.

Typeset in 10.5/15 pt Sabon LT Std by Jouve (UK), Milton Keynes
Printed and bound by CPI Group (UK) Ltd, Croydon, CR0 4YY

Visit www.panmacmillan.com to read more about all our books
and to buy them. You will also find features, author interviews and
news of any author events, and you can sign up for e-newsletters
so that you're always first to hear about our new releases.

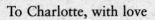
To Charlotte, with love

THE
WINTER
SECRET

Prologue

Xenia thought she had never seen Mama look as ravishing as she did today: her dark hair was perfectly curled, her lips painted a tantalising scarlet so that she appeared to have a mouth made of velvet, her green eyes sparkling below swooping lashes.

She stood at the top of an elegant staircase, the lights catching the diamonds in her hair and at her neck, making them flash like tiny camera bulbs. The real cameras were aimed at her as she stood on her staircase to nowhere; the huge ones straddled by the cameramen like great beasts, the angled lenses hanging from the rig above the soundstage, where they lived with the many-coloured spotlights and the dangling microphones.

Mama wore a beautiful black evening gown, her hair elaborately arranged and studded with jewels. Her shoulders rose white and creamy from the veil wound around her bodice and encasing her breasts. She looked proud, arrogant and unafraid.

Xenia watched from the shadows, almost shivering as the

film approached its denouement. She'd seen so many of the scenes, she knew the story, she knew Mama's lines so well she could almost mouth along with them, and yet . . . it was so real, so fresh, it was like hearing it for the first time. The crowd at the bottom of the staircase gazed upwards, spellbound by the woman on the landing above. 'You've all come here today to find out one thing. You want to know who killed Delilah.'

All eyes were on glittering, beautiful Mama. Every light and every camera were turned on her. Up on her staircase, Mama could see nothing but the glare of the lights. She didn't know what went on in the darkness below, and she must never know. Xenia understood that.

Mama lifted her white arms dramatically, raised her chin and said, 'Do you want to know who killed Delilah? It's very simple. *I* killed her. And I'm glad I did. I'd do it again tomorrow – and so would every one of you!'

A shocked gasp came from the crowd and a murmur of surprise and outrage.

'But you don't know the truth – you don't know the whole story. When you do, you'll understand. And you'll know who's at the bottom of all of this. You see, the real Delilah was dead long before any of you even knew her!'

A gunshot rang out. Mama stiffened, gasped, her expression froze and she clutched her chest. Then she stumbled and sank to the ground, fighting for breath.

A shudder of horror convulsed Xenia.

Mama's lover ran to her side and took her in his arms. 'No! No. Stay with me, Delilah, stay with me!'

But Mama's lashes were trembling, her lips falling open, her body weakening. 'It's no use, it's too late,' she whispered. 'Please, Sam, try not to hate me, won't you?'

'I don't hate you – I love you!' Sam pulled her close to him as the camera soared in for a close up of Mama's beautiful face.

'Please,' she whispered, her eyes shining with tears, 'tell me you love me again.'

'I love you, Delilah!'

'Don't call me that. Call me Sarah. Just once. That's all I ask.'

'Oh, Sarah, don't go. Don't leave me! I love you.' Her lover dropped his head on her shoulder as he wept.

Her eyes closed, her body relaxed, and the camera lingered lovingly on her face, as exquisite in death as in life.

It's not real. It's pretend. Mama is alive.

But down below, in the darkness, Xenia sobbed as if her heart would break.

PART ONE

Chapter One

'Open your eyes.'

I love that voice, thought Buttercup. The car had stopped, the engine was off at last, and in the sudden lucid quiet, Charles's tone seemed particularly intense. It filled her mind even more now she had her eyes shut: that low, husky voice, with a hoarseness that seemed to have been built into it as part of its natural state. It was one of the first things that attracted her to Charles, a sound like velvet sandpaper as he said, *Buttercup Wilcox? That's the most marvellous name I've ever heard.*

They'd clearly arrived somewhere but Buttercup asked anyway, 'Are we here?'

'Of course. Open them.'

Charles had insisted she keep her eyes shut from the time they left the main road. He wanted the first glimpse to be the best, so she got the full impact. She'd laughed and protested but obeyed: life with Charles was full of surprises and they were always delightful and exciting.

Buttercup opened her eyes, blinking in the unaccustomed daylight, and gasped. 'Oh, Charles. It's beautiful!'

She was looking at an exquisite house of golden stone that even on a dank January day looked warm against the cold grey sky. Its narrow diamond-paned windows glittered in what little sunshine filtered through the clouds; its chimneys soared upwards, grand and graceful at the same time. 'Just beautiful,' she breathed.

'It is, isn't it?' Charles smiled with pleasure at her obvious admiration. 'I'm so glad you like it, but poor old Charcombe wasn't always so pretty. You should have seen it when we bought it.' He flung his car door open and jumped out. 'Come on. I want to show you inside.'

He was around at her side in an instant, pulling open her door and offering her a hand to help her out of the low-slung sports car. 'First impressions?'

'It's wonderful.'

He grinned at her. 'Good! You're going to love it, I just know it.'

Charles led the way to the huge wooden panelled door with a great brass doorknob in the centre, a large verdigris lantern in the shape of an orb hanging above it from the porch roof. He opened it, stepping aside to let her go in first.

She hardly knew what to say as she went into a vast square hall hung with oil paintings, its ceiling a riot of colour with painted frescoes of gods, goddesses and fat putti frolicking in the clouds. Marble busts on plinths stood along the walls and in the centre of the room a large round table held a giant globe vase with white hydrangea spilling out in frilly abundance, a fragment of summer in the depth of winter. When Charles had talked about his place in Dorset, she'd envisaged a cottage, a holiday getaway, perhaps a little rough around the edges, a bit make-do.

I should have known better.

Everything with Charles was bigger and bolder than normal life, grander, richer. The London flat he mentioned so casually had turned out to be a penthouse apartment in Westminster at the top of a large house owned by him – very different from her third-floor attic conversion in Fulham. Perhaps that was why he was taking her into his rarefied existence slowly, step by step, as if he didn't want to frighten her off. He'd pretended at first he was a successful business-man, nothing out of the ordinary. It was only now, seven months after their courtship had begun, that she was learn-ing how extraordinary he really was. She was glad it was that way round, that she'd fallen for him before she'd been shown the trappings of his life.

A beautiful black Labrador came bounding across the hall, her claws clacking on the marble floor, barking a wel-come, her tail wagging furiously.

'Who's this?' Buttercup asked, delighted, holding out her hand.

'Oh, that's Tippi.' Charles watched her patting and stroking the silky black head as Tippi looked up adoringly. 'You've won her over, darling. Not that I'm surprised: you win everyone's hearts.'

Buttercup laughed. 'You're intent on making me the vain-est person in the world. Why is she called Tippi?'

'After Tippi Hedren, the movie star. It's rather a joke. Look, I'll show you why.' He turned and led her through a door into a large, light drawing room with a row of French windows looking out over a terrace and the manicured garden beyond. It was furnished in elegant good taste with blue silk sofas, antique furniture, elaborately draped curtains and vases of white roses. Knick-knacks and silver photograph frames sat on polished surfaces.

'What a pretty room!' exclaimed Buttercup, looking about. Tippi pressed against her legs as if unwilling to lose the soft touch of Buttercup's hand on her head.

'Yes, isn't it? It gets light all day and I'm very fond of the view of the garden. But that's not what I wanted to show you.' Charles pointed up at the oil painting that hung above the fireplace, a pair of silver candlesticks on either side. 'Do you know who that is?'

Buttercup stared at the painting. It was a large portrait of a woman, dressed in the style of the 1940s in a white evening dress, her fine dark hair in waves and held back by diamond clips. She gazed out of the canvas, beautiful and self-possessed with a trace of insolence in her striking slanted green eyes and on the dark red lips. 'I don't think so,' she said slowly, puzzled. 'But she looks familiar somehow. Who is she? A member of your family?'

Charles laughed delightedly. 'No! Don't you recognise her? She's Natalie Rowe!'

'Oh! Of course, the actress. Now you say it, I can see it.'

'I can't believe you didn't know her at once – she was a

huge star in the forties. You've seen *Delilah*, haven't you? She was brilliant in it, it made her name.'

'I'm afraid not,' Buttercup said apologetically. 'I've heard of it, of course, but I've never seen it.'

Charles looked at her sorrowfully. 'So woefully uneducated. We'll have to do something about that. It's a classic of the film noir genre.' He gestured up at the painting. 'And this painting was actually done for the film itself. It's in the movie!'

'Goodness.' Buttercup looked at the painting with new respect. 'I'm impressed.'

'Calling the dog Tippi was a sort of joke about film stars in the house. Natalie Rowe lived here, you see, after she made *Delilah*. This picture has been here ever since. Her daughter sold us the house, and left it here with strict instructions it should never be moved. I was rather tickled by the idea, so I agreed. And the old bird lives just down the lane, so I daren't move it now in case she puts a curse on me.' He laughed.

Buttercup laughed too. There was always something extraordinary happening around Charles. It was one of the things that beguiled her so much about him: he made life interesting and unusual, filled it with fantasy and dreams and then turned them into reality. 'What a wonderful story. I'll have to watch the film now.'

'You certainly will. But there's something else I want to show you.'

Just then, there was a rapid knock on the door and a woman walked into the room, her expression anxious. She was casually dressed in jeans, wiping damp hands on them as she entered, her brown hair pulled back into a rough ponytail and her deep-set grey eyes worried. 'I'm so sorry, Mr Redmain, I didn't hear you come in!' Her voice had a soft Scottish lilt. 'I would have come out at once if I'd known you'd arrived.'

'Don't worry, Carol, it's fine,' Charles said cheerfully. 'I was in such a hurry to show off my treasures, I didn't come to say hello. Darling, this is the marvellous Carol, my excellent housekeeper and sorter-out of all manner of problems. She and her husband Steve live here all year round, keeping an eye on everything for me.'

'Hello,' Buttercup said, smiling. So this was another of the very many sorter-outers in Charles's life. He seemed to be surrounded by a team of extremely efficient and trusted helpers who made everything around him run as smoothly as possible. 'Very nice to meet you.'

'You too. Are you—'

Charles interrupted. 'Be an angel, Carol, and get some tea on for us, will you? I want to show this wonderful creature the Redmain Room. Give us twenty minutes or so, and we'll be back to have it in here.'

'Yes, sir.' Carol turned and went out, Tippi following her with a wagging tail.

Buttercup raised her eyebrows. 'Redmain Room?'

'Come on, all will be revealed.'

It was Charles's irrepressible appetite for life that had drawn Buttercup to him at a time when her own existence had been bleak and full of misery. She was reminded of it now as he hurried up the stairs in front of her, eager to share everything with her, and her heart swelled with love for him. He had made her happy again, excited to be alive, after her father's death had left her grief-stricken and hopeless.

With him, I could suddenly see all the possibilities that life could offer.

His enthusiasm was so infectious. He seemed to know about masses of different subjects, and to have travelled everywhere and seen just about all there was to see. Even though he was only a dozen years older than Buttercup, he'd had several careers, founded businesses and lived abroad.

And got married. Had children. Been divorced.

Buttercup tried not to think about that. Someone like Charles was never going to come without baggage, she understood that. She knew about the end of his marriage and had met James and Charlotte, his teenage children. It might not be the perfect scenario but she couldn't help the choices her heart made, and she would rather have Charles and his baggage than a lesser man with a clean slate. It was part of what made him so interesting, after all.

Even now, as they were heading up the stairs, he was talking nineteen to the dozen about the restoration of the house after he'd bought it. True to form, he'd learned all he could about the period and its architecture and styles of art, furniture and fabric. Then, with the help of experts and craftsmen, he'd gone about recreating this place, restoring it to its original splendour.

'I used local carvers and gilders and specialist artisans too,' he said as they walked along a thickly carpeted corridor together. 'Luckily, this part of the world is crammed with the most amazing people, the kind who devote their lives to traditional skills and conservation. Ah!' He stopped before a closed door, his eyes sparkling. 'Here we are. This is the most precious room in the house. It's taken years to create.' He put his hand on the brass handle. 'Are you ready?'

'Yes, never readier.' She smiled, wondering what on earth he wanted to show her. 'Let's do it.'

'Good.' He opened the door and went in, flicking a light switch to illuminate the darkness with tiny concealed spotlights.

Buttercup followed him in, curious and a little trepidatious. The room was small, not much bigger than a box room, and panelled in dark wood. Red velvet curtains hung at the mullioned window and a blind shut out the sunlight outside. Oil paintings of old sea battles hung on the walls, and around the room were glass-topped mahogany cases, carefully lit by spotlights in the ceiling. In the centre of the room was a wooden dais that held a chair and directly behind it a large oil painting of an old ship in full rig. The gold plate on the frame read 'HMS *Cymbeline*'. Next to the painting on one side was a marble bust of a noble-looking man in a tricorn hat, and on the other, an old leather-covered cylinder was mounted on the wall.

'Look,' Charles said, clearly bursting with pride. He waved a hand around the room. 'What do you think?'

'It's . . . marvellous,' Buttercup said, hiding her mild bewilderment. 'What an achievement.'

Charles looked solemn. 'It's been a labour of love to collect this. Museums would give their eye-teeth for some of this stuff. Look at this chair!'

He moved towards it and Buttercup followed. The chair, which looked like a particularly heavy dining chair, was dark wood upholstered with a sandy-coloured velvet on its seat and arms. The back was elaborately carved and, as she got closer, Buttercup saw that there were letters running along the top edge.

'England expects every man to do his duty,' she read out loud. 'Oh, I see. Nelson. Trafalgar.'

'That's right.' Charles looked pleased. 'The original message was that England *confides* that every man will do his duty, but Nelson was persuaded to say "expects" as it was already in the flag signal vocabulary, whereas "confides" would have to be spelled out so it would take longer. They shortened it again for the carving. And look, below that . . .' He pointed to more carved letters below that read '*Cymbeline*' and around them '21 October 1805'. 'This commemorates the ship my ancestor Edward Redmain captained at Trafalgar.' He nodded towards the marble bust of the man in the tricorn hat. 'That's him. And this house belonged to him – he bought it with some of his prize money. That's why I simply had to have it.'

'Goodness,' breathed Buttercup, impressed. 'So was this his chair?'

'Well . . . it might have been. Quite a few were made, to be given to all the ships' officers to commemorate their part in the battle. He definitely would have had one.' Charles pointed at the leather cylinder on the wall. 'But that is most certainly his telescope. And I have his shoe buckles too. And look here, his stall plate for Westminster Abbey – all the captains got one as a reward . . .'

'How amazing!' she'd said, sincerely impressed. 'No wonder you're proud.'

'Edward Redmain was a real hero. And to have his house again – to live in it myself, with his treasures around me – that makes me proud. Hugely proud.' Charles had reached out to take her hand. 'I hope you can understand that.'

'I do, completely.' She hugged him. 'You're so incredible, Charles. Imagine how impressed and overwhelmed Captain Redmain would be, if he could see you now and everything you've done to commemorate him!'

He lifted her face to him and stared at her, his expression serious. 'It means everything to me that you could say something like that. I knew as soon as we met that you are the woman of my dreams, and every day you make me more certain. Darling, I know it's very soon. We've only been together seven months but I'm surer about this than I have been about anything in my whole life. I love you, and I want to marry you.'

Buttercup stared at him, his words sinking in. She had considered it, imagined it, even dreamed of it, but never quite prepared herself for the reality of Charles asking her to be his wife. She felt a surge of happiness mixed with something like peace, as though she'd arrived home after a long journey. 'Oh, Charles,' she whispered. Her eyes filled with tears.

He looked immediately worried. 'Have I rushed things? Have I spoiled it? We can wait as long as you want.'

'No.' She hugged him again, tightly, inhaling the sandalwood and musk of his cologne. 'It's perfect. You're perfect. The house is perfect. We can raise a family here, it's divine. A parcel of beautiful children in this beautiful place.'

'So you will?' His voice cracked suddenly with emotion. 'Because I love you so much – you know that, don't you?'

She nodded, unable to speak for a moment. She felt that Charles alone in the whole world could fill the gap left by her father's death. With him, she could face the future and make a happy life for them both and the family she hoped they would have.

'Yes. And I love you too. Of course I'll marry you.'

Chapter Two

Twenty-two months later

Buttercup came down the stairs in her riding gear, her boots clacking loudly on the marble floor as she headed in the direction of the boot room. In her haste, she almost bumped into Carol as she emerged from the kitchen carrying a tray loaded with a coffee pot, milk jug and cups.

'Sorry!' Buttercup said. 'I shouldn't rush so much but I'm off to meet Phil – he's taken Milky out for some early exercise.'

'It's fine,' Carol said, 'but can I borrow you for a moment? That couple have arrived early and Mr Redmain is still out looking at the pond with Steve.'

She stared at Carol, not understanding, then remembered. 'You mean the couple to interview for the lease on the King's Head?'

Carol nodded. 'They're all alone in the drawing room. Would you mind going to say hello until Mr Redmain gets back?'

Buttercup looked at her watch. 'I've got a few minutes.

I can do some soft-soaping till Charles gets here. Come on, I'll open the door for you.'

They went back across the hall together, and Buttercup followed Carol into the drawing room. Two nervous-looking people were sitting on facing sofas, evidently ill at ease. Buttercup breezed over to the nearest of them, a man, with a hand extended, a broad smile on her face.

'How do you do, I'm Buttercup Redmain. I'm sorry my husband has been delayed, but he'll be here soon.'

The man leapt up at once to shake her hand. He was stocky and rather red-faced with a bald head and heavy stubble. 'Hello. No problem at all. I'm Wilf Tranter.' He gestured to the woman on the opposite sofa. 'That's my wife, Cathy.'

Buttercup looked over at a woman about her own age with a confetti of freckles over her face and a thick mane of chestnut hair. She was struggling to get to her feet from the depths of the soft sofa. 'Please don't get up!' Buttercup said quickly. 'Honestly. We're very relaxed here.'

'Thank you.' The woman sat back. 'Nice to meet you, Mrs Redmain.'

'Please, call me Buttercup.'

'Er ... yes,' the woman said, looking uncertain, as if it would be presumptuous to use such a name, almost like calling her Honey Pie or Sweetie Pops.

'I know, it's a ridiculous name – not my real name, I should add. My father gave it to me as a nickname, after the character in *The Princess Bride*, which was his absolute favourite movie. I'm afraid I was a real daddy's girl – and of course it stuck. Everyone's called me Buttercup ever since I was about

19

three and I can't remember being anything else. Only my headmistress called me Anna, and I used to get told off for being rude when I ignored her!'

The others laughed politely while Carol busied herself pouring coffee and handing out cups.

'What a lovely house you have,' Cathy Tranter said politely, holding her cup and saucer with a trace of awkwardness.

'Thank you.' Buttercup sat down on one of the armchairs, giving Carol a nod to indicate that it was okay to head back to the kitchen. 'It's been a labour of love for my husband – he did the restoration work on it. We're very happy here, I'm sure you'd love the pub and the village.'

'The pub looks great,' Wilf said eagerly. 'It's a terrific opportunity. Fantastic kitchen.'

'Everyone seems really friendly,' Cathy chimed in. 'We had a little wander around the village and we met some lovely people. We met a super lady just outside the shop – she told us all about the local primary schools and which one might be best for our boy, Ollie. He's three, so he only needs a nursery at the moment, but it won't be long before we're looking for a reception place. I'd been looking up schools online, but you can't beat a personal recommendation from a mum who's raised two children in the area.'

Buttercup was suddenly alert.

'She's called Ingrid,' Cathy went on. 'She said she lived near the entrance to Charcombe House. Do you know her?'

It had to be her. Buttercup hesitated, her palms prickling, 'No. I'm afraid I don't.'

'Oh!' Cathy looked surprised. 'She seemed to know this

house very well. She said she's lived in the village for six years.'

Buttercup bit her lip, then said, 'Look, I may as well tell you. If you get the lease for the pub, you'll soon find out. Ingrid is my husband's ex-wife.'

'Oh!' A wave of scarlet flooded Cathy's face as her eyes widened in horror. 'I . . . I had no idea. I'm so sorry if I've put my foot in it.'

'Please don't worry, you haven't. It's okay, I promise. She stayed in the village after the divorce so that her children could be close to their father, and we're all fine with it. My husband and I have only been married a year and a half, and I'm afraid that I haven't got to know Ingrid. I think we all feel that . . .' She hesitated, now awkward herself.

'It's best, I'm sure,' Cathy said quickly, still bright red. Her husband was staring intently into his cup of coffee. 'And very mature of you all to live so close. It must be so nice for the kids.'

'Absolutely,' Buttercup said firmly. 'It's not an issue. Really.'

'Well . . . she seemed very nice,' Cathy said weakly. 'I'm sure you'd get on.'

Wilf shot her a look and frowned.

'We probably would.' Buttercup smiled brightly. 'So, you have a little boy . . . ?'

Cathy, grateful for the change of subject, immediately started talking about her son while Buttercup listened, a smile fixed on her face. It was all she could do to keep her thoughts from straying to Ingrid, whose presence in the village was a constant reminder of the life Charles had before their marriage. She couldn't quite work out why she should mind – after all, the divorce had happened long before she met Charles, and the children were the reason why Ingrid lived in the house outside the gates of Charcombe. And she had no cause for complaint: Ingrid was tactful enough to keep herself to herself. She had never suggested coming to the house or meeting Buttercup. Charles's children, James and Charlotte, came without her. In fact, Ingrid had been a model of decorum. Nevertheless, Buttercup felt the other woman's presence like a permanent insect bite, a source of unpleasant irritation. After all, Ingrid had been here first, the mistress of this house for several years. She'd raised her children here, and even though Charles had been the key mover in the decoration of the house, surely Ingrid's taste and character was everywhere, visible and yet invisible. While there were no photographs of her on display, and none of her possessions, she must have chosen things – curtains, cushions, furniture – and arranged the house the way she saw fit. Who knew if that old pair of boots left in the cupboard had been hers? Or if she had put up the pretty framed pictures of garden flowers in the downstairs lavatory?

How could I ever guess what she was like?

No one spoke of Ingrid to Buttercup, even though all the staff must have known her. She was an unacknowledged presence, a ghost who was everywhere and nowhere, a character who had made her exit from the family drama, but who could not be forgotten: if James and Charlotte were not evidence enough of her existence, there was the fact that she was living so close, her proximity throbbing through the air and making it impossible to ignore her.

It's Charles I feel sorry for. It makes no difference to me, but what must it be like for him, with the ex-wife who broke his heart living at the end of the driveway?

That was what made her dislike Ingrid: she had betrayed Charles and then stuck around as a permanent reminder of the hurt she had caused, without even having the grace to live out of sight of her old home.

Buttercup hoped that there was no trace of that dislike in the bright smile she was giving the Tranters while their conversation flowed over her, only half heard.

There was a sudden change in atmosphere and Buttercup looked up to see Charles coming into the room. As usual, she was struck by how impressive he was: handsome, his sandy hair lightly dusted with distinguished grey, the strong bone structure lending character to his face, his eyes a striking blue. He was invariably immaculately dressed, but casual today in a crisp shirt, soft blue cashmere sweater, jeans and a pair of polished brown Loake's boots.

'Charles,' she said, jumping up, happy to see him.

'Hello, darling.' He was beside her, kissing her on the cheek, before he looked around at the guests. 'Mr Tranter? How do you do, I'm Charles Redmain.'

Wilf looked completely overawed as he stood up to shake Charles's hand, and this time, Cathy got to her feet as well, pushing herself up with a small groan as she did so.

Buttercup saw Cathy Tranter's jacket straining over a large, round belly that hadn't been evident when she'd been sitting back in the depth of the sofa. With as jolly a tone as she could manage, she said, 'You're expecting a baby. That's lovely.'

Cathy smiled. 'Yes! Another one, for my sins. I know I look like I'm ready to burst, but there's actually a month to go yet. I'm due early November.'

Buttercup stared at her, unable to say anything more. She knew she should be offering more congratulations, asking questions, but the emotions spinning through her, making her sway a little under their force, rendered her speechless. Just then, she felt Charles's arm around her shoulders.

'Come on. Come with me.' Charles turned to the Tranters. 'My wife has to get on her way, I'm afraid. I'll just see her out and then we can get on with the interview, if you'll excuse us—'

Wilf and Cathy murmured their understanding as Charles led her gently to the door and out into the hall. Once there, he hugged her tightly.

'You're a brave girl,' he murmured. 'A very brave girl.'

She buried her head on his shoulder. 'It's hard sometimes,' she whispered.

'I know. I could tell exactly what you were feeling. It will get better – didn't I promise that? And you know I'll always be here.'

She nodded, her eyes prickling with tears. A deep sigh shook her shoulders.

He hugged her again. 'There's a good strong girl. Everything will be all right, I promise. Now, isn't Phil expecting you? You should go. A ride will make everything better. It always cheers you up.'

'Yes.' Buttercup managed to smile at him, knowing how he hated to see her unhappy. 'Thank you. You're right. I'll go now.'

He dropped a tender kiss on her forehead. 'Enjoy yourself. I'll see you later.'

Chapter Three

As Buttercup passed through the kitchen on her way to the back door, Tippi looked up from her bed by the kitchen table and wagged her tail. Carol turned from where she was stirring a pot on the Aga top and, seeing the expression on Buttercup's face, immediately asked, 'Are you okay?'

Buttercup stopped and nodded, not trusting herself to speak.

'You don't look it.'

Something about the sympathy in Carol's soft Scottish lilt made Buttercup desperate with sadness and she stopped short, staring at the floor. 'Cathy Tranter is pregnant. She's due in a month.'

'Oh, love.' Carol dropped the spoon into the pot and came over to hug her. 'A month? Oh, sweetheart – that brings you up to the anniversary of – well . . . It's a shame, that's all.'

Buttercup nodded, comforted by the warmth of the other woman's embrace.

Carol stepped back and regarded her with concern. 'I'm

sorry. You don't need that. She should have stayed away when she's that far along.'

'It's not her fault,' Buttercup said, her voice thick with unshed tears. 'She wasn't to know. And I shouldn't still feel like this, after all this time.'

'Don't be silly. You have every right to feel like a mess. Especially as you get closer to – well, closer to the date.'

Buttercup nodded. *The anniversary of when my baby died. That's what we can't say.* 'I'm going to go for my ride.'

'That's a great idea. Just what you need. And lunch will be ready when you get back.' Carol smiled encouragingly at her. 'Off you go now. Try to have a good time.'

Buttercup went out to the Land Rover parked by the stables, jumped in the front and revved up the engine with a roar. The grating sound helped her to release some of the pain she'd felt when she'd spotted that burgeoning tummy on Cathy Tranter. The sight of it had thrown up all the awful feelings of loss and misery, sending them spinning upwards from the place where she kept them closed away. She had hoped that if she ignored them hard enough, they would wither and die like a vase of forgotten flowers; but they refused to do it. Each time she revisited them, they were as fresh and vigorous as ever.

I knew November would be hard, remembering all that sorrow and loss. It's not poor Cathy's fault. She reversed the Land Rover so that she could drive out of the stable yard. *It will get better once the anniversary is over with.*

She knew what would heal her most. After the miscarriage,

27

the doctor had advised her to wait a few months before trying again, but she had been desperate to conceive and refused to wait so they had begun trying right away. Each month that passed with no success made her longing more intense.

She drove over the rough cobbles, through the gate and out onto the gravelled area in front of the house, feeling wretched. Just the sight of the long drive stretching through beautiful parkland to the gates at the end, topped with their stone greyhounds, reminded her how lucky she was.

I have everything. A marvellous husband, a beautiful house, a lovely life. I just want this other thing too – that's all. Just one thing. A family.

By the time she reached Zinch Hill, Phil was walking Milky up and down the lane to warm her up a little. When he heard Buttercup's approach, he pulled Milky to one side and held her on the verge, patting her nose to keep her calm at the sound of the engine, while Buttercup parked.

Phil waved as Buttercup came towards him. 'There you are,' he said, as she strode up. 'I thought I had the wrong place.'

'Sorry,' she said shortly as she took the reins, put a foot in the stirrup and pulled herself easily into the saddle. She leaned down to pat the warm neck. 'Good girl, Milky,' she muttered.

Phil eyed her with a frown. 'Are you all right, BC?'

She smiled, hoping she looked normal. 'Yes, fine.'

He didn't look convinced but only said, 'Okay then. Enjoy yourself. I'll be here when you get back – or text me where to meet you if you need a lift home.'

'I will. Thanks. See you later.' She kicked Milky into a trot and the mare obediently started down the lane, her shoes ringing out on the tarmac. The rhythm provided an instant sense of calm, and Buttercup felt herself relax as she drew in a lungful of fresh air and released it fully. This – the closeness to Milky, the connection with her and the world around them, the companionable isolation and the physical exertion – helped so much.

Milky knew the way and hardly had to be directed to turn off the lane and onto the bridle path. Soon they were climbing up under an archway of trees just starting to turn into their autumn colour, a damp mass of leaves beginning to clog the mud on the path.

If Dad could see me now, she thought wistfully. He'd wanted her to be a star of the pony club, and she'd had riding lessons on a fat little white pony called Jim Bob, taken part in a few gymkhanas and won some rosettes; photographs of her in full kit holding them up sat in pride of place in her parents' home for years. She had not loved riding, however, dreading falls and hating grooming, and had given it up without regret as soon as she could. It was only when she'd moved here with Charles and he was away so much on business, that she'd taken to going to the stables to visit the horses. Something about them, standing patiently in their stalls, waiting and trustful, calmed her and gave her an escape from the grief at her father's death. Phil, easy and undemanding company, hadn't seemed to mind her hanging about and soon she was lending a hand. Where once she'd found grooming a chore, now she positively loved the soothing process of brushing and rubbing, and the way that cleaning tack helped to clear her mind and relax her.

Once she became a regular at the stable, Phil said one day, 'You should take them out, exercise them.'

'Could I?' she'd asked, excited. 'But I haven't ridden in years. I'm sure I've forgotten how to.'

'Rubbish. You never forget. It'll come back soon enough in any case.' Phil had mussy blond hair and a permanent rash of gingery stubble, and was always in work-stained clothes, with dirty hands and black-rimmed nails, but he didn't care how he looked as long as the horses were cared for and the yard was neat. 'You can ride Richelieu, he's Charlotte's. You can borrow a cap, no need for anything else.'

Buttercup had seen Charlotte out riding on Richelieu, a beautiful frisky dappled grey gelding; Topper, the huge bay thoroughbred hunter belonged to Charles, though he rarely rode. 'And does Mocha belong to James?' she asked, looking over at the docile bay mare in the last stall along.

Phil had gone quiet for a moment, murmuring to Topper and pressing a polo mint to the horse's mouth, then he said, 'No, she belongs to Ingrid.'

'Oh.' Buttercup blinked and the atmosphere was suddenly awkward. 'Does she come here to ride her?'

'She hasn't lately.'

Buttercup could hear the unspoken end to that sentence: *Not now that you're here.*

'Actually,' Phil said, 'there's talk that Mocha will go to stables down at the Herberts', so it won't be an issue.'

'Oh. I suppose that's for the best.'

'Yes,' Phil said with finality. 'So, we'll get you saddled up, shall we?'

Nothing more had been said, and not long after, Mocha was gone. Buttercup was glad. She hadn't liked the sense that something of Ingrid's was still here, as though the other woman refused to let go of her hold on Charles and her life here at Charcombe.

How much don't I know about her influence here? What do they know about Ingrid that I don't? But she couldn't ask Phil anything. She owed it to Charles to keep a dignified silence. Buttercup was not going to show any curiosity about her, or give the slightest hint that she cared. Charles had been noble in the face of Ingrid's humiliating betrayal and her brazen impudence at living so close, keeping her horse here, and who knew what other means she had found to maintain a presence at Charcombe . . .

Perhaps she's still in touch with Phil, or with Carol. Maybe she asks about me, gets them to tell her all about Charles and me . . . She could imagine the other woman pouncing on juicy information, making judgements, laughing about her.

I just have to deal with it. After all, we are the adults, we're being civilised for the sake of the children, for James and Charlotte.

But she couldn't help wishing that Ingrid was far away from the new life she was trying to build. Or that she'd never existed at all.

Buttercup took Milky up the gallops and spent a vigorous hour letting her reach her limit, exhilarated by the feeling of speed and power coursing through the mare's body. Milky had been a birthday present from Charles, after he'd noticed how much pleasure she was getting from riding, and the grey mare was the perfect gift. Each time she rode Milky, Buttercup felt released a little more from the burden of mourning, and when it came back, as it always did, it was a little easier to bear.

'You've got more work to do, now, haven't you, girl?' Buttercup panted as they came to a halt, Milky steaming and snorting with exertion. 'More sadness to cure. I hope I'm not asking too much this time. Come on, let's go and find Phil.'

They went back to the woods and walked slowly along the paths to the next vale, where Phil had driven the box around to meet her.

'Better?' he asked, when he'd put Milky in, and climbed into the jeep next to Buttercup.

She nodded and smiled. 'Yes. Thank you. Much better.'

'Difficult morning, was it?' Phil started the engine and they began the drive back to where they'd left Buttercup's Land Rover.

'Not too bad, I suppose. We had a couple over about the pub. They seemed very nice.'

'As long as they serve decent food,' Phil said. 'The King's Head could do with that after the last bloke tried the hot rocks dining experience or whatever it was called.'

Buttercup laughed. 'Hot rocks? What?'

'You don't want to know. Bangers and mash is what we need, make sure they know that. And a decent roast on Sundays.'

'I'm not sure how much say I'll get, but I'll certainly tell Charles.'

'Make sure you do, BC.'

Buttercup smiled at him. He had relaxed with her so much recently. At first he had been a little chilly, perhaps from loyalty to the previous Mrs Redmain, but lately when he saw how much she was responding to the horses, how keen she was to improve her riding and her sheer happiness in it, he had grown friendlier. She liked his lack of pretension and the way he was resolutely unimpressed by the big house, its trappings, and Charles's expensive toys.

Despite their growing closeness, though, Buttercup was always careful not to discuss anything about the past with Phil, no matter how much she yearned to satisfy her curiosity.

'Here we are,' Phil said as they pulled up by the Land Rover and Buttercup prepared to get out. 'I'll see you back at the ranch. And I'll have Milky rubbed down and fed before you get there.'

'You know what? I believe you!' Buttercup called as she slammed the door and Phil pulled away with a grin, Milky in her box behind. 'See you at the stables.'

Back at home, she was tired in a languorous way, her spirits calmer and more content. She had a shower and changed, then went downstairs to find Charles, who was in the drawing room reading a newspaper, while simultaneously scanning his emails on a tablet beside him. The fire crackled in the grate and Tippi lay prone in front of it, lifting her head

and thumping her tail as Buttercup came in, alerting Charles
to her presence.

He looked up and smiled. 'You're back. Was it fun?'

'Very.' She went over to kiss him. She always responded to
his smiles: they made him look boyish and charming, not
that he looked anything like his age. Despite the dozen years
between them, he never seemed much older to her. His sandy
fair hair almost hid the slight grey and he probably hadn't
looked much different since he was thirty. His strong bone
structure and long straight nose gave him a slightly hollow-
cheeked look, and his thin upper lip could make him seem
austere, until he smiled; then his whole face softened and his
blue eyes sparkled, and he radiated merriment that filled her
with pleasure and lifted her spirits.

'How was the interview?' she asked, after kissing his
cheek. She sat down on the arm of the chair opposite him.
'Did you like the Tranters?'

'Yes, I did.' Charles put down his paper. 'They seemed like
good solid people and they're prepared to take on the pub
and make a go of it.'

'So they got the lease?'

'That's right.' Charles smiled.

'I'm so glad it's settled. When do they move in?'

'As soon as we can get the paperwork done. A couple of
weeks, if we hurry. It would be tomorrow if I could sort it.'

'Typical Charles. You want everything now, now, now.'
She laughed. 'You'd have married me the day after we got
engaged if you could have!'

'Of course I would. What's the point in waiting? But I let you have an age to plan the whole thing, didn't I?'

'Four months!'

'Five.'

'Only just!' She shook her head at him, smiling. 'I thought I'd done pretty well to get it all organised by then!'

Charles looked baffled. 'I can't think what on earth you had to do.'

Buttercup made a face at him. 'That's because everything gets done for you! You're very spoiled!'

She remembered how Charles had not seemed to understand even the most straightforward things about booking a venue, or giving the hotel notice of what they would want and how many people there would be, or the intricacies of arranging food and flowers, let alone ordering a dress or sorting out the legalities. But she soon learned the power of what Carol called Mission Control and everyone else referred to as The Hub: the house in Westminster that served as a base for Charles's business, with his penthouse flat at the top of it. Charles's personal assistants, Elaine and Rose, ran his life as if he were the president of a small country, facilitating his travel, business and domestic requirements down to the tiniest detail. In the end, it was Elaine to whom she'd spoken most about the arrangements for the wedding: together they'd chosen the canapés, the menus and wines, the colour scheme, and the stationery. Elaine sorted out the tailor for Charles's suit and probably bought his shoes and tie as well. Buttercup suspected that it was Elaine who had chosen the honeymoon location of Thailand, which Charles told her was his surprise for her, and she certainly handled all the bookings. Sometimes she wondered if Elaine had selected the diamond necklace delivered to her hotel suite on the morning of the wedding, with a handwritten note from Charles telling her how happy she was making him. But Elaine definitely had not written that, and that was the important thing.

But by then, she'd already known how busy Charles was, his mind on dozens of different business deals and projects at any one time, his itinerary jammed with appointments and meetings all over the world. It was no wonder he needed so much support. She had understood and been grateful that Elaine was there to provide the help that Charles could not.

'It was a perfect wedding day, though, wasn't it?' Charles said tenderly.

'It was amazing.' She remembered her joy as she'd walked into that white-and-gilded room in Claridge's, feeling wonderful in her dress and veil, to see Charles, so handsome and smart, waiting to marry her in front of their family and friends. It had been a moment of bliss when he'd slipped the ring on her finger and they were married. Her only sadness was knowing how much her father would have adored giving her away. Her uncle, who did the job instead, made a speech on his behalf and brought Buttercup to tears telling her how proud her father would have been of his beautiful daughter. He mentioned her mother, far away in the nursing home, and they toasted the absent loved ones. Then Charles wiped away her tears and made her smile again. He spoke of her rapturously in his speech, making her blush and laugh with embarrassment. When she looked around, bashful, she saw

beaming faces and pleasure in her happiness, except in the unsmiling faces of Charles's children, who stayed stony and unmoved throughout despite her best efforts to break through their reserve. She'd tried smiles and hugs but it was no good. They were the only dark spot in a bright and beautiful day.

Charles closed the cover on his tablet. 'Darling, I've been worrying about you.'

'Have you?' She felt comforted just hearing it.

He gazed at her intently. 'I hate to see you unhappy, darling. Life can be cruel sometimes, and you've had more than your fair share.'

'I don't know why it's so hard for me to have a family, that's all,' she said sadly. 'Dad's dead, Mum's so ill she doesn't know me and hasn't for years. I haven't got any brothers or sisters. And no matter how hard we try, we can't seem to have a baby.'

He hugged her hard, as if trying to press his own strength into her and murmured in her ear, 'It will happen, I know it will. If you only relax and let it all work itself out naturally.'

Buttercup pulled away so that she could look into his eyes. 'But shouldn't we see a doctor or a specialist or something? I got pregnant so quickly last time, and now nothing's happening. It doesn't feel right.'

Charles said softly, 'Perhaps it was *too* quickly last time. I mean, I was overjoyed just as you were, but we were hardly married before it happened. We've had so little time just for us.' Seeing her expression, he added quickly, 'That's not to say that losing the baby wasn't the most awful, terrible thing, because it was. But if we can find anything to lift the gloom just a little, maybe it's that we have more time for each other. You're only thirty-two. Just wait and see. I think that as soon as you stop worrying it'll happen naturally. Any specialist or doctor you see will tell you the same – it's far too early to do any investigating.'

Buttercup opened her mouth to speak, then changed her mind. She had been on the brink of saying that he couldn't know what she felt. He'd had the joy of fatherhood: holding his own child, kissing the soft, baby cheek and smelling the delicious scent. He'd held plump toddler hands and read bedtime stories, and pushed swings loaded with fat, giggling bundles in hats and wellies. He'd had it, and she wanted it so badly. What harm could it do to see someone who might help them?

But it sounded selfish and accusatory. And she also knew he was right. It was early days. She was young, she'd got pregnant once already. It would all be fine.

'Yes,' she said, and smiled. 'We'll just have to keep trying.'

'That's my brave girl,' he said, and leaned to kiss her softly. 'We'll keep trying. And don't forget, darling – I'm your family now.'

Chapter Four

'Oh, this frightful mess! And you are not helping me one little scrap, you monster.'

Xenia Arkadyoff was lying on her stomach in her bedroom, trying to grapple with the piles of things under her bed. How had it got so bad under there? It was jam-packed with bulging plastic bags, sealed boxes and various suitcases, all smothered in a thick coating of dust. As she fumbled in the darkness, hardly able to see or breathe, the cat insisted on hunting her hand, chasing it and pouncing as it rustled inside plastic bags. She had managed to pull out a couple of them for inspection before she was overcome with a sneezing fit and gave up. It took an age to recover from the dust and summon enough energy to haul herself up off the floor.

'What am I doing?' she said to herself out loud. 'I'm far too old for this, aren't I, Petrova?'

The cat had given up her game and was now washing herself carefully on the rug while studiously ignoring her.

Xenia sighed. It wasn't just age that was tormenting her. Her eyesight was growing increasingly bad and the dust had taken hold not just under the bed but throughout the entire house now that she couldn't see properly to clean.

'Petrova, I need a cleaner, and that's the end of it. I've tried to cope on my own ever since the last one left – what was her name? Anna? No . . . Paulina, that's right – and I can't.' She shook her head at herself. 'I don't know why thought I could. And I can afford help now. And once, though you wouldn't believe it, Petrova, we had lots of servants. My nanny lived with us until I was twelve or so. I think I was twelve when she retired . . .' A picture of Gunter floated into her mind: solid, reliable, very cautious, with her pudgy face and the mud-coloured hair always in a firm bun at the back of her neck. As a girl, Xenia had wondered how she managed to make it look identical every day and had decided she simply never undid it and now it had set like a stone. 'Butlers, maids, gardeners, chauffeurs. Papa knew how to do it properly, he insisted on it. But I'll have you know that I managed alone for years, just Mama and me, so I know what hard work is, don't you worry about that!'

The cat did not seem at all worried but carried on licking her flanks.

'Stupid animal,' Xenia muttered and she went slowly to the window, hobbling a little, stiff from her sojourn on the floor. Pushing up the sash, she let in the cool air. The heat of summer was gone, thank goodness, and the breeze was welcome to clear the air of all the dust motes she had set dancing; she drew in long breaths to clear her lungs.

I must be grateful, she told herself. Here I am, comfortable at last with money in the bank to provide for me, after all those difficult years. If I don't hire someone now to help me, I'm a fool.

The truth was that the hard years had taught her lessons she found she could not forget: she had grown desperately suspicious of people, defensive and afraid, and that was now deeply embedded in her, beyond her control even. Alone with Petrova, in her safe little cottage, she was happy. The idea of inviting others – outsiders, strangers, people who might want to destroy things, take her away – into her home was anathema.

But it was increasingly difficult to cope alone, and it would only get harder.

Xenia looked over the tangle of her front garden to the neatness across the lane, just visible through the branches of the magnolia tree that was sadly in need of a prune. The garden of Fitzroy House looked like a rebuke, with its neat hedges and well-trimmed shrubs, the flower beds still bright with the last of the late summer blooms. She had received letters from that man, Redmain, suggesting she do something about the garden. He had even offered to send his own gardeners down to sort out the mess, and while she would actually have welcomed someone doing what she absolutely could not, she refused and had enjoyed writing a very rude reply telling him her garden was her business and his employees must keep off her land.

He's not going to bully me out of my own house. I know he wants it.

Charles Redmain had wanted Hooke House at the same time as he bought the rest of the estate – Charcombe Park, with its surrounding land, or what was left of it at least – from Xenia. The two gracious houses that stood opposite each other outside the gates of Charcombe – Fitzroy House and Hooke House, twin residences built in the nineteenth century for the unmarried sisters and widowed mother of an owner of the big house – had been rented on long leases when Xenia lived at Charcombe, on virtual peppercorn rents agreed by Papa years before when money didn't matter. The leases had expired when she had sold the Park, and she had added Fitzroy as a separate lot and kept Hooke for herself. Charles Redmain had badgered her to sell it to him, offering to buy her any other house in the village in exchange, but she had refused. Even now, when all hope was gone, when it was utterly impossible, she couldn't help an overwhelming need to stay put, to wait, just in case . . .

'You're a foolish old woman!' she scolded herself. 'Stupid and silly.'

She squinted over the lane at Fitzroy House, which housed the ex-Mrs Redmain. Whatever was happening to her eyesight meant that, bizarrely, it was easier to see across the lane than to see her own hands. She watched for a moment, looking for movement beyond the curtains, but all was still.

Where is she? Away again?

Watching was one of her pleasures. She had watched and observed over the ten years since she had sold Charcombe Park to Redmain and his wife, Ingrid. They had arrived with their two small children and looked around the place, her expression reserved and cautious in contrast to his bubbling enthusiasm and happiness with every aspect of the place.

'But, Charles,' Xenia heard her say as she restrained her little boy, who was trying to climb the rickety back stairs in the kitchen, 'it's a total mess. It will take years to get this shambles sorted out. How can we live here? It's dangerous right now, and it'll be a building site for months.'

'We'll live temporarily in one of the gatehouses, they're very decent,' Charles said airily. 'And it won't take years. Give me six months, you won't know the place.'

Xenia had felt vaguely offended that the wife thought so little of Charcombe, but, really, she knew that the poor house was dilapidated and in desperate need of repair. She had been a bad guardian, despite her best efforts and her promises to look after it, but a house like that took more money than she had. In the end, selling it was her only option. By the time Redmain bought it, she had been existing in just a few rooms, her possessions piled into the most watertight places she could find. Seeing it through their eyes, she could understand why Mrs Redmain had her doubts.

'I prefer the other house,' the wife said quietly as they inspected the kitchen. 'It's far less work and we could move straight in. And there are excellent schools nearby – this is miles from anywhere.'

'I want this one,' Charles had said firmly. 'It was Edward Redmain's house. This is the one. You understand that, don't you?'

The wife had nodded and said nothing more.

It seemed to Xenia a little unfortunate that the poor woman had endured the years of work on the house – it had taken at least three years to restore and remodel it – and now no longer lived there to enjoy the fruits of all that effort and money. She had to make do with Fitzroy House instead, forever shut out of her old home but still within its shadow.

A very strange state of affairs.

A movement caught her attention and she turned her head to squint at the large wrought iron gates of Charcombe Park. In her time they had been rusting and almost immovable, locked most of the time with a huge padlock. Now they were gleaming and moved soundlessly at the touch of a button. The gates were opening, slowly and smoothly, and a car was approaching.

'Who is it this time?' she wondered aloud. She knew them all now: the housekeeper and her husband who did maintenance – they lived in a newly built bungalow in the grounds and were always coming and going; the man in the battered old jeep, who looked after the horses; the cleaners in their small cars or on their bicycles; Redmain, who roared past in his ostentatious sports car, or was driven out in a large silver car.

Spoiled. Rich. Inconsiderate.

And, last of all, the new wife. Xenia had not managed to get a good look at her yet, catching only glimpses of her as she went past in her dark blue car. She had seen blond hair, wide eyes fixed firmly ahead, not looking at either of the twin houses near the gates, intent on wherever she was going. Xenia was sure she knew what kind of woman the new wife was; a greedy young woman looking for a rich husband and a foolish old man marrying youth and beauty was a story as old as time. This woman was no doubt avaricious, manipulative, ruthless. She had seen her chance and captured the fancy of a lonely man who could offer her the life she wanted.

Good luck to her. She'll find out there's a price to pay for everything in the end.

The car drove through the open gates and past the house, but Xenia found that she couldn't focus on the occupant in time to see much. She could make out the outline of the car but the middle was a dark blur, and she tutted in exasperation as her chance was lost. She would have to go back to the doctor before too long about her eyes.

The sound of rustling plastic made her look around and she squinted hard as her focus changed. Petrova had stopped washing herself and was now investigating the interior of one of the bags Xenia had pulled out from under the bed.

'What are you doing, puss?' She went over and hauled Petrova out of the bag, lifted it up and tipped out the contents on her bed. This one contained a mass of old cards, letters and programmes. She knew what they were, she had read them all before: endless notes between Papa and Mama from the early days of their marriage when Mama was still a stage actress. Papa had written to her almost every day: short notes and dashed-off letters for her to read in her dressing room; and she had left questions and instructions for him about all manner of things – telling him who might be dining with them, or what Cook needed to know, or asking his advice – because she would not see him that day. Glimpses of their neat, slanted handwriting – hers rounded and his spiky – filled her with melancholy and yet also brought them close to her again, just for a moment.

She noticed an old theatre programme and picked it up. It was for the first play in which Mama had had a proper speaking role. Inside was the cast list. The hole in the middle of her vision shimmered and blurred the print while tiny black dots flew across her eyes, but she blinked and squinted, trying to make out the words. Mama was third on the billing. On the inside of the programme, a cutting from a newspaper had been pasted. *Star in a night!* was the excited headline, and underneath words that Xenia had read often but that never lost their ability to thrill her.

Last night, a star was born in London's theatreland. Natalie Rowe, a twenty-two-year-old unknown actress, made her debut and captured the heart and soul of everyone who witnessed her outstanding performance as Mrs Crichton in the new play by Gerald Garfield, *Mrs Crichton's Malady*. This paper's critic has called her the brightest young talent for many years, with a glittering future ahead. See page 45 for a full report and review of the production.

Underneath was a grainy photograph of Mama in her costume, her hands buried in a muff, a hat jaunty on her head. Even though the quality was so poor, her beauty shone out.

'Oh, Mama,' Xenia breathed, and ran a finger over the dear face. 'Your glittering future.'

But for a while life *had* glittered, when everything had seemed possible and they believed that youth and success would last forever.

Chapter Five

London 1948

When Xenia heard the clink of the tea tray passing the schoolroom, she leapt up.

'Where are you going, dear?' Gunter asked, looking up from sewing buttons back on Xenia's kilt. 'Aren't you supposed to be doing your French exercises?'

'Mama's awake,' Xenia said, excited. 'Didn't you hear the tray? She's rung for her tea.'

'You shouldn't bother the princess first thing, she hasn't got herself together yet.'

But Xenia loved this time, when Mama was rested and the evening's performance was still hours away, with no one else to take Mama's attention away from her. Ignoring Gunter, Xenia dashed out of the schoolroom and was in Mama's room almost at the same time as the maid, who hadn't even put the tray down yet.

Mama was sitting up in bed against a mound of pillows, wrapped in a peach-coloured ruffled nightgown, her hair tucked up in a silk turban, looking impossibly young and pretty.

'Here's my girl,' she said gaily, holding out her arms, and Xenia kicked off her shoes so that she could jump up on the bed and snuggle up to Mama. 'Mind the tray!'

The maid was setting the bed tray up on its little legs, lowering it down over Mama's lap. It was loaded with a china teapot, cup and saucer, some pills, a glass of water, and a bud vase with a white rose. A small pile of envelopes sat on one side, neatly stacked.

'Thank you, dear,' Mama said to the maid.

'Shall I draw your bath, ma'am?'

'Give me half an hour first.'

The maid bobbed and went out.

Mama put her arm around Xenia and hugged her. 'We can share this tea, if you like. A sip for you, a sip for me. How are you, little Xenia? Are you working hard at your lessons?'

'I don't see why I should do lessons, it's the holidays,' Xenia grumbled.

'It's good for you to remember everything you've learned at school. It's only for a few hours a day. Gunter will take you out somewhere nice this afternoon.'

'Can't you take me, Mama?'

'Perhaps. One day soon. We'll go for tea and visit Harrods. Would you like that?'

'Oh yes, I *would*.'

Mama often made promises to take her out, but they didn't materialise very much. Xenia liked the way that people recognised her mother and made a fuss of her, but Mama found it uncomfortable and preferred to stay at home or to visit friends in their houses, where she didn't have to be on her guard.

'Well, not today, but one day. Gunter will have to do in the meantime.' Mama said consolingly, 'You should ask your friend Rachel if she wants to join you. Shall I telephone her mother?'

'Yes please.' Xenia brightened. Anything was better than being on her own with boring old Gunter, who got frightened crossing the road, and trembled when they got too near the horses being ridden in the park. 'How was the play last night?'

'It was all perfect. Nothing went wrong, even old Roger didn't forget his lines. It helps that we've now stuck most of them around the set so he can rush over and read them when he dries.'

Xenia giggled. She had seen the play on the opening night, feeling very grown up as she went into the theatre on Papa's arm. He'd been so handsome in his evening clothes, a cigarette clamped between his teeth, and she had worn a green velvet dress, a little fur jacket and white gloves. Press photographers outside the theatre had taken pictures as they went in to join the rest of the glamorous crowd in the foyer. The play had been enchanting and Mama was so beautiful and so convincing that Xenia had almost forgotten that the mesmerising woman on the stage was her own mother. She had begged and begged to go again but they had always said it was too late for her to stay up except on very special occasions.

'Did you have a party last night?' Xenia asked disingenuously. She already knew that there had been a party, because she had seen it. It was one of her favourite things: to slip out of bed and sit on the stairs, concealed in the darkness, staring down through the spindles at people arriving. The parties started late, after the curtains came down in the theatres, and the acting crowd began their fun for the evening. The gramophone in the drawing room would be playing, and she could hear the tinkle of glasses and the chatter of voices, and smell cigarette smoke. Papa would stride out into the hall to answer the door, for the maids were in bed.

'How marvellous to see you!' he would boom, that tang of an accent in his voice, to the new arrivals in their dinner jackets and shimmering dresses. 'Come in, my darling, can I make you a cocktail? Natalie is on her way, she'll be so thrilled to see you.'

Xenia had watched the guests last night as Papa ushered them in. She longed to be downstairs with them, all grown up in a long gown, her hair curled, her mouth dark with lipstick. She yearned to look like Mama – so heart-stoppingly beautiful – but when she stared in the mirror, she saw only her own ordinary face, her boring straight hair and her schoolgirl clothes. Mama had arrived last of all, driven back from the theatre wrapped in her fur coat, pale from the effort of her performance but still the most charismatic of them all. As she came into the hall, everyone piled out to greet her, eager to welcome her back. That was how it was with Mama: people sought her attention, and they fawned on her, petted her, offered her drinks and cigarettes and laughed at her jokes. Mama was important somehow, more important than any of the others. She was even more important than Papa, despite

50

the fact that he was an actual prince. It was more than simply her beauty. Xenia knew that Mama was a famous actress whose plays sold out night after night and whose photograph sold magazines and newspapers.

The curious thing was that although Mama loved the theatre and her work, she was also oppressed by it. Xenia could sense that Mama was always disappointed in herself, as though she was never quite the great actress she wanted to be no matter how hard she tried. Her beauty was what people loved, but that meant nothing to her. She wanted to be sublime as an actress, that was all.

That was why at these times, cuddled together with Xenia in her sweet-scented bedroom, when the evening's performance was still only a distant shadow on the horizon, Mama was happy and relaxed and loving.

'I hope our party didn't wake you up, darling,' Mama remarked. 'It did go on rather late.'

'No, no. I slept very well.' Which was true, but only after she'd sat on the stairs until her eyes were too heavy to stay open and she'd gone back to bed. No wonder Mama had to sleep until lunchtime every day.

Mama poured out the tea as she asked Xenia questions, and then she turned her attention to her small pile of post, flicking through the envelopes until she saw one with the printed address of Lawrence Bowman, her agent, on the top corner. Xenia had learned that these letters were the ones of most interest to Mama; she plucked it from the pile and opened it quickly with nervous fingers. Inside were a note and a letter. Mama opened the note and scanned it quickly. Xenia saw it was only two scrawled lines:

Natalie darling, this has just arrived along with a telegram warning me of its contents. Read it and let me know what you think as soon as you can – it's exciting. L.

She glanced up at Mama, who seemed curious but a little anxious.

'How odd,' she muttered, and opened the letter. Xenia could see that it was typewritten, with her mother's name written in ink at the top, and a signature at the bottom, but she couldn't see the body of text. All she could see was the letterhead, a famous logo of a dove. She had seen it before but couldn't place it, so she waited patiently for Mama to finish reading.

Mama put the letter down on her tray, her face ashen. 'Oh,' she said in a small voice.

'Is it bad news?' Xenia asked, surprised.

'No. Not bad news, just—' Mama stopped and stared at the letter on the tray.

'What is it?'

Mama bit her lip, looking worried. 'Lawrence is right, it's exciting, extremely exciting.' She turned to Xenia. 'A film director in America wants me to go there to test for a role in his motion picture. It's a famous part, lots of actresses would love to be cast in the role. They want me to go, at once.'

'But isn't that good?' Xenia ventured. 'You don't seem terribly happy about it.'

'I have the play to think of. And I don't want to leave you and Papa. If I got the part, it would mean I'd be away for months and months.'

Xenia was quiet. That was a horrible idea.

Mama dropped an absent-minded kiss on Xenia's cheek, her mood completely changed from the earlier cosiness. 'Run along now, darling. I must telephone Papa at his office and talk to him at once.'

Xenia got reluctantly off the bed. She knew how it was when grown-up life came to take Mama away from her, and she went quietly away as Mama reached for the telephone beside her bed.

It must have been much more important than Xenia realised, because when she came back in for tea after her outing with Gunter – Mama had forgotten all about inviting Rachel along – Papa was home and her parents were talking earnestly in the drawing room.

Gunter bustled away to take off her coat, while Xenia loitered at the door, listening, slowly unbuttoning her own gaberdine.

Papa's voice was urgent and intense. 'You can't give up this opportunity, Natalie, I won't let you.'

'I know it's a marvellous offer, darling, but—'

'No buts! You'd regret it forever if you let it pass by. Archibald Thomas has already seen the most famous actresses in Hollywood and still he wants to audition you. He thinks you have the talent for this role, and so do I. It will make your career. It's everything I hoped for you.'

'But I'd have to get permission to miss the rest of the run – that won't be easy. Besides which, I could go all that way and not get it. So much effort – for nothing.'

'No, no. Just testing for the role will bring you to the attention of the studios, and who knows what might happen after that? You're bound to meet people of influence, and you've already got friends out there who can introduce you to Hollywood society. I mean it, Natalie, it's the most marvellous chance.'

Mama sounded wistful. 'But I'd be away from you and Xenia for months and months.'

'We'd come with you, darling. We'd make it happen. You wouldn't be alone.'

There was a long pause, and Xenia could imagine exactly how Mama would be: worried, full of self-doubt and yet desperate to please her husband and longing to do the thing she loved the most – act.

Why is it that Mama loves her work so much, and is so afraid of it?

'Paul,' she said softly, 'I'm scared I wouldn't be able to manage the strain. You know I haven't been myself lately. I don't know if I'm well enough for something like this.'

'Nonsense.' Papa was effervescent with enthusiasm. 'You're a little over-tired, yes. Nothing more, my love. This has been a long and exhausting run – they'll let you miss the rest on health grounds alone. A trip to America is exactly what you need.'

'Well ...' Mama sounded both resigned and hopeful, as though she wanted to be convinced by Papa's energy and spirit. 'If you say so, darling ... you know I'll do whatever you think is best.'

'Good. You're a star, Natalie, and you're ready to take on the world.'

There was a pause and then Xenia heard the sound of kissing. She slipped quietly away.

Two weeks later, Gunter took Xenia and her friend Rachel to the cinema. The cinema held no attraction for the nanny, who preferred a nice walk in the park, so the girls were allowed to watch the picture alone, with strict instructions to meet Gunter after the showing.

They had settled into their seats and were watching the newsreel in the darkness when Rachel nudged Xenia hard. 'Crumbs, look!' she said loudly. 'It's your mother!'

Xenia nodded, staring at the screen, wide-eyed. There was Mama, glamorous and beautiful, walking up the gangplank of the great ocean liner, smiling and waving her white-gloved hand at the camera. The newsreel music played jauntily as the narrator explained the action.

'Home-grown star Natalie Rowe is off to try her luck in that land of dreams, Hollywood! After achieving fame on the London stage, the glamorous actress is on her way the United States, summoned by the famous film director Archibald Thomas to audition for the most desirable role of the season – the leading role in the great man's next picture. He's already tested many stars – rumoured to include Ingrid Bergman,

Joan Fontaine and Lana Turner! – but he's still looking for his leading lady. Could our very own Natalie Rowe steal the part for herself?'

The camera panned over the mountain of luggage, neatly labelled 'Princess Natalie Arkadyoff', though the initials on the leather were curling NRs.

'And it may well help that she is also a Russian princess!'

The film showed a swift glimpse of the people on the dockside waving at the departing liner. For an instant it lingered on Xenia, girlish in a velvet-collared coat, beret and strappy shoes, and her father in his greatcoat, both waving.

'Ooh!' said Rachel excitedly. 'That's you!'

'Shhh,' said someone nearby.

Then they saw the liner moving out to sea, the smoke from its funnels trailing behind it in a great black cloud.

'Good luck, Natalie!' said the voice jovially over the crescendo of music. 'Your many admirers at home are all rooting for you!'

Xenia blinked. It was so strange seeing it like that, reduced to a few moments of uncomplicated, happy action. She remembered the drive to Southampton just a few days ago. They all tried to be brave but it was obvious Mama was frightened, and Xenia was sick at the thought of their being parted by a great ocean when she'd never been away from her mother before.

Only Papa had been cheerful, trying to comfort Mama and boost her spirits, talking excitedly about the voyage ahead, the wonders of California, and the promise that he and Xenia would soon join her if she got the role.

Even so, Mama's eyes were bright with tears despite her effort to hold them in. But as soon as they got out of the car in front of the press, she appeared calm and radiant. Only Xenia could know she was shaking as she hugged her and said, 'Be good, won't you, darling? I'll be home soon, I promise. It's only an audition, you know. And if I get it, you'll visit me in California. Wouldn't that be wonderful? Look after Papa for me. Goodbye!'

She had kissed her mother's powdered cheek but by then Mama was distracted by the press photographers and the moving-picture camera pointed at her; she was intent on smiling the right way and not showing she was afraid.

'Goodbye, Mama. I'll write to you!'

'Take care, Natalie,' her father said. 'Do your best, won't you? That's all we can ask.'

'I will, darling,' her mother said, smiling brightly at the camera. 'You needn't worry about me.' Then she turned to her husband, a strange intensity in her eyes. 'I love you, darling. I want to make you proud.'

'I love you too.' He kissed her cheek once more and squeezed her gloved hand.

Then she was gone. They watched until the liner was out of the harbour, then went home.

'You're so lucky,' Rachel sighed. 'Fancy having a film star for a mother!'

'She's not a film star yet,' Xenia said.

'But still. And you on the newsreel! Golly.'

57

'Quiet, you girls!' said someone sitting behind them.

Then the music struck up for the main picture, and Xenia tried to forget that Mama was far away in America.

At least there is still Papa and me. It's up to me to look after him, like Mama asked.

Chapter Six

Buttercup was woken early on Monday morning by the sound of rotating blades thudding as a helicopter landed on the field by the house. Charles's side of the bed was empty and she remembered that he was leaving early for London City Airport to catch his flight to Switzerland for his meeting.

She clambered out of the four-poster bed and went to the window in time to see Charles striding out across the lawn to the gate that opened into the next-door field. Behind him was Carol's husband Steve, who acted as the caretaker, handyman and Charles's assistant when he was in Dorset, with a neat navy travelling bag. A moment later, the little aircraft was taking off, rising vertically until it dipped, turned and sped away east while Steve made his way back across the field towards the house.

Buttercup slipped back into bed, pulling the covers up around her and sighing. The house always felt different without Charles here, as though something vital had been drained from it. It became quieter, as though sliding down into dormant mode until its power source returned to re-animate it.

Coming downstairs later, she saw Agnieska, the Polish girl who came in to clean, dusting vigorously at a marble bust, rubbing it round and round as though she was wiping food off the dirty face of a child.

'Morning,' Buttercup said brightly, as she reached the bottom of the stairs. 'How are you?'

'Yes, very good,' Agnieska replied, glancing over swiftly before returning her attention to the marble bust. Her voice was surprisingly low, and her accent lilting.

Buttercup caught the bitter tang of cigarette smoke and wondered if smoking accounted for Agnieska's pale, pearl-grey complexion, her strangely light blue eyes and the hair that was ashy blond almost to whiteness. She was slender too, quite wraith-like.

Like a smoky sprite. The spirit of a bonfire or a temple brazier.

'And how are the boys?' Buttercup asked. Their names popped into her mind. 'Lukasz and David?'

'They are well,' Agnieska said with a sudden broad smile. 'Thank you.'

'I'm glad to hear it.' Buttercup headed towards the kitchen. 'I'm just going to have a word with Carol. See you later.'

Carol was in the kitchen, as usual, humming as she worked in her usual cheery way. Buttercup had managed to persuade her not to set up a formal breakfast in the dining room when

Charles was away, insisting she would prefer to eat at the kitchen table.

When Buttercup had first arrived at Charcombe after the honeymoon, she was still recovering from the mad whirl of the wedding and the speed of her courtship with Charles before that, and she'd been grateful for the way it ran so smoothly. It had been like moving into a comfortable country house hotel where she and Charles were the only guests, and in any case, they'd still been floating on their post-honeymoon cloud of bliss. But then he'd gone back to work, disappearing for long stretches, and she found herself alone. For the first time, it sunk in that she wouldn't be going back to her flat in Fulham, now rented out, and that she had resigned from her job running an office for a respected kitchen designer, with the intention of finding something else in Dorset, which had so far not led to anything. The full force of her life change had struck her. Where once she'd been busy keeping her flat tidy, commuting and working, as well as enjoying a busy social life, now she was at a permanent loose end.

It wasn't just that she had no job; there was literally nothing that had to be done. There were others to take care of all the cleaning, cooking, shopping and household maintenance. The large, well-equipped kitchen was Carol's domain; she did everything that Buttercup had assumed that she would one day do, from baking bread to making jam, to conjuring up delicious meals at a moment's notice. Buttercup still intended to do those things at some point, but it didn't seem so easy when the kitchen wasn't really hers. She still intended to look for a job of some kind, but her pregnancy put the process on hold and she'd never got back to it, stymied by the depression of her miscarriage. That was partly why she had started to spend so much time in the stables, where there was always work for her idle hands and where Phil didn't seem to mind her on his territory. That, and the balm it provided for her sorrow.

'Morning,' Carol sang out as she noticed Buttercup. She was polishing glasses as the radio played tinnily in the background. 'How are you today?'

'I'm fine, thank you. Charles is away for a few days.'

'I know. Mission Control has been in touch.' Carol grinned. 'He's back on Friday.'

'Oh. Good.' She hadn't known that. 'I'm glad you're on top of it. I must check the online diary.' Elaine kept it updated with all of Charles's movements and usually emailed with any key comings and goings. Buttercup went to the fridge and looked for the yoghurt.

'It's on the table, with your fruit and coffee.' Carol nodded her head at the table, where Buttercup's breakfast was neatly laid out.

'Thanks. I guess I must be a bit predictable.'

Carol shrugged. 'Don't worry, love. It's my job. Have you got some plans for the next few days?'

Buttercup went to the table and sat down. She spooned a mound of soft yoghurt into her bowl. 'I don't know,' she said, adding the berries. They dropped into the whiteness, staining it scarlet. Ever since the interview with the Tranters, she'd felt low again and she knew that it wasn't only the anniversary of the miscarriage. It was the fact she hadn't been able to conceive again. She felt as though she couldn't go on living in a constant cycle of hope and disappointment. 'I might go up to London while Charles is away,' she said. 'I haven't seen my friends in ages.'

'You must miss them,' Carol said sympathetically. She had finished the glasses, and hung her tea towel over the Aga rail. 'Do you all keep in touch?'

'Of course. Lots of messages and things.' Buttercup took a mouthful of tart yoghurt and sweet berries. 'But we used to see each other all the time. It would be nice to catch up with them.'

'Sure.' Carol went over to the fridge. 'Sounds great.'

'So I'll be back on Thursday, before Charles.'

'Fine. Just message me if you need anything out of the ordinary.' Carol was pulling things out of the fridge. 'Are you going to stay in Queen Anne's Close?'

'I'm not sure. I might stay with a friend.'

'Okay.' Carol put a bag of beans down on the counter. 'Let me know what you decide.'

Buttercup ate another mouthful with a prickle of annoyance. It was nothing against Carol personally, but why did she have to explain herself like this? Once she had been able to please herself, do what she liked. Now everyone needed to know where she was and what she was doing when it was no one's business, except Charles's, where she spent her time. She ate her breakfast, feeling out of sorts and irritable.

'By the way,' Carol said suddenly, and Buttercup looked up. 'Agnieska told me that she's got another job. Another cleaning gig.'

'Does she want to leave here?'

'No, it's as well as this, two afternoons a week. But the thing is ... it's down at Fitzroy House.'

Buttercup blinked and said, 'Oh. I see.'

'Do you mind? I thought I should let you know. She's on her own since her breakup, and her husband's gone back to Poland. She probably needs the money.'

She hesitated. 'No ... that's fine. There's no reason why she can't do both, I suppose.'

'Okay.' Carol smiled. 'Have a great trip.'

'Thanks. I will.'

As she drove out between the huge iron gates that led up to Charcombe Park, Buttercup glanced at Fitzroy House. Charles had told her it had been built for the widowed mother and unmarried sisters of a previous owner of the house, where they could live in comfortable dignity after having to leave their home. That was why it was so close, and yet separate, a small distance outside the gate and surrounded by its own garden.

Mothers and sisters, Buttercup thought, with a touch of bitterness. *Not ex-wives. Why can't she go away and leave us alone? It won't be long before the children won't need to live so close.*

In reality, the crossover between the children being home from school and Charles actually being at Charcombe had always been slim. With James at university now and Charlotte near the end of her schooling, they would be moving away in any case, and it looked as though Ingrid would still be at the end of the drive, watching the comings and goings and keeping an eye on her ex-husband.

'Come on, it's a bit bizarre,' her best friend Hazel had said, when Buttercup explained the set-up in Dorset. They had been having a pre-wedding get-together at Buttercup's flat to sort out the last details, just her, Hazel and Polly, her brides-maids, sitting on the floor around the coffee table eating takeaway. 'You've got your husband's ex-wife living at the bottom of the garden! Sounds barmy to me. Unhealthy.'

'Hazel, you don't know the circumstances,' Polly admon-ished her, always the diplomat to Hazel's frank speaker. 'It might make sense to them.'

'Hold on, let me make sure I've got this right.' Hazel frowned, staring upwards as she gathered her thoughts. 'So Ingrid and Charles were married for . . .'

'Ten years,' put in Buttercup. 'I think. Ten or twelve.'

'Right. They buy a fuck-off huge house together and she brings up the kids while he does it up.'

'So far so normal,' Polly said, digging around in her pad thai for morsels of prawn. 'I wouldn't mind that – he could do the builders and stuff. I'd do the fun bits.'

'Then she has an affair.' Hazel fixed Buttercup with an interrogative gaze. 'Do we know who with?'

Buttercup shook her head. 'I can't exactly ask. It looks nosy.'

'Well, what's he told you?'

'He just said that after they decided she should move out, she insisted on living close by to make it easier for him to see James and Charlotte.'

The other two must have heard the defensiveness in her voice because Hazel said in a softer tone:

'You're right, no one knows the circumstances. It's sad for the kids in any case but good they managed to do things in their best interests. As long as she doesn't expect to be your pal, popping up for coffee and biscuits and a poke-around to see what you're up to. Is she still with the bloke she had the affair with?'

'I don't know,' Buttercup said, feeling gloomy. She didn't like all this talk about Charles's other life when they ought to be looking forward to the rosy future ahead. 'Maybe.'

'Perhaps she's regretting having cheated on him, and wants him back!' Hazel said, pointing her chopsticks in emphasis. 'Maybe she's got plans to cosy up to you and then worm her way back in.'

Buttercup felt sick at the thought and pushed her plate away.

'Hazel! exclaimed Polly. 'That's ridiculous. Don't listen to her, Buttercup. It sounds like everyone has been very mature to me.'

Hazel shrugged and dug her chopsticks back into her food. 'Yeah, okay. But you'd better keep your guard up. Does Charles ever see her?'

Buttercup shook her head. 'No. He says they communicate through his office. To be honest, apart from the bare outline of what happened – she had an affair, they got divorced – he never speaks about her.'

'And you've never met her?' Polly said.

'Nope. I've never seen her, except for a glimpse or two when I've passed her house. There's nothing of her in the house either. No photos. Actually, no one ever mentions her. So I don't think she's any threat to Charles and me.'

She saw Polly and Hazel exchange a look and knew what they were thinking: that the whole set-up was very weird.

Well, they're right. Buttercup had left the village and was following the winding narrow roads on her way to the A303. *It is weird.* When she occasionally mentioned Ingrid, Charles would grow a little distant, his mouth setting in a line that meant he wasn't happy. Once, when she'd said heatedly that she wished Ingrid would just go and live somewhere else, he'd seemed to find it amusing, as though he was flattered that Buttercup was jealous of Ingrid.

'She doesn't have to go if she doesn't want to,' he'd said calmly. 'It's the terms of the divorce. I can't chuck her out.'

'Well, she has some nerve living so close, considering she was the unfaithful one. Doesn't she care how painful it must be for you to have her still so near? Can't you tell her we don't want her here?'

'That would most certainly make her stay.'

'Then she's just malicious, that's all. It wouldn't make any difference if she were on the other side of the village. It's not as though she lets the children come up here in any case.' Buttercup had felt a great surge of hatred towards Ingrid, then tried to temper it. 'Does she ever get in touch?'

'Of course not. We communicate through Elaine. She knows Ingrid well. It works.'

Buttercup thought of that as she joined the main road heading for London.

Everyone knows Ingrid. Phil. Carol and Steve. Everyone at the Hub. Even Agnieska is going to know her soon. Everyone except me.

Chapter Seven

It was late morning when Buttercup parked in the under-ground garage below the house in Westminster. She'd decided it was easier to stay in the flat after all, and had emailed Rose to let her know. The answer had pinged back almost instant-aneously.

No problem, Mrs R. All will be ready for you when you arrive. Do you need me to book anything else? I can have Rich standing by if you want.

Buttercup sent her thanks and said that there was no need for Rich to drive her around London this time. When Butter-cup stepped out of the lift by the apartment, Rose, young and chic in a sharp navy trouser suit and dark-framed spectacles, was there to greet her.

'The flat's all ready,' she said. 'And Charles says he'll be online to talk to you later this afternoon if you're in. What are your plans?'

'I'm going out to lunch with a friend, I'm not sure what

after that. I'll probably be in this evening. Goodness, Rose – is that an engagement ring?' Buttercup looked down at the sparkler on Rose's finger. 'Congratulations!'

'Thank you! Jacob finally popped the question in Paris.' Rose smiled happily. She held the ring up so it glittered on her finger under the electric light. 'It's gorgeous, isn't it? I love it.'

'It's stunning. When's the wedding?'

'Next summer.' Rose opened the door to the penthouse flat and led her into the luxurious hall. 'Here you are. Let me know if you're in tonight and I'll order in the steamed sea bass from Riccardo's. I know how much you like it.'

'Thanks, you're so thoughtful. I'd like that.'

Rose had grown to know her well in the last two years. She would even email with reminders when dental appointments were due, offer to book the hairdresser or sort out tickets for shows she thought Buttercup would enjoy, or suggest a dinner reservation at the latest fashionable restaurant.

'You're welcome! Enjoy your lunch. Going anywhere nice?'

'Nothing special, I'm just meeting Polly in her lunch hour.'

'Great. See you later.'

When Rose had left, Buttercup looked around at the flat. Familiar as it was, she was usually with Charles and it was different being here alone. Rose had prepared carefully: her favourite champagne was in an ice bucket on the counter, a bouquet of white ranunculi – her favourite flower – in a vase on the table. No doubt her favourite bath oil would be next to the bath too.

I'm so lucky. It's all lovely. No wonder my old friends think I'm being outrageously spoiled.

People went to so much trouble to make sure she was happy and looked after. She remembered bounding in here almost two years ago, making Charles laugh with her gasps of excitement at everything on offer: the steam room, the fitness suite, the marble bathrooms, the deep-pile carpets and things that moved with a flick of a switch or a voice command.

'Play Chopin's nocturnes!' she had ordered and an instant later, piano music floated out of the speakers. 'Oh wow!'

'The marvels of modern technology,' Charles had said drily, but she could tell that he was enjoying her wide-eyed wonder.

The novelty of it all had worn off now, and she wished the flat could feel a little more like home. She ought to ask Rose to stop doing so much for her, perhaps even keep out of the flat altogether, but it seemed so churlish when all people wanted to do was help her.

Buttercup put her case in the bedroom, and headed out to meet Polly.

Polly was waiting for her in a busy sandwich bar near her office in Holborn.

'Can't be long,' Polly said apologetically as they settled down with their lunch in a booth. 'Big case on.'

'It's lovely to see you, however long,' Buttercup said, shamefaced about her own inactivity when Polly was so busy. She had nowhere to go and nothing she had to do.

'How are things? Tell me everything.'

Buttercup explained how depressed she'd been feeling about the miscarriage and lack of a pregnancy. 'I know I'm young and there's plenty of time, but that's what worries me. Why isn't it happening? I got pregnant practically on honeymoon last time and now nothing. It's turning into an obsession for me, Polls.'

Polly put a sympathetic hand on hers. 'I'm sorry. That's not good. What does Charles say?'

'He says wait. I don't think he necessarily minds if we don't have a baby for a little while longer, and he doesn't seem to realise how much I want to know if there's a problem.'

Polly frowned. 'He doesn't want to find out for your sake?'

'It's not that he doesn't understand how upset I've been,' Buttercup said quickly. 'It's just that he's more relaxed than me, I suppose. He's not in a hurry.'

Polly fixed her with a long look, and then said, 'If you want to find out, you should find out. It's obviously making you unhappy. My friend has just seen a brilliant consultant about her fertility problems and now she's expecting IVF twins. She's over the moon. I'll get the name for you.'

Buttercup felt hopeful. 'Really? That would be great. Please send it to me and I'll see if I can persuade Charles to go.'

'Why not go on your own, if he's too busy?' Polly asked. 'Would he mind?'

'I couldn't do that.' Buttercup shook her head. 'I wouldn't want to go behind his back.'

'So tell him all about it. Tell him you're going to see someone, just to set the ball rolling. Why would it be a problem?'

'I don't know,' Buttercup said slowly. 'Perhaps it wouldn't.'

'Good. I'll send the name when I get back to the office.'

After lunch, Buttercup wandered back towards Westminster, wondering what to do with herself. She had supper booked with Hazel tomorrow night and apart from that, she'd had vague ideas of seeing an exhibition at the National Gallery, perhaps getting her hair done, but when the message from Polly popped into her phone with the consultant's number, she realised what had been in her mind all along.

By the river, she stopped and rang the clinic.

'You're in luck,' said the receptionist. 'I had a cancellation for tomorrow just five minutes ago. Can you come in at ten a.m.?'

'Yes,' Buttercup said firmly. 'I can.'

She had just finished supper that evening and was thinking of taking a shower when a series of chimes alerted her to the fact that Charles was trying to contact her. She clicked a controller at the large flat screen in the sitting room, and Charles sprung to life in front of her. He was sitting at a desk in a neutral hotel room somewhere and staring out at her. As soon as he saw they were connected, he smiled broadly and gave her a jaunty wave.

'Hello, darling. Rose told me you were coming up to town. Did you have a good journey?'

His features were somewhat distorted by the camera but it cheered her up to see his familiar face and the boyish smile.

She curled up on the sofa, tucking her feet underneath her. 'Yes, fine. How are you?'

'Bored witless. But it's all necessary. The new project in Montenegro has run into some problems. We'll sort it out, I'm sure, after another day or two of talking.' He smiled at her. 'What are you doing in London?'

'I saw Polly today, which was nice. I'm going to see Hazel tomorrow night. I'll do some shopping.'

'Shopping? What for? Anything special?'

'I saw something in *Vogue* the other day that I thought would be perfect for the company Christmas party. And my hair needs doing.' Her hand went to her blond hair, cut into a shoulder-length choppy bob.

'You just had it done, didn't you? It looks fine to me.'

'It only needs a trim so I'll pop in for a quick snip. And I want to try a new facialist.'

'Oh. Who?'

'Um.' Buttercup felt a hot pink flush creeping up her cheeks. Charles liked to know details and she usually chattered away, telling everything without any kind of filter. She'd always loved the way he enjoyed all the silly details of her days, from what kind of sandwich she ate to the TV programmes she watched. She had never kept anything back from him before and it was more difficult than she'd imagined. The knowledge of her appointment the following day filled her with an unpleasant sensation of guilt and although she hadn't meant to lie to him, she was already finding herself concealing and telling half-truths. It was on the tip of her tongue to tell him about the consultant but somehow she couldn't say it. 'I can't remember her name! It's on my phone. I'll check it later.'

'Rose will have put it in the calendar. She's good that way.'

'I didn't book through Rose. I didn't want to bother her. You know . . . she's so busy.'

Charles raised an eyebrow. 'It's her job, darling. That's why I pay her a good salary. She's there to make your life easy. Is she not keen to help you?'

Buttercup thought she detected a faint edge of steel creep into Charles's voice. He was a good and kind employer up until the moment that he felt someone had not pulled their weight or was taking advantage of him. Then he could be ruthless.

Buttercup said quickly, 'Rose couldn't be more helpful. But she's busy, and honestly, it's nothing.' She took a breath and then said lamely, 'I don't need her to put everything in the calendar. You don't want to be bothered with all the trivia. Even my hair appointments? A trip to the dentist? It will just clutter up your diary. I mean, it would stop you seeing what's important, like your meetings and your travel . . .'

Charles smiled at her. 'Don't be silly, darling. You're important. You know that. There's nothing more important than you.'

'You're sweet.' She smiled back at him. 'I hope it's not too dull tomorrow.'

'I'll fill you in when it's over. And you can tell me all about this new facialist and what she's going to do to make you even more exquisite. Good night, darling.'

'Good night.' She blew him kisses. 'Good night, good night!' His face vanished and the screen went blank.

The next morning Buttercup went down the stairs past the open door of the office where Rose and Elaine sat at large glass desks with over-sized screens in front of them.

'Hello, Mrs R, are you off?' called Elaine. She was a trim middle-aged woman with short hair dyed solid black, brown eyes rimmed in kohl, and a taste for colourful tunic tops over black trousers.

'Yes, I am.' Buttercup pulled her cross-body bag more tightly to her, clutching it hard. 'I'm out for the day.'

Rich came into view from where he'd been standing in the office, talking to the women. He had a black taxi and was kept on a permanent retainer by Charles to get him around London as efficiently as possible using all the taxi lanes and back-street knowledge at his disposal. 'Can I drive you somewhere?'

'No thanks, Rich.' She smiled at him. 'It's kind of you to offer.'

'Just let me know if you need me, and I'll pop right along,' he said, cheerfully.

'Thank you. I'm having supper with a friend so I probably won't be back before you've gone.'

Rose nodded. 'Understood. Have a lovely day.'

'I will. You too. Bye!'

A moment later she came out on Queen Anne's Close and headed towards Parliament Square, soon losing herself among tourists and people hurrying to work.

From there she walked up through Trafalgar Square, up past Chinatown, thinking of the high jinks she used to get up to with her friends around there. Things were different now: most were settled and starting families, and nights out were few and far between.

Just west of Covent Garden she popped into her old hair salon and got her fringe trimmed. Once she got to Marylebone, she went into a chic café for a coffee, making it last as she watched the world go by until her appointment. She felt disconnected from London these days: the traffic, the crowds, the noise and the smells. She wondered how she could have put up with it for so long when there was the open countryside to ride across, beautiful, full of wildlife and brimming with fresh, clean air.

Perfect for a child. A wonderful place to grow up.

That thought quelled the doubts over whether she was doing the right thing. Just before ten, she left and walked briskly in the direction of Harley Street, nervous but determined.

The tests lasted quite a while: the clinic staff took lots of blood samples, scanned her externally and internally with ultrasounds, X-rayed her and then did a full MRI.

'We'll see what the results tell us when they come in in a few days,' the consultant said when Buttercup was sitting opposite as they went through her notes. She peered at Buttercup through small, wire-framed spectacles; her pulled-back hair made her look like a strict school teacher. 'First things first. I'd like to see you tracking your ovulation and making sure you have sex frequently at the optimum time.'

'I do that,' Buttercup said quickly. 'I have an app, and a thermometer. Charles isn't always around at the right time, but he often is.'

'Okay. Make sure you record everything so we can be certain.' The consultant frowned and clicked some buttons on her keyboard. 'And you've been pregnant before.'

'Not long after we got married, I got pregnant. We were over the moon.'

The consultant looked sympathetic. 'And it didn't work out. I'm sorry.'

'No. It was absolutely . . . awful.'

'You'd be surprised how many first pregnancies do end in miscarriage – sometimes even before the woman knows she's pregnant. But the important thing is that you did conceive. And it was a spontaneous loss of the foetus?'

Buttercup tried to fight the sudden rush of nausea that broke over her. The consultant's language reminded her of the horrible hour in the hospital, when they probed her and spoke coolly of the products of conception. Her little baby; the tiny, flickering life snuffed out and turned into no more than a biological by-product, a bit of waste matter.

'Yes,' she said, trying to keep her voice firm. 'I was over thirteen weeks pregnant and suddenly . . . well, I got cramping and then . . . bleeding . . . and then . . .' She trailed off, remembering the awful strangeness of the little curled creature, more like a fossil than a human, no bigger than the size of her thumbnail, sitting on her fingertips: a large head, tiny dots in it, and minuscule protrusions that would have become limbs. In the hospital she had told them she knew the baby was gone because she had seen it, but they hadn't believed her. She was still haunted by that small curl of humanity. Numb, she had put it carefully in a wrap of lavatory paper and left it on the cistern. Then she had dealt with the bleeding, and driven herself to hospital, not wanting to tell anyone else what was happening. Much later, when she'd returned home, pale and sad, she'd gone to the little wrap and opened it. The pink blob had dried out, leaving only the brittle curve of tiny spinal bones, all that showed what it had been. It had cracked and broken as she moved it, becoming unrecognisable. So she had thrown it into the bowl and flushed it away.

That was what weighed her down so heavily.

'I'm sorry,' the consultant said again, more gently. 'But in a way, it's positive because it means that things have functioned before so we can have a strong confidence that they will again. I'll be in touch when the results come in. And in the meantime, try to relax. Look after yourself, eat well, sleep, and see what happens.'

'I will,' Buttercup promised, relieved, at last, that soon she would know something. Anything.

Charles called her again that evening before she headed out to supper with Hazel.

Buttercup sat on the sofa, half aware of the lights of London sparkling out from beyond the roof terrace outside. Charles, thousands of miles away, was in the same dull hotel room. He asked how she had enjoyed herself and it was on the tip of her tongue to tell everything but something held her back.

I'll tell him when we get the results. No need to worry him before then.

Instead, she talked cheerfully of her afternoon shopping in Marylebone, her impulse visit to the Wallace Collection as she'd walked past on her way to Selfridges, and showed off a few of her purchases.

'Lovely, darling,' Charles said, approving. 'And are you going home tomorrow?'

'Yes, I think so. But I'll drive up and see Mum first.'

'That's a lovely idea. Give her my love.'

'I will.' She appreciated that he always did this, even though they both knew how pointless it was.

'Have a safe journey. I'll let the girls know you're leaving. They'll make sure the car is full before you set off, and they'll alert Carol you're on your way.'

'Thank you.' She smiled at the screen. 'You think of everything.'

Chapter Eight

'Hello, Mum, it's me. How are you?'

Buttercup sat down on the chair near the daybed where her mother lay prone, one leg twitching and rubbing against the other in a ceaseless, repeating pattern. She was dressed in clean neat clothes and her grey hair was brushed, held back by a headband. Her eyes were wide but didn't appear to see anything, and her mouth was open in the toothless way that Buttercup still found it hard to accept. They'd said a couple of years ago that the best thing to do was take out her mother's teeth, now that she was eating only purees and couldn't care for them herself.

Buttercup reached for the cool smoothness of her mother's hand. 'Stacy said you've been doing well. I'm so glad.'

Sometimes it seemed ridiculous to talk to someone who had no awareness of whether Buttercup was there or not, but she didn't know what else to do. What was the alternative? Ignore her? Forget her? She could never do that.

'She knows you're here,' Stacy had said. She was one of

81

the nurses, kindly and reassuring. 'I'm sure she can hear me, and understands.'

'Do you think so?' Buttercup felt like a novice nun who was desperate to believe but full of doubt. 'She seems so far away.'

'She's a gentle one, that's why. Plenty of others here aren't like her. There's a woman down the hall who's violent, it's awful. I always think you can see the soul more clearly when the outside gets stripped away. Your mother is a good one and I think she's still here.'

Buttercup's eyes had filled with tears. She wanted so badly to believe.

'So you must talk to her, tell her what's going on,' Stacy urged. 'She likes it.'

It seemed so difficult to explain her life when everything was so different from how it had been before the illness claimed her mother's mind. The early onset Alzheimer's had begun when Buttercup was a teenager; by the time she was in her twenties, her mother was finding it hard to recognise her and her language had deteriorated badly. Her husband's love and devotion had been unstinting but eventually he had to agree with Buttercup that he could no longer care for her mother alone and they had found a good home where he visited her almost daily.

Buttercup badly wanted her father to have a life beyond caring for her mother, who increasingly had no life at all and was even unaware of what she no longer had. Once, angry at the terrible disease, desperate to be free of it herself, she had shouted at her father, 'Can't you see she doesn't have a clue who you are any more? Go out, live your life, meet someone else! Don't sacrifice yourself, she wouldn't have wanted that.'

Her father had looked at her with an expression that was as close to anger and disapproval as he had ever come. 'She's my wife, Buttercup. I can't abandon her. I'm married – till death us do part. That's just how it is. I couldn't live with myself if I didn't care for her until the end.'

She'd burst into tears of grief and humility in the face of his unquestioning, unstinting love, when her own didn't seem to be as strong. But his end had come before her mother's with an unexpected and massive heart attack, leaving Buttercup utterly bereft. She was sure the loss of her father triggered a sudden descent for her mother: it wasn't so much that she was able to register the fact of her husband's death, but that his visits stopped. Buttercup was now all she had left.

The loss and loneliness had been so great, Buttercup had wondered how she would ever cope. Outwardly, she seemed perfectly fine, going to work, going out, smiling and appearing normal; but underneath she was a churning mess of depression, tears and panic. Her father's signet ring hung on a chain around her neck like a talisman, and she touched it many times a day when the pain struck.

She was holding it delicately between her fingers at a drinks party her boss, Lazlo, had taken her to, standing in a small circle of strangers, not listening to the general talk until she heard her own name pronounced in unusual rasping tones:

'Buttercup Wilcox? That's the most marvellous name I've ever heard.'

She looked around to see a man standing near her, and realised she had not clocked herself being introduced to him.

'I'm Charles Redmain,' he said, and smiled, that odd enchanting animation working its magic. She liked him at once, drawn to the light in his eyes: intelligent, curious, knowing. He was smartly dressed and well presented, his sandy hair neatly cut, his sharp-boned face clean-shaven, his looks distinguished and yet boyish. 'Boring, I'm afraid, compared to you, and not one bit unique.'

'I'm Anna, really,' she said, taken by the way he responded to her name, instead of asking what her parents were thinking of, or whether she liked butter, as most people did.

'Then I prefer Buttercup by miles. Now, Lazlo here tells me you're his assistant and I want to get you an enormous drink to help you cope. He's a ridiculously annoying old fusspot.'

Lazlo, her boss, said, 'Really, Charles!' and laughed.

'He daren't be cross as I'm an investor in his business.' Charles smiled again. 'Would you like that drink?'

'Yes please,' she said, attracted to his vivacity and fizzing charm.

'Good.'

Within a few moments, they were talking intently and he had begun to learn everything about her. When the drinks party ended, he took her to dinner to a discreet but very luxurious restaurant nearby, and over dinner she was surprised to find herself opening up about her father's death, her grief for him, and the void it had left in her life.

'You poor girl,' he said, his expression tender. 'What a horrible time you've had. You're strong and independent, I can see that. But everyone needs a bit of looking after from time to time.' And something in her responded with a chime of relief that her inner weakness had been recognised, not with scorn but with kindness.

The next day forty white roses arrived at Lazlo's office for Buttercup, with an invitation to the opera that week. From that moment, her life lost its bleakness and began to sparkle. Charles treated her like something rare and precious but at the same time assumed she was as energetic and resilient as he was. He brought fun and adventure and, most of all, reassurance into her life. At a moment's notice, she could find herself packing for trip to Paris to see an exhibition or to Rome for the opening of a new restaurant, or be sunning herself on the deck of a boat cruising Greek islands while Charles researched a business opportunity – plans for a new hotel or a harbour complex or any of the many projects he invested in. But at the same, he was full of kindness. He insisted on meeting Buttercup's mother and going along to visit whenever he could.

'I'm just sorry I'll never get to meet your father,' he had said softly, squeezing her hand. 'He sounds like a wonderful man.'

Lazlo was not surprised on the January day when she arrived with a huge aquamarine on her ring finger.

'It was inevitable,' he said simply. 'I saw it when I introduced the two of you that night. Congratulations, sweetheart. We'll miss you.'

'I'm not leaving,' she'd laughed.

'Not yet – but you'll find Charles is a full-time job,' Lazlo said.

She had intended to keep working but once they agreed that they would move full-time to Dorset, it hadn't been possible and she'd handed in her resignation after all.

She'd visited her mother to tell her the news too, radiant for the first time in many months, rapturous with all the details of Charles and how wonderful he was.

Her mother stared into space, her right leg twitching and rubbing against her left, and said nothing.

'You don't have to worry about me any more, Mum,' Buttercup had said softly. 'I'm going to be all right. It's going to be perfect, I just know it.'

It was that reassurance that meant even now Buttercup could not bring herself to tell her mother about the miscarriage or the trip to the consultant. Instead, she talked on about Hazel and the dinner out they'd had the night before, her trip to London, how busy Charles was.

When an hour was up, she bent to kiss her mother's cheek. 'Bye, Mum. I'll see you soon, I promise. Lots of love. Charles sends his love too.'

But as soon as she was in the car on the way home, she wished she'd confided everything.

Passing the King's Head on her way home, Buttercup noticed that there was a car outside the pub.

Is it the Tranters? They can't be there already, can they?

On impulse, she slowed down and turned into the car park as Cathy Tranter came out of the open door of the pub.

'Hello!' Buttercup called, stopping and getting out. 'Are you doing a recce?'

Cathy stared at her, bewildered, then recognition spread across her face. 'I'm sorry, I couldn't place you for a minute!' She came over, smiling, looking far more relaxed than she had at the interview, her copper hair pulled back into a loose bun with ends floating free. 'Yeah, we've come down to take a look and do some measuring up. We're going to be living over the shop, so to speak, and it's a bit smaller than we're used to. Still, a good reason to do some decluttering.'

She was wearing a loose dress with a long belted cardigan over the top to protect her from the autumn chill in the air.

'How are you feeling?' Buttercup asked, indicating the bump.

'Fine, thanks, though it's not easy being pregnant when you've got a three-year-old, I'll tell you that for nothing. Have you got any?'

'Not yet. Soon, I hope.' Buttercup looked over Cathy's shoulder. 'Where's your boy?'

'Inside with Wilf. Come on in and say hello.'

Buttercup followed her into the empty pub and they went through to the kitchen where a small blond boy was sitting on the steel countertop and kicking his heels, an apple held between two hands.

'Olly, say hello to Mrs Redmain,' Cathy said as they went in.

'Hello,' said the boy obediently, and gnawed at his apple like a squirrel, his small white teeth carving out a bite.

'Hi.' Wilf got up from where he'd been kneeling on the floor, inspecting something. 'I didn't realise we had a visitor.'

Buttercup said, 'Sorry to intrude. I just wanted to stop and say how pleased I am that you're coming to live here. When do you think you'll move in?'

Wilf smiled, rubbing his hands on his jeans. 'We'd like to be in by Christmas. That's a good time for pubs. But we'll see. It depends on our house in London and how quickly we can sell it. Lots of unknowns.'

'It would be lovely to have the pub open at Christmas,' Buttercup said. 'Roaring fires, mulled wine.'

'Good old-fashioned pub grub,' Wilf said. 'Venison stew. Roast pheasant with game chips. A good beef pie. Not forgetting a storming burger and the best sausage and mash you'll ever taste.'

'Don't get him started.' Cathy laughed. She shook her head. 'He can't wait to start serving up the best food in the county.'

'The country, actually,' Wilf corrected her.

'Okay, Masterchef. You'll have to get to grips with the kitchen first. A good clean and an inspection for starters.'

'I think it sounds brilliant,' Buttercup said eagerly. 'Just what we need round here. How long are you staying?'

'We're camping here tonight, going home tomorrow.'

'Oh?' Buttercup looked round at the empty restaurant kitchen. 'It doesn't look all that usable.'

'There's the small kitchen upstairs in the living quarters,' Wilf said. 'We'll cook there.'

'Why not come up to me? My husband won't be back till

tomorrow. Come up and have a kitchen supper with me, and tell me all about the plans for the pub.'

Cathy flicked an uncertain look at her husband. 'We'd love to, but there's Olly . . . and it's pretty short notice for you . . .'

'Oh, don't worry about that. The larder's well stocked. And you can bring Olly and put him down to sleep at our house. We've got plenty of room and cots and things for when my friends visit.'

The couple looked at each other for a moment before Wilf said decisively, 'We'd like that, thanks.'

'Good. Come up early, that will give you time to get Olly settled.'

Buttercup drove back to the house in a good mood, enthused by her sudden decision. She explained to Carol about the extra guests and by the time Cathy and Wilf arrived that evening, everything was set up in one of the spare bedrooms and with a toddler supper ready in the kitchen.

'This is so nice of you,' Cathy said, as Wilf sat down with Olly at the table to help him spoon up the pasta and tomato sauce.

'Not at all,' Buttercup replied. 'Carol did all the work.'

'Carol?' Cathy looked around expectantly.

'She's gone home, but she does most of the cooking. It's lovely to have you here.' She watched as the small boy crowed and chatted as he ate his supper, smearing a good deal of it over his face in the process. Tippi stood close by, her tail wagging, hoping for scraps, and quickly licking up dropped pasta. Buttercup wanted to sit down and join in feeding him, but

Cathy was keen to chat and look around the kitchen so she poured glasses of wine for herself and Wilf, and an elderflower fizz for Cathy, then showed her around the kitchen, feeling rather embarrassed that she wasn't sure which cupboard housed the dishwasher or how the fancy sous vide oven worked.

'Wilf will be pretty jealous if you show him that – he's desperate for one,' Cathy said, sipping her drink. 'How long have you lived here?'

'Almost two years.' Buttercup was suddenly conscious that she rarely used the kitchen or laundry, and never cooked or cleaned or shopped. Hazel jokingly called it her lap of luxury and made jokes about Buttercup having forgotten how to use a washing machine and make a cup of tea, but it all added to the sense of not entirely belonging in her own home, as if she were still a newcomer.

'It's so beautiful here,' Cathy said. 'And the countryside! It's magnificent. I can't wait till we finally get out of London and live with this every day.'

'Yes, it is lovely.' Buttercup glanced at the kitchen table, where Olly was swallowing the last of his pasta, coaxed by his father with the promise of fruity yoghurt if he ate two more mouthfuls. A thought came into her mind, strong and clear. *I can't imagine Charles doing that.*

As soon as she thought it, she knew it was true. Charles wouldn't have the patience or desire to sit with a wriggling child, and risk tomato sauce on his shirt cuffs.

Another thought occurred to her. *Is it possible that Charles doesn't want children as much as he claims?*

As soon as she thought this, she felt panicked and breathless, gripped by an impulse to pick up her phone and call him immediately, and quiz him.

But she couldn't do that. Cathy was talking about the forthcoming move. Wilf was wiping up yoghurt, while Olly slurped it eagerly from his bowl, waving his spoon around between mouthfuls.

I have to get on with this evening. But tomorrow I'll talk to Charles.

The feeling of panic began to subside and she forced herself to be calm. Brightly, she showed them up to the spare room, leaned against the bathroom door to watch as Olly had his bath, his parents kneeling beside it to play with him and sponge him clean. When he was dressed in his pyjamas and tucked up with Wilf for a bedtime story, Cathy and Buttercup said goodnight and tiptoed out.

'Thank God that's over!' Cathy said with a sigh.

Buttercup led her down the back stairs to the kitchen. 'But he's adorable.'

'He is. But it's hard work, night after night. Relentless.'

Buttercup felt a deep sense of longing to be up on the spare room bed, the small warm body tucked next to hers, the sweet-smelling head resting on her, the gentle rhythm of a bedtime story filling the air. 'I suppose it must be.' She hoped she didn't sound too yearning.

'You'll find out when it's your turn. I mean, it is wonderful to be a parent, but I couldn't cope if Wilf wasn't a fantastic dad. I never dreamed how tough it would be.' Her hands went over her bump. 'I'm pretty nervous about how it will be when this one's born. If one is hard, imagine what two will be like . . .'

'Yes,' Buttercup said faintly.

'But with Wilf on hand, and both of us around full-time, it will be so much easier than it used to be.' Cathy smiled. 'It's another reason why I'm so happy we're moving here.'

Buttercup was staring at the floor, uneasy again. It struck her that this huge house and all the help within it ought to be perfect for a family. And yet the cosiness of the pub, with its small upstairs flat, suddenly seemed incomparably nicer. Cathy was chatting on, not noticing Buttercup's retreat into silence.

What's wrong with me? I've got everything, it's all perfect, just as I knew it would be. As soon as a baby comes, it will all be complete. And all I have to do is talk to Charles about my worries. It will be fine, I know it.

Her mood lightened over the dinner Carol had left: a chicken casserole with herby dumplings floating in it and garlic green beans, eaten around the kitchen table. The atmosphere was relaxed and cheerful; Wilf pronounced the food excellent and something he might consider copying for the pub menu. As they ate, he held forth about his previous career as a builder and his excitement about the career he'd always longed for, as a chef and publican.

'It's the dream,' Cathy said, her eyes bright. 'We're determined to make it work, aren't we, sweetheart?'

'Yup.' Wilf had relaxed even more as he put away a few glasses of white wine. 'It's a risk for us, I'll be honest. We're selling our London house and putting all the money into this. It's got to work or we are – to be Anglo Saxon about it – fucked.'

'I'm sure you'll make it a huge success,' Buttercup said firmly. 'Will it cost so much?'

'A full refurb,' Wilf said. 'And we're going to convert the outbuildings into accommodation. This is a prime area for holidaymakers. If we get the food right and the marketing, we should be able to make a decent fist of it.'

'We want to start a few local events,' Carol chimed in. 'A food festival, maybe, to showcase local producers. There's so much on offer round here.'

Wilf looked earnestly at Buttercup. 'You've got the big house. We've got the pub. It could be the start of a beautiful friendship.'

She laughed. 'Yes, I'm sure it is! But you'll have to speak to Charles about that.'

'Speak to Charles about what?'

Buttercup jumped at the sound of that familiar, rasping voice. She turned to see her husband walking into the kitchen, his navy-blue travelling bag over his shoulder. Stammering slightly, she jumped to her feet. 'Darling! You're home! How wonderful. I had no idea . . . I thought it was tomorrow.'

'We finished early. I thought I'd surprise you.' He came over, dropped his bag on a chair and kissed her warmly, before turning to look at Wilf and Cathy, who were suddenly quiet. 'Wilf, isn't it?'

'Evening, Mr Redmain,' Wilf said, his ebullience muted.

'Have you moved into the pub already?' Charles lifted his eyebrows. 'Hello, Cathy.'

'Hello,' Cathy replied politely. 'We were visiting today to measure up. Your wife kindly asked us up to supper.'

'So I see.' Charles glanced over the remains on the table, suddenly showing his tiredness.

Buttercup followed his gaze. 'There's plenty left, darling, if you're hungry.'

'I'll have some later.'

There was a pause, and then Wilf, swapping a swift glance with his wife, said, 'We must be on our way, actually.'

'Oh no,' Buttercup said, crestfallen. 'Must you?' She'd been enjoying the casual evening. Through Wilf and Cathy's eyes, this was her home, her domain. She had the sense that when they left, she would go back to being in that strange nebulous position: neither guest nor mistress. A permanent newcomer. The long-time resident at the luxury hotel. 'Are you sure?'

'Yes,' Cathy said firmly. 'It's been lovely but we must leave you two alone. We'll take Olly and get on our way.'

'Olly?' Charles asked, pouring out some wine into a glass.

Buttercup said, 'Their little boy. He's upstairs, asleep.'

'How nice. Well, I'm so pleased you had a charming evening but we mustn't stop you from getting back.'

With a scraping of chairs and polite murmurings of thanks, the evening was over. Buttercup waited in the hall until the Tranters came down with Olly, Wilf carrying him wrapped up in a blanket, a ruffle of blond hair, closed eyes and pink cheeks just visible over its rim.

'Good night, little man,' she whispered as they carried him out to the car. It was ridiculous, she knew, but the house felt colder and emptier without him.

'I wish you'd let me know you'd invited the Tranters for dinner, darling,' Charles said, as they got ready for bed. 'I was looking forward to having you to myself this evening.'

'I'm sorry, I thought you were back tomorrow.' She was sitting at her dressing table, taking off her make-up, swiping away the cold cream and leaving putty-coloured streaks on the cotton wool.

'It was a surprise for you.' He smiled a little tightly. 'I'm sorry. I'm just so tired after the last few days and I was looking forward to seeing you. I've spent all week with colleagues and I just wanted to relax.'

'You can relax with them. They're so nice.'

'Not really. We're their employers.'

'They've bought the lease, that's all. They don't work for us!'

Charles stopped unbuttoning his cuffs and looked over at her. 'I may be a bit old-fashioned, but I don't think it's quite the thing to have the pub landlord and his wife here for intimate dinners, that's all. If you make friends with Cathy, that's different, but . . .'

She looked back, surprised.

He closed his eyes for a moment, then shook his head. 'Sorry, darling, forgive me. I'm tired . . . it's been a long day.' He turned away, and she could only see his back, the creases in his shirt and the trimmed sandy-grey hair at the back of his neck.

She turned to face the mirror, where she could see an expression in her own eyes that she could not quite read.

I need to ask him what he really thinks about having children. But this definitely isn't the right time.

Chapter Nine

Xenia stood at the bay window in her sitting room, squinting up the lane at the gates of Charcombe Park until she saw them swing open and the bicycle she had been waiting for began to edge through the gap. At once, she went quickly to her front door, flung it open and hurried down the path, calling, 'You! Yes, girl, you!'

The slender young woman had pushed the bike through the gates and was on the lane. She turned at the sound of Xenia's voice, staring over with questioning eyes.

Xenia beckoned to her briskly. 'Come here.'

'Yes?' The girl dismounted and walked over tentatively, rolling her bike beside her.

'What's your name?'

'Agnieska.'

'Polish? I see – well, come inside, I want to ask you something.' Xenia led the way back up the path, walking quickly. Her vision might be suffering but she was still fit and her pace was vigorous. 'Come along, follow me. Leave your bicycle there, by the porch. Come along in!'

Xenia went into the drawing room, the girl following. She waved her arm about to indicate the room. 'Can you do anything about this?'

The Polish girl stood silently for a moment, looking around, her expression unchanging. Then she turned to face the old woman. 'You want I clean?'

'Yes, yes. I can't see the dust any more, I can't see what's in front of me. I need someone to clean and tidy and keep it organised for me.'

'Whole house?'

'Naturally. I can't live in squalor.'

'What day?'

'What days can you do?'

Agnieska thought for a moment. 'Thursday afternoon. Friday morning. Other times I am already busy.'

'Friday morning. Four hours. That should be enough to tidy up after one woman. If it isn't, we'll see about adding the afternoon as well. Come at eight.'

'I come at nine thirty,' the girl said in her low voice. 'My children, I go to school.'

'Oh.' Xenia blinked, surprised to be defied with such ease. But she understood that the children going to school was important and she was reassured by the girl's bluntness. It implied honesty. 'All right. I'll supply all your cleaning things, you must use what I want you to use and do it just as I like. I'll pay you well but you must be on time and no coffee breaks or phone calls. My last girl would talk incessantly on the mobile in her own language and it made me so cross.'

98

'Yes,' Agnieska said blankly and Xenia wondered what, if anything, she had understood.

Xenia drew herself up to her full height, which was rather less than it had once been. 'And you are to call me Princess or Princess Arkadyoff. Do you understand?'

'Arkadyoff?' Agnieska's pale eyes glittered. 'Russian?'

'My father was Russian. But I was born in this country. I have never been to Russia, as a matter of fact.' She added stiffly, 'I hope that won't be a problem.'

There was a pause and Agnieska said, 'Problem? No. Fine.'

'Good. Then you can do your first day tomorrow and, if we are both happy, we'll carry on. Bring your passport. '

Agnieska nodded. 'Sure.'

'Then I'll show you out. Till nine thirty tomorrow.'

The following morning, Xenia was awake earlier than usual, fretting about whether she had done the right thing by inviting this stranger into her home.

Not just any stranger, a Polish girl. Papa always talked so disparagingly about the Poles. And perhaps she'll dislike me, or want to steal from me. It's hardly any wonder they dislike Russians, after the years of Communism.

Papa certainly hated the Soviet state more than he could ever dislike Poland. But what the girl would make of working for someone of Russian heritage . . . *Still, she had every chance to say no.*

Xenia did not feel Russian in any way. She couldn't speak the language and had never visited. She had seen her Russian grandmother – the terrifying and elderly Princess Arkadyoff, who had escaped the revolution on board the ship sent to rescue the dowager empress from the Red Guard – only a handful of times and remembered a small, straight-backed woman in old-fashioned clothes, layers of pearls at her neck, grey hair curled and dressed high, who smelt of jasmine and powder. She had sensed disapproval, she had no idea why.

Some of Grandmama's things had come to them after she died: icons, jewellery boxes – empty – bibles in Russian and French, enamelled photograph frames and porcelain trinket pots. Things that had been easy to carry. The rest of the family wealth had been left behind for the Soviets. Xenia wondered what the Polish girl would make of the bits of Russia around the cottage. She had put some of the icons on the wall in her bedroom, along with a large silver crucifix, and in the drawing room were silver-framed photographs of her Russian relations among the pictures of her parents and their friends.

She'll just have to get used to it, Xenia thought. *I'll find someone else if she doesn't do.*

But she hoped that this girl would be the one.

She had taken her customary breakfast of strong black coffee and oat bran porridge and was watching the clock with increasing irritation as the hands crept past nine thirty when there was a light knock at the front door. When she opened it, the girl stood there, pale and monochrome as ever in her black coat with its grey furry hood.

'You're late,' Xenia said curtly, stepping back to let her in.

The girl said nothing but slipped out of her outdoor shoes, dropped a pair of soft-soled slipper-style shoes on the floor and put them on. Then she took off her coat and hung it over the edge of the radiator. She held something out to Xenia but it fell into the black hole in the middle of her vision.

'What's that?'

'Passport.'

'Oh yes.' Xenia took it. 'Thank you. I'll check it. Let's begin.'

She took the girl on a tour of the house, telling her exactly how things should be done to her satisfaction. Agnieska followed, nodding obediently and saying 'yes', although she asked no questions and kept the same, blank expression so that Xenia wondered again how much she actually grasped.

In her bedroom, she looked around and said, 'Polish the furniture and the mirror, clean the windows. Dust, obviously. Keep the silver looking fresh. Yes? But don't touch anything else. Do you understand?'

Agnieska nodded.

'Good. Let's go downstairs so you can get started. And please tell me before you run out of cleaning things, so I can replace them.'

'Yes. Yes.'

They went back downstairs, Xenia going slowly and carefully as she struggled to see the step in front of her. She settled down with a book as Agnieska began to assemble what she needed and set to work; the presence of someone else in the house, someone who was tending to things, was, she found, a comfort.

Sometimes she felt the weight of guilt and remorse for having sold Charcombe Park. For so long she had struggled on alone in that huge house, trying to keep it going by herself, but it had been impossible. Even if she'd worked all day and all night, it would have made little difference. But Papa had made her promise.

'Look after your mother,' he'd said, 'and look after this house. Whatever happens, we mustn't lose it. It's all we have left.'

So she had slaved and toiled, scrubbing and cleaning and doing her best to keep them living in some kind of gracious style. But caring for Mama too . . . it had been too much.

'She's your responsibility now, Xenia,' Papa had told her solemnly. 'You have to take care of her. You know why.'

Xenia did know why. It was her burden and her punishment. It was why she could never escape, no matter how badly she longed to give up. Eventually Papa would come back and things would be like they used to be, in the days when there was plenty, and they lived a life of ease and beauty.

She thought about it sometimes, as she fought to keep the place in order, food on the table for her and Mama, some warmth in the walls of the old house. At first, it wasn't too bad. Mama's films brought in some tiny payments, but sadly, that was not the case with *Delilah* on which she'd secured no royalty. That was one of the reasons Xenia found it too painful to watch when it was shown on the television. Hardly any of the great income it had generated had gone to Mama, its star. It had made her, and broken her too. Xenia couldn't bear to see Mama, so young and beautiful, so full of promise and talent, and to remember the afternoons in the darkness, watching the cameras record her performance for all time: every flash of her eyes, the arrogant pout of her lips, the raised arches of her eyebrows.

That was why she had left the portrait behind at the big house, the place where Mama had last been anything like that fiery beauty she had played on screen. That image was too powerful to bring into this place. Better that it hung in the room where Mama had laughed, smoked cigarettes, drunk martinis and charmed her many friends.

I tried to do as he asked. But in the end, despite my best efforts, I failed.

She felt her shoulders slump. She heard distantly the noises of Agnieska moving around upstairs. It helped somehow, to dispel her burden and take the edge off her fear. Her eyes drooped and she slept.

Xenia was still snoozing when the girl came in holding a plastic bag.

'You want I keep?' she said.

Xenia jumped awake and looked at the girl, bewildered, forgetting who she was and why she was there.

'What?' she said, her voice high and quavery. *A stupid old woman's voice. It isn't me. I hate growing old like this.* 'What do you want?'

Agnieska held out the bag wordlessly. It seemed to contain an animal or a furry toy or . . .

'Oh.' Irritation surged through her and she lifted herself slowly out of her chair. 'What are you doing with that? Where have you been looking?'

'It come out under bed,' she said with a small shrug. 'I find.

You must . . .' She frowned as she searched for a word. 'In the cupboard. And they eat it.' She wriggled the fingers of her free hand and let them flutter away upwards, watching them as they went.

'You mean moths, I suppose. Well, you're probably right. I'd forgotten it was there.' She took the bag from Agnieska. 'It's a coat.'

Agnieska nodded. Xenia pulled the coat from the bag and shook it out, releasing a musty smell of old fur and the tang that came from the silk lining within.

'Mama's coat,' she said, gazing at it. It was so familiar and yet a relic of the distant past. How strange that this should be here, in her hands, when so many other things had fluttered away and disappeared like Agnieska's invisible moths. All the many things she had been surrounded by over her long life. Where were they all? The teaspoons, the underwear, the combs, the tables and chairs, the books and lamps, the clothes she had worn, the umbrellas she'd held, her hair pins, her first watch. Where had it all gone? Some of it was left, here in this house. But there had been so much more.

Here was Mama's coat. She'd worn it on her way to and from the theatre, and then in Hollywood, despite the warm climate. Xenia remembered the cars, long and plush and purring like well-fed cats, that took them all to the studio in the morning and back home to the house on Bristol Avenue in the evening. Mama wore the coat when she and Papa went out to dinner in the evenings, for steak de luxe at Romanoff's or shrimp curry at Ciro's, or to dance and drink at the Cocoanut Grove, her hair curled and shiny, her lips bright with lipstick, jewels glittering around her neck and wrists; she wore it when she went to parties at the homes of other film stars, famous names like Humphrey Bogart, Cary Grant, Mickey Rooney, Lana Turner, Betty Grable ... names that turned out to belong to real people – glamorous like Mama, but real.

The coat was a reminder of those heady, glory days when Mama was on the cusp of her fame, revered for her beauty and her status as a real-life princess, and Papa was her handsome prince, always at her side with a cigarette clamped in his teeth, a hand on the arm of that coat.

Agnieska regarded it thoughtfully, no doubt appreciating the warming qualities of fine sable. 'Very nice.'

'Yes. It is.'

'Yes, yes, put it on.'

'Oh no—' She wasn't sure she could stand the memories.

But the next moment, Agnieska had taken it from her grip and was draping it around her shoulders. The smell was stronger: old damp fur, the slight reek of sweat from the armpits, and ... *oh my goodness. Mama's scent.* A lily-of-the-valley perfume, rich and redolent of spring woods, that made Xenia remember the inside of the trailer on the film set, where the scent had been pumped into it through an air conditioning unit.

She shrugged so that it settled about her shoulders. It fit her perfectly and immediately she felt its warmth.

'Air,' Agnieska said wisely. 'Hang it up.'

'Yes. It needs to air.' Xenia slipped her hands into the pockets. She felt the grittiness of old dust at the bottoms. She opened it up and saw that inside were two inner silk pockets;

she put her fingers into one and felt two slips of paper. She pulled them out and looked at them, one a cloakroom ticket marked 'Chasen's', the other a piece of yellowing lined paper with brownish folds.

Chasen's. Where Archibald Thomas had his booth. Mama dined there with him. She had chilli for the first time, she told me all about it.

She opened the folded paper. It was a page ripped from a notebook and on it were some fading spidery lines, the first written in a strong bold hand and signed *AT*:

You are Delilah, never forget that . . . You are magnificent today, tomorrow, forever.

Below it, written in her mother's sloping hand:

I can, I can, I can. I can overcome this fear. I can do it. I must, I must, I must. For Paul, for Xenia.

Xenia stared at it, then folded it back up and replaced it in the silk pocket.

'Yes,' she said. 'I will air it.'

Chapter Ten

1949

Xenia thought that this must be the closest thing to fairyland she could ever imagine. She was in a magical kingdom where the sun always shone and the air was balmy and warm. The roads were broad and lined with palms, and large shiny cars trimmed with silvery bright metal glided along them. There were neatly trimmed grass verges and then house after house, like she'd never seen before: huge, often white, with swimming pools and endless gardens.

No wonder everyone wanted to come and live in Hollywood.

She and Papa had left England on a drizzly day and crossed over on the *Queen Elizabeth*. Life on the liner had been full of charm for Xenia. It was not at all like a boat, as she'd imagined, but like being in a large and comfortable hotel. Once they were past the last of the land, the vast ocean opened up before them, bigger and grander than she'd dreamed, and so stunningly, frighteningly empty. For days, there was nothing to see but the rolling, white-topped waves of the Atlantic. She knew they must be moving, but it seemed they were perfectly still in the middle of miles of water, not even feeling the waves that broke around the hull far below them.

She shared a cabin with Gunter, who was deathly afraid every night that they would wake up sinking in the freezing water, so slept in her clothes, her handbag clutched to her chest. During the day, when Gunter could be sure that they were still afloat, she was quite calm, and, once they had had their constitutional walk, she was happy to let Xenia roam the great liner and join in the various activities for the young-sters on board. She made friends and joined them for walks on the decks and games, made up and organised. They watched for whales and pods of dolphins, and created an epic hide-and-seek competition that stretched over the entire boat. There was even a screening room, where films were shown for the children in the afternoons.

'Wasn't it marvellous?' said her new friend Patricia, when they came out blinking from watching *Melody Time*. 'Wasn't the duck so funny? I do so love films, especially cartoons.'

'We're going to Hollywood to see my mother,' Xenia told her. 'She's going to be a film star.'

'I want to be a film star,' Patricia sighed. 'You are so lucky! Will you see a film being made?'

'I should think so. I hope so.'

They played at being film stars most of the time after that, and the friendly waiters, their roles explained to them, didn't mind pretending along and coming up to ask for autographs or to offer cocktails of orange juice and soda water and lem-onade champagne in coupes to the small movie stars.

Papa often stayed in his cabin or in the drawing rooms of the liner, sleeping and reading, but every afternoon he would meet her for tea in the lounge, and then they would walk the deck together, talking about what they would do when they got to Hollywood. Xenia had hundreds of questions, and always wanted to hear about the magical story of how Mama had been cast in the role of Delilah.

'She had to audition many times for Archibald Thomas,' Papa told her as they strolled along the deck, her hand in his, 'with dozens of different actors playing the other parts. They filmed her with different hairstyles, and different make-up and costumes, and to see how her eyes and mouth moved, and how she looked on camera.' He smiled down at her. 'She had to kiss lots of actors.'

'Kiss them!' Xenia was shocked. 'Were you very angry, Papa?'

'Oh no. It's only acting. It's nothing, actors have to pretend romance all the time, it's not one bit like real life.'

'That's good.' Xenia was relieved to hear it. 'And did they decide they liked her best?'

'Mama was the best right from the start.' He squeezed her hand. 'It's very exciting, Xenia. Mama is going to be a proper film star, and be famous all over the world. We are very proud of her, aren't we, darling?'

'Very,' Xenia agreed, and skipped beside him with glee.

The evenings were her absolutely favourite time. Gunter would help get her ready for dinner: she had a smart black velvet dress with a white collar and matching black velvet ribbons for her hair. Then she would wait for Papa to collect her, and they would go to the dining room. Papa drank real cocktails while she had lemonade, and they always sat with the most glamorous people on board: beautiful women in long dresses and jewels; handsome men in their dinner jackets who smoked cigars and sported moustaches and oily-looking, slicked-back hair. At least, that was how they appeared to Xenia. Papa looked the handsomest of all, and how he was fawned over.

'Oh, Prince,' the women would say, touching his arm and laughing at his witticisms. 'You're so charming! So witty. So interesting.'

'Tell us, Prince, your opinion of what's happening in Russia,' the men would say, and then they'd listen as Papa told them what he thought of the evil old despot Stalin and how he hoped it would not be long before he died.

Sometimes they talked admiringly of Mama and her career. They had all heard that Natalie Rowe was making an important film with a famous director, and they knew Papa was going to visit her in Hollywood.

'I'm told she is simply extraordinary on film – it's her first real motion picture, you know,' Papa would say with a slight swagger. 'It began just as a little fun for her, and yet now she is on the cusp of becoming a great actress. Naturally, my mother is a little shocked – it's not how she was brought up. She doesn't understand that the world has changed since she was a girl. She still has a horror of actresses and scandal and doesn't realise that today's stars are ladies.'

'Dear Princess Arkadyoff,' they said, as if they knew her. 'She must remember the way things were, before the revolu-

tion. Do tell us – what was the Tsar like? The Tsarina? Those poor grand duchesses?'

'I was just a boy, I'm afraid, far too young to remember,' Papa would say, declining as always to discuss what had happened to his family in the revolution. 'And naturally it was too painful for my mother to speak of.'

Xenia was coming to realise that her family was shrouded in a peculiar glamour, one that she didn't understand at all. She had yet to meet her grandmother or her aristocratic Russian relations, though she knew she had plenty, but that glittering title and a connection to a vanished imperial court fascinated everyone. With a film-star wife thrown into the mix, it was no wonder that the first-class passengers found Papa so thrilling, and he basked in their approval, his dark eyes sparkling with merriment and his lips curving into a smile that revealed his small, slightly yellowed teeth, as he smoked his endless cigarettes. He liked to be at those tables, being deferred to and flirted with. Xenia sat quietly and watched, until he remembered her presence and showed her off to everyone.

The ladies cooed over her: 'The sweet little princess, how old is she?'

'She's almost twelve years old.'

'What beautiful manners she has! And those eyes, just like yours. She'll be a beauty.'

Xenia knew she would never be a beauty, not like Mama, but she liked being fussed over and behaving like a grownup. Then, suddenly, Papa would remember that she was only a child.

'Xenia, that's enough. It's late, you must go and find Gunter and ask her to put you to bed.'

'I can put myself to bed.'

'Off, off, off.' And he would wave his hand at her, or point at her with the lighted end of his cigarette. 'Go away, child! You need your sleep.'

That would be the end of her glamorous evening. But she had learned to creep out onto the deck and peer in through the lighted windows of the dining room. From there, she could carry on watching, unseen. She loved to see Papa animated and smiling. She liked it when the band struck up and the diners took to the floor in the centre of the room to spin and turn, the dresses glittering and shining as they twirled. How wonderful to be grown up and to have the freedom to stay up late and dance for as long as one wanted.

She was watching one particular couple who danced with real elegance and grace when she heard footsteps quite close on the deck, and voices nearby too. It was, she realised to her horror, Papa, strolling out with a cigarette in one hand and a woman's arm tucked through his other arm.

'Paul, you are so romantic,' purred the woman in an American accent. 'I simply don't understand how your wife could bear to be away from you for a minute, let alone six months. You must be so understanding.'

'She is afraid of her own talent. She needs me to realise it for her, to give her the impetus and the strength to harness and tame it.'

Xenia had shrunk into the shadows as they stopped close to her, standing at the railing with their backs to her, half engulfed by darkness and half illuminated by the light from the dining room windows.

Is that true?

The woman said, 'How lucky she is to have you by her side, to encourage her.'

Papa laughed. 'You flatter me. But it's true that, without me, she couldn't be Natalie Rowe. I have created her as surely as Frankenstein created his monster.'

'What a horrible analogy! She's so beautiful—'

'Beautiful without, but damaged and difficult within. I don't mean to sound disloyal but it's not always easy being her husband. Her success and fulfilment, those are my rewards and I ask for nothing more, but it's exhausting, I can't pretend that it's not.'

'You're a saint,' murmured the woman, pressing close to Papa. 'You must love her very much.'

'I do – but I have my own needs ... needs that are not always recognised ...'

Papa's voice had sunk low and Xenia could hardly hear the words he murmured to the woman beside him; then there were no more words and she realised, to her horror, that the couple by the railing were caught in an embrace and were kissing.

Appalled, she darted out from the shadows and around the corner, along the deck to the stairs. She didn't stop running until she arrived, breathless, at her cabin. Gunter was sitting up for her, and scolded her for being late before shooing her into bed. But when Gunter was snoring happily away,

Xenia was still awake, staring into the darkness and mulling over everything she had heard.

Perhaps, she told herself, *it was like Mama kissing the actors. Just pretending.*

But she was very afraid that it wasn't at all like that.

After that, she didn't watch the goings-on in the dining room after being sent away, and she spent dinner itself pushing food around her plate and wondering which of the glamorous ladies Papa had kissed on the deck under the stars. She suspected them all, and soon she began to hate every one of them. They were pretty on the surface – no wonder Papa couldn't resist them – but underneath they were rotten, using their wiles and charms to trick Papa and steal him away from her mother. Poor Papa, he was their victim. She longed for the journey to be over so that her parents would be together again, because as soon as Papa was with wonderful Mama, he would never want to do such a thing again. The important thing was to keep Papa away from the ladies with their make-up and fancy clothes, so she stuck to him like a small shadow until they docked in New York two days later.

After the enormous boat and the long stretch at sea, it was strange to board the small plane and arrive in California just a few hours later. There, at the airport, the sunshine dazzled her and the clothes that had kept her warm on the ocean voyage were hot and uncomfortable.

'Darlings! Darlings!' It was Mama, beautiful in a white dress and sandals, a large straw hat and sunglasses. Perhaps she was trying to be inconspicuous but she stood out like

anything, and everyone stared, wondering who she was. 'Oh Xenia, my sweetheart!'

The next moment, Xenia was held tightly in a sweet-scented hug, pressed hard against her mother. 'Mama,' she said almost wonderingly, and hugged her back.

'Paul!' cried Mama, and the next moment, Xenia was released so that Mama could fly into Papa's arms and kiss him rapturously.

Real, she thought, gratefully. *Not pretending.*

'What do you think?' Mama asked, showing Xenia the sparkling blue swimming pool at the back of the house, set in a garden full of fat pink blooms and glossy dark shrubs.

'It's amazing,' Xenia sighed. She had never seen anything like it. It was as though she'd arrived in a world of heightened colour and scale, after grey, dirty London, full of bomb sites and drabness. Here, nothing seemed ordinary. Even the people glowed with health and vigour, not like the thin, pale, shabby population back home.

The studio had loaned Mama a beautiful house on a road called Bristol Avenue. It was an exotic mansion, with arched doorways and an orange tiled roof. Inside, the rooms were great fields of plush carpet furnished with soft, plump chairs and sofas. Everything seemed vast after the small proportions and spindly antique furniture of the London house. Xenia's room was huge, with a bed with a canopy over it, a pink marble bathroom, and a wardrobe she could walk into.

Papa was delighted. 'This is it, Natalie, you've arrived,

you've really arrived!' He sighed with pleasure, walking about and pointing out everything that thrilled him.

'The studio rented it for me,' Mama said proudly. 'As soon as I got the part.'

Xenia watched carefully for any signs something was wrong between her parents but there was nothing and she wondered if perhaps she'd imagined that horrid moment on board ship. They seemed ecstatic to be reunited, and Mama was happier than Xenia had seen her for a long time, fizzing with excitement to have her family with her and eager to show them the excitements of the new country. She took Xenia to a place called a drug store, where they sat at a long counter on high stools and ordered ice cream floats and banana splits. Mama laughed at Xenia's expression when they were put in front of her.

'This is America, darling, everything is big and beautiful here! You'll see!'

Mama was right: it was a baffling but entrancing, over-sized dreamland.

At dinner, served by dark-haired silent maids, Papa questioned Mama about the film.

'We're over schedule,' she said. 'We began late, the final casting took so long, and the rehearsals went on more than expected. And Archibald is such a perfectionist, we do the same scene over and over until it's absolutely right. He's hired a special coach for me, to work on scenes with, and he makes me stay in my character at all times. He takes me out to dinner and makes me act as Delilah the entire evening. He enjoys that.'

'How wonderful,' Papa said admiringly. A maid put a bowl of salad decorated with boiled eggs and chopped ham in front of him, and he spooned some of it onto his plate. 'He's a true artist. You're lucky to work with such a man.'

'I know.' Mama pushed her plate away almost untouched and lit a cigarette. The glass in front of her was half full of amber liquid bathing a small mountain of ice cubes. 'But it's exhausting. I'm not Delilah, and it's not easy to be a hard-as-nails vamp for hours on end. Archibald demands take after take – he's such a perfectionist. I can't tell you how tiring it is.'

'It'll be worth it, Natalie.' Papa smiled. 'I'm proud of you.'

Xenia, half listening, puzzled over the strange new food put in front of her. She was staring at a pink fruit with dark pips inside it when Mama leaned over, blowing out a stream of cigarette smoke.

'You'll come to the studio tomorrow, darling, and see what it's like. I've cleared it with Archibald. Would you like that?'

Xenia looked up. 'The studio?' she breathed. She hadn't dared to hope she'd be allowed on such hallowed ground. 'Yes please. Patricia would be *so* jealous!'

The film studio was not what Xenia had imagined. She'd envisaged something like a large theatre without all the seats but instead it was like a small town, with office blocks, canteens, warehouses and even its own roads where little open cars, like something from a fairground, trundled back and forth with their passengers. There were vast hangars called sound stages where sets were built for the indoor sequences, and exterior lots where whole towns were built for the out-door scenes.

'Why don't they just use the normal outside?' Xenia asked, when Papa pointed one out to her as they passed in the car on the way to the set.

'It's not as easy as you might think. It's difficult to film something and get it right, especially outside, where the wea-ther or the light might be wrong, or it might not be possible to get the camera in the right position. Just to be sure, they build whatever they need. Those aren't real houses. They're just fronts.'

Xenia stared. The candy-coloured houses looked so real, but they were only pretend, made to fool people. Everything here was part of an elaborate plan to create make-believe that appeared like reality.

Mama had already been there at the studio since early morning, and they were taken to her dressing room: a beau-tiful, luxurious white cabin set up inside the huge warehouse-like set. Mama was sitting in front of a dressing table and a mirror surrounded by light bulbs. She was just having her hair and make-up finished, and she looked beautiful and yet strange. Xenia's expression made her laugh.

'Oh, sweet thing, don't be afraid. They have to make me look like this, because it looks best under the lights, for the camera! I know it's odd, though. I wouldn't go out like this.'

Mama's soft peachy skin was buried under a thick layer of pancake make-up that blotted out every mark and freckle. Her eyes were heavy with false lashes and painted with brown and white shadow. Her eyebrows were blackened and made more arched, and more brown shadows had been added around her cheeks. Her lips were fuller and bigger than usual, outlined in dark red pencil and painted with glossy sticky stuff, and Mama's hair was stiff with a webby covering of hairspray; the fat curls at her shoulders and on her forehead were solid and unmoving. A script sat abandoned on the dressing table before her.

'You look very pretty, Mama,' Xenia said politely, but she thought that Mama looked much prettier without all the paint.

'You're done, honey!' said the make-up woman, lifting off the paper bib that had been shielding Mama's white jacket.

'Thank you, Sissy, you're a genius.' Mama smiled. 'Can you get me a glass of champagne please?'

Papa had been standing watching, a half frown between his brows. 'Champagne, darling?' He looked at his watch. 'Isn't it a little early?'

'I've been up since five. It's lunchtime for me!' Mama said gaily. Sissy was already pouring out a fizzing glass from a bottle sitting in a bucket of ice. Xenia could see that it was half empty. 'Why don't you have one, Paul?'

'No, thank you.'

His tone was uncharacteristically cold. Xenia glanced at him but his expression was unreadable. Then there was a knock on the door and Mama was called to the set.

Archibald Thomas was tall with a round face and black owlish spectacles, and was wearing a bright blue suit and huge brown shoes. He stared at Xenia intensely but only talked to Papa, asking few questions but explaining the day's work schedule quickly, almost brusquely, before directing them off the set. Xenia went to sit in a chair in the darkness next to Papa, and Papa smoked while they watched the scene being filmed. The set – a smart, modern drawing room – looked exactly like a real room, but brightly lit by the lamps hanging from rails in the darkness above. Around its flimsy walls, in the shadows, were dozens of people hurrying about, absorbed in their allotted tasks, but who all subsided into silence and stillness when the director yelled for quiet. Archibald Thomas sat in what looked like a kind of garden chair on stilts, his jacket off now and his sleeves rolled up as he scowled at the set. Beside him, on a much lower stool, sat a young woman in a jersey and kilt, with a clipboard on her knee and a pen poised. Everyone waited, then he bellowed, 'Action!'

A clapperboard snapped, a voice shouted, and everything was focused on the room. A door opened and Mama came in, her head high, a half smile on her lips, the picture of elegance in a black dress with a white bow at the neck and black high heels. She seemed quite different: arrogant, provocative, fearless.

'Well, Sam, I think you're being ridiculous,' she said crisply in a perfect American accent. 'I can't think why you're getting so upset.'

A broad-shouldered man in a pin-striped suit followed her into the room. 'Come on, Delilah, don't act the fool. You know perfectly well why! You've been leading me on, and all along you've been involved with that phoney, Masterson! What's going on? You'd better tell me right this minute.'

Mama gave a tinkling laugh and walked smartly to the side table, where she started to pour liquid from a bottle into a cocktail shaker. She was relaxed and yet too poised to be natural, her eyes bright, her chin held just in such a way to tilt her face towards the camera. Her expressions, though, were barely noticeable – tiny movements of her eyes and a tightening of the lips or a small smile – and her voice was low and mellifluous.

Is this acting? Xenia thought. *It's not like in the theatre.* There, voices boomed, faces contorted, gestures were huge.

Mama turned to the man, holding out the drink. 'You're overreacting, Sam. There's no need for all of this.'

Sam took the drink and put it on the side, then grabbed her by the arm. 'Don't fob me off, Delilah, I'm warning you. I've had about enough of it. I'm crazy about you and you know that! Why . . . there's something about you that drives me mad.'

'And is that my fault? I never asked you to feel that way.'

'You know you did. Right from the start, you've always known your power over me. You can't just expect me to stop feeling when it's not convenient for you any more.'

'I've never wanted that. I'm telling you, you've got it wrong! I . . .' Mama stared at him insolently, her chin high, her green eyes flashing, her body tense and then, suddenly, all the fight went out of her and she wilted. When she spoke, it wasn't in Delilah's strong, confident voice but in her own, soft, English tones. 'I'm so sorry, I've forgotten my line!'

'Cut!'

Everyone around the set came back to life, dashing about to reset the scene, powder Mama's nose, adjust the cameras and chatter among themselves. Archibald Thomas strode over, towering over Mama, and began talking to her in low, urgent tones.

'What's happened?' Xenia whispered to her father. 'What's going on?'

'She made a mistake,' Papa said. He sounded tense, his voice wound up and his teeth gritted. 'They'll have to do it all again.'

Five minutes later, they were ready to go again. Once more, Mama strode confidently into the room, and talked to Sam in her haughty yet flirtatious way. They carried on past the point where Mama had flagged last time.

'I'm not seeing Masterson, except as a friend. He's helping me with my career. It's good to have someone who does. Someone who cares about what I'm going to do with my life.'

Sam's eyes flashed. 'There's more to it than that, I know it! You'll not treat me like this and get away with it.'

'Let go of me.' She pushed Sam's arm off her, her face scornful. 'What are you going to do about it? I'm not your . . . your . . . your . . . *thing* . . . oh no, that's not right. Oh, I'm so sorry!'

'Cut!'

They did the scene over and over, until Xenia felt she knew all the lines herself. Her lips moved along in the darkness as the little vignette repeated itself, always the same until at some point, Mama would forget her line, sometimes one she had delivered perfectly in the previous take, then she would wilt and apologise. The tension around the set grew stronger and fiercer, until Xenia herself wanted to burst into tears when Mama made yet another mistake, and she could feel Papa's frustration.

'Cut, cut!' yelled the director. 'Let's take a break for lunch.'

Mama turned and ran for her trailer, her hands over her face.

Papa got up and followed her, leaving Xenia alone in the dark.

'Natalie, what on earth was wrong with you today? You've never been like that before, never! You're always word perfect, you pride yourself on it.'

'I know that, Paul. Do you think I don't?'

They were in the car, being driven home from the studio, Xenia tucked between her parents who were talking over her head. Papa was still tense, not angry but indignant, almost bewildered. Mama sounded tired, as though everything had been drained from her.

'Why are you drinking on set? That can't possibly help.'

'Paul, it's fine!' Mama sounded agonised but it was impossible to see her face. She wore huge dark sunglasses and the collar of her fur coat hid her mouth and nose. 'Please. It relaxes me. That's all. I don't get drunk, if that's what you're saying.'

'You can't jeopardise this chance, Natalie. It won't come

your way again.' Her father leaned back in the seat. 'They'll sack you if you go on like this, then where will we be?'

'It's the pressure, Paul, sometimes it's unbearable ...' Mama's voice was shaking. 'I find it so hard. I didn't realise ... Everything, this whole film, all these people's hopes and expectations, their jobs, their futures ... all on me.'

Xenia snuggled close to her, wanting to push some of her own strength into her mother's body. It was fearful to see Mama like this but she trusted her eyes: Mama might have made mistakes today, but she had also been sublime. Even with all the pretence, the make-up, the flimsy walls and boiling lights, the stopping and starting of scenes, the endless repetitions, Xenia had believed in Delilah and all her machinations.

Papa said softly, 'Don't doubt yourself, Natalie. You can do this. We'll stay until the film is finished and make sure of it.'

Mama said nothing but looked out of the window of the car into the evening twilight. Xenia saw her fist was clenched and her knuckles were white with the force of it.

Chapter Eleven

Thanks so much for the other night! We had a great
time. We can't wait to move in to the village and get
going, I'll let you know when we have a date. Love
Cathy xxx

Buttercup read the text over as Milky walked slowly along
the lane, hoping the Tranters hadn't thought Charles rude,
even though he had made it so obvious that he didn't want
them there. Perhaps they felt it was understandable, when
he'd just returned from a business trip.

I hope so. It would be nice to have a friend in the village.
So far the wives of Charles's hearty country friends had
kept their distance, no doubt feeling a loyalty to Ingrid. They
probably thought Charles was a fool and she, Buttercup, was
a gold-digger. But what did it matter? They weren't her
friends, and never would be – they were older than she was,
for one thing, most of them at different stage in their lives,
with children growing up and the end of school years in
sight. Cathy was different: a newcomer, a woman around her

own age with a young family. She was, by natural justice, in Buttercup's territory. It was only right that she should be her friend.

'Put that phone away!' called out Phil from behind her. 'Don't think I can't see what you're doing!' He was riding Topper, the large bay hunter Charles had bought when he'd planned to learn how to ride in the field, but he'd never had the time.

'Sorry!' Buttercup put the phone into her waistcoat pocket.

'You come out here for a reason – to get away from all that. So don't spoil it.'

'Aye, aye, sir.' She made a mock salute.

He came up and rode abreast of her. 'You're bored. You wouldn't be looking at that phone all the time if you weren't.'

'That's a bit harsh.' She laughed.

'I mean it. What are you going to do with yourself down here? You're too young to mope about that house all day long. What did you do with yourself when you lived in London?'

'I was assistant to a kitchen designer. I helped very rich ladies choose incredibly expensive appliances and calmed them down when they got upset about finishes, and cabinet handles, and the wrong shade of white.' She laughed. 'They drove me mad, but I enjoyed it.'

'Lots of people like that down here,' Phil remarked. 'Lots. Everyone's always doing a new kitchen, it seems to me. Mr Redmain knows people with big houses. You should ask around, maybe.'

'Maybe I will. I thought that I might be busy with other things, you see. A family.' She felt her throat tighten and forced herself to breath out slowly. Milky swayed underneath her and she noticed that the hedges were full of sloe berries.

Phil nodded. 'It doesn't have to be one or the other, does it? And you might find it takes your mind off the waiting.'

'You're probably right.' After a moment Buttercup said, 'Are you married, Phil? Any children?'

'Nope. I never found the right girl. But I'm hopeful. And if she has kids, so much the better. I wouldn't mind a ready-made family.'

'That's what I thought about James and Charlotte. I was looking forward to getting to know them, but we never see them. They haven't got used to me yet, I think.'

'Give 'em time. Young people never like a newcomer, especially if they feel protective of their mum. They're good kids, though.'

Feeling that the personal tone of their talk had given her an opening, she said hesitantly, 'Phil, can I ask you something? I don't want to be nosy – and there's no need to answer if you don't want to – but . . . what was Ingrid like? Sometimes I feel as though everyone but me has met her. And she lives so close. It's such a strange situation.'

Phil said gruffly, 'I understand. We all liked Mrs Redmain. She's different from you though – I couldn't say exactly how, but different. She had quite a job, running this place and bringing up the children more or less single-handed. Mr Redmain was away a lot then, just as he is now. But she was pretty cheerful most of the time. Friendly.'

'I suppose that it must have been a shock to everyone when she ran off like that . . . ?' She asked casually but there was no disguising the leading nature of her question.

Phil frowned. 'I don't know anything about that,' he said shortly. 'And I wouldn't talk about it if I did.'

Buttercup flushed, ashamed at herself for asking about Ingrid's departure when she'd told herself she never would. 'No. I'm sorry. I won't mention it again.'

'You're all right,' Phil said, then pulled Topper back so that he was riding behind her again, the hunter's hooves ringing out on the lane as they walked. Buttercup was glad he couldn't see her embarrassment any longer.

Back inside, she found Charles in his study, where he was sitting solemnly in front of three giant flat screens, observing the state of his investments around the world.

'Hello, darling,' he said absently as she came in. 'What can I do for you?'

After leaving Phil at the stables, everything they discussed had been whirling round her mind. She sat down and said, 'I've been thinking . . . we haven't seen James and Charlotte for ages. It's half-term soon, isn't it? We could ask Charlotte to stay and see if James wants to come too for a day or so.'

'I've seen James recently,' Charles said, his eyes on one of the screens. His hand moved a computer mouse and he clicked down. 'In London.'

'Have you?' She was surprised. 'You didn't say . . .'

'We meet sometimes. Now he's at university, it's easy

enough for him to come into town. We have dinner, chat, he stays the night and goes back the next day.'

'You didn't mention it.'

Charles's gaze slid towards her. 'Do I need to?'

'No . . . no, I suppose not. But we are all family, aren't we? I'm not going to get close to your children if I never see them or know what's going on in their lives.'

Charles frowned. 'But they're almost grown up, they don't need a stepmother like young children might. They have their own mother, after all. I think they see you more as a friend than a relation.'

She felt wrong-footed. 'I see,' she said lamely. This hadn't been her vision of what her life with Charles would be like; she'd seen herself growing close to his children, not trying to supplant their mother but bringing an added richness to their lives. She wanted to be a kind and sympathetic listener, there to absorb their teenage angst when they weren't getting on with their parents or had confessions they were too afraid to make to them.

A polite friendship was not what she'd expected. Perhaps at first, but not forever.

When the reality of her relationship with Charles's children had been different from her rosy fantasies, she'd told herself it was only to be expected; they were still traumatised from their parents' divorce and bound to see her as an interloper. The first time she had met them at the London flat, they had been stiff, formal and unsmiling, replying to her questions with cool, polite brevity. Charlotte, fourteen years old, looked like Charles with blue eyes and her sandy-coloured hair;

James was seventeen and taller than his father, gawky and dark-haired, hazel eyes behind glasses.

'Do you think they liked me?' she'd asked anxiously afterwards, when Rich had picked them up to take them back to Dorset.

'Naturally they liked you,' Charles said, surprised. 'I love you, so they will too. How could they not?'

But it seemed to Buttercup highly likely that they could not. What was more surprising was that it didn't seem to occur to Charles.

The next time she'd seen them had been at the wedding. She heard much later that James had been violently ill in the lavatories at the hotel after drinking too much champagne but she had been quite unaware of it at the time.

After the wedding, she had still never been able to get close to either of them, partly because they simply wouldn't stay in the same room as her for long, and certainly not on their own. Whenever they visited, they skittered away as soon as they could and avoided her. Even riding had not brought her closer to Charlotte, as she hoped it might. Charlotte went out at odd times, gave up on rides when Buttercup offered to join her, and hid in the stables and even the horse boxes when Buttercup came to look for her. It was hard not to feel slighted. How could she be understanding, affectionate and giving if they simply wouldn't let her?

And here was Charles, not even trying to bring her and James together.

Now she thought about it, her dreams of what life would be like had never been reinforced by Charles. She had bubbled and enthused and told him her hopes and dreams. He had listened and nodded, but he had never agreed or disagreed. He would simply embrace her and tell her she was adorable or charming or sweet, as though indulging the fantasies of a child. Not once had he said, 'Yes, we will make that happen.' Or: 'That is what I want too. Let's plan how to do it.' He had never confided his feelings. And she had never questioned it. Well, she would start.

'I think we should definitely have Charlotte to stay during the half-term,' Buttercup said firmly. 'She and I could go riding together.'

'I can certainly get Elaine or Rose to ask Ingrid how Charlotte feels about it and if it suits their plans. She may be doing something else.'

Buttercup stared at him, exasperated. 'Don't you care if she comes or not?'

Charles tutted and looked up. 'Obviously I'd like her here. But it's not possible simply to dictate to young people, especially when they don't live with you.'

Tears sprang to Buttercup's eyes. 'I'm only trying to do my best!' she cried. Gripped suddenly by despair, she turned and ran to their bedroom, throwing herself down on the bed and crying hard, frustration and anxiety coming out in a stream of hot tears. A moment later, Charles was beside her, sitting on the bed and stroking her hair.

'I'm sorry,' he said gently. 'I didn't mean to be unfeeling.'

She mumbled into the pillow, her breath hot against it: 'I want a baby. I want us to be parents.' She lifted her head to look at him as he bent over her. She thought of how much she loved him, how dear and inspiring and wonderful she'd found that face, with its strength and determination, and the surprising tenderness that could spring suddenly, meltingly, into the mouth and eyes. 'Do you want that, Charles?'

'I want you to be happy.'

'Yes – but do you want another child? Do you want to have a baby with me?'

His blue eyes scanned her face and returned to her gaze. 'Of course I do.'

She sat up, sniffing. 'Do you mean it? Honestly?'

'Yes,' he said firmly. 'If it's possible, then I want a baby with you.'

'Not just to make me happy, though. For yourself?'

He smiled. 'Yes. For me too.'

She threw her arms around him, elated. 'Oh, Charles. I'm so happy you said that. I've been worried that you didn't want another baby.'

'If it's possible,' he said, hugging her back, 'then I do.'

Chapter Twelve

Charles was working in his study again when Buttercup settled down at the desk in the drawing room with her computer, a cup of tea steaming gently by her side. It was raining outside, the sky slate-grey and blurred with the downpour. She shivered, feeling the chill despite the radiators going full-blast and the fire burning in the grate. She felt better since the reassurance Charles had given her, sure again that they were united in their hopes for the future, and she'd also come to a decision: she would write that email to Lazlo suggesting she could look into promoting him in the area, perhaps start finding new clients for him.

She was just drafting it when the door opened and Agnieska came in, a bucket of cleaning things in one hand, cloths in the other. When she saw Buttercup, she looked startled.

'Sorry, I come later,' she said, and started to leave.

'No, no, it's fine. You won't disturb me.' Buttercup smiled reassuringly. 'Honestly, go ahead.'

'Okay.' Agnieska looked uncertain but she came in and moved about in her silent way.

She watched Agnieska for a moment as she dusted the frame of Natalie Rowe's portrait and then turned back to her screen. On a whim, she brought up her social media account and typed Charlotte's name into the search engine; her profile came up, locked and visible only to friends. She gazed at the picture: it was Charlotte cavorting on a beach in bright sunshine, frozen in a wild star jump of joy, her sandy hair bleached silver blond. Before she could change her mind, she sent a friend request. It was ridiculous that they weren't in contact. She had decided to wait until they were closer but it seemed that she would have to get the ball rolling.

Then, after a second's hesitation, she typed in Ingrid's name as well. She was the first result: Ingrid Redmain. The profile picture was a full-length shot of her in a summery dress, flanked by James and Charlotte in similarly smart clothes. Ingrid was wearing sunglasses and smiling broadly. It was impossible to make out much of what she actually looked like. She could be any average-looking dark-haired woman.

Buttercup clicked on the profile but it was set to private and it wasn't possible to see anything more than her profile pictures. Buttercup began to type in the names of the wives of Charles's country friends, the ones she had met at dinner parties and drinks parties, who smiled coolly and were polite but distant. They had evidently known Ingrid. Most also had their profiles set to private, but one dippier type had left all her security wide open to whomever looked. Buttercup's finger hovered over the mouse and then she sent a friend request to the dippy woman. The gateway towards Ingrid.

But why on earth do I want to know anything about her? I know enough. She cheated on Charles and ended their marriage. Fine.

And yet, she had been feeling more drawn to the house beyond the gates. Perhaps it was knowing that Agnieska was working there too. Perhaps it was because of the knowledge that everyone around her knew that mysterious dark-haired woman, and perhaps what had happened here when the marriage had imploded.

Even if she made a link to Ingrid, what then? It was impossible to imagine that they would ever actually talk to one another. And what could an unfaithful wife tell her except to justify her own bad behaviour by painting her ex-husband in a bad light?

She clicked the page shut and felt a chill tremble over her skin. She shuddered lightly and pulled her jumper down, wondering why she couldn't feel the warmth of the fire burning in the grate. *What am I doing? If Charles thought I was interested in Ingrid . . . well . . . he wouldn't understand. And he certainly wouldn't like it.*

Immediately she wished she hadn't sent that friend request, but it was too late. She looked over at Agnieska, who was plumping cushions and straightening the cashmere throws. She realised that she had intended, casually, to ask her if she had started work at Fitzroy House and what it was like there.

I can't do that. I mustn't. She shook her head and closed her computer down. *I'm playing with fire. I must stop it.*

To assuage her guilt, she was extra loving and sweet to Charles, and he responded with pleasure to her spoiling of him. They had a lovely afternoon together, and he asked Carol to set the table in the small dining room, and make something special for them. He went down to the cellar for a good bottle of wine and they had a romantic evening, talking and laughing like the best of friends.

Which we are, she thought, full of love and tenderness for him, and she reached out to stroke his hand.

He raised his eyebrow, smiled and gave her a sideways look. 'Does all this charm have anything to do with your ... er ... temperature, my darling?'

She laughed. 'You know, for once I wasn't thinking about it. Now you mention it, it might be about the right time.' She thought for a moment. 'Yes, we're in the zone from today. Shall I take a reading?'

'There's no need.' His thumb rubbed over the back of her hand, and he fixed her with an intense look. 'Whether or not your temperature is doing its duty, I intend to have my wicked way with you.'

Her stomach turned in a delicious swirl of anticipation. 'You must have read my mind because that's exactly what I'd like.' She felt a burden lift from her. She had been letting her brain go into overdrive, and her silly suspicions were ground-less. Why would Charles make love to her at her fertile time if he didn't want her to get pregnant?

Maybe tonight ... maybe we'll be lucky this time.

The next morning, Buttercup woke to find Charles already up and the bed beside her empty.

Downstairs, Carol passed on a message. 'He said he'll be back later, but he's got to go to an early meeting. Steve's driving him up to London.'

'Okay, that's fine, thanks, Carol.' Buttercup smiled happily. She replayed moments from the previous night and hoped, joyously, that everything that was supposed to happen was taking place right now in the mysterious inner darkness that was such an intimate part of her, and yet remained so unknowable.

'Breakfast is set out for you in the dining room,' Carol said as Buttercup bounded out of the kitchen.

'Thanks!' she called, heading off.

She was eating bircher muesli and thumbing through emails on her phone, wondering when Charlotte might accept her friend request and if Lazlo had got her email, when it rang suddenly and made her jump. The name flashed up and she answered.

'Hello, Rose?'

'Hello, Mrs R, sorry to disturb you. I just wanted to ask about a payment.'

'Yes?'

'Your credit card statement has come in for settling, and

there's a name we don't recognise. I just want to check it's bona fide.'

Buttercup felt suddenly cold. 'Yes?'

Rose said, 'It's a Harley Street clinic, but not any of your usual practitioners. The date is when you were here in London, so you may have arranged the appointment yourself. It's called Barrett Singh. I looked it up – it's a foetal health and fertility clinic.'

'That's right.' She tried to sound unflustered. 'Yes, I arranged it. Please make the payment.'

'Okay, Mrs R,' Rose said cheerfully.

'Thanks so much. Is there anything else?'

'No, that's it. Have a wonderful day.'

'Thank you.' She put the phone down on the table and stared at it, unseeing. Her good mood had disappeared in an instant. She had completely forgotten about the credit card payment. Charles had given her the card after they married, and it had been a little exciting to know she could hand over that piece of plastic and have anything she wanted. She'd intended to use her own money for luxuries, though. After all, she'd always been independent and paid her own way, except for a small inheritance from her father that she put towards paying off some of her mortgage. She'd never known the strange freedom of wealth. But despite her good intentions, slowly but surely, encouraged by Charles, she'd grown accustomed to using her married accounts. As a result, they always knew where she'd been and what she'd spent: Charles's bankers and accounts and assistants and managers. They knew what she'd bought as Christmas presents and what her haircuts cost. They knew when she'd had a facial or been to the gym or needed new underwear. They had access to the smallest details of her life and routine, they could probably describe her activities better than she could. They certainly knew more about the cost of, say, keeping Milky than she did.

And whatever they knew, Charles could know. Perhaps he did know.

She felt a rush of panic at the idea of him finding out that she'd been to a fertility clinic behind his back. No matter how she tried to explain it, it would look like deception. He had never yet been properly angry with her, and she knew with deep certainty that she didn't want to provoke that anger.

Picking up the phone, she rang Rose back.

'Mrs R?'

'Rose . . . I wonder if you can do me a favour. Would you kindly not mention to my husband about that appointment?'

There was a brief pause, then Rose said, 'I never volunteer anything about your movements.'

'Does my husband ever ask?'

There was another, longer pause. 'Well, I . . . I suppose he does sometimes ask.'

'Does he?' She was surprised. She told Charles whatever he wanted to know, why did he need to question the staff? 'What does he ask?'

'Mrs Redmain, I can't go into what happens in the office.'

'I'm not interested in what happens in the office. This is about me. I wondered whether, for example, the accountants pass my bank statements to Charles. Obviously, there's no reason why he shouldn't see them, but I'd like to know.' She tried to keep her tone light, not wanting to alert Rose to any anxiety on her part.

Rose's voice dropped down a tone. 'Mrs R, I can't talk about it. I'm bound by confidentiality agreements.'

'About my bank statements?' Buttercup laughed. It came out a little too shrilly. 'Surely not.'

'About a lot of things and it's better not to risk getting things wrong. I can only suggest you talk to the boss about it all, I can't get involved. I'm sorry.'

'But, Rose – you won't tell about Barrett Singh, will you? It's something I'd like to discuss with Charles in my own time.'

'It's not up to me.' Buttercup could hear the strain in Rose's voice. 'I don't have any control over it. I'm sorry.'

'Okay, I understand. But maybe just hold that statement back for a month, will you? Until I've had an opportunity to talk to Charles about it? It's just so personal, I'm sure you must understand that. Please . . . ?'

She heard Rose's breath escaping in a worried sigh as she thought. Then she said quickly, 'All right. I can hold it back a month without any questions being asked. But then I'll have to put it in the file.'

'Thank you, Rose. Thank you.'

'You're welcome, Mrs R. But please – talk to him, won't you? Much better that way, I promise you.'

'Yes. Thanks again.'

As she put the phone down, feeling dazed and thinking over what Rose had just said to her, Carol came in, breezy and good-humoured as always, holding a tray for the dirty dishes. She started loading it up.

'Everything okay?' she asked. 'You're feeling all right, are you? You look a bit pale.'

'I'm fine, honestly.' Buttercup looked up at Carol with a smile. She saw – or did she? – Carol's eyes flick to the screen of her phone, which was still alight and showing her email inbox. She moved her hand to cover it and when she looked back, Carol was busy putting the empty yoghurt dish on the tray and stacking unused plates.

She had the sudden and uncomfortable feeling that there were more eyes on her than she had ever understood.

Chapter Thirteen

'The results are ready for you now, Mrs Redmain. We were going to email them today and post a hard copy to your London address.'

'Oh no, please don't do that,' Buttercup said into the phone, relieved that she'd called the clinic before the documents went into the post. She was standing outside by the railings at the edge of the park. The rain of the morning had stopped and the weather was suddenly clear, cold and blue, with only the rotting detritus of the leaves blown down in the rainstorms to recall the recent deluge. 'Can you hold them for me? I'd like to collect them in person. Tomorrow, if that's all right?'

'Yes, that's fine. We'll hold them for you till then. Thank you, Mrs Redmain, and see you tomorrow.'

The phone went dead before she could ask the receptionist what the results actually were, but perhaps she wouldn't have been allowed to read them in any case. She had suddenly decided that she didn't want such delicate, personal material sent to her electronically, though she didn't know why it mattered. She was glad she had stopped the hard copy arriving at the London house.

I can wait till tomorrow. And maybe, just maybe, I'm pregnant already.

The idea filled her with a rush of joyous warmth, and a sudden wild fascination with whatever might be happening inside her. She longed to know. She imagined telling Charles the happy news, and how she might find some funny way to do it, something they could remember for years afterwards. 'Do you remember when I said . . . and your face . . . you realised what I meant! And then we had our darling . . .'

The joy faded and her anxiety returned. It all depended on what the results were. What if they told her that she had serious fertility problems and could never bear a child? Or that she would need serious, lengthy and expensive interventions?

I need to know before I tell Charles about going to the clinic. But I must tell him before he finds out I went behind his back.

She walked back towards the house, feeling low. She'd married thinking that there would never be any secrets between her and her husband. One of the things that had made her so sure about Charles was the certainty that he was her best friend; she could tell him anything – and she did. She'd opened her heart to him, and shared whatever was in it without any censorship. But now, by omission, she was being deceitful.

How did I get like this? Hiding something so important, so integral to us.

She had the discomfiting thought that she had been

pushed into this position, and yet she wasn't entirely sure how. But her conversation with Rose kept replaying itself in her head and adding to her sense of anxiety. She wanted to know more about what went on in Charles's office.

When I go back to London, I'll see Rose and talk to her about it.

The good weather held as she drove into London, negotiating the traffic right to the heart of the city, where the Houses of Parliament, built in spikily confident Victorian Gothic, flew their bright flag by the river, and the Abbey sat beside it in all its ancient magnificence.

She arrived at the Westminster house in the early afternoon, and stopped at the office on the way up to the flat, putting her head around the door to look for Rose.

Elaine looked up from the computer screen on her large black desk as Buttercup came in. 'Good afternoon, Mrs R. How was the drive?'

'Fine, thanks. How are you, Elaine? Busy?'

Elaine smiled. She looked so familiar, her short black hair in that business-like crop and the splashily coloured tunic top coordinated with coral lipstick, yet Buttercup felt that she hardly knew this woman, despite her key role in Charles's life. 'It's always busy with Mr R!' she said perkily.

'Where is he today?'

'Meetings in the City. Dinner at the House with a couple of MPs. He's sorry he won't be around to see you until later. You are staying, aren't you?'

'Yes, for tonight.'

'Good. He'll be pleased. What brings you to town?'

'Just a whim. I want to do some shopping and my friend Hazel promised to take me out to a new club she's joined.'

'That sounds nice.'

Buttercup looked about the office. As always, it was pristine and well organised. Elaine's in and out trays were empty, as Charles hated to see piles of paper. Buttercup hoped that there were boxes of unsorted stuff hidden away in filing cabinets and cupboards, to make this whole set-up a bit more human, but somehow she doubted it. Elaine was probably every bit as pernickety as Charles. 'Is Rose around?'

'She's got the afternoon off to do wedding things. She'll be in tomorrow.'

'Okay.' Buttercup tried to look casual. 'I thought I might ask her advice about some things in the flat. Could she come up and see me tomorrow when she gets into the office?'

'No problem. I'll tell her. You're sure I can't help?'

'That's kind of you, but I thought Rose might . . . Well, I don't want to bother you. Just send her up tomorrow when she gets in. Thanks.'

She turned away quickly before Elaine could repeat her offer, and headed up the stairs to the flat. Inside, she let out a long breath. It was strange how stressful it could be trying to conceal things in this environment. She couldn't say anything without thinking first about what she was giving away.

Buttercup put down her things, and went out again almost immediately, heading towards the clinic, thinking only of the results waiting for her there.

*

LULU TAYLOR

'You're afraid to tell your husband you went to a fertility clinic?' Hazel hissed over the white linen tablecloth. 'Buttercup, how many kinds of wrong is that?'

They were sitting in the dark basement dining room of Hazel's club, and Buttercup had not been able to keep the results of the tests to herself. But explaining about the trip to the clinic was just the preamble to the main event and Buttercup was taken aback by Hazel's reaction to the news of her appointment there.

'Well—'

'And, I might add, you kept it very quiet when we last met!' Hazel added, looking hurt.

'I'm sorry. I should have told you. And I should have told Charles. You're right – it's not normal.'

'Not *normal*? It's completely weird that you went without him in the first place.'

'I know.' Buttercup looked down, ashamed. 'I shouldn't have done it. I'm not surprised he'd be outraged about me going behind his back.'

'No – it's not that.' Hazel laughed mirthlessly. 'Oh my God, it's not that. Don't you see? It's the fact that you felt you had to go on your own! Why wouldn't he go with you to find out what the hell is wrong?'

'He doesn't think anything *is* wrong.'

'Excuse me, I must have missed the part where Charles qualified as a doctor and specialised in obstetrics and gynaecology with a sideline in fertility problems.' Hazel made a face. 'I don't mean to sound snide but what the hell does he know? If you're anxious about it, then he should have been

146

happy to go – no, scratch that – he should have been the one *suggesting* it.' She sighed crossly. 'You have nothing to apologise for.'

Buttercup stared at her friend, startled by the strength of her response. There was a vehemence she'd never heard before when Hazel talked about Charles. 'I've always felt you're not that keen on him, but you've never voiced any criticism of him. Not to me, at least.'

Hazel bit her lip awkwardly, then said, 'Oh, honey. I don't want to be unfair to him and I don't want to stick my oar in when you're so happy.'

'Yes, I *am* happy and he treats me amazingly.'

'Almost too well.'

'That can't be why you don't like him! Is it because he's divorced? Older than me?'

'I do like him,' protested Hazel. 'But it's more the way he's so . . . all over you.'

'He's my husband,' Buttercup said coolly. 'And we're only two years married. Of course he's all over me.'

'It's more than just romantic. I mean – don't you find it at all stifling? He keeps you sitting in that huge house all on your own, endless staff to run your life. I can't reconcile that with my old Buttercup, that's all. You were always so independent, so energetic . . .' Hazel shook her head. 'I'm worried that it doesn't make you happy.'

'That's up to me, not to Charles. As it happens, I've been thinking about getting back to work. I've sent Lazlo an email asking if he'd like me to start networking for him in Dorset.'

'Great idea. But what does Charles think about it?'

'I haven't told him yet. I'm sure he'll be completely supportive though.' Buttercup fought down a sense of rising irritation with her old friend and what she was implying.

'I hope so. I just don't like the fact that you're afraid of his reaction to the fertility clinic.'

'I'm not afraid,' she said obstinately, then suddenly remembered her anxiety when Rose told her that Charles would see the bank statements, and her bewilderment that he should ask about her movements. She pushed that quickly out of her mind.

Hazel took a sip of her wine, then she said quickly, 'Sorry, Buttercup, I've been totally heartless. What did your results from the clinic say?'

'It's good news. In a way.' Buttercup bent down and pulled a sheaf of paper from her bag. She unfolded it and flicked through the attachments: scans and tables and graphs and statistics and all the conclusions they led to. 'There's nothing wrong with me. I should be getting pregnant. There's no explanation as to why I wouldn't.' She passed the pages over to Hazel, who took them and flicked through with interest. 'It seems I'm as normal as normal can be. So it's unexplained infertility . . . we can only keep trying for now.'

Hazel glanced up from the report. 'Or it's not you. It's Charles.'

'I think the fact of James and Charlotte rules that out. So I'm back where I started. We want a baby but I'm just not getting pregnant.' Buttercup eyed the glass of wine she was sipping, and put it down. She picked up her water instead. 'Not so far.'

'You need to talk to Charles. Make sure he knows exactly how you feel. Tell him that you need his support and he's going to damn well give it. You need to be strong with him. Explain that if you don't get pregnant soon, you want more tests.'

'You're right. I'll tell him tonight. I know he'll be fine with it.' As she said it, she was certain she was right. She would explain, and Charles would understand.

'Good. I want you to be happy, Buttercup, honestly I do. You deserve it.'

Buttercup arrived back at the flat before Charles did, and went straight to bed, telling herself she would talk to him about the clinic in the morning. When he came in, trying to tiptoe but crashing about, smelling of wine and whisky, she was almost asleep in any case. She was only half aware as he threw his clothes over the back of a chair, pulled on pyjama bottoms and then snuggled up beside her, one arm snaking around her and pulling her tight.

'Good night, my darling,' he murmured, kissing her hair. 'My sleeping beauty. Good night.'

Chapter Fourteen

Buttercup and Charles had breakfast together the next day, and although she meant to raise the subject of her tests, in no time he was standing up to leave. 'I'm off to work, my love. Meetings, meetings, and then a trip to Geneva again.'

'Another one? When will you be home?'

'I'll be back for the weekend.'

'That's good. I had a message from Cathy Tranter. They want to open at the weekend, with a Bonfire Night party. I said we'd go.'

Charles made a face as he put on his jacket. 'A Bonfire Night party? Oh.'

'I think we should support them.'

'Let me think about it, darling. I'm sure it will be brilliant fun but I don't know if it's quite my cup of tea ...' He put his hand to his forehead suddenly. 'I forgot to tell you! I bumped into Lazlo last night, quite by chance. He said to say thanks for your email but he's not planning on expanding the business at the moment, he has more than enough to keep him busy.' He gave her a quizzical look. 'Were you thinking of going back to work?'

Buttercup felt obscurely disappointed, not just that her idea would come to nothing but that Lazlo hadn't bothered to write to her himself. Still, she reminded herself, he was always rubbish about getting in touch. *That's why he needed me.* 'Just an idle thought. It doesn't matter.'

'Fine. Don't forget to text me when you get home.' He picked up his coffee cup and drained the last of the liquid. 'By the way, Charlotte isn't coming to Charcombe at half-term. She's meeting me in Geneva instead, I'm going to take her for a few treats while we're out there. That's okay, isn't it?'

'Er – yes. Of course. It's a shame not to see her though.'

'You will soon.' He kissed her. 'Bye, darling.'

And he was gone.

It was just after 9 a.m. when there was a knock at the door and Rose put her head round. 'Hello?'

'Come in, Rose, come and sit down.' Buttercup beckoned her over to the long low white sofa with its view over the terrace to the rooftops of London. 'Would you like a coffee or something?'

'I'm fine, thanks.' She came over, smart in a navy dress, her eyes a little apprehensive behind her spectacles. 'Is everything okay? Elaine said you want to ask me something about the flat?'

'I do want to ask you something, but not really about the flat.' Buttercup sat down and Rose did the same, smoothing her dress underneath her as she perched gingerly on the edge of the sofa. 'But it's about the talk we had the other day.'

Rose looked a touch uncomfortable but said airily, 'Fire away, Mrs R.'

'I've been thinking about it and I've realised that I don't understand the office, or how you and Elaine work with my husband.'

'Elaine does all the personal stuff,' Rose said quickly. 'I just do admin.'

'Yes. But what does that entail? How does it affect me? I suppose I thought that things were just ticked off, filed away . . . I knew that the bank statements would be looked at, of course, but I didn't realise that it's all so scrutinised. I don't have anything to hide, but I'd like to know what goes on.'

A worried expression flitted over Rose's face. 'I just have to be careful, that's all. I can't talk about it.'

'Even to me? I only want to know about the bits that pertain to me, can't you talk about that?'

'No, only to Elaine and the boss. I've had to sign some pretty strong confidentiality agreements.'

Buttercup frowned, puzzled. 'Let me get this clear. You can't tell me things that are about me? To do with my life?'

'I would need to clear it, that's all. I'm happy to ask what I'm allowed to disclose. But they're going to want to know what you've said to me and why you want to know these things.'

'Why shouldn't I know them?'

'Because there's no need.' Rose looked pleading, locking her hands together around one knee, and knitting the fingers.

'It all goes on so nicely. You get everything you want, we do everything for you. Honestly, it's just . . . admin.'

'Then what's the harm in telling me about it?' Buttercup was surprised; she'd imagined this would all be straightforward – Rose would tell her the procedures around her personal admin. What was the big secret? She hadn't expected such a reluctance to say anything at all.

Rose sighed, and looked away, biting her lip.

Buttercup said gently, 'I don't want to put you in a difficult position, Rose. And I won't tell anyone what you tell me.'

'But if they find out, they'll know it was me.' She turned to face Buttercup. 'You don't understand – if there's any suspicion that I've broken a rule, I'll be out. Just like that. No excuses, no second chances. They'll sack me so fast, I won't have time to unpack my desk drawer. I've seen what the boss is like. He won't be disobeyed, and he doesn't like mistakes. And he hates disloyalty.'

Buttercup stared at her, a strange feeling turning in her stomach. This didn't sound like Charles. She knew he put a high price on loyalty, but that was a good thing, wasn't it? He wasn't the way Rose was making him sound: ruthless and unforgiving. He was fair, she knew that, and a great boss. How could he inspire such loyalty from the people around him if he wasn't? It wasn't just that he paid good salaries, surely.

I am loyal, I know that. But what if Charles decided I wasn't?

'I don't want to be dramatic about this,' Rose said in a low voice, 'but I'm getting married in the summer. There's a wedding to pay for, and we're saving up for a deposit on a flat. I can't afford to lose my job. I'd rather say as little as possible.'

Buttercup leaned in towards her and said in the same quiet tone, 'Rose, do you trust Jacob? Do you intend to be open and honest with him all your life, and want him to be the same?'

Rose hesitated and then said, 'Of course.'

'Then you surely understand that Charles would not mind me knowing what goes on with my information here in the office.' Buttercup watched Rose absorb this. 'Or do you know differently?' She studied the other woman's face and saw her chance. 'Please, Rose. I won't tell anyone, I promise.'

Rose looked as though she were wavering.

Buttercup said, 'I know Charles keeps track of where I am. That's only natural. I can see his online diary whenever I like. But is there more to it than just the diary? I have a feeling that there is . . . I think I'm more monitored than I know, and you're all in on it. Is that right?' She leaned forward even closer. 'And is that how you would want to be treated, Rose?'

Rose stared at the floor, evidently thinking. Then suddenly she looked up. 'Okay. I can't see that it will do any harm but I can't tell you much because I don't know much. All the information that concerns you is passed to Elaine, who collates it into a file and makes a weekly report that goes to the boss. I've never seen a report but I think it includes a timeline of your movements, plus all the financial information about what you've spent, where and when. There's a database with the details of your activities – hairdressers, beauticians, trainers, memberships, clubs, friends . . . everything.'

'A database?' echoed Buttercup, shocked. 'Really? But why?'

'It's for security reasons.' Rose looked at her solemnly from behind her spectacles. 'You must know that you're a potential kidnap target.'

'That's why I'm monitored?'

'Of course. Mr R would do anything to protect you. It's all for your own safety.'

Buttercup let out a breath, perplexed. 'How does it protect me? I don't think I'm threatened that much, am I? We're not famous or royal or anything. I don't understand.'

'It's just what happens. I don't know the reasons. It's for security, that's the only thing I've been told.'

'Am I being followed?'

Rose shook her head, smiling. 'No! It's nothing like that. Honestly. It's my job to go through statements that come in from the accountants, approve them for payment or flag up anything unusual. That goes to Elaine and I supposed she puts it in the report.'

The report. On me. It sounded so odd. *But it's to keep me safe, that's all there is to it.*

Rose went on: 'And I will have to give her the statement we discussed quite soon, or she'll ask questions.'

Buttercup sat back against the sofa cushions. 'I haven't told Charles about my appointment at Barrett Singh yet. I'm picking my moment and he's away so much. Can you just approve the payment and not flag it up to Elaine? That way

I'll have time to discuss it all with Charles. I don't want him to find out before I can tell him myself, I'm sure you can understand that.'

Rose looked wary again. 'If she notices, she'll ask me why I didn't mark it for her attention.'

'Can you risk it for me, please, Rose? What would she do if she found out?'

'Not much, I suppose. Remind me of my job.'

'So . . . you will?'

Rose hesitated, then said: 'All right, I will. Just this one time, okay? I don't want to get involved in any secrets.'

'No. I promise. Just this one time.'

Buttercup showed Rose out and then went to stand at the terrace windows, looking out over the London skyline.

He wants to protect me, like any caring husband. What's wrong with that?

Perhaps he was taking his duty to look after her a bit too seriously. He knew she had no parents, no family that she was particularly close to; he clearly felt that he was her guardian as well her husband.

I must talk to him about that. He doesn't need to be intense about me. If we discuss it, I'm sure he'll understand. All I have to do is be honest with him and everything will be fine.

PART TWO

Chapter Fifteen

Xenia found, to her surprise, that she looked forward to Agnieska's visits. She couldn't think why, as they barely spoke to one another and her English was too bad to have a real conversation, but having someone else in the house was a pleasurable novelty, and it broke the sometimes shattering loneliness of being by herself so much.

She didn't go out often, and certainly avoided the kinds of activities that other women her age were doing: the craft clubs, the gentle rambles, the history society. She doubted that she would be welcome at the over-60s lunch club, even if she wanted to attend such a thing. The villagers did not have much to do with her. When she went into the shop at the other side of the village, they went quiet and wouldn't look at her. She was served with a cool politeness.

She knew why. She had brought it upon herself by speaking her mind and refusing to let them succeed in their quest to break her and force her out during the worst times, when Papa was gone and she was forced to care alone for her mother.

The villagers had not helped. They had turned against her, starting up petitions to have her removed and Mama taken away. Nasty letters arrived, berating her for the state of the house and the grounds, demanding she cut down trees or clear thistles or whatever it was that annoyed them. They sent social services and council officials – bossy people who had told her what to do and what regulations she had to obey, what stipulations she must fulfil.

Me. One woman against all of them, the only thing between Mama and—

Something awful. Being taken away and being shut up and having all her hopes ruined. As if she could have survived that!

'He'll come back to us, won't he?' Mama used to ask plaintively.

'Oh yes,' Xenia would say firmly. 'He'll come back one day.'

When busybodies came around to see what conditions they were living in, Xenia learned how to deal with them. She had found that epic rudeness worked well, particularly with the timid-looking young women who knocked on the door.

'Get off my property!' she would shout. 'You're trespassing. Get off or I call the police!'

'Mrs Arkadyoff, please—'

'Mrs Arkadyoff!' Scorn filled her voice. 'Who do you think you're talking to? I am Princess Xenia Arkadyoff. My grandmother was second cousin to the Tsar of Russia! Who are you? Nobodies! How dare you presume to tell me what to do! Get out of here – go away.' She would stand, eyes flashing, in front of the door, arms out like the angel at the way in to Eden, refusing them entry. Sometimes that was enough to send them on their way. At other times, they would persist, barging inside with their clipboards and prying eyes, looking about and making notes. She would shout and scream until they could take no more, and left.

Afterwards, letters would arrive in their horrible brown envelopes with their computer-generated labels, her name always misspelt. She ignored them. Things must stay as they were: just her and Mama, alone again, waiting patiently for the day when Papa would return, as he had promised.

That was years ago. These days, she had learned to hold her tongue more than she used to, especially now that she had no choice about where she could shop. The car sat unused in the garage because she didn't dare drive; she couldn't see what was right in front of her. So she couldn't go to the supermarket and shop in peace; she had to use the village shop or starve.

Agnieska did not know any of the past hostilities and would not understand if someone tried to explain them to her. She turned up, did her work and went away again. The only thing she did not do was say when supplies were running low. She never mentioned that at all, which Xenia found frustrating. But where once she would have berated her, told her exactly what she was doing wrong, she kept quiet. She had a sense that she might need this girl's help and it would not do to alienate her, as she had the others.

Agnieska put her head around the door of the drawing room. 'I go now.'

'Yes.' Xenia looked over at her. 'Thank you.'

Agnieska nodded and slipped away to put on her outdoor shoes. Xenia followed her into the hall.

'Are you cycling today?' She looked out into the chill grey of the late October afternoon. It was raining again, and the sky was low, full of heavy, iron-coloured clouds. The lane outside was muddy, the potholes full of water the colour of strong tea.

'Yes.' Agnieska was pulling on her coat.

'Don't you drive in this weather?'

'I have no car.' She spoke in her customary uninflected way. It was neither good nor bad that she had no car. Just a fact.

'Where do you live?'

'Galston.'

'Oh.' The town five miles away: a pedestrianised shopping mall of concrete and high street shops, ringed by industrial estates; a hodge-podge of housing: modern estates, crumbling old terraces, a few streets lined by gracious Edwardian villas with large gardens. She could guess that Agnieska would live on one of the estates, in a house with narrow doorways and low ceilings, all the rooms just a little too small to be properly furnished, so they always felt crowded. 'And where do your children go to school?'

'Elmhurst Primary. Two miles from the house, but it is a good school.'

'You all walk there every day?'

'Yes, or on the bus.' She shrugged. 'It's fine.'

'If you say so.'

Agnieska turned to the door. 'I go. I have the other job.'
She turned back and said, 'Money?'

'Oh, yes. Here it is.' Xenia handed over the wages and
watched as Agnieska pocketed it, pulled up her hood and
went out, skipping down the front steps to where her bike
rested under the lean-to. She wheeled it out through the gate
and turned left, heading back up the lane towards Charcombe Park.

Xenia leaned out a little further into the porch and
watched as she walked up the lane and then over the road
and into the driveway of Fitzroy House.

*Ah. She's working for the other wife too, is she? I didn't
know that.*

That afternoon, Xenia walked to the churchyard to visit
Mama's grave, as she did every week, to lay something from
the garden below the carved wooden cross that marked her
resting place. Usually she cleared away whatever she had left
there the week before. Sometimes she found a wreath or a
bouquet left by an admirer who had made a pilgrimage to
visit Natalie Rowe. Occasionally the cross was draped in
velvet or with a rope of pretend pearls, or a photograph of
Delilah was pinned to it. Xenia always removed those things,
so that the cross could be seen properly; it was very beautiful, carved with delicate emblems of flowers: roses, lilies,
daisies and daffodils. Mama had loved to gather them when
they were in bloom around the house. The cross meant a
great deal to Xenia. When news of her mother's death had
become public, she had received many letters. Most of them

had been fan letters but one had stood out, addressed to her in swirling calligraphy. It was from Luke Ashley, asking if he could make a cross for Mama's grave in memory of the years he and his family had spent living at Charcombe, and Xenia had gratefully accepted. Luke had come to deliver it himself – Gwen, he told her, was too ill to travel – and brought his boy with him, though he'd been much older by then.

'We loved your mother,' Luke had said, and she'd known he meant it. Mama had been more than Natalie Rowe to them, more than Delilah. She'd been real, no matter how troubled and broken she was, and they loved her anyway. The fans only wanted to know about the glamorous young woman with her exquisite face and incredible talent. When all that was over and gone, they had melted away.

Xenia stood in front of Luke's cross in its quiet corner of the cemetery. Below Mama's name was carved her year of birth and of death, each letter and number perfectly formed. Looking at them, she remembered Luke in his workshop, with his chisels and hammers and carving tools, creating beauty out of plain blocks of wood. He had been talented, there was no doubt about that, and Gwen too. She had painted exquisite botanical oils in miniature, on tiny pieces of china and glass or minute stretched canvases. The two of them had brought something special and unexpected to the house, something that she had in the end been grateful for, no matter how much she had disliked the whole idea of strangers living at Charcombe to start with.

A gust of bitter wind blew under Xenia's scarf and made her shiver. She laid down the berry-laden branch from the shrub in the garden, placing it carefully on the ground under Mama's cross, and then went into the church to escape the cold before she walked home again. It was not a Catholic church, but it was all she had, and she still savoured the aroma of old candle wax and the musty, dampish smell of the ancient stone and hymn books.

Where are Luke and Gwen now? Are they dead?

For years, to pay the bills, she had leased bits of Charcombe to people who wanted it. The park was grazed by sheep and cattle, the garages housing a few old wrecks and stored possessions. One day, a tall, thin man with wild brown hair, wearing jeans and a loose purple shirt, had driven up to the house in an old VW to suggest a plan. He had an idea that he would run a residential artists' collective at the house, to teach young people artisan skills that were in danger of being forgotten. Skills like carving, gilding, carpentry and silk-screen painting. He would live at Charcombe with his wife Gwen and their children, while the young people would come and go.

The idea had not appealed to Xenia in the least, but they had been prepared to pay good money and she was in dire need, and so she had agreed to it on a trial basis. She and Mama had moved into rooms on the second floor and Gwen and Luke took all the bedrooms on the first floor. The large reception rooms became studios and communal spaces. The stables were workshops where furniture was made in the traditional style, stone was cut, wood carved, glass melted and remade. They even made a forge in the old pigsties. A large round table built by Luke from wood cut down in the park had taken pride of place in the empty dining room, the grand mahogany furniture long since sold off, and provided space for thirty people to eat at the same time.

Those had been happy days, Xenia thought. Unexpectedly happy. She had expected to hate the invasion of uncultured youth but instead, she had been surprised by the way the house had felt alive, with children running about, creative energy sparking everywhere, the parties and the laughter.

Like the old days, when we first arrived at Charcombe. And there was Harry. How could I forget him? Where is he now? Is he dead too?

It had all come to an end, as everything did. Luke got tired of it, Gwen got painful, twisting arthritis and couldn't work any more. The students stopped coming. They cleared out the stables and the house, and went, leaving only rubbish behind. Then she was alone again, in the great whistling space, wishing she could have it back the way it used to be, in the glory days.

The glory days!

It made her think of Mama when she was at the height of her power, before everything conspired to break her.

Chapter Sixteen

1950

A governess came to the house on Bristol Avenue but Xenia found the lessons deathly, and the sight of the tantalising swimming pool below too much to bear. After the third session with the governess, she went outside into the bright sunshine to find her mother, who was sitting on the terrace under a large sun umbrella, wearing her dark glasses as usual, recovering on one of her rare afternoons off. Papa sat nearby reading *Variety*.

'Please, Mama, mayn't I have my lessons on the set? Then I could come out and watch when I'm allowed a break.' She draped her arms around her mother's neck. 'I'm lonely here!'

She knew it was a good card to play, because her mother felt guilty there were no brothers and sisters to keep Xenia amused.

'I don't know . . .' Mama put down her drink, clear liquid over dissolving ice cubes, and looked over to her husband. 'Paul, what do you think?'

'What?' Papa looked up from the newspaper he was

reading, talking over the cigarette between his teeth. 'What did you say?'

'Xenia wants to do her lessons on set.'

Papa thought for a moment. 'Let her, if you want. In fact, why bother with the lessons? You should dismiss the governess. It's only a few days more, and she'll learn plenty on set with a book or two to keep her occupied when she's not watching the filming.'

The filming was going well. Papa went to the set every day and at home, he and Mama worked on her performance. The lines were no longer a problem, because they were said all day long: over the dinner table, in the sitting room, on the terrace, while Mama was swimming up and down the turquoise waters of the pool, and late at night. Xenia knew the role herself, she'd heard the lines so often.

Mama leaned on Papa more than ever, looking to him for all the reassurance she needed. But Xenia felt that Papa's patience was growing strained and close to snapping; she felt it in the restrained irritation he exuded and the way he frowned and grimaced when Mama walked over to the drinks table in the evening.

One night she'd heard Papa talking loudly in the drawing room and had sneaked downstairs to listen.

'Put that down,' Papa was saying. 'It doesn't help, can't you see? It makes it all worse!'

'Please, Paul, I need it.'

'I don't understand, Natalie. You can act, can't you? How hard can it be to say your lines and be on your mark? You've never had a problem before.'

'It calms me down. I'm frightened, when they all expect so much of me. I know how much is riding on this film, and how everybody is waiting for it. They expect me to be so wonderful – I got this amazing part instead of all those other actresses, so I must be special! It's a nightmare . . . all those eyes turned on me, the cameras, the silence I have to act into. It's not like the theatre – I can't see the audience there, and anyway, they love me. I can give to them, it's easy. But on the set . . .' Mama's voice rose with passion. 'They all hate me, Paul! I can feel them waiting for me to spoil it, so they can hate me more.'

'You're imagining things. Do you think they want to waste time and money with your mistakes? Don't be so stupid.'

'No! That's just it. They're all against me.'

'Archibald isn't against you. I think he believes in you. He's desperate for you to succeed, that's why he takes you out all the time and tries to help you with your part.'

'He knows it's too late to replace me. But he hates me for not being what he expected. He thought he was getting one of those steely professionals, like Crawford, or Stanwyck. And he got me! Please, Paul, let me have a drink, it makes me braver, it makes me stronger . . .'

'You're being foolish, it spoils your looks and makes you slow.'

'Don't you love me any more?' She sounded plaintive, desperate. 'I saw you looking at that girl who plays the secretary. I know she's beautiful. Is she more beautiful than me?'

'That's ridiculous and beneath you. Listen to me, Natalie, no more drink until the film is over. But you can take these to help you sleep. The studio doctor gave them to me when I told him about your problems. The blue ones are best to sleep, and the white to wake up with . . .'

Xenia crept away, afraid. She remembered Papa on the boat, telling that woman how damaged and difficult Mama was. Could he be right? Xenia had always known that Mama was hard on herself and didn't believe she was good enough, but Xenia thought that was a loveable quality, like modesty or humility. Perhaps, after all, it was a terrible affliction that undermined her and stood in the way of her ever properly enjoying her success or reaching her potential.

But Papa is here. Papa will look after her.

It was the tone in Papa's voice that frightened her the most. Mama leaned on him more than anyone else in the world. If Papa ever did grow bored of her fears and difficulties, or if she ever stopped being the wonderful Natalie Rowe . . . what then?

'Darling, when you come to the set, will you bring something for me?'

Xenia pushed her covers away, blinking. It was growing light outside her bedroom, the sky baby blue with pink streaks as the golden sun rose for another blazing day. Mama was sitting on the end of her bed, already in her jacket, her hair in a turban and her face bare, ready for the drive to the studio. Xenia yawned and said, 'Yes, Mama.'

She pulled a large silver Thermos out of her bag. 'Can you fit this into your school bag?'

Xenia nodded.

'Then will you bring it in with you to my trailer when you come? But don't tell Papa, will you? He doesn't understand that I need my tonic to help me on the set. It's such a long day.' She leaned over and put the flask on the night table, then looked into Xenia's eyes. 'Tell me honestly, do you think I'm still pretty?'

Xenia stared back at her mother. She could see dark circles under her eyes, and the whites were crazed with red lines at the edges. Her skin had a greyish pallor and hollows under the high cheekbones. The doctor had put Mama on a strengthening diet of mostly eggs, meat, milk and spinach, but she seemed to be getting thinner and thinner.

'Absolutely,' Xenia said emphatically. 'You are the most beautiful woman in the world.'

She meant it from her depths. Mama's green eyes, the arched brows, the soft dark hair and the exquisite cupid's bow mouth below that straight nose with the faintest upturned swoop at the end – Xenia could not conceive of greater beauty. The make-up lady, Sissy, would cover the dark circles and the blotches on her neck and add the colour to her face with rouge and plump her cheeks with those brown and white shadows. Drops of special liquid would make her eyes sparkle white again. Then she would be back to her lovely self.

Mama engulfed her in a hug. 'Oh, thank you, darling, thank you! What a wonderful daughter you are. I know I can depend on you.'

When she was gone, Xenia opened the flask and sniffed the contents, but there was almost no smell, just a faint astringency, like something from the medicine cupboard. She packed it carefully into her school bag to take into the studio with her books.

On set, Xenia lingered in the darkness as usual, mostly tucked away on her little chair. She had put the flask by Mama's couch in her trailer, and instead of reading the book of Greek myths she'd been given to study, she watched the goings-on: the sets being changed, the props laid out or refreshed, the cameras and lights being adjusted. It was all so interesting.

Mama knew her lines, at least. Her trouble seemed to be keeping herself still when the camera stopped rolling. She often appeared to be swaying slightly, and she frequently disappeared into a dreamy state, her eyes turning up towards the great lights hanging from their bars as if gazing into the heavens. A sharp shout from Archibald Thomas would usually bring her back, and a talk with Papa – rapid whispers at the corner of the set, or a quick conference in the trailer – could also restore her. And when filming began, she was still able to project that strange quality that looked like a kind of inner stillness. Xenia knew it was something special because she'd heard Archibald Thomas talking about it to the assistant director.

'Don't you see what I mean?' he'd murmured. 'It looks like nothing when she does it and then, on the screen . . . on the rushes . . . she's sheer magic. I've rarely seen such luminescence. It's why we can believe men want to kill for her love.

That's why she's Delilah. If we can just keep her on the right side of sober until the end of filming . . .'

Today, Mama was in a beautiful evening gown, her hair dressed and her make-up perfect. The scene was a New York nightclub, and it was full of glamorous women but none of them could hold a candle to Mama. Xenia watched Mama being whirled around the dance floor by the handsome actor who played the man she loved. When they had dialogue to record, she and the actor stood still on a piece of moving floor that turned them around from side to side, as though they were dancing, but kept them in front of the camera while the other dancers moved around them, back and forth in a semi-circle.

Then someone had the idea that it would be fun for Xenia herself to appear in the scene, as one of the coat-check girls.

'Put her in one of the black dresses and do her hair, she'll look quite grown-up,' said the script editor, a friendly faced young woman with dyed red hair and glasses shaped like a cat's eyes. She smiled at Xenia. 'It'll be fun! Something to tell your friends when you get back to England, huh?'

They put it to Archibald Thomas, who laughed and said it was fine if Natalie was happy.

'Do you want to, darling?' Mama asked, smiling.

Xenia was stunned. To appear in Mama's film, even as one of those mousy creatures who took the coats? It was too exciting to think about. 'Yes please,' she said breathlessly.

They put her in a make-up room, not Mama's trailer but a room with dozens of metal chairs in front of one long mirror, where they painted the faces of the extras and bit part actors. The long table was scattered with pots of grease in different colours, palettes of coloured powders, tubs of brushes and hundreds of balls of cotton wool, some stained brown and red and discarded. A gum-chewing girl stood beside her, looking quizzically at Xenia's face in the mirror.

Xenia stared at her reflection. It was so familiar and so ordinary, a world away from Mama's velvety beauty: a round, pale face; startled blue eyes. Her nose was like her mother's in that it had an upward tilt at the end, but hers was chunkier, like Papa's. Her mouth, though, had that sharp little cupid's bow and pointed upper lip, and small soft cushion of a lower lip, that did look like Mama's.

'We can do something with you,' the make-up girl said. 'You got a real pretty face.'

'I have? I don't think so . . .'

The girl laughed, showing the wad of gum between her teeth. 'I love your British accent, you sound like Basil Rathbone!' She leaned in so that Xenia could smell her pepperminty breath. 'They say you're a real princess too – is that right?'

'Yes, it is.'

'Well, what do you know? A real princess. My very own Snow White. Let's make you look gorgeous, Your Majesty.'

It seemed to Xenia that she'd spent an hour having her face dabbed and stroked with brushes and pencils before the girl said, 'You can look!'

And Xenia opened her eyes to a completely different

person. She looked like a grown-up, this stranger in the mirror, with her shimmering eyelids, thick dark lashes and bright red lips.

'Oh!' she said, astonished. She didn't look exactly like Mama – no one could – but she looked glamorous and . . . *pretty? Yes, I look pretty!*

'We don't have time to do your hair, but I've got a wig or two we can try,' the girl said confidentially, 'and then we'll get you into a dress.'

Going out onto the set in her black dress – plain, apparently, but still the most glamorous and grown-up thing she had ever worn – and with her new face and hair, she had the tiniest inkling of what it must be like to be Mama, and it was terrifying. Everyone was looking at her. All over the set men turned to stare and a few of them whistled their appreciation. She felt as though every person on the huge sound stage was looking at her and evaluating her and how she looked. The cameras, large from behind, looked gigantic when standing before them, their staring single eyes focused directly at her, and the light from above was dazzling, filtered through cellophane squares of red, blue, yellow and green.

And I'm not even the focus of their attention. No wonder Mama is so scared of it all.

And yet it was heady. To be Mama – so beautiful, so desired and so important – must be lovely too. Xenia had nothing to do but take coats from extras as they came and went. She didn't even take Mama's coat, because that was a speaking role and she didn't have the right to talk in the film, but she stood next to the girl who said, 'Good evening' and 'Here's your ticket'. She could only hope she didn't look too stupid, because she had been stunned by Mama as she came by with the camera rolling. The strangest thing was that she didn't seem to be her mother at all, but this haughty arrogant woman, Delilah, who drove everyone to madness with her beauty and her reckless, selfish behaviour.

When it was all over and they carried on with the next scene, Xenia kept on her grown-up clothes and all the make-up, and hid in the darkness at the edge of the set to carry on watching, still somehow feeling like a part of Mama's world. It had been terrifying and yet . . . utterly addictive.

So that's acting.

'Hello, you beautiful creature.'

She heard the voice deep in her ear, and felt a hand at her waist and then at her chest, where it stroked over the beginnings of her breasts. It was a man, with a low and growling voice. He was short and she could tell by the smell of his antique cologne – ancient leather and smoke – that he was old. He had an actor's voice: over-pronounced, smooth.

'You are exquisite. So young and so enticing. There's so much I'd like to teach you.'

The voice buried itself deeper into her ear and became a tongue, wet and tickling, sounding like a storm in her head. Revolted, she pulled away, pushed off the hand and ran off as fast as she could, not stopping until she was back in the make-up room, and in the comforting company of the gum-chewing girl.

'You okay? You have fun?' she said, dropping her magazine and standing up. 'Want me to get that stuff off you?'

Xenia nodded, panting. She wanted all the paint and artifice gone. It was too dangerous after all.

No wonder Mama was so afraid, if this was what her beauty caused her.

Chapter Seventeen

On the way back to Charcombe, Buttercup made her usual detour to see her mother, glad of the time in the car when she could think without distractions. She was alone, just another anonymous vehicle on the motorway, without any watchful eyes upon her.

Unless my car is tracked. Or maybe I'm being followed.

She flicked her gaze up to the rear-view mirror as if she might see someone tailing her. A few cars back was a London taxi, despite their distance from the city, and she thought suddenly of Rich and his black cab – perfect for blending into the background.

Would Charles get him to follow me?

Then she shook her head and laughed at herself. 'Watch out,' she said out loud. 'You'll make yourself paranoid if you're not careful.'

Nevertheless, she couldn't help thinking of that report, carefully compiled by Elaine and put in front of Charles every week, detailing all her movements and keeping a close watch on her. At least Rose had agreed to slip the clinic through. With any luck, Elaine wouldn't notice and if she did, well . . . Buttercup would have talked to Charles by then in any case.

She stayed with her mother for a couple of hours, talking some of the time of inconsequential things, reading to her, or just sitting in silence and watching her. Stacy had said Mum was on a course of antibiotics for an infection, and Buttercup wondered if the drugs were working. There was no way of knowing if Mum was in pain or felt out of sorts; she seemed, as always, deep in a dream world, far away from everyday reality. What was going on in her mind? Was she dreaming? Or could she hear and understand? Maybe there was nothing at all; perhaps she was drifting in darkness, just a step away from death itself.

Buttercup reached out and held her mother's hand. 'Don't die yet, Mum. Please.'

When she'd been younger, she'd been tormented by the idea that she wanted her mother to die – partly so Mum could escape the monstrous encroachment of the disease as it robbed her of the life she had loved; and partly so Buttercup too could be free from the awfulness of watching it creep over her like gangrene up a limb, and the long-drawn-out grief as she was slowly taken away and yet remained. Now, though, it was dreadful to think of her slipping over the border and into oblivion, her light finally extinguished. Her mother was still here, warm, alive and existing, still tied to this world by a tiny thread. If it were cut, Buttercup would be entirely alone.

Except, she reminded herself, *there's Charles.*

*

When she got back to Charcombe, the weather had turned again; rain exploded in a riotous patter on the windscreen, the wipers going full pelt. Autumn had taken a turn from crisp gold and orange to the slatey grey, chill dark of oncoming winter. It was getting cold. As she stopped outside the gates of the house and waited for them to slide open, she couldn't prevent her gaze from moving to the right to where Fitzroy House stood obscured by neat hedges and the magnolia tree. It seemed to be in darkness and closed up. When had she last seen any sign of life there? The fact was, she tried not to look so that she couldn't be caught attempting to catch a glimpse of Ingrid, and she couldn't remember how long it had been since she'd seen a light in the window. Perhaps, with Charlotte away, Ingrid was on her own travels.

It's none of my business in any case.

The gates were open now and she pressed down on the accelerator; the car shot forward to fly up the driveway to the house.

Tippi came bounding out to welcome her back, excited and barking, her tail thumping against the car door as Buttercup climbed out, laughing. The rain had eased off but the whole courtyard was dripping and slippery with wet.

'There, there, girl – did you miss me?' She patted Tippi and lifted her bag out of the back seat.

'Good trip?' Phil was coming across the courtyard pushing a red bicycle, his hair damp and his puffy jacket rain-spotted.

'Yes thanks. Are you off for a bike ride?'

'What?' He looked down, surprised, as though he hadn't

seen the bike before. 'Oh this! No, I'm fixing a puncture for Agnieska.'

'That's nice of you.'

'If the weather clears, I'm going to ride tomorrow morning if you fancy it.'

'Yes please.'

Phil looked up at the sky, squinting at the rain clouds. 'Let's hope it dries up a bit before the bonfire party at the pub. It'll be a washout if it carries on like this.' He wheeled the bike into the stables, and Buttercup headed inside, Tippi at her heels.

Buttercup shivered. She was sitting in the drawing room trying to warm up and wondering why the heating wasn't having any effect, scrolling through her social media. She saw that a notification had popped up so clicked on it and found that Caroline, the gateway to Ingrid, had accepted her friend request and sent a message.

> **Hi! So lovely to hear from you. We must have you and Charles over for dinner soon. I'll ping some dates. Hope you're well. Caro. xxx**

Buttercup stared for a moment and realised she was holding her breath. It all depended on what security settings Ingrid had selected. She may have protected herself but forgotten that friends of friends could see more than she realised. Her fingers trembling lightly, she went to Caroline's page and her list of friends. There was Ingrid's profile picture.

She clicked on it and was taken straight into her page. It felt like a mysterious door in the wall being opened and revealing a secret garden to her. She sat very still as she scrolled downwards, oblivious to everything but the pictures on the screen in front of her. Ingrid was not a prolific poster but there were occasional photographs with captions, and the comments underneath gave some clues as to what was going on.

Buttercup found she was looking at a picture of Ingrid standing with James outside what must have been his school. Ingrid was without her sunglasses this time, and Buttercup could see the warm hazel eyes like James's, crinkled at the edges, a round pleasant face, and shoulder-length dark hair that fell in soft waves. She was wearing a flowered tea dress that showed a slim figure, and high espadrilles that tied in blue ribbons around her calves.

She looked nice, ordinary, a normal woman on the edge of middle-age standing proudly next to her young son. Nothing like the hard-eyed vamp or desperate flirt that Buttercup had imagined. The caption read: 'My boy is all grown up. School is over, now he's off to university. It's still so hard to believe!'

Underneath friends had written their comments agreeing how time had flown and how mature James looked. 'You look lovely, Ingrid!' wrote one. 'Love the dress.' Ingrid had liked all the comments.

The next series of photographs were flowers and gardens. Buttercup passed quickly over them and stopped on a more curious picture: a knight in armour on horseback accepting some kind of prize from a woman dressed like something from a picture book in a red velvet gown and a cone-shaped hat adorned with a swirl of veil. 'Winning all the honours at the tournament in Cologne' read the caption.

'Ooh, clever Joachim! Doesn't he look handsome?' was one of the comments.

Who on earth is Joachim?

Buttercup carried on downwards, past more pictures of garden flowers and then to a post that was only text. It read:

Please understand that I cannot talk about recent events. My friends can contact me via email but I will not be commenting on this forum in any way. Thank you.

Buttercup looked at the date and saw that it was almost two years before she'd met Charles. Ingrid must be talking about the divorce. There were several likes but only one external comment: 'I can't believe Charles is treating you like this after everything you did for him. What an utter shit. You're so much better off.' Underneath that, Ingrid had written, 'Can't say anything. Appreciate your support though.'

Buttercup stared, reading it over and over again. What was Ingrid saying about Charles? Relations were civil, amicable. Had she been making up stories about her ex-husband?

'Can I get you some coffee?' Carol's voice broke into her thoughts, and she jumped violently, pushing down her computer screen so that it was not visible.

'Oh! Er – yes, thanks. Actually, I'm done here. I'll come to the kitchen. I just can't get warm in here, I don't know why.'

'It's always icy everywhere, except in the kitchen, thanks

to the Aga,' Carol said, not appearing to notice anything amiss. 'I'll see you there then.'

Did she see anything? Surely she couldn't have. Buttercup let out a shaky breath. *Anyway, Carol's lovely, she isn't a watcher.* But she thought of all the times Carol had casually asked her where she was going and who she was seeing. Did she contribute to Elaine's reports?

She shook her head. *I've got to stop thinking like this, I'll drive myself mad if I don't. But that was a close thing. I don't want anyone to know I'm looking at Ingrid's profile.*

In the kitchen, Buttercup at last felt some warmth seeping into her bones. 'I think this is my favourite room in the house,' she remarked, sitting down and picking up her mug of coffee. She wrapped her chilly fingers around it and savoured the heat.

'It's the cosiest, that's why,' Carol said, coming to join her. 'How was London?'

'Good, thank you. I popped in to see Mum on the way back.'

'How is she?'

'All right, as far as I can tell. Getting on top of her infection.'

'Bless her.' Carol gave her a sympathetic look. 'It's terrible to lose your mother to that awful illness, she's still so young . . .'

Buttercup nodded. 'Thanks, yes it is.' She sipped her hot coffee and looked at the other woman sitting across the table. Carol was always cheerful, ready to help, friendly without being interfering or over familiar. She was part of the house, an integral part of what made it home. *I live with her as much as I live with Charles. Maybe even more. What an odd thought.* 'How long have you and Steve worked here?'

'Oh, a long time. Eight years, I think. Ever since the children left home.' She shook her head. 'It's gone so fast.'

'So you were here when Charles's previous wife lived here.'

'Oh yes.' Carol's demeanour and cheerful tone didn't change and she held Buttercup's gaze. 'She was here for about two years after we arrived. James and Charlotte were still quite young then. Absolute terrors they could be, racing around like mad things. Out on their ponies half the time, thank goodness. In the summer, they were in and out of the pool, dozens of friends around.' Carol smiled. 'It's quieter now, that's for sure.'

'It sounds nice,' Buttercup said wistfully. She could almost make out the echoes of children's laughter and hear the slap of wet feet running on the warm stone beside the pool.

'Children always make a house a home,' Carol said, and her smile instantly disappeared. 'Oh, I'm sorry. I know . . . Oh, I've put my foot in it.' Her hands went to her face. 'I'm an idiot.'

'Don't be silly,' Buttercup said, forcing out a smile. 'It's absolutely fine. It's not your fault. And you're right – houses like this do need children. I'm sure that will happen in time.'

'Of course it will,' Carol said, taking away her hands, two spots of pink on her cheeks showing her embarrassment. 'Of course.'

*

Buttercup went upstairs slowly. She had been on the brink of asking Carol about Ingrid: what she was like, how the marriage had imploded and what Charles had done. It seemed that some people thought Charles had behaved badly – had he? Could he be blamed for that when his wife had betrayed him? But she couldn't ask Carol those things, it put her into a very difficult position.

So how am I ever going to find out? And, in any case, should I want to know anyway? It's the future that matters, not the past.

When she arrived at the first-floor landing, she noticed the door to the Redmain Room was open and there were sounds coming from within. Going over, she looked in and saw Agnieska crouching on the floor, scrabbling about, gathering what looked like white triangles off the floor.

'Agnieska? What are you doing?'

The girl looked up, her eyes wide and frightened. 'Sorry!' she cried, even paler than usual. 'It was accident!'

'What happened?' Buttercup went in and saw that a commemorative plate lay smashed into large pieces on the floor. 'Oh no! Did you knock it off the wall?'

Agnieska nodded, her eyes filling with tears. 'Accident!' she whispered. 'I'm sorry.'

'Oh dear.' Buttercup bit her lip. 'Charles is so incredibly careful about all these things. Did Carol tell you to clean in here? I'm sure it's best if she does it in future, just to be on the safe side.'

Agnieska was looking back at the pieces, obviously no longer understanding her. 'I throw away?' she suggested.

'No! No, don't do that. Here, give the pieces to me. Maybe we can mend it.' She picked up the largest piece of plate, looking at its rim of gold and the delicate painting at its centre. Around the edges were black letters. She dreaded the thought of delivering the news to Charles. Agnieska passed her the other pieces in silence, but her eyes were eloquent. She was afraid.

Buttercup looked at her earnestly. 'I'll try and get it fixed. But don't clean in here again, Agnieska. I'll tell Carol she must do it. Okay?'

The girl nodded, got to her feet and picked up her bucket of cleaning things. 'Thank you,' she said quietly, and fled.

Buttercup stood looking at the broken plate in her hand and sighed heavily. It was ridiculous that they should be so upset over a plate. But it was most likely irreplaceable, or at least expensive. No doubt Charles was insured, but he wouldn't see that as a comfort.

She took the pieces and went downstairs to find Carol.

Chapter Eighteen

By the time the evening of the bonfire party arrived, the weather had cleared and it was crisp and cold again. Buttercup had arranged for Milky and the other horses to go down to the Herberts' yard for the evening, to keep them well out of the way of the display. She put on a long coat and a woolly hat to keep out the chill and drove down to the pub, where dozens of cars were already parked. It was busy out the back of the pub. The villagers, no doubt curious about the newcomers, had turned out in a large number. Children were running about, excited, or lining up impatiently at the barbecue where Wilf was grilling burgers and sausages, to be laced with onions, stuffed into rolls and then smothered with ketchup. Grown-ups were keeping hold of jumpy offspring or clutching cups of mulled wine and hot cider while they waited for the main event: the bonfire and the fireworks in the field behind the pub. Lanterns hung at intervals on cast-iron poles, shedding a gentle yellow light, and the back of the pub was festooned with twinkling fairy lights.

'Thank you so much for coming!' Cathy said, coming up. She gave her a kiss on each cheek. 'We appreciate the support.'

'Don't be silly, I wouldn't have missed it!' said Buttercup. 'It looks brilliant.'

'Are you here all on your own?' Cathy asked, looking about for Charles.

'Yes, I'm afraid so.'

'You look rather lonely all by yourself.'

'I'm fine, honestly,' Buttercup said firmly. 'He's often away, I'm used to it. He's gone from Geneva to Rome but he's coming back the day after tomorrow.' She waved one arm out towards the pub. 'I can't believe you've achieved all this in less than a week!'

'It's been kind of crazy,' Cathy said, her eyes sparkling. 'I don't know if I'm coming or going. The fact it's dark hides a multitude of sins, believe me. But it's great, isn't it? So many people! Look at all the kids! My mum is here looking after Olly. Goodness knows what time we'll get him to bed. Oh! Sorry, I've got to go, Wilf is waving at me—' She was off, weaving through the crowd, her bump more evident. She turned back to shout, 'Come down tomorrow for a coffee and a catch-up!' and then was gone.

Buttercup stuffed her hands in her pockets and started to wander about. She had rarely been to the King's Head, despite it belonging to the estate. It had been empty for most of the time she had lived here, and anyway, Charles was not a pub man.

She moved about, enjoying the anonymity of the darkness. No one seemed to recognise her with the bobble hat and her upturned collar, and she didn't know many of the villagers. After a while, she took up a position in a dark area, out of the lantern light, where she could watch proceedings and sniff the sweetly enticing caramel scent of frying onions. Children were suddenly illuminated by glittering golden fountains as they waved sparklers about, and then shadowed again when they burned out. Her attention was caught by a familiar face visible in the lantern light that, for a moment, she couldn't place. Then she realised it was Agnieska, looking different with a large furry grey beret on the back of her head, muffled up in a dark coat. She was holding hands with two small boys, also bundled in puffy coats and wearing gloves, their small white faces visible in the darkness. Agnieska was smiling and talking to them rapidly.

How nice to see her off duty. She looks happy. It's good to see that she's recovered from the plate-breaking incident.

She watched as Agnieska and the children made their way towards the burger stall, then lined up herself for a cup of spicy mulled apple juice. She was sipping it in the darkness near the pub when the display started. The crowd quickly formed a semi-circle around the field where dark figures darted back and forth, setting off fireworks: small sizzlers first, to get things going. The oohs and aahs began, children whooping at the rockets whooshing upwards, then the display became flashier, with whirling Catherine wheels, and bangers that popped noisily in the night air, sending out red and blue sparks that flickered fast and died rapidly. The fireworks climbed higher, and exploded into bigger, brighter rings of red, blue and golden rain, exploding thousands of stars against the inky night.

'Oooh,' murmured the crowd.

Buttercup became aware of a ragged noise behind the murmurs and cries of delight, a kind of shout that was growing towards a shriek. She began to make out words:

'What do you think you're doing? What is this? What's going on?'

She looked out over where the crowd were turning and muttering.

'Silly old bag.'

'It's that mad woman from the house down the lane.'

'Someone shut her up, please! We're trying to have a nice evening here . . .'

Buttercup went towards the shouts and saw an elderly lady in a fur coat, her white hair dishevelled and her eyes panicked and wild. She was ignoring those close to her who were trying to talk to her, and shouting out into the darkness: 'This is unsupportable, I won't have it! These frightful bangs and crashes! We are terrified, do you hear me? You must turn it all off at once.'

It's the woman from the other house – the one who sold Charcombe to Charles. The princess. She looks in a state.

The mutterings were growing louder and angrier. The people closest to the old woman were frustrated that she was ignoring them. She saw a nearby woman give the old lady a quick shove and another said, 'Real fur, is it? Disgusting!'

Buttercup sensed the mood turning ugly, and she began to make her way through the crowd towards her, but she was impeded by the people watching the fireworks. Then she saw a grey beret moving ahead of her, and realised that Agnieska had reached the old woman's side, taken her by the arm, and was talking to her gently.

The princess remonstrated, but her voice lowered and she listened to Agnieska's low murmur. People began to lose interest and turn away. A moment later, Buttercup saw the Polish girl leading the old woman away from the pub, back down the lane towards her house, the two boys following behind, clutching their hot dogs.

That was kind of her. I didn't realise Agnieska knew the old woman.

She turned to back to see a circle of golden stars in the sky behind her, and the crowd sighed with pleasure at its beauty.

Buttercup went back to the pub the following morning to see Cathy.

'Welcome to the King's Head!' Cathy said, leading her into the bar area. 'We're still in a state in here, I'm afraid, even though we did everything outside last night.' She looked around and put her hands on her hips so that her bump looked even bigger than before. 'There's plenty to do in here, as you can see.'

Buttercup nodded. The room was full of higgledy-piggledy stacks of chairs and tables, and the bar was covered in boxes and glassware and bottles. 'I won't keep you long.'

'Don't be silly, it's nice to have a break. And I've just got the coffee machine working, so we can have a nice cappuccino or something. What do you fancy?' Cathy headed behind the bar to a large shiny silver machine.

'Cappuccino would be lovely, thanks.' Buttercup remembered suddenly how, during her last pregnancy, she had completely gone off coffee. Did that mean she wasn't pregnant? *It's only a couple of weeks. I'm sure that kicks in later.* 'It's getting there, though?'

'Oh yeah. The decorating is done. Once we've got the stock sorted, we'll do the last twirls and whirls. Wilf is busy setting up the computer system and the till, and sorting the kitchen.' Cathy sighed and smiled. 'There's so much to do. But if everything arrives, we'll be able to run a soft opening next week, try the menu and get the hang of the kitchen and train the staff. Then, the grand opening after that.'

'Wow. I'm impressed. And it looks great. Love the light fittings.' Buttercup looked around. The walls had been painted a chalky blue and adorned with antique brass wall lights. Old prints had been put up and the fireplace set up with a huge iron grate full of logs. 'It's going to be gorgeous.'

'Thanks.' Cathy smiled as the coffee machine roared, hissed and released a cloud of steam. 'I hope so.' She came over with the two froth-topped cups. 'Can't find the chocolate powder, I'm afraid. Next time.'

They cleared two bar stools of detritus and sat down.

'So – did you see the crazy old lady who came and shouted at everyone last night?' Cathy stirred the foam into her coffee.

Buttercup nodded. 'Yes, poor old thing. She looked quite upset.'

'I feel bad. I should have let her know about the Bonfire Party – I thought all the posters would be enough but perhaps she didn't see them. I'm going to send a note apologising. Apparently she calmed down quite quickly. I've seen her a few times, actually. She came out and shouted at the removal vans when we were moving in. Is she completely bats?'

'I think she's a bit eccentric, but I haven't been properly introduced to her. All I know is that she sold the house to Charles a while ago. Her mother was a film star – Natalie Rowe. They lived together in the house for years apparently, with the whole thing falling to bits around them.'

'Natalie Rowe? Wow, that's amazing! I love *Delilah*, it's one of my favourite films. She's Natalie's daughter?' Cathy shook her head. 'Unbelievable. I'd love to ask her about her mother, but I'm not sure what kind of reception I'd get.'

'Maybe you should get to know her. Don't try to be too pally though, Charles said she's very particular about being called Princess.'

'*Princess?* What is she, a Disney fanatic or something?'

'No – she actually is a princess, a descendant of some Russian prince . . . imperial family . . . that sort of thing.'

'Weirder and weirder. And kind of fantastic.' Cathy laughed. 'And they said moving to the country would be boring!'

Buttercup walked back home thinking about her own lack of activity in comparison with Cathy's energy and enthusiasm for the pub, how busy she was despite being on the brink of giving birth.

She puts me to shame. I need to do something to engage my mind. I'll call Lazlo, she thought, *and ask him if he's sure he doesn't want me to look for clients down here.*

As she passed Fitzroy House, she glanced over. It still appeared shut up, with no signs of life there at all. Where was Ingrid? For so long Buttercup had wished that Ingrid would just disappear so that she could forget all about her. Now that she had, she was thinking about her more than ever. It didn't make sense.

As she walked up the drive to the house, she felt a dull ache in her stomach and when she got back to the house, she found that her period had started, bang on time. The ovulation tracker, the temperature taking, the fervent lovemaking had done nothing at all.

She gritted her teeth in sadness and frustration, feeling hopeless and miserable.

Why isn't it working? Why?

Chapter Nineteen

Charles arrived home the following day, and he came in, cheerful and zinging with his usual energy.

'Darling! You are a sight for sore eyes. Come here.' He enfolded her in his arms and sighed happily. 'I've wanted this very much.'

'Hello, sweetie. Welcome home.' She kissed him. 'How was Rome? Did Charlotte wear you out?'

'We certainly made the most of it.' Tippi came bounding up and Charles rubbed at her ears and stroked her head. 'Good girl, Tippi, good girl. Glad I'm home, eh?'

'Carol's bringing some tea.'

'Wonderful, I've been longing for some. Let's go and sit down by the fire and enjoy some home comforts.'

They walked through to the drawing room together, Tippi following.

'So you had fun?' Buttercup sat down in an armchair as Charles threw himself on the sofa and crossed his legs, Tippi settling at his feet.

'When we weren't marching about the Colosseum or

down the Via del Corso, we were drinking a lot of prosecco. You'd be surprised how much Charlotte could get through.'

'She's only sixteen,' Buttercup said, surprised.

Charles shrugged. 'She's growing up. But rather excitingly, I managed to find a little souvenir of Nelson in one of the antiques shops. I'm going to put it in the Redmain room. And how have you been here without me?'

'Fine,' she said. She told him about the bonfire party, and how the old lady had started one of her tirades. Charles laughed.

'Oh, she's harmless, if noisy,' Charles said with a laugh. 'She's always liked dashing out to have a shout at anyone she thinks is up to no good. She used to rant at Charlotte regularly when she went by on her pony. We all got used to her.'

'What did you think of her when you bought the house?' Buttercup said.

'Bonkers,' Charles said simply. 'Driven quite mad by the old place. You should have seen it then, the state of it – she should never have been allowed to live here all by herself. The agent told me that she'd been here for decades, ever since she was a girl, looking after her old mother, renting the place out to various tenants on condition she could stay here. The mother had died some years before we saw the house, and the old girl stayed on, desperately trying to hold the place together. Rather a sad story, by all accounts. She'd completely devoted her life to her mother. No wonder she's gone barmy. Still, I expect she's got enough money now to pay for some decent care when she goes gaga.'

Buttercup looked up at the portrait over the fire. It seemed so melancholy to think of that beautiful, spirited woman ending her days here, in a house crumbling around her ears; and her daughter sacrificing herself to her mother's care. 'So the daughter never married. She never had her own family.'

'No, I don't think so,' Charles said carelessly. 'Where is Carol with that tea? I'm parched.'

Buttercup looked back at the woman in the picture. *Her daughter had no family. No children. Charles's children taken away by their mother after just a year or two. What's wrong with this place? Why can't there be a family here?*

As if to remind her of the emptiness of the house, Buttercup got a text that afternoon from Wilf Tranter.

Delighted to announce the safe arrival of Bethany Blue Tranter this morning at 4.10 a.m. Weighing 7lbs 3oz. Mother and baby doing well.

Attached was a photograph of an exhausted-looking but smiling Cathy holding a fuzzy-haired white bundle. Buttercup smiled and texted back her congratulations, then stared into space for a while, thinking of her disappointment, then pushed it aside and rang up to order a bunch of flowers and a big box of chocolates to be sent to the King's Head from her and Charles, with their love.

Over dinner that evening, Charles talked excitedly about his Montenegro project which was finally getting close to being signed and sealed, and about a new plan for a mining deal in Australia. They were finishing up with coffee when he said:

'How's your mother? Was she all right when you popped in on Tuesday?'

'Yes, she seems okay.' Buttercup frowned. 'Did I tell you I was going to see her?'

'You must have – or you told Elaine or Rose, and they passed it on.'

'I didn't think I had,' she said, thinking back, trying to remember.

'Oh.' Charles shrugged lightly. 'You usually go and see her on your way back from London. Perhaps I just assumed . . . anyway, what does it matter? You did see her, didn't you?'

'Yes.'

'Well then. I hope you gave her my love.' He gave her a playful look and said, 'How are things with the ovulation cycle? Am I on call at the moment?'

It's the only thing about me he doesn't bother with, she thought suddenly. *How odd. He knows everything else, but he doesn't bother with that*. 'I'm afraid it's no go again this month.'

'Oh darling! I'm sorry.' He looked at her sympathetically. 'I know you must be disappointed. Try not to be too down-hearted.' He reached out to take her hand. 'We'll keep trying.'

'Yes,' she said, and it was on the tip of her tongue to tell him about the clinic, but instead she said, 'Cathy and Wilf had their baby. It's a girl.'

'Did they? That's splendid news.' He leaned over to kiss

her. 'But she won't be half as fabulous a mother as you will. It's bound to happen soon. I know it.'

With Charles home, the peculiar tension he brought to the house returned. When he was away, the house was quiet, only half alive, running on familiar lines; but he brought a sense of unpredictability and possibility. It was one of the things Buttercup had most loved about him when they first got together, along with his certainty and experience. He seemed to have the key to how life should be lived. Buttercup, reeling from the loss of her father and appalled by her mother's descent into a shadow existence, had been enraptured by his verve and energy, and his determination to squeeze the most from every minute. Sometimes, at a stuffy dinner or a tedious social event, she could sense him getting bored and edgy, and soon he'd making their excuses and tugging Buttercup away. Outside, he would whisk her into the little Alfa Romeo and fly along the country roads back to the house, saying, 'Weren't they desperately dull, darling? A load of old bores. Why don't we go to Paris this weekend and see *La Bohème* at the Opera?'

And within a few hours, a new adventure would be beginning.

But it's been a while since we did anything like that. It was Charlotte he took to Geneva and Rome this time.

Buttercup was sitting in front of her computer, writing an email to Hazel, and she stopped short, frowning. It was true. They hadn't done much together for a while; Charles had been travelling so much, and she had stayed here, doing far too little with her time.

She had a sudden vision of Elaine passing the report of her activities to Charles, saw him sitting at his desk, opening it up and inspecting the details of what she'd been up to and what she had spent. There wouldn't be much of interest this time, if Elaine didn't spot the clinic. Why did he need to know anyway? How did it contribute to her security for him to know what she'd been doing?

She trusted him when he said he was off to Geneva or Rome or was staying in London. It never occurred to her to check on him.

I trust him. Doesn't he trust me?

A sudden shout from upstairs made her look up from her screen, and she heard Charles calling down the stairs.

'What the hell has happened? Carol, can you come here?'

Buttercup stood up, concerned, almost tripping over Tippi, who was on the floor at her feet, and hurried out into the hall. Charles was on the landing above, leaning over the banister.

Carol came running out of the kitchen, looking anxious. 'What is it, Mr R?'

'Come here please.' He marched away.

Carol and Buttercup exchanged anxious glances and then headed for the stairs, hurrying up to the first floor. The door to the Redmain Room was open and inside Charles was swearing.

'What is it?' Buttercup asked, suspecting she knew the answer.

'Where's the damn plate?' Charles spluttered, pointing at

the gap on the wall where it had hung. 'I came to put my new acquisition in the cabinet, and I saw at once that it's missing.'

Carol glanced at Buttercup, opened her mouth to speak and then stopped.

Buttercup stepped towards Charles. 'Don't get upset, darling. There was an accident. The plate was broken. Everyone is terribly sorry and Steve has taken it to a specialist repairer in Exeter, they say they can mend it—'

'Broken?' Charles hissed. He whirled round to face Carol. 'Was it you?'

'It wasn't Carol,' Buttercup said quickly.

He turned to stare at her, his eyes hard and accusatory. 'It wasn't you, was it?'

'No, no!'

'Then who?'

'Does it matter? It was an accident—'

But he cut across her. 'Of course it matters. No one is allowed to touch the things in this room, let alone break them. Who was it?'

Buttercup couldn't lie, but didn't want to throw the blame on someone less able to defend herself. She glanced at Carol, who looked nervous now.

'Who?' shouted Charles.

Buttercup said in a small voice, 'It was one of the cleaners. Agnieska. But it was an accident, she was devastated!'

'Is she here?' he asked brusquely.

Carol said, 'She's cleaning out the boot room—'

Charles strode out of the room, heading downstairs. The

two women followed, Buttercup feeling powerless to restrain him and desperate that he shouldn't take it out on Agnieska.

But it was a vain hope. He found her in the boot room; she was on her knees, scrubbing the floor, the boots and shoes in a pile outside. Agnieska looked up at him, her eyes wide and bewildered.

'There's no room for mistakes in my house. Collect your things and go, your services are no longer required.'

Agnieska seemed to understand, a look of horror going over her face. 'Please! I'm sorry . . .'

'That's it, I'm afraid.' Charles's voice was steely and Buttercup suspected there was little chance of his changing his mind. 'Carol will pay you a fortnight in lieu.'

He turned and marched away down the corridor, his shoulders set.

Agnieska turned anguished eyes to Buttercup. 'No? I have to go?'

'I'm so sorry,' she said, putting out a hand towards her. 'If only I'd got the plate back before he noticed. It's such bad luck that he went in there before it got back from the mender!'

Agnieska didn't understand all of it, but she knew it was hopeless. 'I get my things,' she said dully.

'I'm sorry,' Buttercup said again. She looked at Carol, whose mouth was set in a grim line. 'Can you sort Agnieska out? Please give her two months' wages. I'll give you the money myself.'

'Fine,' Carol said quietly. Her expression was difficult to read. 'Come with me, Agnieska.'

Agnieska followed her out, her grey eyes filling with tears. Buttercup watched them go, then marched back up the stairs to Charles's study.

He was sitting at his desk monitoring his computer screens as she came in, looking up coldly as she stood in front of him. 'Yes?'

'Charles, that was unforgivable! You can't sack her for breaking a plate!'

'I can and I have.'

'She's a single mother with two small children and three cleaning jobs to keep it all going! It's completely disproportionate to fire her for one mistake.'

Charles was staring back at her, his blue eyes icy. 'That's my decision. She's my employee, not yours.'

'But she's got so little and you've got so much! What does one plate matter?'

'It matters a lot,' he said in a quiet tone.

Rose's words in London suddenly came into her mind: *I've seen what the boss is like. He won't be disobeyed and he doesn't like mistakes.* She could see it now: that steel-trap ruthlessness Rose had described but in which she hadn't quite believed.

Charles was still staring at her. 'Trust, you see. I wouldn't be able to trust Agnieska any more. I gave her access to my most precious possessions, and she's shown herself unworthy of the trust. Do you understand?'

'I honestly believe you're being unfair. I can't believe you would be so unjust!'

Charles stood up and went to the window. For a moment,

he gazed out over the parkland, grey and spikily bare under the winter sky, then said in a tone that was now calm but still measured, 'Let me try to explain. Life here is special. You must know that. Inside my circle, life is lovely. It's safe and comfortable. When someone crosses me, they move outside my circle. Outside, it's cold and miserable and unpleasant. Sometimes, very sadly, someone who has been a trusted and valued insider must be put out – like a sinner being shut out of heaven. And once you are out, you can never come back in. That's how it is with Agnieska. She's out, and can never come back. That's my decision, I'm afraid.' He turned back to look at her. 'Now, darling, I must get on, if you don't mind.'

Buttercup opened her mouth to protest again, then realised that there was no point with Charles in this mood. She had never seen him so cold and resolute, and she didn't like this side of him at all. 'Fine. I'll see you later. I'm going for a ride.'

Chapter Twenty

Xenia was in the front garden looking for Petrova the cat, although it was also a good opportunity to stare down the lane at the comings and goings at the pub. The obvious preparations for the hoped-for influx of new customers bothered her. She had grown accustomed to the pub sitting in quiet desolation with an empty car park and a silent beer garden. It had not been particularly noisy when it was occupied, apart from the occasional party, but she couldn't help fretting.

That awful thing they had last week – the bangs and crashes! Poor Petrova was so frightened! What will all these cars mean for her? It will be their fault if she's killed.

She had received a note pushed through her letter box only the day before:

Dear Princess Arkadyoff,

We are writing to apologise for not warning you in advance about our Bonfire Night event. We thought our posters advertising it had provided notice, but we understand that we should have personally let you know

what to expect when we held our Bonfire Night party.
We are usually considerate and intend to stay on the best
of terms with all our neighbours, so we are mortified at
this lapse. Please accept our sincere apologies and we
hope you will come in to visit us for a complimentary
drink and have a look at our new venture.
   Yours sincerely,
   Cathy and Wilf Tranter

She had read it over twice and then laughed at the idea that she might go into a pub. She had never visited a public drinking establishment – no lady did – and she was not about to start. If they were as considerate as they claimed, they could begin by cancelling their outdoor events forthwith.

She considering ringing up the pub to give the Tranters a piece of her mind but decided against it. Still, she was more vigilant than ever about what they were up to down there, and on the lookout for an opportunity to tell one or both of them exactly what she thought. Standing in the cold garden, she craned her neck over the top of the hedge to see if she could make out what was happening, but her eyesight was no longer up to it.

The sound of soft sobbing made her turn her head. Squinting through the black fuzzy hole in the middle of her vision, she saw Agnieska coming through the gates of Charcombe Park, wheeling her bicycle as she went.

'Agnieska, what's wrong?' she called out.

The girl looked up, her grey eyes pink with tears. 'Oh – nothing. I am fine.'

'Don't be silly, you're crying. Come in at once.'

Agnieska hesitated, then wheeled her bike over towards Hooke Cottage.

Xenia hurried to open the gate, wishing she could move with more agility. She was still fit, but her limbs were creakier and her back had a tiresome curve in it that kept her permanently bent. 'Come on, come inside.'

A few minutes later, she had the kettle on the stovetop while Agnieska sat weeping at the kitchen table, her face buried in her hands.

'Sweet tea,' Xenia announced, putting it down on the table. She sat down next to the girl. 'What's wrong?'

Agnieska sniffed and looked up with large, watery eyes. 'I am sacked. No job.'

'From the big house? Why?'

'Accident. Plate . . .' Agnieska mimed dropping something from a great height. 'Whoosh! Smash.'

'Oh, you broke something.' Xenia frowned. 'They sacked you over a broken plate? That seems rather harsh. What kind of plate was it?'

Agnieska looked at her sadly, uncomprehending.

'Normal plate?' Xenia asked.

'No! Special. Old.'

'I see. Oh dear. It still seems disproportionate, my dear. Did Mrs Redmain dismiss you?' Seeing the look of confusion, she said slowly, 'Missus gave you the sack?'

'Missus? No – Mister. The boss. He is so angry.' The grey eyes welled again. 'He tell me to go.'

'Ugh, that man . . . a Napoleon complex if ever I saw one.

He's always needed taking down a peg or two.' Xenia broke off suddenly, remembering her attempt to take him down a notch and its consequences. 'Well, you're better off without it.' She touched Agnieska's arm. 'Don't worry, dear.'

'The money.' Agnieska sniffed. 'The money, I need it.'

'We'll just have to think of something else, that's all.' Xenia hesitated and then decided to say what had been on her mind for the last few days. 'You were kind to me the other night, with the fireworks.'

Agnieska looked at her, nodding at the word fireworks. 'Yes.'

'I appreciated it. No one else would speak to me politely. You did. Your little boys are well behaved too. Here is my idea. Can you drive?' She mimed moving a steering wheel to make sure Agnieska understood. 'Drive?'

The girl nodded. 'Yes, I drive. I have licence.'

'Good. I have a car, but I can't use it because my vision is getting so bad. So – about how this. You drive the car for me. I will insure it. You can take me shopping or on visits, whenever I need to go somewhere. Perhaps you can even help me with shopping. And you can use it over the winter for you and the boys, when you need it yourself.' Xenia smiled at her, realised what an unaccustomed expression that was these days. 'There! Isn't that a good solution?'

Agnieska frowned, baffled.

Xenia sighed with irritation. 'Oh dear, let's try again.' She fetched a piece of paper and pencil so she could draw simple sketches of cars and people to explain, squinting to see the paper as well as she could. 'Here – this is you and the children, two little boys. See? Good. Here is my car, and me. YOU' – she scrawled arrows pointing the Agnieska figure to the car – 'drive ME to the shops. And YOU and the BOYS go to school when it's cold . . .'

When Agnieska understood what was being said, her face cleared like the sun coming out from behind a cloud. 'Ah! You give me car!'

'Well, not quite, but—'

'Oh thank you, thank you.' She leaned over and put her arms around Xenia and hugged her. 'Thank you so much. I understand. I use it for you, and for me. You are so kind.'

Xenia stiffened under the girl's touch, and then relaxed. 'You're welcome,' she said formally. 'We will have to draw up some terms, but yes . . . you can use the car and I hope it will help you.'

The feeling of having done something good and useful stayed with her all afternoon after Agnieska had left. It reminded her what it was like to feel wanted and needed, the way she had when she'd had Mama and the house to look after.

'My darling Xenia,' her mother would say, gazing at her with soulful eyes. 'You are a saint. My angel. I don't know what I would do without you.'

But that was before I betrayed her.

She pushed the voice out of her mind. What good did it do to think of that now, when it was all so far in the past? The image of Mama's grave floated before her eyes and her mind went to Luke and Gwen.

She had not thought of them for years, and yet they had

come to mind twice in a few days. Perhaps it was because she'd been thinking about Agnieska's sons, who had seemed such nice, well-behaved little boys at the fireworks party. It had occurred to her that she could give Agnieska a Christmas gift: some nice treats, and presents for the boys. What did little boys like, besides chocolate? She had only ever known one small boy, and that was Luke and Gwen's son, Gawain. Luke had loved Arthurian legend: his huge round table that sat thirty was a tribute to it. The name of his boy, and that of his daughter, Isolde, were also Arthurian. She tried to remember Gawain as he'd been when Luke and Gwen had lived at the house thirty years before: a small, solemn thing with coppery hair and eyes of almost the same colour, freckles and skinny legs. He'd bicycled, and played with a football and read books.

They won't do that now. It's video games, I think. And television.

She had dreaded the thought of children at Charcombe but in the end she had grown fond of both the drifting Isolde, who was thirteen and always falling in love with the young carpenters and blacksmiths, and Gawain, who was like a curious puppy – constantly prowling and finding his way into places he shouldn't be. He often got himself into mischief, plummeting out of trees, tripping over and grazing his knees, getting entangled in something. One day, he picked up something in the workshop and cut himself, and Harry had brought him to the kitchen to be cleaned and bandaged. Xenia, washing up at the sink, had tended to the cut and decided it wasn't bad enough to need stitches.

'We don't have to take him to the doctor,' she'd said firmly. 'He'll be fine.' She was relieved that he hadn't been badly hurt, especially with Luke and Gwen away for the day. She'd looked sternly at the little boy, who hadn't cried but had been fascinated with the ruby blood that spilled from the cut on his hand. 'Don't play with the tools, Gawain. They're not toys!'

'That's what Dad says,' the boy replied.

'Keep out of the workshop, young man,' Harry cautioned him. But when the boy had run off, proud of his bandage, he'd smiled at Xenia and said, 'I like him around, really. He's good company. I'll make sure I keep the tools out of his reach next time.'

That was the first time she and Harry had properly spoken to one another.

I mustn't think about that. It does no good. She shook her head. *I'm considering Christmas presents for little boys, not dreaming about Harry. I shall get them chocolate, then. I can't go wrong with that.*

She didn't want to feel melancholy; she had enjoyed the warm inner glow that came from helping Agnieska.

I will do something that makes me happy.

That was a cup of tea, a large slice of coffee cake from the tin, and settling down on the sofa with the electric heater beside her while the television played one of her favourite programmes about people buying houses in the country. She liked to shout loudly at them, and tell them in no uncertain terms that they were making a mistake, either for buying or not buying, although her fuzzy vision was spoiling her enjoyment.

Petrova sprang up beside her, turned around a few times, then settled down to snooze beside her while she watched a useless couple refuse a perfect property and yearn after quite the wrong one. She finished her cake, put her empty teacup to one side and before long, her eyes were drooping and she snoozed, then slept.

When she woke, she thought she was still dreaming. She was in a familiar world, peopled by voices she recognised. She heard one voice in particular that fell into her ears like the sweet strains of a long-forgotten but beloved piece of music.

'Well, Sam, if that's the way you feel about it—'

'I do. Goodbye. Forever.'

The slam of a door. A sigh.

Xenia blinked and tried to focus on where she was. She looked at the screen, which was a fuzzy black mass in front of her.

'Oh, Sam,' said the sweet voice. 'You fool. If only you knew the truth.'

Slow footsteps. Another voice, not sweet this time. Horrible. Smoothly repellent and bringing the bitter taste of sickness to her mouth.

'Well, well, Delilah. It looks as though you've finally managed to shake him off.'

'It's your fault, Julius! You're the one behind all of this. Why won't you let me tell him the truth?'

'You know why.'

Xenia moved her head to the side so that she could focus on the screen.

Mama.

So beautiful! In her prime – the lustrous curling hair, the eyelashes, the flawless complexion . . .

False lashes, pancake make-up. But still . . . nothing can dim her beauty.

And next to her, that horrible man. She could feel his tongue in her ear, hear the heavy rasp of his breathing and it sent a shudder of revulsion through her as powerful as the one she had felt so many years before.

There he was on the screen, suave and neat, his tiny moustache perfectly trimmed – *except that I know how it felt, the coarse hairs on my skin* – his manicured hands – *on my chest* – his small sharp eyes bright with intelligence.

'You're mine, Delilah. You're my creature. My creation. The sooner you learn to accept that and put that lunk out of your mind, the better.' He smiled as the music rose. 'You'll understand that the only possible way is to do as I command.'

She was overcome with disgust.

I hate him. I hated him then, and I still hate him. He was the beginning of the end.

Chapter Twenty-One

1950

'I don't want to go to the studio, Mama,' Xenia whispered. She lay in bed and pulled the covers right up to her chin, staring at Mama over the top of the apricot-coloured sheets.

'Not go?' Mama looked bewildered. 'But you love going! We've almost finished the film now. Today I'm filming the car crash, don't you want to see that?'

Xenia was sorry that she would miss it. Mama had explained that she would not be in the big scene of the crash when it was filmed outdoors – a double would be in the car because they couldn't risk her getting hurt. But in the studio, she would sit in the car with a film of the outside moving while the camera stared in at her, which sounded strange but would apparently look fine on screen, as if the car were travelling along a mountain road. Xenia couldn't change her mind though. 'I can't, Mama. I don't feel well.'

'Don't you, darling?' Mama put a hand on Xenia's forehead. 'You don't have a temperature. But if you feel sick—'

'I do,' Xenia said hastily.

'Then you must stay in bed. I'll see that the maid brings some iced water for you.' Mama kissed her. 'I hope you feel better soon. I don't want you to miss the finale, we're filming that tomorrow or the next day.'

'I will.'

Xenia watched her mother go, knowing she would feel perfectly all right because there was nothing wrong with her. Papa had told her this was the best thing to do to protect Mama and keep her happy, and so she was willing to sacrifice seeing the end of filming, to please him.

Someone must have seen what that man did to her in the darkness, because Papa had come to see her that evening, when she'd been sitting reading in the school room to take her mind off it, his expression grim. 'Xenia,' he'd said, 'did the man who plays Julius . . . did he try anything with you today, when you'd finished the scene?'

Xenia blushed violently, and felt ashamed. She said in a small voice, 'Yes, Papa. He kissed me. After I was in the coat-check scene.'

Papa looked grimmer than ever. 'On your mouth?'

'Well, no, not on my mouth, it was more . . .' Xenia crinkled up her nose as she remembered. 'It was in my ear. And he put his hand on my . . . on me – here.' She laid a palm lightly on the centre of her chest, too embarrassed to show where the man's hand had actually landed and how much force he'd put into his caress.

Papa began to pace the school room, his fists clenched. 'I'd like to punch that cad,' he said, his voice strange and tight as though he was talking through his gritted teeth. 'He didn't hurt you, did he?'

'No.' Xenia shook her head. It was true. It had been horrible but not painful.

'What did you do?'

'I pushed him, and I ran away,' she said, hoping that had been the right thing.

'Good. I'm sorry that horrible man touched you, my darling. He's a beast.'

'Should we tell Mama?' ventured Xenia, feeling less ashamed now that Papa knew that she hadn't wanted the man to kiss her.

'No!' Papa declared vehemently. 'We mustn't do that. She'd be devastated. She'd walk off the film, or she'd have him sacked, or she'd refuse to work with him. It would destroy everything.' Papa came over and sat down on the desk where she was reading, looking at her intently while he reached for a cigarette from the silver box in his pocket. 'She could easily cause a scandal, Xenia. News will leak – everyone loves a whisper of bad behaviour like this. Then it will blow up and the film will be lost in the storm of gossip. Do you understand? The film would be lost – all the hard work we've all put into it, all the anticipation for it, everything the studio has done to stoke expectations – it will all be wasted. Mama's one chance would be gone.'

'I don't want that,' Xenia whispered.

'None of us do. That's why we must hide the truth from her. So that we can protect her, and she can work. Will you do that, Xenia?'

'Of course I will.' She gazed back, hoping he understood that she would do anything to protect Mama.

'Good. Then stay at home for now. I'll talk to Archibald and explain, and he can get that bounder off the set as soon as possible. He'll understand that Mama mustn't know anything about it. He knows perfectly well what she's like, that any suggestion that you'd been hurt would put her in a terrible state.'

'Of course. Can I . . . can I go back to see the last scene? Mama promised I might?'

Papa thought for a moment. 'If that man is gone, then I don't see why not.' He smiled at her. 'You're being very brave. It's the right thing for Mama, and we both want that, don't we? We're so close, the film is almost done. And then everything will be fine.'

Papa must have spoken to Archibald Thomas and sorted everything out, because the actor who played Julius was gone when Xenia went back to the studio to watch the last scene being filmed before they moved to the outdoor locations. Xenia felt proud of herself for helping Papa to protect Mama from anything that might upset her. She realised now that everything rode on Mama being strong and happy, and they must all do whatever was necessary to help her. That was why, with shooting going on longer than expected, Xenia was sent home alone so that she could start the new school term, crossing the ocean on board the great liner with only Gunter for company. There were no glamorous dinners this time: they mostly ate in the cabin, early so that Xenia could get a good night's sleep and Gunter could knit herself out of the fear that they would sink at any minute.

When they were back at the London house, it felt as if they had never been away, and everything that had happened in California was just a strange dream. She could almost have believed that, if it hadn't been for the fact that Papa and Mama were still there, so far away.

Mama wrote to her often from the film set, filling pages of writing paper with her scrawling handwriting:

Darling Xixi

We are on location at the moment, it's so disconcerting. I'm still in my trailer but instead of stepping out into that great big sound stage, I exit into the garden of a beautiful house, where we are filming some of the outdoor scenes. I'm sorry you were so upset on the last day at the studio. I didn't actually get shot! I'm still here, I'm fine.

Papa is so glad that we are almost finished filming. Then he will come home to you! I'm afraid I have to stay a little longer away from you, in case I'm needed for reshoots. And then we will have to do our publicity for the movie before it is released, but I hope I can come home before then and return when they need me. It might be months more before it is in the cinemas. But Papa always knows best.

I'm sending you all my love, darling. Write and tell me how you are. I'll write back to you soon too.

Mama xxx

The letters smelt of lily-of-the-valley and cigarette smoke. Xenia kept them under her pillow and read them at night when she couldn't sleep.

It was another month before Papa came home, and Mama was not with him.

'She's staying in California,' Papa explained, home at last from his ocean voyage. 'It's important she's there while the buzz builds for the picture – other directors will want to see her. And she must be seen at all the best parties and with the right people.'

'Don't you want to be there, Papa?' Xenia asked, worried. She felt sure that Mama should not be alone.

'She was becoming very anxious about you here by yourself. In the end, it was better to return. I've left her in the care of a very responsible lady who knows how to look after her. And there are things to be done here before she gets back.' He smiled at Xenia. 'Our lives are about to change, my dear. Just wait and see.'

The motor car roared down the long road past Andover and out towards Salisbury, the engine grating with every gear change.

'Are you excited, Xenia?' Papa said, casting a glance at her, smiling broadly before turning back to the road. 'Look, darling, that's Stonehenge!'

She turned to look across Papa at the circle of stones in a field at the side of the road. 'Oh yes.'

'I think you will love this house,' he said confidently. 'And Mama will love it too.'

'But, Papa, do we need another house?'

'Naturally. We have our London home, and we need our country place. That is just how it is for people like us. It's how we live. It's how a famous actress like Mama ought to live.' The film had opened in America and broken box office records, and Papa couldn't hide his excitement that everything had worked out as he'd hoped: Mama was a great star, there were more offers for films and it was certain that she would be nominated for acting awards after the rapturous critical reception of *Delilah*. 'We'll make a wonderful place for her, one she will love.'

If it makes Mama happy, then it must be the right thing to do.

An hour later, they drove into a small village, past the village green and a public house with a faded sign hanging outside that read 'King's Head Tavern and Hostelry'. Then down a lane, past a pair of twin stone houses, and they were outside a pair of large iron gates that stood open, framed by pillars with elegant stone greyhounds on top.

'Here we are!' Papa announced. 'Charcombe Park. A grand country seat. Reduced for a quick sale.'

The motor car roared up the drive, through velvety parkland. Deer grazing under oak trees looked up startled and bounded off as they passed. Then the house came into sight: a gracious manor in a classic shape in golden stone, with elaborate chimneys and mullioned windows. 'It's beautiful!' she said, awed.

'Yes. Exactly right,' Papa said, beaming with satisfaction. 'Ah – that must be the owner.'

The current owner of the house, a thin, gaunt-faced man with a bald crown and a shabby tweed suit, came out to meet them. He wanted a quick sale, he said, because death duties were doubly onerous. His father and then his elder brother had died within a week, leaving twice the amount of duty to pay.

'It's insupportable,' the man said as he showed them around, sadness etched into every part of his face. 'I simply cannot bear it. The cost, I mean. We must sell.'

He took them all over the house, and when they had finished their tour, Papa was more effervescent than ever.

'It's perfect,' he said. 'Quite beautiful.'

'Yes.' The owner sighed. 'It is a great sorrow to me that we will lose this place. I hope you'll look after it.'

'Of course we will,' Papa said firmly. 'You don't need to worry about that. The house will be in safe hands.'

On the way home, Papa said, 'What did you think? Isn't it beautiful?'

'It seemed very old, there were hardly any bathrooms,' Xenia ventured. Perhaps the comfort of the house in Hollywood had spoiled her more than she'd thought.

'There's work to do, certainly. We'll get on with it as soon as we can.'

'Didn't you think it was cold? All the rooms seemed chilly to me.'

'We'll put in new heating. Besides, old houses are always cold. We'll warm it up all right!' Papa slapped the steering wheel with excitement. 'I heard that a well-known film director lives nearby. We'll be at the heart of a whole new world. It's perfect for us, Xenia. Perfect!'

Xenia said nothing more. What did it matter if she hadn't really liked the house, despite its beauty? She had felt oppressed inside it, and had been glad when they'd come out through the great front door to the open air. But Papa had set his heart on it, and he was always right.

Mama came home just a few weeks later. They went to the airport to meet her from her flight, and the place was alive with anticipation. The film had opened all over the world to the same ecstatic reception, and it seemed that everyone had seen it. News reporters and cameramen jostled for the best position behind the barriers that held them back on the Tarmac outside, ready to record the return of Natalie Rowe after so many months away and such a glittering success. Crowds of well-wishers and fans pushed up against the temporary railings or stared down from the airport windows. Xenia and Papa stood in front of the barriers, windswept by the breeze from the runway, waiting for the plane to taxi to a halt, the steps to be pushed to the door and the little hatch in the side to open.

As soon the door swung back, the cheers began, and suddenly Mama was there, standing at the top of the stairs, glamorous in her fur coat and dark glasses, her hair glossy, her red lips shining in a bright smile as she waved and acknowledged the welcome. She came down the steps from the aeroplane slowly and gracefully, every inch the star, to be met by an airport official and escorted across the concrete to Papa and Xenia. When she reached them, she fell into Papa's arms and then took Xenia's hand, kissed her and whispered, 'I'm so happy to see you again, my sweet child. Let's go home.'

Inside the airport, more crowds of admirers and fans were held back behind barriers, screaming, jumping up and down and calling her name. Some held out books for her to sign and sighed with pleasure as she passed.

'Oh, Natalie! Talk to us, Natalie! Please give me your autograph. Delilah! Please talk to me . . . We loved your film. We love you, Delilah!'

Mama waved but did not stop. She held Xenia's hand tightly and hurried on, her high heels clicking on the tiled floor as they went. She seemed tense.

In the chauffeur-driven limousine, she was shaking. 'It's like this everywhere,' she explained. 'People – everywhere! They want to own me, possess me. Sometimes I think they want actual pieces of me, and they would be happiest if they could tear me into bits in a frenzy.'

'But it's wonderful, Natalie,' Papa said serenely. 'They love you. They want to see more of you. The most important thing we can do is decide which film you will do next.'

'I'm tired, Paul. I need a rest,' Mama said.

'You're absolutely right, darling. A rest is what you shall have. We have a special surprise for you.' Papa's gaze slid to Xenia and he winked. 'Haven't we, Xenia?'

'Yes.'

'Oh?' Mama looked at Papa, eyebrows raised, her expression slightly anxious.

'Don't worry. You'll love it. But all in good time. We're going home first, so you can have a good long sleep after your flight.'

But at home, there were more reporters with cameras waiting outside, waiting for a glimpse of Natalie Rowe. As they got out of the car, flashbulbs exploded and the reporters shouted questions. Papa had put his arm around Mama and hustled her quickly inside, saying, 'There'll be an interview later, boys, but leave us alone for now, can't you?'

Xenia followed along behind, clutching Mama's handbag to her chest and keeping her eyes half shut against the popping lights and all the chaos. She was relieved to be inside, away from all the noise and ruckus.

Inside, with her coat off and shoes discarded, Mama went to the drawing room window, and then shrunk away. 'They're still outside! How awful.'

Papa came in, lighting a cigarette. 'You should be pleased, Natalie. This is an index of how popular you are, how much people want to see you. This will translate into work and money and success. We must desire this. Encourage it!'

'But I don't like it,' Mama said in a thin, nervous voice.

Papa went to her and embraced her. 'You don't need to worry. I'll look after you, I promise. You'll never be hurt. I'll always be here to protect you.'

Mama seemed to sink into his arms, her head on his shoulder, her eyes closed.

'Now,' said Papa in a jolly voice. 'Tea!'

That evening after dinner, Mama came up to Xenia's bedroom and sat on the side of her bed, and they talked for a long time. Mama's eyes filled with tears when she said that Xenia had become a young woman while she had been away. She told stories of what it had been like to make another film, which she'd done while they were editing *Delilah* – 'Done and dusted in three weeks, can you imagine that? Sly Manikee is a different kind of director to Archie, that's for sure!' – and of the marvellous parties she had been to in Hollywood. 'There was an actual elephant there, Xenia, can you believe that?'

'Are you glad to be home?' Xenia asked. It was wonderful to have Mama back; just looking at her made Xenia feel full to the brim with a kind of peaceful happiness, as though, after a long time of being askew, things were right again with the world.

'I'm so happy to be with you.' Mama hugged her tightly again. 'But I know Papa has lots of plans for us. He wants us to have parties, meet everyone, show ourselves off. I'm so tired. I need to rest.'

'Papa will understand. He's just happy to have you back at home with us.'

'I know, darling. I know.' Mama sighed. 'He wants what's best for me. We must always do our best to please him, mustn't we, little Xenia?'

*

Papa threw his arms wide, gesturing expansively to the whole of the drawing room of Charcombe Park, furnished in exquisite silks and mahogany furniture.

'Isn't it wonderful, Natalie? Don't you love it?'

Mama stood there, looking bewildered, not quite able to take in what was happening. 'This is our house?' she said wonderingly.

'Yes! And I thought that we could hang your portrait right there.' He pointed to the wall above the fireplace, where there was a space exactly suited for a painting. Mama's portrait, the one that had featured in the film, had arrived in a wooden case packed with straw and a note from Archibald Thomas, congratulating her on her nomination for the most famous movie acting award of all. Papa had kept the secret of the house for two months while the workmen finished, and he had told Xenia to keep it too. He'd taken her with him to antiques dealers and auction houses, to help him choose all the things they needed for a house like this: endless beds and chests of drawers and wardrobes; antique chairs, tables and sofas; paintings; fine china, silver and glass; champagne coolers and giant porcelain tureens.

All so that he could unveil the house as a magnificent surprise for Mama, finished and complete. His excitement was infectious, but Xenia could tell that Mama was aghast at the size of the house.

She went to the French windows and gazed at the view of the terrace, and the velvet smooth lawns and topiaried pyramid bushes. When she turned round, her eyes were anxious and she said seriously:

'Paul, this is too much.'

'It was reduced!' Papa said, looking hurt at even this mild remark. 'We can afford it in any case.'

'But – it's not just the cost of the house. A place like this must be kept up, repaired. We'll need staff. The garden alone . . .' Mama looked around her, tense again. 'And there is something about the atmosphere here, I don't feel comfortable.'

Xenia went over to her and slipped her hand into hers to give her strength. She knew what Mama meant. She felt the same, despite the obvious beauty of the place.

Papa looked sulky. 'That's ridiculous, it's a magnificent house and we will make it our own. You only have to make one film and we'll have enough money to keep it going for years.' His ebullience returned. He walked over to Mama and took her hand in his. 'We're rich now. And there're the expectations from my mother as well. Even if you never work again, we're sure to be all right. Don't you see? At last we can begin to live like civilised human beings, the way we are supposed to.'

Mama's grip tightened on Xenia's hand until it was almost too much. She wanted to pull away but didn't see how she could when she was held so tightly.

'Very well, Paul. I can see it's too late in any case. It is beautiful.' She managed a smile. 'I'm sure we'll be happy here.'

'Oh, we will, Natalie. I can see it all now.' Papa looked around, his eyes shining. 'This will be our home forever.'

Chapter Twenty-Two

Buttercup got back from her ride, put Milky in the stables and sorted her out for the evening, and was running up to the stairs to take a shower when she almost collided with Charles on the landing.

'You're back,' he said. 'Good.'

She couldn't read his mood: he seemed flatter than usual, without his normal ebullience. Was he feeling bad about the sacking of Agnieska and Buttercup protesting against it? 'Yes . . .'

'Good. Meet me in the drawing room later. I have a surprise.'

'Okay, but—'

'I'll see you there at seven sharp. Don't be late.' He vanished back into his study.

Buttercup was apprehensive as she showered. A surprise from Charles was usually a good thing: a new adventure or a generous present or exciting news. For the first time she was not sure that she would like a surprise he had for her. The side of Charles she had seen that day had shocked her.

Throughout her ride, she'd been replaying how he'd acted and what he'd said.

Life here is special . . . it's safe and comfortable. Inside my circle, life is lovely. He was right about that: she had known nothing but safety and comfort since she'd met Charles. She could see now that that was what she had been craving: her life had been full of chaos, uncertainty and sadness, and Charles had appeared like a guardian angel to sort everything out for her. But despite the trips abroad and the houses and holidays, in reality, her life had shut down more and more since she had met him. She had no job. She hardly saw her friends. She had no independence and little freedom to do what she liked without answering to someone. He was right, life inside his circle *was* lovely; she had a husband she loved and who adored her, a life of luxury, so much to look forward to . . . and yet . . .

She thought of how he was surrounded by people whose mission in life was to make sure that everything ran the way Charles wanted it to – because he paid their wages. He paid the bills, so he could dictate how everything should be. That ought not to apply to Buttercup, his wife, and yet she had fallen into the same mindset as everyone else: Charles was the sun, the focal point, and they all orbited around him.

It's all on his terms. That's not what I expected in our marriage. I thought it would be give and take.

No doubt, from the outside she seemed to be a pampered, spoiled wife with a husband who indulged her. She had never wanted to be that person.

And the truth is the opposite of that. We all dance around

Charles. He's the one who is pampered and spoiled. Of course, he earns the money, but he makes sure that he calls the tunes as well. And I'm complicit in it. I even hide my sadness and stress about getting pregnant, in case it bothers him.

She had challenged him over Agnieska and he had made it clear that her objections meant nothing at all. They carried no weight whatsoever. Instead, what he'd said sounded ominous, almost frightening.

Ingrid had crossed him. She was no longer here, not a trace of her. The only sign that Buttercup had that she actually existed, besides James and Charlotte, was her social media profile.

What if Charles thought I had tried to cross him?

She had never told him about the fertility clinic, and the longer she left it, the harder it got to confess. He had not liked her taking Agnieska's part one little bit. Was that a smaller version of how he would react if he knew about her appointment?

Perhaps he already does know.

She started to feel nervous about whatever Charles might have in store for her that evening.

At seven Buttercup came down the stairs to the main hall, dressed in an emerald green velvet jacket over a silk T-shirt and jeans, just in case Charles planned to whisk her away somewhere. The house appeared to be empty. There was no noise from the kitchen, no Tippi pattering over the marble to greet her.

She stopped in the hall and looked around, but she could

see no one. There were security cameras trained on the front door, their dark glasses eyes inscrutable and red dots flashing to show they were recording. The marble busts looked towards her with blank, colourless gazes. The drawing door was closed and no sound came from behind.

She walked over and put her hand on the doorknob. Slowly she turned it and opened the door to darkness within, only the faint glow of pearly light from somewhere to provide any illumination. She stepped inside and could make out nothing but massy shapes where she knew the furniture stood. Suddenly a torch flicked on, shining in her eyes and blinding her for a moment before the beam moved off her face.

'Come this way.' It was Charles's rasping voice. The beam slid onto the floor in front of her, lighting the carpet and then moved ahead of her to show where she should go. Bemused, she followed the pool of light as it moved across the room to one of the armchairs, which had been turned to face the back of the room. The curtains were pulled tightly shut and she could see very little at all, but when she reached the chair, she saw a small table beside it and the other armchair next to it, also facing the far wall. On the table was a bottle of wine chilling in an ice bucket and a plate of food.

'Sit down. We're almost ready.'

Buttercup said lightly, 'This is very mysterious!'

'Shh, no talking please.'

She sat down obediently and heard Charles moving around behind her. Then he said, 'All systems go.' A moment later he was in the other armchair, and the torch was off. The next instant, she heard a flourish of violin music and at the back of the room, a famous logo appeared, huge and in shades of black and white: a dove surrounded by an olive wreath. Letters appeared and she read: 'Columbine Pictures proudly present . . .'

Charles, she realised, had set up a movie screen, a proper room-sized screen that stretched across the back of the drawing room; the sound of an orchestra filled the air around her as the letters curled majestically across the screen:

DELILAH

And then the names of its stars: Natalie Rowe was the first. The credits flashed up as the music played.

A private showing. Just for me.

She looked over at Charles, who was grinning at her in the light from the screen. He leaned over and said, 'Didn't I say you should see this film? I don't know why it's taken me so long to get around to it. I'll pour you a drink – sit back and enjoy it.'

When it finished an hour and a half later, Buttercup was sniffing and wiping away tears. The screen went blank, Charles got up with the torch and a moment later, he had switched on the lights and fetched her a tissue from the box on the bureau.

'Did you like it?' he asked. He dabbed at her face with the tissue, and she took it from him so she could blow her nose.

'It was wonderful,' she said, her voice still thick with emotion. 'But so sad at the end! Just when it looks as though everything is going to work out for them—'

233

'That rotter Julius got her in the end.'

'He was a monster! But it was clever, all the way along, you thought Natalie was Delilah, and then you discover the truth and it's such a shock!' Buttercup sighed. 'She was amazing! What a stunner.'

'And there she is.' Charles gestured to the portrait over the fireplace.

Buttercup turned and gasped. She'd seen the portrait dozens of times but it had never meant much until now. The living, breathing creature from the screen – so enchanting, so fascinating, ethereally beautiful – was right there on the canvas, in this house. She saw the painting as it had been in the film, hanging in Delilah's apartment, a symbol of her success and power. 'Oh my goodness!' she exclaimed. 'That's the actual picture from the movie! I knew that but it didn't mean anything till now.' She shook her head in wonderment. 'It's so hard to believe that Natalie Rowe actually lived here. That woman existed in this house!'

'She didn't just live here. She died here too.'

'Actually in the house?'

'Oh yes. Years later, when she was an old woman, with her dotty daughter.'

Buttercup stared at the painting, trying to take it in. *From that beauty with the world at her feet to an old woman dying. Like Mum – all the life lived behind her, all the chances gone and over.*

From somewhere in her mind, a voice spoke loudly and clearly.

That mustn't be me. I mustn't miss my chances. Not while I still have time.

The next morning, Charles left for another business trip, to Shanghai this time. It had been a pleasant evening after the private movie showing. Charles declared it such a success, he wanted to get a proper cinema room built at the house so they could repeat their movie night.

'The golden oldies only at first. We need to round out your film education. If you'd never seen *Delilah*, what else haven't you seen?'

She'd laughed and enjoyed his enthusiasm, getting caught up in plans for the cinema. She put the rupture between them out of her mind. He was her husband and she trusted him. He might have a temper and be controlling, but that was why he was such a success. She loved him despite those qualities when he had so many other wonderful attributes.

As he was leaving, Charles said, 'Darling, I meant to say – the Christmas party needs arranging, we've left it rather late. Can I get Elaine to email you the guest list for checking so we can get the invitations out?'

'Yes.' Buttercup was glad of something she could do. 'I'd love to help. Have her send it through.'

'Thank you, you're an angel.' He smiled. 'Goodbye, darling, I'll be home soon, I promise.'

As promised, an email arrived that morning from Elaine with the guest list for the Christmas party, and details of all the arrangements. Charles always threw two parties – one for the village, as he put it, and one in London, his corporate party, with business bigwigs and long-time contacts all invited. Buttercup had nothing to do the London one, she only had to turn up looking glamorous and make small talk with men in suits. The one here at the house was different, much more enjoyable. It included everyone who worked for them and their families, along with neighbours and friends from all over the county. The atmosphere was excited and jolly, the house looked beautiful with great sparkling trees, festoons of ivy, holly wreaths and twinkling lights. The fires would be lit, and carol singers in hats and scarves would gather around the flaming brazier in front of the house. There was mulled wine and champagne and spicy sausages on sticks and mince pies and trays of Christmas treats for the many children. A snow machine blew pretend snow on the terrace, and a jolly Father Christmas would visit, accompanied by two real-life reindeer and a sackful of presents.

Buttercup sat down after breakfast to check the guest list, updating it and adding new names – the Tranters must be invited.

I wonder how they're getting on. Busy, I expect, with the new baby. I must call in and see them.

She went back to the list and saw that Princess Arkadyoff was also on it. The old lady was always included but never came. It crossed her mind to delete the name, but she stopped herself. Just because their hospitality was never accepted was no reason not to offer it. Instead she hesitated, then added Agnieska's name plus two children. She wrote next to it: 'Please check with Carol for surname, address.'

Charles will never see her among five hundred or so others. And why should she and the children miss out on a party and presents? She deserves it. He'll never know.

She had finished the list, ready to scan and send back, when she looked up and found herself staring at the portrait of Natalie Rowe over the fireplace. The words she'd heard in her mind came back to her:

I mustn't miss my chances.

After a moment, she leapt up, went to the boot room and put on her coat. Tippi appeared, panting eagerly and wagging her tail, so Buttercup picked up her lead and put it in her pocket, and strode out into the yard, Tippi following. As she went past the stables over the cobbles, she waved at Phil, who was just bringing Topper out to exercise him, but didn't stop to talk. Instead she walked out into the chill air, enjoying the sharpness in her throat and lungs, heading out of the estate and up the hill while Tippi ran ahead, exploring happily. At the top of the hill she stopped and looked back down on the house, with its sloped tiled roof and many chimneys. The reception was much better outside than it was in the house, and there would be no listening ears there either.

The call was answered almost before it rang. 'Buttercup, sweet thing, is that you?'

'Lazlo! Yes of course it's me. How are you?'

'Busy and missing you, you scallywag. I'm run off my feet and could do with your help.' Lazlo's dramatic tones quietened and he said, 'Your replacement is hopeless, nowhere near as good as you. Fancy coming back?'

Buttercup laughed. 'You read my mind! But you weren't too keen on my idea of recruiting clients for you down here, and I wondered if we could have a chat about it.'

'Sorry, what are you talking about?'

'I sent you an email, remember? Then you bumped into Charles and told him it was no go. You said you were too busy to think about expanding the business . . .'

'Email?' She could hear Lazlo's confusion, but he was always so disorganised, it wasn't a huge surprise.

'Yes, I wrote to you! You talked about it with Charles. He passed on your message.'

'Darling, I haven't seen Charles since your wedding.'

She stared blankly out over the wintery parkland, the house so serene and secure at its centre. 'Yes, you have.'

'Nope! I'm dozy but not that dozy. And I'm sure you didn't send me an email, I would have remembered that! Emails from you are like gold dust.'

'I . . . I'm sorry, I must have got confused.' She shivered. Tippi crashed about in the bracken, making her jump.

'Do you want to think about coming back to work? I'd love that! Let's meet up and talk about it.'

'Yes, I'd like that. Maybe after Christmas, when things have quietened down?'

'Sounds great. I'll see you at Charles's Christmas party in any case.'

'Bye, Lazlo.'

'Bye, Buttercup.'

*

Back home, Buttercup went into the drawing room where she'd left her computer, pushed open the screen and fired it up. A moment later, she was in her email account, searching for the sent email to Lazlo. It wasn't in her sent folder, so she did a search and found her email sitting in the drafts folder. She had never sent it at all.

She stared at the screen, blinking in astonishment. *I never sent it! How did Charles know about it?*

She had a vision of the screen left open, the draft email on it, someone taking a look and closing it down. Who? Agnieska? Hardly likely with her limited English. Charles himself? He'd been away when she wrote that email, if she remembered rightly. Then surely it had to be Carol – snooping and reporting on her. And Charles had thought she'd actually sent the email to Lazlo. But why did he make up the story about meeting Lazlo and talking to him?

To stop me getting a job? That has to be it.

She stared, still shocked, at the email in her drafts folder. It had never been sent. Charles had definitely told her that Lazlo had seen it. But he hadn't.

Chapter Twenty-Three

'Hello, Rose?'

'Mrs R!' Rose sounded jovial but Buttercup thought she detected just a tiny hint of strain in her voice. 'What can I do for you?'

'I'm coming up to London tonight but I won't see you then. Listen, can I ask you a private question?'

There was a pause and Rose said brightly, 'Sure! Elaine's on the other line right now.'

'Okay. Obviously, there's a limit to what you can say, I understand that.' Buttercup stood by the French windows in the drawing room, looking out over the garden. It appeared chill and dead in the dull afternoon. 'I want to know if I can take a look at the file Charles has on me. I want more information.'

Rose said nothing for a moment and then, slowly, 'That might not be straightforward. It's not really my area.'

'I know.' *It's Elaine's territory. The guard dog.* Buttercup knew that there would be no breaking through Elaine's defences. She'd been working for Charles almost all her adult life and was utterly, steadfastly loyal; she would no doubt keep his secrets to the bitter end. Charles had told her how, after Elaine's husband had died, leaving her with three small children and no money, he had offered her the lifeline of a job that she could fit around her family. As the children had grown up and gone away, Elaine had become ever more devoted to Charles's welfare. It wasn't unusual for her to go with him all over the world, and she knew everything about him. 'But Charles said she's joining him in Shanghai today.'

'That's right. Later today.'

'Good. Then at least we can discuss it openly when I see you tomorrow.'

'Fine, Mrs R. I'll have the flat ready and waiting.'

It was late afternoon and Buttercup was putting her bag into her car, ready to be on her way, when Phil appeared out of the darkness, muffled up in a coat and scarf against the icy wind blowing across the yard.

'BC?'

She jumped, her mind elsewhere, then smiled when she saw him. 'Phil, hi. How are you?'

'I'm all right,' he said gruffly. 'You off somewhere?'

'Christmas shopping in London.'

'I wanted to have a quick word with you if I can.'

'I'm actually just about to leave – will it take long?'

'No, not at all.' He stared at her, his hands thrust deep in his pockets, his eyes hardly visible in the light from the court-yard lamp. 'It's about that poor Polish girl. Carol told me what happened. It wasn't right,' Phil said gruffly.

'I totally agree, and I asked my husband to reconsider but I'm afraid he was a bit upset.' She hesitated, then said quickly, 'I'll try again when he's home, no doubt he'll have calmed down by then and will be in the mood to be more generous. I'd love to have Agnieska back, and you know Charles . . .' She trailed off, wondering suddenly if any of them knew Charles. *Least of all me.* She finished weakly: ' . . . his heart's in the right place.'

Phil stared at her for a moment longer, his shoulders hunched, then said, 'If you say so.' He turned on his heel and marched away into the darkness. Buttercup watched him go, before climbing into the car to start her journey.

On the way out of the gates of Charcombe, she noticed that, for the first time in a long time, the lights of Fitzroy House were on.

So Ingrid was home at last.

London was already dressed for Christmas. The lights were up: frosted peacock feathers glittered down Bond Street, ethereal blue angels hovered with outstretched wings around Piccadilly. Oxford Street and Regent Street flashed with Disney figures and blockbuster film promotions. Shop windows were crammed with candy canes and snow and gift-wrapped boxes.

Buttercup reached the flat late in the evening, had a cold supper and went to bed. The next morning, she headed out early to do some Christmas shopping and returned to the Westminster house in the afternoon in a taxi loaded up with her bags and boxes. One of the security guards took charge of them and carted them all upstairs in the lift while Butter-cup took the stairs so that she could call in at the office on the way. Rose was there, sitting at her desk and staring at her screen, tapping on her keyboard.

'Hi, Rose.'

Rose looked up and smiled. 'Hi, Mrs R. You went out first thing?'

'That's right. I needed to do some shopping. I've got half a dozen godchildren to buy for.'

'Let me know if you want anything wrapped or sent.'

Buttercup came into the office and put down her handbag so she could slip off her coat. 'You make my life so easy, Rose, do you know that? All the little things people usually struggle with – even like finding the tape and the scissors, or getting the time to do the wrapping – you take all of that away from me.'

Rose smiled. 'That's my job.'

Buttercup sat down in the black leather chair in front of Rose's desk and fixed with her a candid look. 'Can we speak openly here, without being overheard?'

'Yes. We're not bugged, if that's what you mean. At least, I don't think so. Say whatever you like.'

Buttercup wondered if Rose's cheerful demeanour, so different from the nerves and trepidation she had shown last time, was a defensive technique. Maybe she had already decided not to help but was just playing along. She said: 'I'm sure you remember our telephone call. Things have changed a bit since I last spoke to you, and I'd really like to get more of an idea of what's in my file, and exactly how many people are reporting on me. You see, I don't believe any longer that it's all for the sake of my security. To be frank, I think the kidnap story is rubbish.'

'Okay,' Rose said slowly. 'That's what I'm told.'

'Do you believe it though?'

'I think . . . maybe they're being a bit over-protective.'

'Just a bit.' Buttercup leaned towards her. 'And I'd like to get to the bottom of it so I can persuade Charles that he doesn't need to worry about me quite so much.'

Rose looked doubtful, rubbing her fingertips nervously over her keyboard and pursing her lips. 'Like I said, I don't deal with any of that. Elaine takes care of it.'

'There must be quite a lot of paperwork. So where does she keep the files?'

Suddenly agitated, Rose leaned across her desk, frowning. 'You want me to access the files and give them to you to look at?'

'Bingo.' Buttercup smiled at her. 'You've got it in one.'

Rose exhaled a long breath, shaking her head and frowning behind her spectacles. 'Mrs R, that's sackable stuff, you know that. I'd have to open Elaine's locked filing cabinet.' She glanced over at a shiny black padlocked cabinet in the corner of the room. 'That's top secret.'

Buttercup followed her gaze. *So that's it. Everything is in there.* 'Do you know the code?'

Rose said nothing.

'You do, don't you?'

She bit her lip and looked guilty. 'Elaine once had to tell

it to me, when she needed me to get something for her while she was abroad with Charles.'

'And she hasn't changed it?'

'She has. She changes it every week. Then she sends herself an email with the combination in it.'

'So it's in her email folders?'

'It should be. And I know her password.'

'Great.' Buttercup looked at her intently. 'I want to look in the cabinet. Will you open it for me?'

'I want to help you.' Rose sighed and pushed her glasses back on her nose. 'But if I get found out, I'll be sacked.'

'It's a risk, I can't pretend it's not. But I won't tell, I promise you that.'

'They'll know it was me. It couldn't be anyone else.'

Buttercup could see that Rose was becoming less keen to help her, more scared of the consequences. She knew her chance was slipping away. 'Rose, please, I'm begging you. You know that Charles is monitoring me. I think he might have people actively spying on me – and not only for my protection, like he says. I'm beginning to feel like I'm not in control of my own life, and it's eating away at me. I'm beginning to suspect everyone, even Charles himself. Maybe even my emails are being read. Who knows how far it could go? I just need to know what's actually going on. That's all.'

Rose shifted uncomfortably. 'I don't want to get involved with the boss's private life. I've already told you more than I should.'

'I don't know what else to do, Rose. I'm powerless. Everything is hidden from me. And listen to this: I barely know what phone network I'm on, and I've certainly never seen a bill. I've never taken our car to be serviced and rarely put petrol in it. I've never been in our cellar. I don't know how many rooms there are in my own house. It's not normal! It might sound like I'm just a bored rich wife, but it's much more than that. Gradually, I'm being closed in. And I think people are watching me all the time, even sabotaging my attempts to get a job, and I don't know why! It's beginning to drive me mad: sometimes I feel like I'm paranoid and other times I'm sure I'm right. Please, Rose. I need to know what's going on.'

Rose stared at her desk for a while and then said in a low voice, 'All right. I'll do it. Jacob said I was an idiot to get mixed up in this, but I can't just stand by and do nothing. I can see that there is some weird stuff happening, though I don't know any details. So I'll open the cabinet for you.'

Five minutes later, Rose had the combination for the cabinet, and she went to the padlock, Buttercup following. Now that the answers were so close, she could feel her heart racing. Rose took hold of the padlock and turned the dials. One by one they fell into place and when they were all in a line, the lock clicked obediently open.

Rose pulled the top drawer open; it was full of hanging files, each one carefully labelled and full of paper. Though tidy, it was bulging with information. Buttercup began to read the labels, her heart pounding and a sick feeling in her stomach.

'Oh my goodness,' she whispered. 'This is unbelievable.'

Rose said nothing, blinking behind her glasses.

'I mean . . . utterly unbelievable.'

With shaking hands, Buttercup began to leaf through the files, so she could read every label: 'BR – phone records'; 'BR – internet history'; 'BR – medical history'; 'BR – childhood info'; 'BR – credit card'; 'BR – social circle'; 'BR – employment'; 'BR – horse riding' . . . Each file bulged with paper and there were dozens of them.

Buttercup turned to Rose, her eyes wide, trembling with shock. 'But this is all about me!'

Rose nodded, also looking astonished. 'I had no idea there was this much. I looked in the other drawer. It's kind of . . . a bit *too* much.'

Buttercup turned back. It was worse – much worse – than she'd thought.

Chapter Twenty-Four

'Be careful, be careful!' quavered Xenia, standing at the door of her bedroom and watching Agnieska anxiously as she dusted the top of the chest of drawers. 'Don't break anything.'

'You have much things,' Agnieska grumbled, lifting up another photograph frame to wipe underneath.

It was true that the room was full of ornaments and bibelots. Every surface had something on it: enamelled picture frames, porcelain snuff boxes, silver trinkets, jewellery cases – empty, mostly. When Xenia left Charcombe Park, there had seemed to be little that remained from the great load of possessions that had been assembled over those years when they had lived in grand style. Roomsful of furniture had been sold or thrown away. What was left that was precious from those days she kept here, in her bedroom, and whenever Agnieska was in there, she found it hard to keep away, just in case. Now that she knew that Agnieska had broken an antique plate at the big house, she fretted all the more that something might get damaged.

Agnieska picked up the crystal star, one of Mama's many awards for *Delilah*, and began to polish it.

'Be careful!' cried Xenia. 'Don't drop that. And be careful of the other ones, too – they are all real, you know!'

Agnieska put the star down, turned to her and put her hands on her hips. 'It's okay!' she said firmly. 'Don't watch me. Go away.'

Xenia murmured and then, obediently, went back downstairs. The rest of the house was furnished from a mail order catalogue, along with a few pieces of what had remained from the big house – but she had left an awful lot behind. Much of it was too imbued with unhappy memories. She kept only the things that reminded her of the good times, and of Mama. She had no qualms about letting go of the rest. The great kitchen table had been dragged outside by two village men and, at her request, put on the bonfire in the garden, along with mouse-infested mattresses and all the broken bits and pieces wanted by nobody. She had been glad to see it burn to ashes.

Xenia went downstairs to find Petrova and make a cup of tea. She drank gallons of it as the weather turned colder outside. She liked to pull the curtains shut, have the lamps lit and the electric heater on, and make herself a cosy nest in which she could keep warm and comfortable while she watched the television. Sometimes she felt she could never feel cosy enough, after the years in the great house, that grew draughtier and draughtier as it fell apart. Trying to keep her and Mama warm had been an endless task.

'Mama, we must go, we must find somewhere else!' she

would say as they shivered under blankets in the drawing room, huddling close to the fire. She would build a barricade with chairs and old curtains to keep the heat in and when the cold was at its worst, they would put their mattresses there and sleep in front of the fireplace.

'We can't leave,' Mama insisted. 'He'll come back. He promised. How will he find us if we've moved away?'

'All right, all right,' Xenia would say. How could she refuse? Instead she devoted herself to keeping them going, but it grew ever harder. The money was all gone, only Mama's residuals from her films kept them fed and clothed, with running water and electricity. Xenia was far too proud to apply for benefits, though she must have been eligible for something.

She took great pleasure in the cottage, weather-tight and warm, and the purring cat who curled on her lap and whose presence kept her from shouting too loudly at the television.

But Agnieska's presence brought her comfort too. She liked the sound of the other woman moving around, humming and singing to herself as she worked, the distant buzz of the vacuum cleaner. No one had spoken to her firmly or said the words 'go away' to her in decades, yet somehow she didn't mind, knowing that Agnieska did not mean to be unkind – quite the reverse.

They had taken a shopping trip together, which had not been exactly straightforward, as Xenia had felt that Agnieska drove far too fast and dangerously, and had called out instructions from the back seat, which Agnieska simply ignored, probably because she had not understood them. By the time they arrived at the supermarket, Xenia had been extremely tense and she had begun shouting as soon as they got out of the car.

'What did you think you were doing, you silly girl? You nearly killed us on the roundabout, I saw that bus even if you didn't – and my eyes are failing me! You went far too fast . . . !' She was quaking with fury.

Agnieska fixed her with a clear grey gaze, put her hand on Xenia's shoulder and said quietly, 'It's fine. Not fast at all. And we are here. Everything is okay.'

Xenia had taken three quick, gulping breaths and forced herself to be calm. She was right. They were there. Agnieska had stayed with her all the way around the supermarket, helping her reach things, opening the fiddly plastic bags for the vegetables, listening calmly while Xenia complained that there were no sensible paper bags, and pushing the trolley when it got too heavy. Then after the checkout, she loaded the car, took Xenia to the bank and to the chemist, waited while she went to the library to get some large-print crime novels and some audiobooks, then drove her home and helped unload the car.

It had been a relief when it was all over, and an even greater one to see Agnieska drive away in the car, knowing that she would fill it with petrol and check the tyres and do all the things Xenia found so difficult.

When Agnieska had finished, Xenia came out to see her in the hall.

'What are you doing over Christmas, Agnieska? Are you going back to Poland?'

'No, not this year. My mother comes here. Christmas with my family and my sister, and my husband's sister too.'

'But when the school holidays start, you'll be too busy to come here until January?' Xenia said, worried. She had got so used to seeing Agnieska once a week that she didn't like the thought of being alone for the three weeks of Christmas and New Year.

'I still come,' Agnieska said with a shrug. 'My mother will look after children.'

'Oh, good. Excellent. Here's your money, and thank you.'

'Bye.'

'Goodbye.'

Xenia watched her go, comforted. Then she turned back to the warmth of her little sitting room, the early evening game show she enjoyed so much, and a doze.

Chapter Twenty-Five

1952

They had only been at Charcombe Park for a week or so, and Mama was still recovering from her journey, when Grandmama arrived to visit from her house in Paris, bringing with her some family portraits for the new house. Papa sent their new car with a driver to collect her from the station and when it drew up, hurried out to kiss her hand and offer her his arm. Her maid got out too, loaded down with bags.

From her bedroom window upstairs, Xenia got her first glimpse of her grandmother: a stooped woman in a long coat with a wide fur collar that sat over her shoulders like a shawl, moving slowly with the help of a silver-topped walking stick. Steely grey curls emerged from under a hat with folds in it, like a turban, and two emerald-green feathery sprays pinned to it. Xenia knew she must go downstairs at once, and she checked her reflection in the mirror on the way out, tucking a stray curl behind her ear, then ran along the corridor, only slowing when she reached the first-floor landing, where a grand and gracious staircase led down to the hall. She could hear voices from the drawing room as she approached, then she knocked and went in.

Grandmama sat in pride of place on the white and gold sofa, her coat gone so that her blue brocade dress could be seen. Around her neck were ropes of pearls, and a blue sapphire brooch with a great tear-drop pearl hanging from it glittered at her breast. Her face was lined, collapsing around the jowls, and her small blue eyes – so like Papa's – blazed out of its soft, powdery whiteness, staring at Xenia as she came in.

'Oh, here is Xenia,' said Mama, who was sitting on another sofa nearby, looking pale and nervous but still elegant in a green suit, a string of pearls at her neck. 'Say hello to your grandmama.'

Xenia stopped in front of the old lady, curtseyed and said politely, 'How do you do, Grandmama.'

'How do you do.' A smile flickered around the thin lips. Her voice was deep and a little cracked with age, but still strong. It had the faintest hint of a foreign accent in the well-accentuated English. She looked over at Papa who was standing by the fireplace. 'Well, *mon Paul*, she doesn't look like you or Natalie.'

'A mixture of us both, I think.' Papa smiled. He seemed stiff but also, Xenia thought with surprise, a little afraid.

'You may sit down, child.'

Xenia went and took her place on a neat little armchair opposite the fireplace.

'The tea will be here in a moment,' Papa said, his gaze flicking to the door. 'I'm sure you would like some, Mama.'

How funny. She is his mama! It was almost impossible to imagine this old lady as a young woman and Papa as a baby. It seemed to her sometimes that grown-ups had always been old and she would be eternally young. *Papa is all grown up and still afraid of his mother. Although I can see that she is rather frightening.*

Her grandmother's dignity came blazing out of her. There was no question that she was a person of stature and importance. It wasn't only the jewels she wore; even though she was bent with age, she seemed to be stiff and straight and haughty.

A real princess, Xenia thought. *Is that what I am expected to be?* She tried to adopt her best princess manners and said politely, 'How was your journey, Grandmama?'

'Extremely tiresome. The boat train from Paris is not much better than cattle transport. I have survived but I'm certainly too old to do anything like it again. Next time, you must come to me, I'm afraid.'

'I'd like to go to Paris,' Xenia said eagerly. 'I've never been.'

'I know that only too well. For some reason, your father has never brought you.'

Papa said, almost stuttering, 'Xenia has her studies, and Natalie her work—'

'Indeed.' Princess Arkadyoff looked around the room. 'You have done extremely well for yourself, that's clear. You live in style.'

'I'm happy to say that my investments have paid off handsomely.' Papa looked over at his wife with pride. 'And Natalie has enjoyed a huge success, as you know.'

'I do know.' The old lady raised her eyebrows at Mama and said, 'In my day, an actress was hardly a fitting match for someone like my son. A man might spend his leisure hours with her, but he would never marry her. He would never *elevate* her.' Grandmama paused and then said, 'Do you intend to carry on acting?'

Mama looked paler than ever, glanced at Papa and then back at Grandmama, seeming to be at a complete loss. 'I don't know. I suppose so,' she said, helplessly. 'Paul wants me to, don't you, Paul?'

'Times have changed, my dear mother,' Papa said stiffly. 'Respectable people are actresses. Here, they are made dames and considered to be women of stature.'

Grandmama sniffed. 'That is most peculiar. I don't believe that taking an actress wife is something that Nicholas would have done. He was set on marrying Countess Palinov but goodness knows what happened to her. After their palace was requisitioned, they left for the country where they were no doubt murdered in their beds.'

'How terrible,' Mama said in a small voice.

'One prays they escaped,' Papa said fervently.

'Hmm. Well, it was a long time ago.' Grandmama looked around, frowning. 'My dear boy, where is that tea? I'm quite fainting with thirst.'

Just then the door opened, and the maid came in with the tea tray. Xenia was sent away, back to the nursery.

Grandmama stayed only three days, and before she left, she sent for Xenia.

'You seem a good child,' Grandmama said when they were sitting together in the drawing room in front of the crackling fire. 'How old are you?'

'Thirteen. Nearly fourteen.'

'Do you go to school?'

'Papa says I must go back to school in London soon, but I don't much want to.'

Grandmama was regarding her gravely. 'You seem a sensible child, despite everything. A shame about your mother, but there we are.'

Xenia didn't know what to say. Mama was practically perfect, and everyone in the world loved her. It seemed contrary to think anything else.

'Now.' Grandmama smiled a thin-lipped smile. She looked as imperiously elegant as always in a turquoise dress, her customary pearls in thick ropes around her neck. Her hand went to the sapphire brooch sparkling on her chest, the large tear-drop pearl glimmered beneath. 'Do you like my jewel?'

'It's beautiful.'

'It should be. It was a wedding gift to the Empress Maria Feodorovna. Many years ago, I accompanied her into exile and she gave it to me. It is extremely precious and valuable. One day, it shall be yours.'

Xenia stared at it again in wonderment. The jewel of an empress was to be hers? She could hardly imagine owning such a thing, the responsibility seemed too great. 'Thank you,' she breathed. 'I will be ever so careful with it.'

'You are my only Arkadyoff grandchild. My son Nicholas was killed in the revolution, murdered by the Bolsheviks. He should have fled but he stayed.' There was a pause while Grandmama seemed to compose herself. 'Your father was just a boy. My youngest. He has grown up in exile and never understood what we went through. He cannot be blamed for what he has become.'

Xenia blinked at her grandmother. Here they were, sitting in a grand house. What had Papa become that Grandmama did not approve of?

'Come and kiss me, my dear. When this jewel is yours, you must look after it, do you understand? It may be all you have in the end.'

Xenia went over obediently and kissed her grandmother's powdery-smelling cheek. Her gaze drifted to the sparkling blue jewel on the front of her dress.

Will that truly be mine? I can't believe it.

After Grandmama returned to Paris, Mama and Papa went back to America, so that Mama could attend the awards ceremony in which she was nominated as the best actress of the year. This time, they flew, Mama heavily sedated by special injections to keep her calm as she was so terrified of aeroplanes.

Xenia returned to London with Gunter, to follow her old routine, going back to school with her friends and marching around the chilly park in the afternoons with boring old Gunter, who now walked so slowly and was going deaf. Xenia felt she was too old for all this now, and longed with all her heart to be in Hollywood with her parents. Instead, she had to make do with watching the newsreels at the cinema. When Mama's triumph was reported, Xenia went as often as she could, to see Mama in her wonderful gown going into the ceremony on Papa's arm, sparkling and gorgeous, and then posing with her golden statuette, smiling and evidently delighted.

At last Mama will be happy, Xenia thought. *What could make anyone happier than to be beautiful, rich and successful, a film star and a princess?*

But when her parents returned and she joined them at Charcombe, Xenia found everything was worse than before. Mama was sick: wracked by a cough, thin, pale and feverish, her green eyes enormous in her hollow-cheeked face. She could hardly speak when they finally arrived home, but went at once to bed.

'What's wrong with her?' Xenia asked, frightened. 'Does she have a disease?'

'A kind of disease,' Papa said, looking pale and ill himself. 'It's a breakdown. The journey home was simply terrible. She panicked and needed several people to restrain her from trying to leap out of the plane. They almost diverted us, but I managed to calm her.'

'What's a . . . a breakdown?'

'It's hard to describe. Her nerves are tired. She needs complete rest, peace and quiet.' He hugged Xenia. 'She'll get well again, dear one, if we can only help her. Then she will make a film like *Delilah* again. That's her destiny, I know it.'

It was obvious to Xenia that making another film was not something Mama would be capable of for some time. There was no question of her acting. Too sick to do anything at all, she was put to bed in the large bedroom in the east wing, where she had a view of the garden as the winter finally began to make way to spring.

For as long as Xenia could remember, Mama had slept patchily. At times, she was exhausted and had to sink into unconsciousness for long hours, but mostly she was full of energy, so much that she barely knew what to do with it. She would be up at dawn, arranging everything just so, fulfilling hundreds of tiny tasks with ceaseless activity. She could keep going all day and late into the night when, despite drinking several martinis and plenty of red wine with dinner, she would still want to play games and sing songs when others were flagging and desperate for bed.

But now, ill and utterly lacking in energy, she was forced to remain in bed and sleep and at last she seemed to find some peace. The view of the garden and the park beyond seemed to comfort her. When she gained a little more strength, she drew up plans for the garden and how lovely she would make it, to please Papa.

Xenia brought her bowls of nourishing soup and cups of tea, and refused whenever Mama asked for cigarettes. Slowly, her mother grew brighter. She gained weight, the cough eased off, the colour returned to her face. She came downstairs more and more.

'Are you well again, Mama?' Xenia asked, hopefully, as they sat together on the terrace in the weak spring sunshine, wrapped in coats and blankets.

'I think so, darling. I hope so.' Mama leaned her head back

to let the sunshine fall on her face and closed her eyes. 'I don't want to be ill again, it's the worst thing in the world.'

'You won't be,' Xenia said stoutly.

'I can't bear to be a burden on you and Papa.'

'You could never be that, Mama. Never, never.'

Mama took her hand and held it tightly. 'Dearest Xenia. What did I do to deserve you? Of course I'll get better. You'll see.'

Chapter Twenty-Six

Buttercup stared at the contents of her life, all carefully organised and labelled, made to look orderly and controllable. There they were in front of her: fat hanging folders full of information about all her comings and goings, her history, her friends . . .

I just don't understand why he would need this!

'Does Charles read all of this stuff?' she asked, still unable to take it in.

'He certainly gets sent it. I don't know if he reads it all.'

Buttercup pulled out a file labelled 'BR – internet history' and took it over the table. She sat down and opened it as Rose went back to her desk and continued her work.

In front of her were dozens of printouts going back over the time that she and Charles had been married, beginning as soon as she started using the laptop Charles had given her as a present not long after they met. Every website she had visited since then was listed.

But it's unbelievably tedious!

She flicked back to the time just after her engagement

where the search history bulged with wedding dress designers, florists and caterers as she'd done all the research for her wedding.

Why on earth would he be interested in all of this?

It wasn't just that he was curious. It was the fact that it had all been downloaded, printed out, looked at and filed away, like evidence for some very long court case.

As she went on through the records, remembering searches she had made and websites she had visited, she realised that actually they gave a clear window onto her personality and her views, her likes and dislikes, the things that caught her fancy, from recipes, to diet ideas, to the latest yoga craze. So much could be learned about her, from which news websites she read, to where she shopped, to where she might like to go on holiday and what she was planning to buy Charles for Christmas.

So the monogrammed briefcase was no surprise, I guess, she thought grimly as she saw the page history: product, shopping basket, payment confirmation. *Unless he got the report after Christmas. But maybe it explains why he got me that necklace I had no idea he knew I liked.*

She found herself sighing in frustration because she would tell him all this, if he asked her. She probably had told him plenty. But he still wanted to see it in black and white, as though he didn't trust her.

Her heart ached as she flicked forward to the time of the miscarriage, and her searches for information and for help; the forums she'd visited, the bereavement pages she'd read and, later, the tips for increasing fertility and investigating a lack of pregnancy.

So he knows how much I care. There's no doubt about that. A wash of sadness came over her; he knew how much the hunger for a baby had possessed her, and yet he'd still told her to relax and wait, that it would all be fine, as though that would relieve the oppressive need to know why she couldn't seem to have another child.

And yet, weirdly, he won't find out about the fertility clinic from my internet searches, because I never looked it up online.

Then she realised that her phone records and credit card statements would fill that gap.

He really can find out everything he wants.

She gathered up the pile of printed pages and pushed them back into their folder. Putting them back in the cabinet, she selected another file she hadn't seen at first, this one labelled 'BR – Charcombe reports'. Taking it back to the table, she sat down to inspect it. It contained printouts of emails written by Carol, one for each week she had lived in the house. Buttercup pulled one out dated after the miscarriage and started reading:

Mrs R is still in low spirits. I heard her crying today when she was in her bedroom and she didn't come out until almost midday. She ate almost nothing but I managed to persuade her to have a bit of soup before she went out riding. She seemed a little better when she got back. She stayed in the stable with the horses

**until the afternoon, then she came in and watched
television. She had a bit of supper this evening, just fish
and greens, and went to bed quite early to read. My
opinion is that she seems a bit more stable than she did
last week.**

There was more, a short paragraph for every day of the
week, like a diary but all about her.

Oh Carol.

She felt a weight of sadness drop on her. So Carol was a
spy, after all. All the cheery chirpiness and calling her 'love'
and pretending to look after her, and all along she was reporting back to Mission Control, like some kind of double agent.
So it was most likely Carol who'd snooped on the email she'd
written to Lazlo and told Charles about it, assuming she'd
sent it. Then Charles had made up some kind of weird story
to stop her pursuing a job and, no doubt, being less available
for him.

A thought struck her. *Carol might have seen that I've been
looking up Ingrid.*

But what did it matter? Her internet searches would show
that soon enough.

She sat back in her chair, overwhelmed by it all. There was
virtually no move she had made for the last two years that
wasn't known about, and she had been almost completely
unaware of it. She'd known that the Hub knew where she
was, arranged appointments for her, smoothed life out for
her. She hadn't guessed they were a secret service, gathering

information, collecting facts to pass up the chain to their boss, for whom no detail was too small to be of interest.

She leafed through more of Carol's reports, and something caught her eye:

Mrs R started her period today, on time. She is not pregnant.

So he did know. No detail too small. Well, he knew what I'd eaten for breakfast for two years, why wouldn't he know my cycle too?

But it brought a bitter taste to her mouth. She looked up at Rose.

'You must have known about this, Rose.'

Rose looked over. 'What?'

Buttercup gestured with a print-out towards the filing cabinet. 'All this. You must have known how much they were watching me.'

'I had an idea,' Rose said softly, looking shame-faced, 'but they kept it back from me as much as they could. I'm not quite in the inner circle, you see.'

The circle. Charles's circle. His lovely circle where life is lovely. But is it?

'But you had a feeling?'

'Yes, because of what's in the other drawer.'

Buttercup looked slowly back at the other drawer. There were three. She was contained in the top one. 'What's in it?'

'The stuff about Mrs Redmain—' Rose stumbled over her words and said quickly, 'the other Mrs Redmain.'

Buttercup went to the cabinet and put back the files containing the information about her, then pulled open the second drawer. There were many more of the bulging hanging files, now with 'IR' in their labels. She pulled out a file titled 'IR – Fitzroy House', taking it out with trembling hands. 'Oh my goodness.' It felt suddenly so invasive, to have all this confidential information in her possession. *There's still time to put it back.* But she couldn't do that either. She had to look.

She took the file back to the table, sat down and opened it. The first page was a recent utility bill. She began to rifle back through the papers, and found it was mostly administration: council tax, water, gas and electricity. There were bills for work on the house and grounds. *So Charles pays for everything.* Then she found that she was looking at an itemised phone bill, dated only last month. She saw at once that Charles's mobile phone number was listed several times, with calls lasting sometimes a minute and sometimes up to half an hour.

Oh my God. How often does he talk to her?

It was the same on all the other bills she looked at. She stared at it, shocked. Charles had most definitely told her that he had no contact with Ingrid, it all went through Elaine. But he had lied to her.

She closed the file and went to pick out another. This one had no title. Slowly, she opened the cover and looked at the first page. It was a legal letter about custody arrangements. Only recently, it seemed, Charles had queried Ingrid's right to take Charlotte out of the country.

Why would he do that? He took her to Rome himself only a few weeks ago.

The letter had an air of long-suffering irritation:

> *Your client will not cease to make these vexatious*
> *objections whenever my client wishes to go on holiday*
> *with her daughter, even though it is well established that*
> *there is no flight risk ... your client has been able to*
> *take his daughter abroad without objection from my*
> *client ... please confirm as soon as possible that your*
> *client will consent to this trip and desist from further*
> *action in this matter now and in the future ...*

Buttercup knew nothing of ongoing custody issues, or that Charles was frequently making objections to Charlotte going away. She was too perplexed to feel angry, almost too overwhelmed by the rush of information engulfing her.

But the truth is that I don't know anything at all.

She turned over the papers until she found something else that caught her eye. Another legal letter from the same firm of solicitors, who must represent Ingrid.

> *My client demands the return of her family property and*
> *memorabilia including irreplaceable photograph albums*
> *that contain precious photographs of deceased family*
> *members. All have been previously itemised and sent to*
> *your client via your office. Your client agreed verbally to*
> *do this some years ago and my client accepted that he*
> *would act in good faith. As there is no written*

agreement, we cannot enforce this request in the courts
but must ask again, in the interests of ongoing
relationships, that your client makes good his promise . . .

He has her property and won't give it back. Where is it?
What is it besides photo albums?

She kept reading. The letters were dated only a few months ago. It was quite clear that Charles's relationship with Ingrid was alive, even if it were of a litigious nature. She flicked back through more letters. This was correspondence to do with the divorce, the children and more. She went back further, through the years to the time when Charles and Ingrid divorced. Surely . . .

Ah!

She had stumbled on a letter, several pages long, dated before the divorce, but clearly laying out the terms of the agreement. It was signed by Charles and Ingrid. She began to read the terms, going as fast as she could to take it all in quickly. It was agreed that Ingrid must live at the property Fitzroy House until Charlotte turned twenty-one. She was forbidden from moving anyone else into the house without Charles's express consent. She was not allowed to deny reasonable access by Charles into the house. In return, all upkeep and household expenses would be met by Charles. A car and private healthcare were provided. All expenses relating to the children, including education, would be met by Charles. A one-off payment would be made, along with monthly alimony which would cease on remarriage.

So it was Charles who insisted on the arrangement all along. Not Ingrid, after all. She shook her head, shocked.

Her eye was caught by another file, entitled 'Joachim von Bertram'. She had seen the name Joachim only recently. The image of Ingrid's webpage came back to her; the name had been mentioned under the picture of a knight. She picked up the file and opened it. A photograph fell out; it showed an intense-looking man, well built with close-cropped black hair, a dark moustache and beard. He was handsome but what caught the eye was the suit of bright armour he was wearing, richly engraved across the breastplate. Behind him was a magnificent stallion in equine armour and a flowing scarlet cloth worn from neck to tail under his saddle that swept to the ground, embroidered with a coat of arms of black, white and gold.

The same man I saw on Ingrid's page.

There were further photographs: of jousting knights in full armour wearing helmets topped with plumes and visors lowered, galloping down the lists at one another with lances at the ready. They made an extraordinary sight.

'Do you know why this would be in Ingrid's file?' Buttercup asked, holding up the first picture.

Rose looked over. 'Sir Lancelot? I've got no idea.'

'His name is Joachim von Bertram and he seems to be some kind of jouster or a medieval re-enactor, or something.'

'No. Sorry. I don't know.'

'There's tons of stuff about him. He has to be her boyfriend.' Buttercup looked over at Rose, and shrugged. 'I didn't know being a jouster was even a thing.'

Rose made a face. 'It's not your everyday profession ...' Then she looked suddenly enlightened. 'Wait, I remember Elaine telling me that they used to have jousting in the gardens of Charcombe Park in the summer. She said they used to have jousters to stay for a month and they would put on shows. And there would be birds of prey displays and stalls and an old-fashioned fair. It was great, apparently, it brought loads of people into the village. But they don't do it any more.'

Buttercup stared down at the photograph of the handsome knight. 'I think I can guess at why they don't. He must be the man Ingrid had an affair with.'

Rose's phone buzzed and she picked it up. 'Yes?' Her expression changed to one of panic. 'Okay.' She dropped the receiver and said urgently, 'It's Rich. He's on his way upstairs right now. Get the file back in, quick! He mustn't see it. He's the boss's man to the core.'

'Oh my God.' Buttercup instantly became clumsy as she pushed the papers into their files. She gathered up the jousting one, shoving the photograph of Joachim on the top, closed it and returned it to the hanging file. *Was it below this one? Or that one? Which one was on top? The admin file, I'm sure it was that one.*

Rose was at her side. 'Quick, give them to me, he'll be here any second.'

'I ... I can't remember how they go!' She put the admin file at the front and slid the divorce file in behind it. 'There!'

Rose scooped up the hanging file, went over to the cabinet and put it in the drawer, while Buttercup got up and slid

Elaine's chair back into place. She could hear Rich's whistle as he got closer. Any moment he'd walk in through the door and see them. Rose got the file on the runners and fumbled to get the drawer shut. Just as Rich reached the door, she pushed it shut but there was no time to secure the padlock. She left it and raced across the room, sitting down in front of her screen just as Rich came in. Buttercup stood frozen on the spot, staring at the doorway, her heart pounding.

Rich sauntered to Rose's desk. He was only wearing a T-shirt despite the cold outside. 'Hello, Rosy Posy – oh! Mrs R. I didn't expect you here today.'

'Hi, Rich. I've been out shopping but it was so cold and dark out there, I came in for a gossip with Rose.' She hoped her voice sounded normal. Her eye was suddenly caught by a piece of paper covered in handwriting. It was on the table and definitely hadn't been there before. *It must have slipped out of the file.*

'Sounds nice.' Rich looked at both of them. 'You okay? You both look a bit . . . I don't know . . . shaken.'

Buttercup improvised. 'I . . . I just told Rose a sad story about a friend of mine . . . she's . . . she's ill.'

'I'm sorry to hear that.' Rich turned to Rose, and in the moment he did that, Buttercup reached over and scooped up the paper. 'Rose, is it all right with you if I do some work here this afternoon? I'm doing some stuff for the boss and I need to access the system.'

Rose nodded. 'That's absolutely fine.'

'Great.' Rich ambled over towards Elaine's desk.

Buttercup said brightly, 'I'll leave you to it, I think. I'm going upstairs to sort out my shopping. See you all later!'

'Bye, Mrs R,' Rich said, barely looking up from where he was logging on to Elaine's computer.

Buttercup picked up her bag and coat, keeping the paper out of sight.

Rose, white-faced and her fingers visibly trembling, said nothing.

Chapter Twenty-Seven

Upstairs in the flat, Buttercup closed the door and leaned against it, still trembling. It had been close. Rich had almost seen them with the cabinet open and files on Elaine's desk. She hoped that Rose had found an opportunity to secure the padlock before he noticed it was open, but there was only a slim chance that he would spot that, surely.

She went through to the sitting room and sat down on the sofa, gazing out unseeing over the already darkening London skyline. Lights below were flashing and twinkling, as streams of traffic moved slowly below the streetlights and Christmas decorations. Buttercup was almost numb from everything she had felt in the last hour, confused by everything she had learned, and at such a pace.

I don't understand. Why does he need to do it?

All the subterfuge and lies and concealment; the spying and watching and pretending. Did Charles think he was some kind of spymaster, a master controller, keeping tabs on his underlings?

I don't understand him. I thought I did, but I don't.

She was torn between outrage, sadness and bewilderment, but most of all she felt as if she had taken a misstep and lost her balance, feeling the world move beneath her unexpectedly. She had regained her balance but everything had changed, though she didn't quite know what from, or what to.

Who is Charles?

She knew the answer to that: he was a successful businessman, a charming raconteur and energetic embracer of all life had to offer, a father and her husband. She had fallen in love with that Charles, and taken him at face value too.

'My mother brought us two boys up as best she could when my father did the dirty and ran out on her, leaving her penniless,' he'd told her. 'Then she married again, and we lived in France with the stepfather until I got sent away to boarding school here in England thanks to a bequest from my grandfather. My brother was always her favourite, she made no secret of that. She still finds it hard to tell me how well I've done, no matter how high I climb up the tree. But Robert, in his little place in Austria composing music no one has ever listened to and never will ... he's a triumph, naturally.' Charles had laughed and his blue eyes had sparkled over the top of his glass as he drank his wine.

She'd laughed too. Perhaps there was something in what he said that she had missed. *But what is he so frightened of?*

Someone could only control that much if they feared loss, surely. She thought of the young Charles, the one who had lost his father.

'Did you ever see your father again?' she'd asked, when it

had come up in some conversation. 'He left your mother when you were seven years old, and that was that?'

'Funny you should ask. Actually I decided to find him about ten years ago. I hired a private detective and had him tracked down. He didn't want to see me, but I insisted. We had a lunch together, at the best restaurant in Brussels, which was where he was living. I made sure he knew what I thought of him walking out on us, and what I'd achieved despite him – and that he'd never see a penny of it.' Charles had grinned. 'He was not well and rather poor, with wife number three sitting next to him hoping for a handout. That was my little revenge on him. Not noble, but there we are.'

Buttercup hadn't blamed him. She'd been utterly on his side. 'Good! I hope you told him what for!'

'He knew how I felt by the end of lunch, let's put it that way.'

Because outside Charles's circle, life isn't lovely any more.

Buttercup looked down and realised she was still holding the piece of paper she had taken from the office. She hadn't meant to walk away with anything from the file, but here it was. A letter. Turning it over, she saw that it was signed by Ingrid. It was addressed to Charles.

Looking at it, she felt at once she shouldn't read it. Then she almost laughed out loud.

'I shouldn't read it!' she exclaimed. 'I should respect Charles's privacy. As if he's respected any aspect of my privacy for the last two years! Ha!'

She began to read, slowly making out Ingrid's scrawling handwriting.

Dear Charles

I understand that you're hurt and angry and that you believe I have done you the worst wrong imaginable. In some ways, it's easy for you to believe that because sexual infidelity is, as everybody knows, a sin. But you are not blameless in this, though I know you want to think that you are. Why do you think I wanted to betray you in this way? Is it because I'm simply wicked, and must be punished? Do you think I succumbed to lustful desire for Joachim and acted on it without any thought for you and your feelings?

You must know in your heart that isn't the case.

For years I have tried to tell you how unhappy you were making me. I longed to work and you forbade it. You destroyed my friendships by not allowing my friends to visit. You alienated my family with your attitude to them, and eventually shut them out of our lives altogether. Worse than that is the way I was always, constantly spied on. Do you think I didn't know that all the staff were paid to report on me and what I did and who I saw? You controlled everything about my environment, from the money I spent to the food I ate. You chose my clothes, my jewellery, my shoes. You made every decision about the children without consulting me. You treated me not as a wife and a partner but as your possession, owned by you.

I have tried to tell you this, many times. I wanted the old Charles, the one I married. Loving and caring and

*full of fun. But you would not listen to me. You made
me feel isolated, unloved and desperate.*

*I didn't mean to fall in love with Joachim, but it
happened. He honestly, genuinely loves me, and he has
opened my eyes to what my life is like. There may not be
a future for the two of us – he's younger than me, less
battered and bruised – but his love has given me the
strength to do what I should have done years ago, and
get myself and the children out.*

*I know you will never forgive me for this, and that
you'll continue to obsess over my infidelity as though
it's all that matters, and ignore what I am saying in this
letter. You'll carry on trying to punish and control me,
and I will have to put up with that until the children are
grown and I can be truly free. Maybe Joachim will wait
for me, I don't know. But in the end, I did this for me,
for my survival. I hope one day you can understand.*

> *Yours*
> *Ingrid*

At the bottom, in Charles's handwriting, were two words
in hard capitals: *TREACHEROUS BITCH*.

Buttercup put down the letter, her eyes wide and every
nerve alert. Adrenaline flooded through her, making her heart
pound.

Oh my God.

Every word Ingrid had written – apart from her explanation of her infidelity – could have been written by her,
Buttercup.

Her hands were shaking and she stared into space, panicked and almost disbelieving. Why hadn't she seen it clearly before? Ingrid was right. Charles saw his wife – whether it be Ingrid or Buttercup – as a possession, not a person. Another of his precious acquisitions, to be kept locked away like the things in his Redmain museum. His anger over the broken plate was a faint echo of the rage he must have felt at another man winning his wife's love, taking her away, making love to her . . .

No wonder he watches me so closely too. Perhaps he's afraid that the same thing will happen again if he's not careful.

Buttercup shook her head in bewilderment and confusion.

But what am I going to do? I know the truth about Charles – what should I do?

One thought came into her mind, clear and utterly adamant:

This has to stop. Charles has to understand that he can't do this to me. It's the only way.

Buttercup left the next morning after a restless night of broken sleep and bad dreams. She wanted to be at home now, in her familiar place. This flat was too much Charles's territory. She called in to see Rose on the way out.

'Is everything okay?' she asked, glancing over at the filing cabinet, which was locked again. 'Did Rich notice the cabinet was open?'

Rose shook her head. 'No. I locked it again after he left. But I'm sorry, Mrs R, I'm not going to open it again.

I shouldn't have done it in the first place – I daren't get involved. Yesterday was such a close shave and I can't afford to lose my job.'

Buttercup nodded. 'I understand. Thank you for helping me.'

She had been going to ask Rose to open the filing cabinet again so she could replace the letter, but she would keep it for the time being. The chances of it being missed were surely slim to non-existent.

'Goodbye then, Rose,' she said, picking up her overnight bag. 'I'll see you soon. And don't worry, no one will know what you did for me. I promise.'

She barely saw the road on the drive home, her mind was so busy mulling over everything she had learned. Phrases from Ingrid's letter played in her head, each one chiming like an echo of her own experience.

She wondered about the affair with the jouster. It seemed so romantic, so crazily old-fashioned to fall in love with a dashing knight on a charger, but she could imagine the thrill of watching a man in full armour riding a stallion bedecked in scarlet and silver. There would have the ground-shaking thud of hooves as the horses galloped towards one another, the clash of wood and steel as the lances met or struck on a shield, the cheers and shouts of the crowd in support of one or other of the riders. It must have been incredibly exciting.

And, yes, romantic. No wonder Charles is obsessed with the whole thing. He loves heroes – like his beloved Captain Redmain – but he could never be like that himself. He isn't big or macho or strong. Ingrid certainly picked someone guaranteed to make him feel inadequate. Even so, I'm sure it's beyond him to understand how she could prefer a travelling jouster over all his money and luxury.

Now, she realised, when she thought of Charles, she could no longer see the exuberant, affectionate man she married; she was not quite sure yet what she saw instead.

And he's lied to me about so many things. What else might he be lying about?

As she came into the village and drove down the lane towards Charcombe Park, she had a strong impulse to stop and call in at Fitzroy House. In the light of what she had learned, she felt now as if she knew Ingrid, that they had a kinship, and that she was the only other person in the world who knew how Buttercup felt. She slowed the car, but the sight of the lights on in the house drained her courage, so she drove on through the gates and up the drive.

The view of Charcombe Park looming at the end of the drive filled her with a kind of dread. The house she had once loved seemed like a prison now. Once inside, she would be back in her gilded cage, waiting for her master to return. She had a strong urge to turn the car around and speed away while she still could.

But I can't. Where would I go? I can't throw my marriage away without trying to put it right. Perhaps if I talk to him, if I'm honest with him, we can find a way through this. I'll tell him about the clinic, tell him I know that he monitors me. I'll see if I can make him tell the truth about Ingrid too. If we can just be honest with each other, maybe we can still save this.

I'm not going to let this end without trying to save it. I owe him – and myself – that much.

Chapter Twenty-Eight

1952

There was no more talk of Xenia going back to school that summer. Mama's health seemed to improve along with the weather, and as it grew warmer, life seemed to get better. During the week, Mama rested or pottered in the garden, while Papa oversaw the decoration and went off to buy more antiques to fill the old house. At the weekends, there were the parties. Glamorous people arrived from London: stars of the films and theatre, writers, composers, artists, lords and ladies and society names. There would be a riotous two days, full of laughter and indulgent with food and drink. Mama, slender but stunning, was always the most beautiful, shimmering woman there, and it was hard not to look at her all the time when she was in the room. She smoked at the weekends, and drank her cocktails and wine at dinner.

'But,' Papa said confidentially to Xenia, 'we're keeping an eye on her, aren't we? We won't let her get sick again.'

The fun brought colour to her mother's face, and she seemed to thrive on the weekend social gatherings, staying up late to play games and dance, and oversee the hospitality that they lavished on their guests: huge breakfasts, elegant lunches, proper afternoon teas, and the long dinners that started with cocktails on the terrace and ended, sometimes, with champagne and skinny-dipping in the old pool in the early hours.

'I say, Natalie, good shot!'

Mama laughed, shielding her eyes from the sun to see where her ball had hit the court. 'It was a hopeless shot, Johnnie. Lucky, that's all!'

'Don't be silly, you're a natural.' Johnnie, handsome and elegantly sporty in his long tennis trousers and open-necked shirt, looked over to Xenia, who was sitting in the umpire's chair, supposedly keeping score but constantly forgetting. 'Isn't she, Xenia?'

'She's getting better,' Xenia said diplomatically, which made them laugh. Mama looked so spindly in her tennis dress, her legs pale and thin, and she moved with the awkwardness of someone unaccustomed to running about.

'I never was any good at tennis at school!' she called out.

'Then now's your time to learn,' Johnnie said. He held the ball up. 'Watch out, I'm going to serve.'

Xenia watched the ball looping slowly through the air. Johnnie was giving Mama an easy time of it, but then, everyone was. The theatre people and artists who came down all knew Mama had been ill and they treated her with a cheerful delicacy, simultaneously acting as though she were normal, and on the point of total collapse. Johnnie managed just the right tone; he had been in a play with Mama years before and stayed her friend ever since, close enough to tease her and be sure she knew he was joking. His wife was sitting on the terrace with a small group, drinking tea in the afternoon sunshine, while others were splashing about in the pool. The summer was past its best, the grass withered and cracked, the garden looking thirsty after a dry fortnight.

Mama whacked the ball and it sailed back and out of the court. 'Sorry!' she called, holding up her racquet. She sighed and rubbed her hand over her face. 'I think I'm about done with tennis for now, Johnnie.'

'Of course, darling,' he said, picking up the ball and pocketing it. 'Let's get some lemonade.'

'Lemonade!' Mama looked outraged. 'Champagne, you mean. Come on.' She beckoned Xenia and they began to walk off the court and up the small hill to the lawn where the house opened to the terrace. As they went up, Xenia saw Papa coming out of the house, holding a piece of paper. He saw them, and started towards them. 'Natalie!' he called.

'He's got news by the look of it,' Johnnie said. 'Telegram. Might be from the good old US of A.'

Mama prodded him. 'Don't be silly, I'm not that important any more, not after more than a year away.'

'You'll still red hot, darling.'

Papa had reached them, his expression grave. 'Natalie, Xenia. I've had some news. It's Grandmama. I'm sorry to say that she has died.' He looked at the telegram. 'Peacefully on the evening of the eleventh. They didn't rush to let me know, did they! My sisters are dreadful, they really are. No doubt they've been ransacking the jewellery boxes already.'

'Paul, I'm sorry,' Mama said, her eyes wide.

Johnnie murmured, 'Yes, sorry, old man. Always a loss, one's mother.'

Papa shrugged. 'It's no shock at her advanced age. But I appreciate your sympathy.'

'Poor Grandmama,' Xenia said in a small voice, a rush of sorrow coming over her.

'Go inside and get changed, Xenia,' Mama said, patting her shoulder. 'You look far too hot.'

'I shall have to go to Paris at once, there'll be things to sort out.' Papa hardly seemed to notice her. 'A funeral. The will and so on.'

'Don't worry about us, we'll be fine,' Mama said quickly.

'We'll go home right away, in the circumstances,' put in Johnnie.

'Don't do that!' Papa clapped him on the shoulder. 'Stay and have fun, look after Natalie for me. She was a killjoy in life, my mother, no need for her to be one in death as well.'

Papa was gone for a week and when he returned his mood was black, and not from grief for his mother.

'She left me almost nothing,' he declared when they were together again. 'It's insulting. To my older sisters, who married imbeciles and ratbags, she left money and jewels. To me, a few mouldy old pictures and some personal effects.'

'No money?' Mama said, smoking rapidly. Her bracelets jangled at her wrist with the constant movement.

Papa shrugged. 'A thousand pounds. Nothing. Her villa was rented. Her will said, "In view of the fact that my son has married a successful actress, he will require no further monetary support from me and thus shall receive tokens only."'

Xenia looked anxiously at Mama, who went instantly white.

'I see,' she said in a high voice, stubbing out her cigarette. An instant later, she reached for another from her silver case. 'So I've cost you your inheritance.'

'You know her ridiculous ideas about the acting profession. Bitter old bitch.' Papa reached into his pocket and brought out a sealed packet. 'By the way, Xenia, she left you this.' He passed it to her.

Xenia took it and opened it carefully, pulling the string from the red wax stamped with an eagle crest, and snapping the wax disc open so that she could pull apart the paper wrapping. A blue box came out. She opened it and lifted out the cloth bag inside. Within that was a velvet case. Inside that was the blue sapphire brooch with the ring of diamonds and the tear-drop pearl glowing beneath. She gasped. So Grandmama had remembered her promise. But the reality of it was more overwhelming than she'd imagined.

'What is it?' Mama asked, curious.

Xenia was speechless, she could only turn the box to show them the contents.

'That pretty trinket,' Papa said carelessly. 'Well, I'm glad she remembered you. You are her sole Arkadyoff grandchild. The one princess left. It's only right you should have it.'

She stared at the jewel that glittered in the lamplight. *It's an empress's jewel. I can never be worthy of it.*

*

In the autumn, the London house was sold and Xenia did not go back to school there but stayed at Charcombe and went to a small school on the other side of Gorston where there were only eleven pupils, all girls of differing ages, taught by two elderly sisters and a retired clergyman. Mama went away to make a film, her first since she'd come home from America, but only to studios outside London – close compared with filming in America. At Christmas, they were reunited at home for the celebration, with a twenty-foot tree in the hall, extravagant gifts, and ever-flowing hospitality. But there were ominous signs in Mama's behaviour. In the run-up to Christmas she was either hectic, racing around to ensure everything was exactly as it should be, awake till all hours to complete it all, or in such low spirits that she could only lie in bed with the curtains closed, miserable and unable to move.

Papa sent for a doctor from London, who said she must drink less and sleep more. That would cure both the feverish activity and the depression.

Mama laughed when they told her. 'I can't sleep unless I drink! That's the whole key to it. If I don't knock myself out with martinis, I'll be awake all night.'

So Papa sent away for more of the pills Mama took when she couldn't sleep, and more of the pills she took when she couldn't get out of bed. She began to lose weight and gain that glittering, hollow look she'd had before. It was impossible to stop her though.

'I'm having fun, Paul, isn't that what you want?' she'd ask gaily as she reached for another cigarette. 'It's Christmas, we must have fun!'

'Balance, and moderation, Natalie!' Papa cautioned.

'Pah to that!' Mama laughed. 'What's the point when we don't have a clue what will happen tomorrow? Come on, let's get Johnnie and the gang down for New Year.'

Papa agreed because he thought Johnnie and his wife were good for Mama, but even they couldn't restrain her. Over the New Year, Mama didn't go to bed for two days, and nothing Johnnie or Pearl said could calm her down.

It was a relief when it was dull, boring, cold January again and the parties were over. Mama seemed to settle down a little. Xenia worried that she was almost too calm now, and this was the first sign that she was starting a downward swoop into the other phase of her nervous condition: an utter lack of energy as a deep blanket of misery settled on her.

She watched her mother carefully as they walked in the garden one icy morning, watching for the deadness in her eyes that signalled the onset of sadness. 'I'm glad it's just us at home now,' she said, pulling her coat closer around her. 'It's great fun to have parties, but I like it when it's peaceful too.'

Mama was wearing her fur coat against the cold, the collar turned up to keep out the chill. 'You said home!' she exclaimed, looking at Xenia over the furry top. 'You called this place home. Is that what you think of it?'

'Of course. This is our home, isn't it? We don't even have our London house any more.'

'That's wonderful.' Mama smiled. 'That's what I want for all of us. A home where we can be happy. I want it for Papa, because he wants it so badly.' Her mood seemed to change in an instant and she sighed. 'I'll miss it when I go.'

'Go? Go where?'

'Papa wants me to make another film, a big one this time. I still owe the studio that made *Delilah*, you see. They say I must go back to America.'

Xenia felt afraid at once. 'You're not well enough, Mama, you need to stay here for a while longer.'

'I must go. We don't have the money we need, and Grandmama left us nothing. So I have to earn it. If I don't, who will?' She gestured towards the house. 'You're not a baby any more, Xenia. You must know that all of this costs a fortune to run.'

'But you shouldn't go if you're ill!' Xenia protested. 'Papa is wrong to make you.'

Her mother turned on her suddenly, her eyes flashing. 'And you know best, do you? Better than Papa? How dare you talk to me like that, how *dare* you? He is the most wonderful and most caring husband in the world, he would never hurt me, and yet you accuse him of wanting me to suffer! *You* are the one who wants me to suffer, you're the real little beast around here, taking everything and ungrateful with it! Get out of my sight, you horror!'

Xenia gasped, shocked that Mama would speak to her in such a way.

'You heard me, get out of my bloody sight!'

She turned and ran all the way back to the house, up the stairs and into her room, where she collapsed sobbing on her bed. Much later, when she had recovered herself and her red eyes were not so swollen, she crept back downstairs. Mama was in the drawing room, reading while a cigarette burned in the ashtray beside her. She looked up as Xenia came in, and smiled.

'Hello, my darling, how are you?'

Xenia went up to her, penitent. 'I'm sorry about before, Mama,' she whispered. 'I didn't mean to criticise Papa.'

Mama smiled again, bewildered. 'My dear girl, I don't know what you're talking about.'

'On our walk – you were so angry . . . you shouted . . .'

She shook her head. 'No . . . no. I don't think so. Did I? No. I simply don't remember, my darling.' She picked up her cigarette and took a long drag on it. 'Be an angel and make me a drink, will you? I'm quite parched.'

The sudden furies appeared more often after that: they came without warning, were over rapidly, and often immediately forgotten. When the film in America was confirmed and a date set for her departure, Mama did her best to rally. She stopped drinking and smoking, she ate the diet recommended by her doctor, took her pills, and went to bed early every night. During the day, she wanted to spend as much time with Xenia as she could, doing jigsaw puzzles in the library, playing Chinese chequers or doing hands of patience together. It seemed to keep her on an even keel.

'You are her medicine,' Papa confided as he and Xenia sat together after dinner in the drawing room. He was smoking a cigar and cradling a large glass of whisky. 'You can work miracles, dear Xenia. She responds to you.'

'She adores you, though, Papa.'

'Yes. But I can't seem to break through when she falls into one of her states. You weren't here when she had her last attack of nerves. She turned on me like a wild cat, talking to me in a way I've never heard from her before, swearing and using such awful language. It was most distressing. And then afterwards, down she swoops, knowing she's done something awful but barely able to remember it. When I tell her, she hates herself for talking to me like that.' Papa sighed. 'And she will not see the doctor any more. She absolutely refuses. That's why you must go with her to America and help her to make this film.'

Xenia stared at him, stunned.

'Don't look at me like that, child,' he said testily. 'I thought you hated school.'

'Not so much any more – and don't I need an education?'

'You seem perfectly well educated to me.' He leaned towards her, his blue eyes intense. 'Don't you see, if Mama can't work, all of this' – he waved his cigar around the room – 'will go. She must complete another film. You understand that, don't you?'

'I suppose so.'

'It will only be a few months. You can go back to school when you're home again.'

'Won't you come to America too, Papa?'

'I believe that at the moment, I do more harm than good. I wish it weren't so, but it is. So you must go in my place.'

'I see.' She bit her lip, quailing at the thought of supporting Mama all on her own through the strain of making a film when it had taken all of Papa's strength to get Mama through *Delilah*.

'Good girl. I'm proud of you. Now run along and go to bed.'

As the time for departure grew closer, Mama seemed to improve and show signs that her energy was returning and that there would be a period of calm and normality.

As she and Mama left Plymouth on the *Ile de France*, bound for America, Xenia hoped that this time, the normality had returned for good. She left the empress's jewel hidden in her bedroom in its velvet box.

Chapter Twenty-Nine
1953

Far away from Papa, Mama seemed balanced and in control as the preliminaries for the new film began. This time there were other stars of equal stature: a newly arrived young beauty of pneumatic sexuality with china-blue eyes and platinum blond hair, and a moody actor who took his art extremely seriously and had little truck with the princess and her English manners.

Xenia accompanied Mama wherever she went, a secretary and assistant as well as a daughter, staying attentive to her mother's moods. As rehearsals began, she was proud of the way Mama composed herself, full of dignity and prepared to work with all her might to do the best she could with the role, putting in long hours studying her lines and practising the mannerisms of her character. She was soon obsessed with thoughts of the woman she played: Rhonda was a cool sophisticate floored by passion for a younger man despite the fact that they were both married.

Mama and Xenia sat for hours in the trailer, talking to the make-up and costume designers about the kind of woman her character was, how she would dress and look. With the props manager, Mama discussed what might be in Rhonda's house, on her bedside table, in her handbag.

'It's so important that everything is right, if I'm going to inhabit my character,' Mama said.

With Xenia, she discussed the character herself, and what made her behave the way she did. 'It's vital to explore the nature of her love for Anderson,' Mama said, and began to talk to Xenia as if she were not a sixteen-year-old girl, with no experience yet of the world and of men and passion, but a mature woman who could analyse the forces that drove people into each other's arms, no matter what the conse-quences.

'Love makes you feel so alive,' Mama said, a cigarette held between her fingers. She was in a bathrobe with cold cream all over her face, but she was still exquisite and the dreamy look in her eyes made her even more extraordinary. 'That's why it's impossible to resist. When you have to make the choice between feeling as though you don't know what your purpose is, and the utter, heady magnificence of someone else knowing you, desiring you, bringing you to life in every nerve of your body—'

'Doesn't she feel that for her husband?' Xenia asked tim-idly. 'She must have, if she married him.'

'Once she did, I expect, or perhaps something she thought was love – it's easy to mix it up with admiration and attrac-tion when you don't know any different. Not all married couples are as lucky as Papa and me, still like lovers in the first flush of romance. Most people find that their love turns stale over time. They don't please each other the way they used to. Rhonda feels as though her husband doesn't see her any more. Then she meets Anderson, and he sparks that passion in her.'

'But how, how does it happen?'

Mama smiled, her eyes knowing. 'Oh darling, that's the mystery. You meet hundreds of people, and then one day there's someone who makes you feel quite different. They draw you to them and, if you're lucky, they are drawn to you. Soon you only feel your true self with that person, and they bring you such joy that you need them like a drug. That's love, darling.'

'And that's how you feel for Papa,' Xenia breathed. How extraordinary that people met other people they could love all the time. How else could there be so many married couples?

'Yes. And that's how you'll feel one day. It will be the greatest adventure of your life.' Mama leaned back, closed her eyes, and took a long drag on her cigarette.

Rehearsals were over, the sets were built on the enormous sound stage, and filming began. Xenia, sitting in the shadows, was fascinated by this film in a way that she had not been with *Delilah*.

Perhaps I was too young to understand it. But I'm older this time . . .

The actor who played Anderson was impossibly handsome, with brooding dark eyes and a mop of black hair that was long at the front and heavy with hair cream, unlike the other men on and off the set. His mouth, full-lipped and expressive, was often sulky yet full of a promise that made her stomach tingle pleasantly when she looked at him. Soon he was all she thought of. At night, she constructed elaborate fantasies where the beautiful blonde who played his wife had an accident and she, Xenia, was asked to take on the role, and Anderson would kiss her on the set only to find that he loved her for real. And then something . . . something extraordinary would happen.

Making love would happen, Xenia told herself with a thrill, though she wasn't exactly sure what would take place beyond the stories she had heard at school, some of which were frankly unbelievable.

Her infatuation with Anderson meant that for a while she was blind to the signs of Mama's growing nervousness. Her mother wanted to stay at the set until late, working on her lines and blocking her every move, learning her marks and thinking about the kind of gestures Rhonda might make. At home, her light was on into the early hours but she was up with the sun, eager to be back on set. Then she began to be morbid. The blonde actress who played Anderson's wife started to play on her mind. Sometimes she was envious, pacing around her dressing room, her eyes intense.

'She's at the start of everything, it's such a delicious place to be! She's so young and so pretty. She's an unwritten page, all of it lies ahead of her.'

'But you're a proper star, Mama,' Xenia protested. 'And she doesn't have your elegance and style.'

'Maybe. But she's got sex appeal.'

'She's nothing *but* sex appeal,' Xenia countered stoutly.

Mama laughed. 'You're right. She's just a repository for fantasy. How wise you are, little Xenia. I'm an actress, a real actress, and I mustn't forget it.'

But the envy began to turn to something dark and morbid. Soon, Mama talked incessantly of the baby-faced blonde and her remarks grew vicious, her language filthy. 'She's a tramp who's slept her way up the career ladder,' she would spit, putting on her lipstick with a shaking hand. 'She's trying to seduce Sly and everyone else too. She wants to see me put in the shade because she thinks I'm past it. She's sex mad, and stupid with it.'

Xenia hated it when Mama became coarse like this, and had no idea how to respond. What good would explaining do, in any case? The blonde did flirt with everyone but in a kind of desperate way, as though it was the only method she had to make people like her. And she did concentrate on the men, but then, the set was full of men. Her real mistake was to treat Natalie like some kind of wise old mother figure who might give her the approval she seemed to crave. Natalie wanted no part of that relationship. Soon she was obsessed with the idea that there was something brewing between the girl and the actor who played Anderson, and that seemed to send her into a jealous fury, as though the feelings her character had for him had possessed her for real.

At home in the evenings, in the house they'd rented on South Crescent Drive, Mama drank her favourite martinis and raved about the vileness of what was going on between the young actors, or stared into space and spoke of Papa and her fears that he would stop loving her. Perhaps he was with someone else while she was far away in America, making this bloody awful film. He'd leave her for someone younger and more attractive, and her life would be over.

Xenia was helpless before her mother's fears. No matter how often she told her that she was beautiful, desirable and successful, the woman of Papa's dreams, whom he would love forever, Mama became convinced that her looks were fading and that he would leave her.

The filming proceeded quickly. Sly Manikee, the director, liked to work chronologically and that was possible in this drawing room drama, set inside. As the passion and intrigue between the characters grew more extreme, so Mama's spirits seemed to intensify until she lived in a state of nervous tension, calming herself with drink and pills that Xenia thought, in reality, only made things worse. At night she paced the floors of the house, muttering and trying to place phone calls to England to reach Papa and demand that he tell her who he was sleeping with, but she always lost patience and hung up before they connected her.

Xenia couldn't sleep either. She haunted her mother like a little ghost, growing pale and wan herself through lack of sleep and fretting about what might happen. She wrote letters to Papa begging him to come and calm Mama down, but he wrote back that she was doing a fine job and that it wasn't worth his coming when filming was almost over.

'Hey, little lady,' said a drawling voice behind her as she loitered on set one day. 'How are you?'

Xenia turned and found herself face to face with her dream. He was smiling at her with his charming lopsided grin, his brown eyes warm, one lock of dark hair falling forward over his face. Her stomach plummeted and turned in a sickening and yet pleasant tumble. 'Oh,' she stammered. 'I'm . . . fine, thank you.'

'You don't look so good. Are you sure you're okay? You're awfully pale.' He put out a hand and rested it lightly on her arm. It seemed to burn where he touched her. 'I know you have quite a job looking after your mother. She's on the flip side of sane, isn't she? You're too young to have that kind of responsibility, I'd say. Where's your dad?'

'Papa is at home in England,' she said, her voice sounding high and prim next to his drawling American accent.

'Papa's home in England, huh?' He mimicked her clipped tone. 'Well, well. Then he ought to get over here, I think. Before your mother loses it completely.'

Xenia was torn by the desire to talk, to tell him everything – all her hopes and dreams and worries – and by her loyalty to Mama. 'I think she'll be all right,' she said lamely.

He shook his head. 'It still shouldn't be your responsibility. I said as much to Sly, but he won't listen. Well, whatever happens, it won't be your fault. Remember that, okay?'

She nodded as he turned and sauntered off, leaving her longing more than ever.

'I saw you!' Mama turned on her, green eyes flashing with rage, fists clenched. She was in costume for the next scene, a nightdress and slippers, which seemed all the more incongruous, paired with her towering fury. 'You're like that blonde slut! You were trying to seduce him, weren't you? Trying to prove that you've got what I haven't! Little tart! I thought I'd brought you up better than this.'

Xenia stared at her, aghast. She knew what her mother was talking about, but she was horribly mistaken. Except . . . she did love Anderson and long for him to kiss her and hold her and . . . A hot blush exploded across her cheeks.

'Guilt is written all over you,' spat Mama. 'You're cheap! You're cruel and cheap. How could you do it to me?' Tears sprang into her eyes and she moaned pitifully. 'Why do you want to punish me? My own daughter! How could you?'

'But I don't want to punish you—'

The tears vanished, the snarl was back, Mama's beautiful face contorted with the horrible emotions possessing her. 'You think I'm finished, do you? Washed up? Dried-up old hag? Is that it? Well, just you watch me.' She marched out of the trailer, Xenia racing behind her, frantic, desperate to stop her, knowing it was her responsibility to hide Mama's state from everyone else.

'Come back, *please*, what are you going to do—?'

Her mother strode out onto the set. As usual, it was full of people as another shot was set up. Electricians, carpenters, sound engineers, grips and dolly operators, swarming over the scaffold that surrounded the set, all over the cameras, up in the lighting rig, everywhere.

'No, Mama!' cried Xenia desperately, but it was no good. The actor and the blonde looked up startled from the scene they were running through as, in full view of everyone on set,

Mama stormed up to the girl, raised her hand and slapped her hard across the face. While the girl was still gasping with shock and pain, she pulled the actor close, sunk her fingers into his hair and put her lips on his, pressing hard in a kiss, her tongue coming out to probe his closed mouth. It all happened so fast, but an instant later, the actor was pushing Mama away, his expression disgusted; the girl was sobbing hysterically, pointing at Mama; people were rushing onto the set to pull Mama away, while she screamed abuse and resisted their efforts to remove her.

'Let go of me, you fuckers!' she yelled as they wrestled her back to her dressing room.

'For Christ's sake,' yelled Sly Manikee, 'get that fucking maniac off my set!'

Xenia burst into tears and ran to the ladies' room to weep, ashamed of the awful stranger her mother had become.

Chapter Thirty

Here I am. Home.

Buttercup had parked the car on the gravel at the front, instead of her usual place near the back door in the yard. Visitors and Charles usually parked here. She went in at the front door, where the security cameras recorded all arrivals and a moment later, as she put down her bags and took off her coat, Carol came into the hall from the back, wiping her hands on a towel.

'Hello there!' she said brightly. 'How was London?'

'Very nice, thank you.' Buttercup found she could hardly look at Carol, knowing what she did about her. She could imagine Carol going back to the kitchen right now, taking out her tablet and making some notes: Mrs R seemed a bit downcast when she got back, and much less friendly than usual.

'I was just about to head off home actually,' Carol said, not seeming to notice Buttercup's detachment. 'I've got the rest of the day off. There's soup on the stove, and a casserole to go into the oven for later.'

'Thanks.' She managed a smile, relieved that Carol would be going. 'You think of everything. Enjoy your day off.'

'I will.'

Buttercup took her bag upstairs and checked her emails. There was one from Charles – a few brief lines asking how she was – and one from Rose filling her in on his return from Shanghai in three days' time. So she had three days to work it all out and plan what she was going to say to Charles. It would need careful thought if she was going to strike the right note. She sent back a breezy reply saying she was looking forward to seeing him.

Going downstairs, she found her attention caught by the flash of a red dot: one of the security cameras aimed at the stairs had come on, alerted by her movement. A sick feeling washed over her: she was watched and monitored, she knew that, but the cold, hard evidence of it was still horrible.

On impulse she went to the electrics cupboard in the back corridor and opened it to see a complicated-looking control box, but the labels under various switches helped. She found the one labelled 'CCTV system' and flicked it off. Immediately she felt much better. Then she noticed the wireless router that controlled the internet access to the house and after a moment, pressed it to off. The light went out. The house was offline.

Buttercup giggled. She had just thrown a blanket of invisibility over the house by cutting its connections to the outside world. Better than that, she had freed herself from all constraints. Carol was gone, the cleaners were not here, the cameras were off. There was only Tippi about, dozing in the kitchen by the Aga most likely.

Buttercup went to her bag and took out her wireless ear pods, linked them to her phone and set an energetic playlist going loudly. Bouncy, upbeat pop exploded in her ears. 'Silent disco!' she shouted at the top of her voice, and kicked off her ballet slippers so that she was wearing only her fine cotton socks underneath. 'Let's *dance*!'

Sliding and jumping over the slippery marble floor of the hall, she danced with all her might, singing along to the track, not caring what she might sound like to anyone listening. She wriggled and bopped, leaping about and grooving hard, using the whole great room as her personal dance space, feeling the energy flowing through her as she threw her whole body into movement, her blood racing as she danced.

As the song finished, she was panting and bright-eyed, elated by the rush of endorphins in her blood, feeling better than she had for weeks or even months. Tippi was standing at the corner of the room, her tail wagging, watching her curiously.

Buttercup turned down the music and pulled out one of the earbuds. 'Sorry, Tips, do you think I'm completely mad? I'm not, I'm just so happy to be properly alone for the first time in so very long.'

Just then, a great thud reverberated around the room. Buttercup gasped loudly, jumping with shock, before she realised it must be the brass knocker on the front door, so rarely used that its sound was completely unfamiliar.

'Oh, fantastic.' She rolled her eyes at Tippi. 'Who could that be? Surely not the postman!'

She slid over on her cotton socks and turned the great brass doorknob, pulling the huge door open as she did. Standing in front of her was a tall man, solidly built in a dark coat, jeans and heavy lace-up boots, thick coppery russet hair and warm brown eyes. He took Buttercup in, her single earbud, the phone sticking out of her pocket, her socks, jeans and sloppy sweat top, her hair pulled back into a messy ponytail and the flush in her cheeks. 'Hello,' he said uncertainly. 'I'm looking for Mr or Mrs Redmain – they're the owners, aren't they?'

'They are. I'm Mrs Redmain. How can I help you?'

Embarrassment dropped over his face. 'Ah – I see. I'm awfully sorry, I didn't . . . you look so . . . Sorry.'

Buttercup held up a hand. 'It's fine, honestly. But it's jolly cold here with the door open. Perhaps you should come in.'

'Thanks.' The man stepped into the hall, looking about curiously as he did, a look of bemused awe on his face. 'Wow, this place has changed.'

'You know it?'

'Yes, I do.' He turned to smile at her, showing even white teeth, his eyes full of easy charm. 'I used to live here.'

'Really?' Buttercup frowned, pulling out her other earbud and putting them in her pocket. 'I thought that before Charles, the house belonged to the princess for years.'

'That's right. Xenia Arkadyoff. We lived here when she owned it.' He was gazing around, his eyes moving around the room, taking it all in. 'What a transformation. Those ceiling paintings look incredible now they've been restored.'

'Sorry – your name is?'

He remembered himself with a start. 'Excuse my rudeness, I'm a bit overwhelmed being here after so many years. I'm Gawain Ashley. Sorry to turn up out of the blue like this, I tried to arrange something with Mr Redmain's office but couldn't get very far with them.'

Buttercup nodded. She could imagine that there were many levels of protection in place before a stranger could reach Charles. 'My husband's away right now, I'm afraid.'

He looked beseechingly at Buttercup. 'Would you mind terribly if I took a look around? For old times' sake?'

She stared at him for a moment. *He seems genuine, not much like a murderer.* She smiled. 'Sure. Why not? Would you like a coffee or something?'

'Yes, please,' he said, grinning back. 'That sounds great.'

She led him through to the kitchen where he was even more overcome with astonishment.

'This is amazing,' he said, as she put the kettle on to boil. 'You would simply not believe what this room used to look like. I wish I'd brought my old photos now so I could show you. When we lived here, this was pretty much unchanged from the nineteen twenties. I remember the range in that fireplace where you've got the Aga – an old cast-iron thing. An old butler's sink, not a picturesque one at all. A copper to boil hot water, cracked black and white tiles, and a huge old table in the middle of the room. And the whole place was cold and draughty.' He turned to Buttercup, smiling. 'It's so different.'

'But how did you come to be living here?' Buttercup asked, spooning coffee into the jug.

'She rented out the house and outbuildings to my parents. My dad died recently. He was a furniture maker and carver, and he believed passionately about passing on the old skills before they died out. So did my mother – she was a painter of miniatures. They had a dream to create a kind of artists' commune here, with all the room they needed for creating things. Charcombe seemed absolutely perfect and it was so decrepit that it was cheap.'

'So the princess lived here with you?'

'That's right. She obviously needed money badly, the place was in an awful state and she lived here more or less alone, looking after her mother who was pretty old and sick by then.'

'You mean Natalie Rowe.' Buttercup thought back to the shimmering screen presence, the flawless face and graceful figure. 'What was she like?'

'I was just a boy – this was back in the late eighties – and I was pretty frightened of her, if I'm honest. She wandered about, crazy white hair, dreamy, sometimes crying and wailing, sometimes happy and singing, always looking for someone called Paul.' Gawain laughed sheepishly. 'I thought she was completely cracked, of course, but I was only about seven. Golden Age movie stars meant nothing to me, and she certainly didn't look like one in any case. My parents showed me her portrait but I didn't think it was really her.'

'We've got that portrait.'

'Have you?' Gawain looked interested. 'I'd love to see it again.'

'Let's take our coffee through and I'll show it you.'

They took their mugs into the drawing room and Buttercup led him to the portrait over the fireplace. He stared at it, shaking his head.

'That's the one. Wow. Now I can appreciate who she was.'

They both stared for a while at Natalie's portrait, thinking of her chin held high, her eyes haughty, her arrogance and beauty.

'How long did you live here?' Buttercup asked.

'About four years. Then my mother developed arthritis and couldn't work any more. My father started caring for her, and the collective came to an end. We moved to the seaside after that. Not long after we left, my mother was diagnosed with motor neurone disease and she died a few years later.'

'I'm sorry to hear that,' Buttercup said sympathetically. 'And about your father too.'

'Thanks.' Gawain smiled at her. 'It was going through all his stuff that made me think of this place. I suddenly thought that there might be a book or something in this old house – the work my parents did here, the life of Natalie Rowe. I thought I might be able to do a kind of double biography of them and the overlap here at Charcombe.'

'You're a writer?'

'Journalist. I write features, some TV criticism, an occasional column. But I'm always looking for that book project that means I can retire from the freelance rat race and get my head down for a year or so.'

'That's impressive.'

'You're very nice to say so, but I wish it were.'

A thought occurred to Buttercup. 'If you're interested in the house, then you should see the Redmain Room.'

Gawain looked quizzical. 'The what?'

'Come on. I'll show you.'

She led him upstairs to the first floor and led him into the tiny museum, telling as they went some of what Charles had told her about Captain Redmain and his exploits.

'I had no idea about this.' Gawain went to the first display cabinet and studied the contents. 'Captain Edward Redmain, captain of HMS *Cymbeline*. This is great. I mean, he's not exactly famous but everyone loves the story of Trafalgar.' He looked over at Buttercup, his eyes bright. 'This could be another angle on the story I'm thinking of. It could be a triple biography.'

'Or the story of the house,' Buttercup suggested, 'and the extraordinary people who've lived here.'

'Yes.' Gawain nodded, looking back at the bust of Captain Redmain. 'Great idea. It brings it full circle that it's now in Redmain hands again as well. Maybe that means a change in fortune for the old place. Perhaps it's happy again.'

'What do you mean?' Buttercup asked, puzzled.

'Nothing . . .' He frowned thoughtfully. 'Just that – well, the sad story of Natalie, and Xenia, and my parents' project failing and Mum getting ill . . . it's all a bit grim, isn't it?'

'Do you mean there's something wrong with the house?' Buttercup asked, alarmed.

'Oh, don't listen to me. I've got a vivid imagination. They're all old stories, they don't matter now. Listen, I've booked a room at the pub tonight and I might stick around a bit longer to do some research. Would you mind me coming back sometime?'

'Of course not. You should probably talk to the princess as well, I'm sure she'd love to see you.'

'Xenia? She's still alive?'

'Yes, she lives in Hooke House, just near the gates. She's getting on and a bit eccentric, she sometimes shouts at the locals, but she seems okay.'

Gawain looked astonished. 'I assumed she'd be dead by now. I never even looked her up. I'll definitely call in and see her.' He laughed suddenly, throwing back his head. 'She really *was* frightening. What a temper! She was cross with everything and everyone, angry at the world, I think. I avoided her. I'd run away, go off to play. My parents were kind to her, though. Later, she softened up completely. Once Harry came.'

'Harry?'

'Oh, just someone who used to live here when we did. Can I take your email or something? Then we can keep in contact.'

'Yes, sure.' She gave him her address, reminding herself that she should switch the router back on.

'Thanks for the tour,' he said, putting his phone away once he'd loaded her details. 'I enjoyed it a lot.'

'You're welcome. I hope they're treating you well at the pub.'

'Spoiling me rotten!' he said with a smile. 'Just the way I like it. Thanks again. I'll be in touch.'

Chapter Thirty-One

When Carol came in the next morning, Buttercup was already up and dressed, and had finished her breakfast. Now that she knew what was going on, she wanted to have as little to do with her as possible.

'You're up and about early,' Carol said cheerfully, going over to the dishwasher.

'I'm going out for a walk with Tippi. I might be a while.'

'Any preferences for dinner?'

'No. Whatever.'

Carol frowned, pushing back her light brown hair behind her ears as she bent down to pull out the dishwasher shelf. 'Is everything all right, love?'

'Yes, fine, thanks,' Buttercup said coolly.

'You seem a bit . . . not yourself.'

'Oh? You know me so well, after all.' Buttercup smiled sweetly. 'I can't imagine what it would be like here without you.'

Carol's expression grew concerned. 'Have I done something to upset you?'

'No. Everything's just the same as ever,' Buttercup said, forcing herself to sound normal and fighting the impulse to tell Carol exactly what she knew. Something told her to keep her cards close to her chest for now. Anything she said would go straight back. It was hard to hide her feelings, though, which was why it was best to avoid Carol if she could.

'All right,' Carol said slowly. She started bustling about in the kitchen, unloading the dishwasher. 'Oh, I got a message from Mission Control last night asking if everything was all right with the internet service here. Apparently the house went offline for a bit.'

'Oh yes, it went a bit funny, so I turned it off and rebooted it.' Buttercup put down her coffee mug. 'It seems fine now.'

'Good. I'll see you later then. Will you be back for lunch?'

'For God's sake, Carol, I don't know. I can look after myself, okay? Just leave me alone.' And she marched out of the kitchen.

So much for staying completely normal.

She turned and looked back at Charcombe Park, golden and beautiful against the winter sky, smoke trailing up from one of the chimneys. The old house looked inscrutable, her windows reflecting the pale sunshine. Buttercup thought of Gawain Ashley and his life at the house.

We're all just borrowing our time here. We move in, live our story, and move on. The house stays, changing with the owners but always here.

She turned back and strode on down the driveway, glad to be away from it and free. Tippi strained at the lead that

Buttercup clipped on her just before they went through the gates and out onto the lane.

'Come on, girl, you have to be on the lead here. Won't be for too long.'

A gust of wind buffeted her for a moment, freezing her cheeks and biting her fingers, and Buttercup shivered as they went along the muddy lane, past Fitzroy House. She couldn't help looking at it as she passed, but no lights were on and there was no car in the driveway. Ingrid must be out.

The strangeness of the proximity of her husband's ex-wife hit her anew. But where she'd once resented Ingrid's insistence on staying so close, she now saw that the other woman had not had a choice.

All along it was Charles who made her do it. And he's still controlling her. She remembered the lawyer's letter, demanding the return of photograph albums and property. *Where could they be? I've never seen anything like that.*

More secrets. More things hidden away, out of sight, so they wouldn't cause any problems.

Not for much longer. I'm going to bring it all out into the open.

The pub had just opened when she reached it, but she went around the back, ringing the intercom that connected to the upstairs flat.

'Hello?' It was Cathy's voice, fuzzy over the wires.

'It's Buttercup.'

'Come up!' The buzzer went and Buttercup pushed the door open. Inside, she hooked Tippi's lead to the stairs, gave her some treats and said, 'Wait here, Tippi, I won't be long.' The dog obediently curled up at the bottom of the stairs to gnaw her treat while Buttercup went quickly up to where the door to the Tranter flat stood ajar. She pushed it further open and went inside. Cathy came out of the sitting room, holding a white blanketed bundle that she was jogging gently.

'Hi!' she said, in a half whisper. 'Lovely to see you! I'm just getting this one off to sleep after her morning feed.'

'Oh!' Buttercup cooed quietly. 'Let me have a look? Oh, she's gorgeous, look at that face! She's almost asleep already.'

'I'm going to put her down and I'll be right with you.'

'You bet.' Buttercup went into the sitting room, messy with toys and newborn equipment – a baby gym, blankets, a feeding cushion and muslins. When Cathy joined her, she said admiringly, 'You've got her well trained! Down for a nap, just like that?'

Cathy sat down and grinned. 'I'm still on babymoon. She's still really sleepy. She'll perk up soon and then it will be a different story, so I'm just enjoying it right now.'

'I was hoping for a cuddle . . .'

'You'll get one, don't worry – she'll be awake in about twenty minutes.'

'Good, can't wait. Now . . .' Buttercup produced the bag she'd brought with her. 'Present!'

'You shouldn't have!' Cathy exclaimed with delight as she brought out the beautiful baby girl dresses Buttercup had bought in London. 'These are gorgeous, thank you! I have to admit, I'm loving the girl stuff, it's so much prettier than boys' clothes.'

They talked about the birth and new babyhood over cups of instant coffee, and how Cathy was coping with two and a pub to run. 'Good pub staff,' she said simply. 'And Wilf's brilliant and my mum is staying – she's out with Olly at playgroup. So I'm fine. Loving it actually, because Bethany's so easy.' She fixed Buttercup with an inquisitive look. 'How are you? You seem a bit down.'

'Well . . .' Buttercup knew there was a limit to what she could say but Cathy was so friendly, so easy to talk to. 'Just a bit of . . . Charles and I are having a difficult time, that's all.'

'I'm sorry to hear that.' Cathy looked sympathetic. 'If it's any consolation, we all have our rocky roads, you know. Every marriage is difficult, don't believe the people who look like they're having a marvellous time, they're just really good at hiding the trauma, or they're having a purple patch. I've wanted to leave Wilf at least half a dozen times but never enough to do it, and things always get better with a bit of talking and some give and take. It sounds like a cliché but it works. You two make such a fabulous couple. Honestly, talk to him and see what happens. Have you tried that?'

'Not really,' Buttercup admitted.

'There you are then. Try it, before you give up on it.'

'You're right, I will.'

Cathy smiled, then cocked her head. 'Hello – I think madam is awake. Looks like you're going to get that cuddle.'

Buttercup unhooked Tippi's lead from the stairs, deciding to go out through the pub and take a look at what had changed since she was last there. As she walked through with Tippi, admiring the results of the makeover, she saw Gawain Ashley sitting at one of the tables, a black coffee and a plate covered in croissant crumbs in front of him, reading a book about the Battle of Trafalgar. Just as she looked over at him, he glanced up and saw her. A smile broke over his face and he waved at her.

'Hello! What are you doing here?'

Buttercup went over, Tippi pressing close to her. 'I was just visiting the landlady. They've got a new baby.'

'I know, I heard all about the birth last night when I was at the bar, being served by the landlord.' He made a face of comical bewilderment. 'I mean, I like babies and everything, but I haven't got one yet and I don't know if I'm quite ready to hear about the more gruesome aspects of the whole process. I like to think about the bit that involves dinner, moonlight, sweet romance . . . that bit.'

Buttercup laughed.

His brown eyes twinkled at her. 'Why don't you sit down and have a coffee with me?'

'Well . . .'

'Come on, sit down.'

'Okay then. Just for a minute.' She slid into one of the chairs while he went off to order the drinks. He came back with two cups and put a cappuccino down in front of her. Buttercup had picked up his book and was reading it.

'Interesting reading?' he asked, sitting down. 'I've never been that interested in it myself, but since we talked, I've decided to find out more about that period, Trafalgar, and the people involved. It could provide some interesting background for the biography idea. I'm off to Portsmouth tomorrow, actually, to do some more research.'

'And have you seen the princess yet?'

'Not yet. I plan to go there today. I'm looking forward to it, though I'm a bit apprehensive about my welcome.' He smiled at her again. 'I appreciated that you let me in yesterday, and showed me round. It was kind of you.'

'I enjoyed it.' She smiled back at him, noticing the golden glints in his dark copper hair where the light hit it from the window. He had such an open, friendly face, and she was drawn to the warmth in his eyes. There was a candour in them that appealed to her.

'I think I'll come back here after I've been to Portsmouth and have a bit more background for my idea. I wondered if I might be able to take another look around the Redmain Room . . . if it's no trouble?'

'I'm sure that would be perfectly okay. Charles loves showing off his collection and he'll be back by then. We're having a Christmas party next week, you're very welcome to come if you're still here.'

'Thanks, I'd like that.'

'I'll send an invitation here, to the pub.' She smiled at him again, glad that they were definitely going to meet again. He was interesting – not fizzing and unstoppable like Charles, but more measured and thoughtful.

Not that I'm making comparisons. He's different, that's all.

'Have a great trip,' she said, and called Tippi to heel for the walk home.

*

As she headed back, Tippi bounding off the lead once they were through the gates, she checked her phone and found a message from Charles.

Back this evening, darling. Can't wait to see you. Cx

She put her phone back in her pocket with a sigh. Usually she'd be so happy that he was coming home. Now she was dreading it and the conversation they had to have. But Cathy was right – talking was the only thing to do. She was going to do everything she could to make it better.

Chapter Thirty-Two

Xenia told Agnieska that she should come three days a week, if she could fit it in.

'Yes, no problem,' Agnieska replied. She was cleaning the bathroom mirror while Xenia stood in the doorway, watching. 'I have only you and the Fitzroy House.'

'You could do the ironing for me, and some other jobs around the house. The under-stairs cupboard could do with a clearout.' She was only suggesting another day because she'd grown to like having Agnieska around and had woken in the night certain that, without Charcombe, Agnieska might think about leaving the village for a more regular job in Gorston. Panicked, she'd decided to offer the other day. In the daylight, the idea that Agnieska might leave seemed less probable; things were going well and the car arrangement suited them both. She said, 'If you need more work, you should ask at the pub too, now that they're open and taking in guests. They must need a cleaner.'

'Pub, yes.' Agnieska nodded. 'I will ask.'

After a moment, Xenia said, 'The lady at Fitzroy House – is she there? I haven't seen her but her car is back sometimes.'

'Yes, she is home.'

'Ah. Do you know where she's been?' Xenia was embarrassed to seem nosy but she couldn't help an interest in the woman in the house over the way.

Agnieska shrugged. 'Away.'

I suppose her lack of language works for all of us: she can hardly start giving away any intimate details when she can barely describe the curtains.

Xenia watched Agnieska polishing until the girl turned around and gave her the warning look that meant she didn't like being observed and would Xenia please go away, so she went slowly downstairs, looking out in case Petrova decided to dart up and get under her feet.

The fact was that Ingrid Redmain was intriguing: so close and yet remote. Xenia kept an eye out for what was going on, but there wasn't much to see. Ingrid kept herself to herself. Lights went on, curtains opened and shut, her car came and went, demonstrating that she was about. People appeared at intervals – her friends, her children, the online grocery delivery. And occasionally that man – her ex-husband, of all people – visited, parking up the side lane where his car was not visible and walking down to the back door. Once, Xenia, crossing the road and standing in the lane to pretend to look for Petrova, had heard the woman telling him to go away:

'Charles, you have to stop coming round. I mean it. I'll have to get an order out if you don't. Talk to me through the lawyers, you seem to enjoy that, considering the number of letters I get!'

'This is my house and I'll come as often as I like,' he retorted in that curious, husky voice of his.

'Don't be ridiculous. You don't have any right to burst in whenever you wish, no landlord does. Please don't harass me. You can't stop me living my life, however much you might want to. You don't control me any more.'

Xenia had hurried away, afraid to be seen. He hadn't been around since then. That was months ago, in the summer, when the hedges were high and the trees bright with acid-green leaves. Ingrid had been away ever since the autumn. Well, who could blame her? The only surprise was that she had returned just when it was so bitterly cold. The weatherman on the radio had said that more icy weather was on the way from Siberia, bringing snow with it. Thank goodness she had her cosy cottage with its thick curtains and bright lamps.

This cold weather made her remember Charcombe as it had been in the worst days: freezing, leaking and horribly uncomfortable. There had been glorious summers, though, when the park, a haze of grass and meadow flowers, buzzed with insects and tiny fluttering white flags of butterfly wings. Life was so much easier when it was warm, with long days, brightness and bounties of fruit and vegetables from the garden. Mama's spirits had lifted then too, as she drifted about collecting armfuls of the flowers she loved most, and it was possible to forget for a while the horrible injury that had been done to her. It was worst in winter, when the cold came and Mama would sink into misery, crying for Papa and remembering, in some part of her muddled brain, what had been done to her and the life she had lost.

I can't think about that.

She settled down in front of the television. Half an hour later, Agnieska looked in.

'I go now,' she said briefly. 'You need shopping?'

'No, thank you, dear. But I do have a doctor's appointment on Friday if you can take me to that.'

'Doctor?' Agnieska nodded; she knew the routine for medical appointments. 'Sure. Yes.'

The front door closed behind her and a moment later Xenia heard the car engine as Agnieska drove away. Petrova climbed onto her lap, purring, and she changed the channel to a programme about life for people who moved abroad, which was almost as good as the countryside one.

She was absorbed in the story of a couple opening a restaurant in Spain, when a sudden instinct made her turn around and she saw, to her horror, a young man standing in the doorway looking straight at her. She opened her mouth to scream as panic surged through her, but he spoke before she had time to draw breath.

'Princess Xenia? Princess Arkadyoff? Please don't be frightened, I rang the doorbell but there was no answer, and then I saw the door was on the latch . . .'

Stupid Agnieska! She left the door open! It will be her fault when I'm found stabbed to death! She stifled the scream but shouted instead. 'The bell doesn't work, you should have knocked! Who are you? What are you doing in my house? Get out, get out!'

Petrova woke up, stiffened with the noise and pattered away. The young man looked instantly fearful and put up his hands in a gesture of peace and goodwill. 'I'm not going to hurt you – I'm so sorry if I've frightened you. You know me.'

'I certainly do not. I've never seen you before in my life.' As she said those words, his face seemed to resolve into a different, more familiar one, and she suddenly felt that perhaps she had seen him somewhere before after all, but when and where she could not say.

'Yes – you once knew me quite well.' He smiled at her, his eyes beseeching; she noticed that he had warm brown eyes and thick, chestnut brown hair. 'My name is Gawain Ashley.'

She stared at him, her mouth open, astonished.

'Do you remember me? I'm Luke and Gwen's son.'

A flash of memory illuminated in her mind: a small boy running around the stable yard in shorts and a T-shirt, with bright auburn hair, waving a sword around.

'Yes . . . I remember you,' she said slowly. But it was hard to reconcile that small boy with the huge man standing in front of her. Then she remembered that she had also seen him as a gawky youth, when he'd come with his father after Mama's death to deliver the carved cross that stood at her grave. He'd looked more like this man then, but she still would not have recognised him. 'What are you doing here?'

'I've come back,' he said simply. 'I've wanted to for years, just to see if it was the same as I remembered it. I was last here as a sulky teenager, and didn't take much notice of the place. Then Dad died and it gave me the jolt I needed to actually do it. So here I am.'

'How did you find me?'

'I went up the big house first, and the lady there told me you still lived here. I wanted to come and pay my respects, if that's all right.' He looked a little sheepish. 'I am terribly sorry about barging in. I should have phoned ahead. It never occurred to me that I might give you a fright, turning up unannounced.'

'You certainly should have thought about that, a great man like you walking into an old lady's home,' she grumbled. 'Very thoughtless.' She felt calmer now. 'Well, never mind. You're here, and what's done is done.' Petrova jumped back up the sofa beside her; she stroked the soft fur and the cat settled down and closed her eyes. 'You'd better come in and sit down.'

She made them both tea and Gawain took off his jacket and settled in an armchair, looking enormous in her small sitting room.

'I'm sorry to hear about your father's death,' Xenia said when they were settled again, the tea tray on the small table between them.

'Thank you. It was quite recent. I wondered whether you might have seen his obituary in the papers. Mum went quite a while ago. She was already ill when we left Charcombe and then she developed motor neurone disease. Dad looked after her to the end.'

'My condolences,' Xenia murmured, and thought of Luke thirty years before, sitting at the round table he'd built, working on new designs. He wore sloppy jeans and a torn shirt, his brow furrowed in concentration as he drew. He had a sloping chin that virtually disappeared when his jaw went slack as he worked. Behind one ear was a spare pencil and a pocket knife for sharpening was tucked into his belt, and his hair was grey and haphazard where he rubbed his scalp while thinking. Gwen would be in her studio, surrounded by brushes and palettes crusted with wild swoops of colour, as she bent over a tiny canvas or square of wood or ceramic to paint a tiny but perfect flower. A twisted turban kept the hair out of her face and she wore flowing kaftans in riotous ethnic designs, always with her favourite apricot lipstick, a curious, garden-party kind of choice. 'I remember them fondly. They were kind to me.'

'They were both good people. Honest. They were always searching for integrity in the modern world, trying to find a way to stay true to art and to morals. I try to follow their example, though it's not always easy.'

Xenia was quiet for a moment, remembering. When she thought of Luke and Gwen, it was always in the brightness of summer, the house alive with their students, ringing with talk and laughter. In the evenings, bottles of homemade wine and kegs of local beer came out, and they would sit late into the night, deep in conversation or singing songs with the accompaniment of whatever instruments were played by community members. At first, Xenia had found it unbearably intrusive, but Mama was drawn to the music like an enchanted child, creeping closer to be part of the magic circle. Somehow, the two of them became part of it: not singing, but accepted, sitting with everyone else, listening to the rhythms and harmonies of folk songs and old-time favourites she had never heard before: Bob Dylan, Joni Mitchell, the Beatles, the Stones ... *Harry loved those the best. He loved to sing.* She said wistfully, 'The time you lived at the house was a happy time for me and my mother. I wasn't very welcoming at first, I know that. Your parents were so patient, very understanding about Mama. In the end, they helped me. I'll always be grateful for that.'

Gawain looked at her sympathetically. His hands were spread out on each armrest and he had crossed his legs so that one foot stuck out into the room. He seemed incredibly vital, a buzz of energy in her usually quiet sitting room. 'It's twenty years since she died, isn't it? I remember my mother showing me some of the notices and features in the papers at the time. I hadn't realised until then what she meant to people – too young to understand, I suppose. They weren't going to let someone like her pass without comment, were they? I was proud to have known her.'

'She was a great star,' Xenia said simply. 'I only wish you could have seen her in the glory years, before ... before she changed.'

'I'm sure she was amazing.'

Xenia inclined her head in agreement and sunk her fingertips into the soft fur at Petrova's neck, rubbing until the little cat pushed back her head with pleasure, purring. 'But I don't understand why you've come here. The house is owned by new people. You wouldn't recognise it – it's quite different, they've put a lot of money into making it beautiful again, the way it used to be long before you lived there. Not that it will make the slightest difference, regardless of how much money they spend on it. As far as I'm concerned, it will always be a place of misery and suffering.'

Gawain raised his eyebrows. 'That's interesting. Why do you say that?'

Petrova's purr filled the room for a moment before Xenia spoke. Gawain waited patiently until she was ready.

'The man who sold the house to us had suffered awful misfortune, and from the start I felt that was a bad omen. And, in fact, my mother never wanted the house at all, but she accepted it because Papa wanted it so much. I loved it because it was our home, but there was something about it that never felt right, not comfortable, like a shoe or glove that doesn't quite fit.' She smiled at Gawain with a trace of awkwardness. 'The only time I was happy there was when you and your family lived with us. Just think, in all those years, that was the only truly happy time.'

'I'm sorry to hear that. Surely there were other occasions . . .'

Xenia shook her head. 'Not really. Nothing that lasted. From the moment we arrived, things worsened for us. The house was always a burden. The cost of running it was part of what forced Mama back to work when she was in no way capable of such a thing, and that in turn sent her spiralling into the very worst of her disease. And that brought about the ruin of everything.' She leaned towards Gawain and said very clearly, 'You see, my dear boy, the place is cursed. It always has been and it always will be.'

Chapter Thirty-Three

1953

After the scandal of Mama's behaviour on the set, she stayed at home for a week in a darkened room, seeing no one. She was permitted back to the studio to film what remained of her scenes. Luckily most of the picture was complete but there were some reshoots needed; since the blonde actress refused to be in the same room as Mama, they were filmed separately and the film edited to make it seem as if they were together. Everyone else was remarkably forgiving and kind; they knew Mama was ill and they all remembered the marvellous, entrancing Delilah, and loved her still.

Once the final few shots were finished, Mama went back to the house and collapsed completely, unable to do anything but lie in bed, weeping, occasionally falling into a frenzy and calling wildly for Papa, before sinking into a grim and miserable torpor that nothing could lift her out of. This pattern went on ceaselessly for three days, with Mama refusing all food and only drinking water.

'I don't know what to do, Papa!' Xenia cried, over a crackly line to England. She had barely slept herself, trapped in a nightmare of Mama's despair, living every moment of it with her until she felt she was going mad herself. 'You have to help us.'

'Poor Xenia.' Papa sounded desperately worried but was obviously trying to control it. 'We need to get her home as soon as possible. Do you have a doctor there?'

'Yes, the studio sent a doctor and a nurse. They keep sedating her, but she's only calm for a while, then it all starts again!' She started to weep, longing for home and Papa. 'I can't do it any more.'

'You've been so brave and strong, only a little while longer now. I've made arrangements for you to come home. Are you listening, Xenia? Pay attention, it's most important. You're coming home.'

The next day, a new nurse came to the house and, once Mama was dressed for travel, injected her with a powerful sedative. Zombie-like, Mama allowed herself to be put in the car to the airport and then onto the plane. The nurse came with them, and topped up the sedative when needed through the long flight home. All the way back, Mama remained in her absent state, not sleeping or awake, but a living shell of her former self. Xenia, exhausted and glad of the presence of the nurse, slept at last.

Papa, looking grim and sad, was there on the tarmac as they disembarked in London, accompanied by two men in suits. He hugged Xenia but only looked at Mama. 'Oh, Natalie. Oh, my poor dear.'

She appeared hardly to notice him and made no protest as

the men stepped forward and escorted her to where a private ambulance waited near the terminal. Obediently, she climbed into the back and the doors were shut.

'Where are they taking her?' cried Xenia, agitated. 'Where's she going? I thought we were going home!'

'Somewhere they can help her,' Papa said, holding her tight.

'Where?' Her eyes filled with tears and she pressed her cheek against the scratchy wool of his jacket.

'A hospital.'

'She'll hate it, she won't be able to stand being away from us.' The tears began to flow and she sobbed. 'When will she come home?'

'My dear, I can't say. When she's better. We can't help her any more, you must see that. Come along, let's go.'

Charcombe Park felt empty, only half alive without Mama, but it was also peaceful, the strain of her illness mercifully absent. Xenia, exhausted by everything she had been through in America, slept and slept. She dreamed of Anderson all the time, wondering if perhaps he might try to contact her, and took long walks so that she could fantasise about him coming to England to find her. There was no one to mind her now, for Gunter had retired while Xenia was in America, moving to a little cottage by the sea, and Xenia could live in a haze of daydreams with no one to interrupt her. One day, in the village shop, she saw an old film magazine from America that had an article about him, so she bought it and cut out the pictures to stick on the wall by her bed. She talked to him at night before she fell asleep. There was also a big feature on the blonde actress, adorned with pictures of her in a swimsuit, sitting in a giant martini glass while looking astonished, and in a tight white dress on a long pink sofa, posing happily with a fluffy white cat the same colour as her hair. Those photographs made Xenia feel sick; she didn't see the candyfloss sweetness, the smile and the pout, but the scarlet mark on the girl's face where Mama had slapped her, her look of horror, the screech of outrage. She ripped them up and burned them in the grate.

It was late summer when Mama returned, a thin shadow of her former self, with a defeated air but quiet and calm. She was muted, and oddly sweet like a scolded child determined to be good again. She spent long hours sitting outside in the sunshine, as if soaking warmth into her bones and blood, coming back to life like a butterfly fresh from the chrysalis.

'Look!' Xenia said, showing her the newspaper. 'The film is a success. This critic says your performance is a work of great artistry.'

Mama looked at the article with only a flicker of interest and said, 'How nice', as though she barely remembered making the picture at all.

'Listen to this.' Xenia read from the piece. '"Miss Natalie Rowe returns to a form we've not seen since *Delilah*. She captures perfectly the spirit of desperation and the force of forbidden passion in her portrayal of Rhonda."' She smiled at Mama. 'Isn't that wonderful?'

'Wonderful,' Mama agreed, but she didn't seem to care at all, even though she was nominated for awards, and won several, brought to the house by friends and colleagues and received by her with the same lack of interest. They made her happy in a vague way, as if they were part of a life long forgotten that meant nothing to her.

The truth is, Xenia thought, *I doubt she will ever act again. Perhaps that's a blessing, considering what it does to her.*

'What was the hospital like?' she asked once, when Mama was sitting as usual in the sunshine in the garden, watching the birds flutter about the lawn and the shrubbery.

'Horrible!' Mama shuddered. 'They locked me away as if I were insane. I had no say in anything. They gave me ice baths and medicine and fed me on the most disgusting things I've ever eaten in my life. I didn't know how to tell them that I was perfectly fine, and quite as sane as they were. The more I told them that, the more ice baths they gave me. So I stopped saying anything and just smiled like an idiot. Then they decided to stop the baths and give me normal food again. Isn't that silly?'

'And being ill . . . ?' ventured Xenia. 'What is that like?'

A shadow passed over her face. 'Imagine the worst nightmare there could be, knowing that you're trapped in it and you can't wake up. The harder you try to escape it, the worse the horror and fear become until you'd rather die than carry on.' She looked tired and scared just talking about it. 'But when that feeling goes away, something else happens. I'm filled with an energy like nothing else, a sense that anything is possible and I can do it all, and I'm full of light and sparkle, bigger than the world and immensely powerful. Darling, it's a marvellous feeling!' She laughed but it quickly faded and she looked bleak again. 'But it isn't worth the horror.' She reached out for Xenia's hand. 'I'd do anything to be better again. Anything.'

To Xenia, it seemed that Mama was not merely happy to be home, but grateful. She was adoring around Papa, who treated her kindly while maintaining his distance, as though she were someone he'd once known well but could only vaguely remember. He spent more time away from her, reading in the library, out walking, taking trips alone to London on business. When he was at home, Mama was clingy and affectionate, pulling his hand to her cheek, kissing his fingertips, calling him to her whenever she could. When she tried to embrace him, he stiffened a little before accepting her arms around him.

'Do you love me still, Paul?' she would ask him, holding out her hands beseechingly.

'Of course, dear,' he'd reply politely, but almost at once, he'd ask her: 'Are you better, Natalie? Are you well?'

Mama would reply, 'Oh, almost, Paul. I can feel it, I'm making such progress!'

But Xenia could tell that Mama remained in the same delicate, sensitive state, and did not seem to be getting anywhere close to her old self. She was trying hard – she didn't smoke or drink – but she remained as fragile as glass, just a tap away from shattering into a thousand pieces.

In the autumn, no one even mentioned the possibility of Xenia returning to school. Instead, as the summer faded and the garden lost its bloom, the illness came back, in waves this time. First, the low spirits, where she would often be found mumbling incoherently to herself, or lost in intense thought, that sunk downwards into a depression. That led to a heightened nervousness that climbed to full-blown hysteria, when she could not stop herself from falling into a frenzy, shouting and wailing, trying to hurt herself and attacking anyone who came near her, first with words and then with fists, though her intention was not to hurt anyone, merely to prevent them from touching her.

'You want to send me away!' she would shriek, as the maids or even the gardeners tried to manhandle her back to bed so that the doctors could be summoned with their sleep-inducing medicine. 'You want to put me back into that hospital, lock me into an institution and drive me truly insane!'

The only person she would not lift her hand to was Xenia. Papa, unable to bear seeing her in that state, did not come near her at all. The longer Mama went on being ill, the more he could see that the woman he had loved so much and whose future was so glittering and bright was lost to him.

'It is time for special measures,' Papa declared when Mama was no better. 'I'm getting the real experts involved now. Proper doctors, with scientific methods.'

Dr Hanrahan duly arrived. He was distinguished-looking, with handsome grey eyes and wings of silver hair at his temples. He brought with him a white box with dials and switches on the front of it.

Mama was upstairs, pacing her bedroom and bathroom like a caged animal, shouting occasionally to be let out when she wasn't mumbling disjointedly to herself under the watchful eye of a nurse.

Papa and Xenia sat with the doctor in the drawing room, Xenia apprehensive while Papa, dressed like a country squire in tweeds, seemed excited. 'Tell us, Doctor, what you're going to do.'

The doctor gestured to his white box. 'I'm going to help your wife, Prince Arkadyoff. I will cure her of this awful condition.'

Xenia leaned towards the doctor, filled with astonished hope. Was it really that easy, with that little box? 'You can do that?'

'Yes. This treatment is widely accepted as being efficacious for the kind of mania Miss Rowe is displaying. Let me explain. I'll administer a general anaesthetic of sodium pentothal mixed with a muscle relaxant, so that she'll feel no pain. Then, while she's unconscious, I will attach electrodes to the side of her head – both sides, in her case, as bilateral shock will be more effective for her condition – and pulse an electric current through the brain. That will cause her to convulse, and when she wakes, you'll find that she is normal again.' The doctor smiled reassuringly.

'Just like that?' Xenia said, disbelieving and yet ready to hope.

'This will cure her?' Papa demanded.

'Yes, I believe so.'

'Then what are we waiting for? Let's start at once.'

*

The treatment took place in Mama's bedroom and Xenia did not see the shocks administered. She could not bear even to listen at the door, in case Mama screamed, or she heard electricity buzzing through her mother's head. It made her think of the films of Frankenstein's monster, hit by a fearsome bolt of lightning, jolted into life. It was difficult to understand how a current shooting around her brain could help Mama, but Xenia knew she had no choice but to trust the doctor knew what he was doing. At least he seemed to know what was wrong, and had a name for it. *Mania. That's what Mama has.*

She remembered Sly Manikee shouting to get that maniac off his set. He'd been right – but calling someone a maniac was an insult. It was scornful, contemptuous. *But poor Mama can't help it. She'd do anything to be well.*

Mama emerged from her treatment the next day, pale and, to Xenia's horror, with two burn marks standing out vividly on her forehead, but eerily calm. The doctor stayed for several days and administered six doses of the electro-convulsive therapy. On the sixth day, he packed up his box and said, 'I'm delighted to announce that the treatment has been a complete success. Miss Rowe is cured.' Then he went away.

Xenia rushed to Mama and hugged her with delight. 'You're better! I'm so happy!'

Mama smiled in her absent way, as though the matter hardly concerned her.

Papa was exuberant. 'There, Natalie! You're well! You'll soon be making a film as great as *Delilah* again.'

'What are you talking about, Paul?' Mama asked with a laugh. '*Delilah*? I've never heard of it.'

Great patches of Mama's memory disappeared. The doctor told them that the memories would return in time, but until then, she had large blanks in her mind. It didn't seem to bother her; if anything, the loss of her past seemed to set her free from anxiety. Perhaps, Xenia thought, that was why the shock treatment worked.

Except that it didn't work. For another year or so, Mama was fine. There was talk of her acting again. They went on holidays, touring the south of France, flying to Italy and visiting friends. But when Mama heard that Archibald Thomas had died suddenly of a massive heart attack, it triggered the depression that heralded the return of the mania. That struck with full force on a train in Italy on a blazing hot day, when Mama, agitated since they boarded, went into a full frenzy and began running up and down the train, throwing anything she could get her hands on, then tearing off all her clothes. She was wrestled by Papa and a guard back into their private compartment. Xenia, frantic, was the only one who could eventually calm her and persuade her to get dressed again.

Papa was so appalled he couldn't look at her, even when Natalie was calm once more. She sobbed and cried and apologised, for she knew she had done awful things, even though she couldn't remember them. Papa could not bring himself to speak to her.

Back at home, there was more ECT, more induced convulsions, more treatment. But Mama was no better.

Chapter Thirty-Four

Buttercup came in through the back door, chilly and glad of the warmth from the kitchen. She sorted Tippi out and took off her coat, then headed into the pleasant fog of cooking smells and heat from the range.

Carol was chopping onions and she looked up through teary eyes as Buttercup came in. 'Och, these are strong!' She wiped her eyes with the back of her hand. 'I'm making a vegetable chilli for tonight, apparently Mr Redmain wants that for supper. Something spicy, he says, and very warming.'

'Great idea. Nothing like home cooking when you've been travelling.'

'Cold out, is it?'

'Very.'

Carol carried on chopping. 'It feels like Mr R's been away a long time.'

'Yes. It'll be lovely to have him back.'

Carol glanced at her. 'I expect you'll be glad to have some company, you've been on your own for too long. That's my opinion, anyway.'

Buttercup shrugged. She wasn't going to get drawn into a personal conversation with Carol. She could imagine the report now:

Mrs R seems a bit withdrawn and lonely. She's down in the dumps and has something on her mind that she's keeping to herself.

Then they'd all start watching me harder than ever.

'Honestly. I'm fine.'

Carol had finished with the onion and picked up a butternut squash to peel. 'I've been thinking that you don't have any friends here these days.'

'No – they're all busy with young families, and most are still in London. It's difficult to get them down here.'

Carol nodded. 'It leaves you rather lonely though, doesn't it? A bit isolated. Just remember, I'm always here if you need a chat.'

Buttercup blinked at her. Carol had never said such a thing before.

Carol was concentrating hard on the butternut squash, peeling away long orange and grey ribbons of skin. She said in a casual tone, 'I thought Mr Redmain was a bit too harsh on poor Agnieska. I know she broke his precious plate, but she was truly sorry about it and was always such a good worker: reliable, conscientious. I was sorry to lose her, and I felt that it was an overreaction, if I'm honest. But I hear she's doing all right.' She looked up at Buttercup with a smile. 'I know you were concerned about her, and you arranged those extra wages for her, so I thought you'd like to know she's managing, just in case you were worried.'

'Okay. I'm glad to hear that. Thanks for letting me know. I appreciate it.' She smiled back tentatively. 'I'm going up-stairs for a bath now. I'm chilled to the bone.'

'Sure. See you later.' Carol turned back to her preparations.

That was weird. Buttercup went slowly up the stairs, not seeing them but thinking about Carol. *What made her say that? Is she trying to let me know that she's not as much on Charles's side as I thought? It's going to take a lot more than that before I can trust her again, that's for sure.*

In the bath, as the hours melted away until Charles's return, Buttercup realised she was feeling rather sick. The time was approaching, there was no way she could put it off. Every-thing had to come out into the open, and that meant she must be honest too: she would tell him frankly what she knew and how.

Except I promised Rose not to reveal her part in it.

Buttercup splashed warm water over herself, frowning. It would be difficult to be entirely honest without doing that. Fine, she told herself. I won't tell him that I've read any documents or know some of the history between him and Ingrid. I'll ask him to tell me the truth – all of it.

A small voice in her mind piped up: *but he didn't have to tell you he never sees Ingrid. He didn't have to tell you that she was the one who insisted on living in Fitzroy House. Why has he never mentioned the issues with her, why hasn't he shared that with you?*

Protecting me, she insisted to herself.

But that inconvenient little voice wouldn't be silenced. *He's lied to you, right to your face. You wouldn't have minded contact with Ingrid if he'd been honest about it. And he's spied on you.*

It was harder and harder to convince herself that the desire to protect her might be the reason. *Then why?*

The voice said: *To protect himself, to keep you ignorant of what he's really like. So you don't do what Ingrid did, and leave.*

She sighed sadly. All that effort, all that work, all that vigilance to stop something happening – and only bringing that possibility closer with the lies and control that were used.

But I believe that if we're open and honest with each other, if I talk to him and explain how I feel, we can make this better. He's not behaved well with Ingrid, but he was deeply hurt and, no matter what her letter says, she was unfaithful to him. He can't be expected just to get over it. Charles has an intense nature, she must have known that before they got married. He was always going to react badly.

She pulled herself up mentally.

Are you making excuses for a bully? she asked herself. *Why should Charles be allowed to be controlling and vengeful and spiteful, just because it's his nature?*

She splashed lightly in the warm, scented water.

He has to tell me the truth. He has to promise he's changed. That's the only way we have a chance.

*

Buttercup's stomach was still fluttering nervously when she came downstairs a little later, having dressed carefully for Charles's return in a dress he admired, and with her hair loose and flowing as he liked it.

She heard the crunch of the car on the gravel and went to the front door, opening it and standing in the pool of light from the hall, looking out into the dark night where the car's lights glowed like the eyes of some giant wolf. She shivered in the freezing air, watching as Charles climbed out of the back and walked across the gravel towards her, holding his coat and briefcase. He looked exhausted.

'Darling, it's so wonderful to see you.' He kissed her wearily.

'Welcome home, Charles – you look completely bushed.'

Inside she could see clearly that he was grey and tired, not at all like his usual energetic self.

'This trip has taken it out of me.' He put down his things, slinging his coat on to a nearby chair. 'Sorry to be a party pooper, but I'm going to have a bath and then go straight to bed. I'm feeling pretty ropy, actually. Tell Carol she must save my chilli until tomorrow night.'

Charles went upstairs, leaving her watching him, concerned. It wasn't like him to be shattered. A trip to Shanghai, packed with all the usual meetings and dinners and late nights, was bound to take it out of him, but he had never flagged quite like this before.

Sometimes I forget he needs taking care of. Our talk can wait till tomorrow.

*

Coming back through the hall after telling Carol that Charles wasn't eating this evening, Buttercup saw his tablet on the table. He would definitely want that, he hardly ever went to sleep without perusing it first, and he often put on a meditation app if he couldn't sleep. She scooped it up and headed up the stairs to their bathroom. She got to the door and was about to knock and announce herself when she heard Charles's voice rasping away loudly inside.

She paused, realising he was talking to someone while in the bath. *He must be on the phone.* She didn't exactly mean to listen, but his voice came quite clearly through the door.

'What are you talking about, Elaine? . . . You're in the office? Well, that's dedicated, I told you to go straight home . . . Yes . . . Are you sure? Is anything missing? . . . Does Rose know the combination? . . . All right. She's the only person who could have touched the lock, isn't she? But I don't see why she should have if she doesn't know the combination.'

Buttercup realised her heart was pounding and her grip on the tablet had tightened so much, her fingers were stiff.

Charles went on. 'Listen, calm down. If nothing is missing, then perhaps you simply don't remember the way you put the padlock on . . . Do an initial search tomorrow and we'll have a more thorough look later in the week when I'm back in the office. Chances are it's a slip on your part. Don't panic . . . Listen, just a thought – can you make sure my medical files are all intact? . . . Thank you, Elaine. I'm sure it's fine. We'll speak tomorrow.'

Buttercup heard him click off. She stood outside the door, her mouth dry, hardly able to move.

Oh God. Have I got Rose into trouble? I must warn her. And I still have Ingrid's letter. I must get it back in the file before Charles notices it's missing.

She gathered herself together and tiptoed quietly away, Charles's tablet hugged close to her chest.

Chapter Thirty-Five

The next morning, Charles slept uncharacteristically late. Buttercup left him in bed, got dressed quietly in the dressing room and slipped downstairs. It was pitch-black outside and she could tell that the temperature had plummeted.

It's almost December. But it's pretty cold, even so.

She went into the drawing room where the fire was already lit. Carol was up and about then.

Buttercup rang Rose on her mobile. Rose answered at once, her tone surprised.

'Mrs R? This is an early call.'

'Yes, I expect you're still at home. Sorry to disturb you. I just wanted to warn you—'

'Yes?' There was instant panic in Rose's voice.

'It's okay – but Elaine has sussed that the cabinet has been touched—'

'Oh my God! Oh no!'

'Calm down, it's okay! She's told Charles and he thinks she made the mistake herself – the lock was on backwards or something like that. He doesn't think it was you. So all you have to do is tell Elaine that you didn't notice anything wrong and never touched it. Okay?'

'Oh my God.' Rose's voice sounded panicked. 'You don't know what Elaine's like, she has a bloodhound's nose for lies. Shit, I'm going to be fired. *Fuck*.'

'You can do this, Rose,' Buttercup said firmly. 'Just be calm and tell her you never touched it. If the worst happens, and she thinks you opened it, tell her that I ordered you to do it and you had no choice. But I think she's ready to believe you. The important thing is to stay relaxed. So deep breaths ... You'll be fine. I promise it's going to be okay.'

Once she'd ended the call with Rose, Buttercup felt her own anxiety rising. It was all very well keeping Rose calm, but she was worried about what might happen next.

I don't want her to get sacked, I promised her I would look after her. I need to get to London and put that letter back, just in case.

Charles was still grey and exhausted when he came down for breakfast.

'This trip has completely taken it out of me,' he said. 'I don't feel at all well. I probably need some vitamins or something. I might see the doc and find out what he advises.'

Buttercup poured some coffee for him. 'I think you should. Get Elaine to make an appointment. Or go to the surgery here, if it's quicker.'

'I'd rather see my doc in Harley Street. He knows me.' Charles smiled wanly. 'I'll pop up as soon as I feel better or get him down here if I get any worse. I've told Elaine to

LULU TAYLOR

clear my diary for a bit. That way we can have some time together.'

'I'd like that.' She smiled back, feeling a little of the old affection for him returning. Maybe, just maybe, there was a chance for them, if they could talk it out. But this wasn't the time for a confrontation or a heart to heart. She would wait until he was feeling stronger.

'You work far too hard, you obviously need a rest. It's the Christmas party here next week, you'll want to be better for that, so take it easy.'

'Ah yes, the party. I can't miss that.'

'That reminds me – we had a visitor while you were away.'

Charles's gaze flicked up at her, instantly enquiring. 'Who?' he asked sharply.

'A man who used to live here when he was a boy.' She told him what Gawain Ashley had recounted of his time at the house. Charles listened, interested, while he picked at his yoghurt and fruit salad, and drank his coffee.

'Well, well,' he said when she'd finished. 'That's intriguing.'

'I asked him to the party, if he's still around.'

'Good, I'd like to meet him. Anything that can shed light on the history of this place is of interest to me, as you know. I always wondered what went on during the years that old woman was here with her mother. Another piece in the jigsaw of Charcombe Park. Film stars, sea captains and now painters. Excellent.' He took a sip of his coffee.

'He's thinking about writing a book about the house and Natalie Rowe, and he was very taken by the story of Captain

348

Redmain. He's going to Portsmouth to do a bit more research.'

Charles frowned. 'I'm not sure about that. I don't think I want someone writing a book about my house.'

Buttercup was surprised. 'I thought you'd want a wider audience for Captain Redmain's exploits.'

'You don't know everything,' Charles said crisply. 'It's my damn business and my damn house. I'll explain that to this Ashley person when I see him.' He stood up. 'Actually, I'm not feeling at all chipper. I'm going to go back to bed.'

Buttercup watched him leave, feeling wrong-footed again. Somehow she'd angered him, but had no idea how.

He's not well. We'll sort everything out when he's better.

Charles went to bed and immediately fell asleep. When he woke later, he was feverish and headachy, wanting only to sip water, take a pill and sleep again. Anxious, Buttercup looked in on him every few hours, until he was awake again, bleary-eyed and evidently ill.

'You'd better keep your distance,' he said in a tired voice, 'just in case I've got something catching. Sorry, darling, this is very boring for you. Can you pop up to London, see some friends or something?'

'I don't want to leave you when you're not well.'

'There's nothing you can do. Honestly, I just want to sleep this thing off. I'm good for nothing for at least a day or two.'

Buttercup thought of Ingrid's letter, upstairs in her bedside drawer. This was her opportunity to return it without being interrogated. 'If you're sure . . . I wouldn't mind going up to do some Christmas shopping.'

'Good idea.' Charles smiled weakly. 'I'll feel better knowing you're occupied. You go, and by the time you're back, I'll be back to my old self.'

Buttercup got to London late in the afternoon, and asked Rose to come up to the flat.

For once, Rose seemed faintly reluctant. Elaine glanced over and Rose immediately said she would be up there as soon as possible. Ten minutes later, she was knocking at the door. She was hardly inside before she said vehemently, 'I'm not touching that cabinet again!'

'No – you mustn't,' Buttercup said, leading her inside. 'Did Elaine ask you about the padlock?'

Rose nodded. 'I was an idiot. It slipped off when I was relocking it and I put it on backwards without noticing. It just snaps shut, you see. But when Elaine asked if I touched it, I stayed calm, like you said, and denied it. She hasn't said anything else about it.'

'Okay. Good. Listen, a piece of paper fell out when I was putting the files back together, and because Rich was here, I couldn't tell you. So I took it away and I'm going to put it back tonight, but I need the combination for the lock.'

Rose looked agonised. 'I told you, I don't want to have any more to do with this!'

'Just the code, Rose. Elaine and Charles are going to check the files next week. They mustn't find the letter missing.'

'This is the last thing,' Rose said, gazing beseechingly from behind her spectacles.

'The last thing. I promise.'

'Okay. I'll get it for you. I'll send you a text later. But then I'm done.'

To keep her story straight, Buttercup headed out dressed up and made up at six o'clock, saying a cheery goodnight to Elaine and Rose as she went. She considered actually seeing a friend, but decided against it. She needed the flexibility of being on her own. 'Don't stay too late,' she called out.

'Goodbye, Mrs R, have a nice time,' Elaine said.

'I will – thank you!'

It was freezing cold outside and she was wearing heels, so she hailed a taxi and asked for Duke's Hotel in Piccadilly. When she got there, she went to the bar and ordered a single martini, which she drank extremely slowly while reading a book. When it was finished, she went outside, hailed another cab and went back to the Westminster house. It was dark, except for the lights she'd left on in the flat upstairs, and she rode up to the penthouse floor in the lift. Inside the flat, she got changed, ditching her heels for sneakers and putting on a pair of jeans. Then she took Ingrid's letter out of her suitcase, read it one more time and made her way quietly downstairs.

There was no reason to be quiet – there was no one else in the building, she was sure of that. Nevertheless she moved as silently as possible as she went down to the office. Rose had told her there were no internal alarms, so she didn't have to worry about setting anything off. Even so, she was nervous and on edge, and jumped at the slightest creak on the stair as she went down.

The office was deserted, the desks left tidy and all the lights switched off. She put on the overhead light, then padded over to the filing cabinet. She took her phone and photographed the padlock so that she would be able to put it back exactly as it had been, then used Rose's code to open the lock.

She pulled out the hanging file and found the folder on Ingrid, which she assumed must have contained the letter. Taking the letter carefully from the top of the cabinet, she pushed it into the folder at random. There was no way of knowing exactly where it had come from, so she might as well trust that its presence there was the main thing. No one was likely to remember exactly where in the folder it had been, were they?

She went to shut the drawer and then stopped. Here she was, at the repository of all Charles's secrets. There was no one about. What was to stop her looking through everything?

Fear. This is spooky, here in the office at night, where I shouldn't be, looking at things I'm not supposed to see.

But Charles was far away, asleep in Dorset. Elaine was at home. What was there to be afraid of?

They are about to go through this cabinet to check no one has been here. If I start disturbing things, they are bound to notice.

Yes, she needed to play it safe. She'd already sailed too close to the wind. She shouldn't push her luck. Instead, she should close the drawer, go upstairs and watch some television with a nice cup of hot chocolate.

That's what I'll do.

But as she was pushing the drawer shut, her eye was caught by another file tab: 'C. Redmain, Medical'. As soon as she saw it, she stopped and remembered Charles asking Elaine to check his medical files were intact. And he'd been saying he wanted to see his Harley Street doctor. She wondered if something had been wrong with him lately and whether he'd made some appointments with his doctor. She knew he wouldn't tell her that. It was the kind of thing he kept strictly private.

I could have a quick look, she thought. *It won't take a moment.*

She pulled the file out, carried it over to Rose's desk, sat down and began to read.

Chapter Thirty-Six

1959

'It is too much,' Papa said simply. 'It's too painful, Xenia. It's intolerable.'

Xenia gazed at him with scared eyes. 'What do you mean, Papa?'

She was almost twenty-one but there was no question of a party for her. There had been no parties at Charcombe Park for years, and even visitors were no longer welcome unless they knew and understood the situation. If they were not frightened by Mama's condition, if they loved her even when she was attacking them verbally or using foul language, looking a mess in a filthy dressing gown, then they could come. But not many were able to manage that.

Papa got up and began pacing around the library. He was wearing his favourite velvet smoking jacket and tasselled slippers, warmth against the cold January weather outside. They seemed incongruous with the subject matter they were discussing. 'Without money, we simply can't continue as we are. Mama can't work in her condition.'

'But I thought we had enough money, once we sold the London house. You said the money would last for years.'

Papa looked at her crossly. 'Don't be so foolish. The money realised by the sale ran out a long time ago. We are in a difficult position. The ECT hasn't worked, that much is plain.'

'It works in a way,' Xenia said hopefully. 'It stops the attacks.'

'Only temporarily. They always come back. And with her memory shot to pieces, it's all she can do to learn her own name, let alone a script. We need a permanent solution.'

'But there isn't one!' she cried in despair. 'That's the whole point.'

'Except . . . perhaps there is. We have one last chance. I've found another doctor. One who promises that he can bring Mama back to her old self. But it means an operation.'

'She'll never agree,' Xenia said quickly, shaking her head. 'She won't go into a hospital.'

Ever since her stay in the sanatorium that had doused her in ice baths, Mama had developed a pathological hatred of hospitals. The doctors and nurses who visited the house had to wear ordinary clothes before she would allow them near her. Xenia quailed at the thought of trying to force her inside a hospital or anywhere near a ward.

Papa turned to stare into the crackling fire in the grate. 'I know that. She won't need to go into hospital. We will do the operation here. The doctor assures me that it's quite possible as long as we take the proper hygiene precautions, and I agree with him.'

Xenia stared at the flames as they flickered against the

sooty back of the fireplace, dancing over the top of the logs. *Could Papa be right? Perhaps we do have one last chance to cure Mama. It was his idea to try the ECT, and it most certainly helped.* 'What is this operation?'

'It's performed on the brain. It removes the rotten part, the part that's driving her mad, and leaves the rest, which is healthy. Then, at last, she will be better – permanently.'

Xenia stared at him, bewildered. 'But isn't an operation on the brain extremely dangerous?'

Papa became instantly angry. 'Obviously there are risks, which is why I've hired the finest surgeon I could find, one who's properly qualified in this area, with a one hundred per cent success rate. He has cured dozens of cases like this.'

Xenia frowned. 'Then why haven't we heard of him before?'

Papa sighed, still irritated and defensive. He evidently wanted to be praised for his discovery, not questioned and doubted. 'The procedure is a little controversial, it's true. You know what the medical establishment can be like – resistant to change, unprepared for challenges to its accepted practice. But this is going to work, Xenia! We will get Mama back this time, I have every confidence.'

'I don't know. I'm not sure . . .' Xenia said. An operation on the brain? Surely the risks were far too great. She felt uncertain, prepared for once to tell Papa that she didn't agree with him, but he was such an unstoppable force. When had she ever managed to stand in his way?

'I *do* know,' he said firmly. 'I've asked the surgeon to come here and perform the operation as soon as possible.'

'Shouldn't we ask Mama what she thinks before we operate on her brain?'

Papa's face changed completely in a moment, his expression fiercely angry. 'Ask a lunatic?' he yelled, throwing up his hands. 'Ask a madwoman? You're crazy yourself if we think we should listen to her. No, Xenia, she isn't capable, you know that. We know best. She hates the way she is, we hate it too. This is her last chance. We are going to take it.'

By the time the surgeon arrived for the operation, the weather had turned dark and relentlessly cold. The snow was falling hard and settling over the house and grounds like a blanket as the car carrying the surgeon and his ominous black bag, his anaesthetist and nurse, drove up to Charcombe Park.

'This is the answer for Mama,' Papa had insisted. The papers arrived in the post and he signed them. He told Xenia to sign them too because the surgeon required two signatures in order to operate. 'She will be grateful to you forever,' he declared.

And so she had signed.

'We will operate as soon as the room is prepared,' the surgeon said.

'Even though it's dark?' Xenia asked, shivering with cold in the hall.

'We need electric light in any case, to see clearly. Night is better, in some respects.'

Xenia watched, scared, as they set about preparing. The kitchen was chosen. It was warm from the range, and could easily be scrubbed down; water was close at hand, and the hanging lights over the kitchen table would provide the right illumination. The kitchen table itself was large enough to double as an operating table, with plenty of space around it.

Upstairs, Mama was in her room, unaware of what awaited her until, when at last the room was ready, Xenia and Papa brought her downstairs, blinking in her white night-gown, bewildered until they went into the kitchen and she saw at once what was intended: the table was covered in a green cloth, a tray of obscene-looking instruments on a stand next to it. A huge gas canister with a mask attached by hoses was close by, and a machine to monitor the heart. Next to them stood the nurse in white and the doctors in their hos-pital coats and masks.

'No, I won't, I won't!' Mama turned terrified eyes to Xenia. 'Please, darling, no, don't let them touch me.'

'But please, Mama, they want to make you better!' Xenia said, struggling with her mother, her own eyes filling with tears.

'Natalie!' shouted Papa. 'This is your cure, this is the answer!'

'No!' cried Mama, trying to shake them both off. 'I won't do it. Leave me alone, how can you do this to me?' She started to weep.

Xenia couldn't take it any more. She dropped her mother's arm. 'I won't make her, if she doesn't want to. Can't you see it's wrong?' She began to sob. 'It's all wrong.'

Mama shrieked and tried to tear her other arm free of Papa's grip. He held it tighter, and yelled over her:

'Please, Natalie, for me! For Paul! Do it for me!'

His voice seemed to reach her. Suddenly Mama quietened. She stopped struggling and turned to look at Papa, her eyes beseeching through her tears. 'Paul ... I want to make you happy, you know that. I dream of it. Will you ... will you love me again if I do it?'

'This is your cure,' he said urgently. 'It will make everything the way it used to be. You and me. Everything.'

'Do you promise? You'll stay with me, no matter what?'

'I'll always stay with you,' Papa said firmly. 'But you must do this. For me.'

Mama took a deep breath. She glanced at Xenia and smiled a tiny smile, as though trying to convince them both of her courage. 'Then ... I'll do it.' She turned back to look at the doctors, and clutched Xenia's hand so tightly it felt like a vice. 'All right. I'm ready. I'll do it.'

She took a step towards the surgeon as the nurse advanced, only her eyes visible above her mask, and put out her hand.

PART THREE

Chapter Thirty-Seven

When Buttercup left London, she did not drive home as she had planned. Without informing anyone, she drove north, towards her mother's nursing home outside Cambridge.

When she reached there, though, she did not stop, but pressed on until she reached the icy windswept Norfolk coast. She drove on to Cromer and parked on the seafront. It was not long after lunch but the sky was already darkening, a reminder that the shortest day of the year was drawing near. The beach was deserted except for one or two hardy dog walkers, and she made her way across the sand, feeling the wind whip up her hair and coat it with sea salt. As she walked, the numbness that had possessed her for the last twelve hours began to wear off and at last the tears came, as she had hoped they would, if only to relieve the unbearable pressure within her.

There was salt on her tongue, where her stream of tears seeped in at the edges of her mouth and left little briny drops inside. Her nose ran, and she mopped it with a tissue every now and then, turning her face away when she passed anyone so that they wouldn't see her crying.

This is why I can't see Mum. All of this has to come out first.

She wanted the ice-cold sea wind to lash her and hurt her, and the bitter cold to burn her fingertips and chill her feet. She thought of throwing herself into the frigid waves, or impaling herself on the spikes of the seafront railings. She wanted to pick up driftwood and beat her head with it, or strike herself with a rock. But why she had this urge to hurt herself, she had no idea. Perhaps it was because she longed to be free of the mental anguish that gripped her, and looked to physical pain as a distraction or release. It was as if her inner being had swollen and enlarged to become a giant receptacle for endless, bleak misery and towering frustration. Her small outer shell struggled to contain the massive void within her, dark emotions swirling like a black hole, drawing in misery and hurt.

She walked to the edge of the water and when the wind was at its fiercest, battering her ears and face, she turned herself into it, leaned into its buffeting strength, and yelled at the top of her voice, a shout that became a scream that morphed into high, animal sobs. When she had nothing more to let out, she mopped her face with the screwed-up, sodden tissue and went back to the car.

When she arrived in Cambridge it was early evening but there was still time to see her mother. She went into the brightly lit reception, hung for Christmas with garish tinsel and assorted decorations, while a blue and silver artificial tree flashed in the corner. Stacy was not on duty but the nurse on the desk told her that Mum's new medication had completely cleared her recent infection, as far as they could tell.

'It would be easy enough if she could let us know everything was better,' the nurse said. 'But she can't, poor love!' Then she peered closer at Buttercup's face. 'Are you all right, dear?'

'I'm fine. Just a slight cold.' She smiled. 'I'm not infectious any more.'

'All right then. Go along and see her but we're serving dinner in twenty minutes.'

Buttercup went in, and saw her mother lying there exactly as she had been on all of her recent visits. The sight was, somehow, comforting. She seemed peaceful, her leg moving in its familiar rhythm – rub, rub, rub, against the left one – her hair clean and with a ribbon tied in its white locks.

I want to tell her. But I can't. Just in case she can hear me and she understands. I can't hurt her. I have to bear this on my own.

So instead she talked in a brittle, merry voice about Christmas at home, how Milky was getting on, the visit from Gawain Ashley, and everything that was on her mind except the awful thing that weighed her down like a rockfall.

The desk nurse put her head around the door. 'It's dinner time, love. We're coming to take your mum to the dining room.'

Buttercup nodded. 'That's fine.'

She didn't want to leave, though, and instead she watched while they moved her mother off her daybed and into a wheelchair. She was strapped in securely, her body held upright within the sides of the chair, and then they pushed her out into the corridor, her eyes still closed, her head lolling.

'Come on, dear, off we go!' said one of the nurses, a young girl with heavy eyeliner and a pierced nose. She glanced at Buttercup. 'Are you coming?'

'Oh – yes. Yes, I will.' She followed them along the corridor to the dining room. Inside, the staff were corralling a crowd of elderly people, evidently in different stages of dementia. Some were docile and obedient, others confused, some truculent. The staff moved among them, talking and gently manipulating them into chairs. Buttercup's mother appeared to be the most removed from the world, although the noise of the dining room and the heavy, savoury smell of dinner seemed to wake her and stimulate her into remembered activity; her eyes opened and her mouth moved.

'Dinner time, love!' the pierced nurse said gaily, and wheeled the chair over to a table, where she proceeded to tie a giant bib around Buttercup's mother's neck. She glanced at Buttercup. 'Better safe than sorry, eh?' She settled herself beside her in a chair and picked up a bowl of puree. Buttercup sat down opposite her mother and watched as the nurse scooped up a spoonful of brown puree and inserted it gently between her mother's lips. 'There, that's nice, isn't it? Do you like that?'

Her mother seemed to be awake, blinking slowly as she sucked at the puree-covered spoon and swallowed the contents.

Like a great big baby, thought Buttercup. She stared at the bowl of puree as the nurse lifted another spoonful. Then she said, 'Will you let me do that?'

The nurse looked surprised, then said, 'Be my guest, love' and held out the spoon. Buttercup moved round to the other side of the table and pulled up a chair next to her mother. She took the spoon and the bowl and carefully gathered up a quantity of the puree. Then she held it out to her mother and pushed it gently into her mouth.

She must have done this for me once. It's only natural that I do it for her now. It seemed like the human pattern: the strong caring for the weak, who became strong as the strong became weak and the care was reversed. Buttercup fed her mother another spoonful. She seemed to eat it with enjoyment.

This will never change. It's all she has. This is her life, until it ends. The only pleasure left to her is the taste of food on her tongue. That's all she can respond to.

A thought struck her suddenly, cutting through the blackness inside her like a lightning bolt searing a night sky.

But I'm still strong. I'm not weak yet and I have power. I can change. I can make things happen. I can escape if I want to.

A load seemed to lift off her shoulders in an instant.

Yes. I can do it. And I will do it.

She glanced up at her mother and, to her astonishment, her mother was staring back at her, looking at her directly for the first time in years. And, briefly but assuredly, a smile crept over her lips as she looked into Buttercup's face.

*

367

Buttercup drove into Cambridge and booked herself into a hotel by the river not far from the city centre. It was comfortable but not particularly beautiful, each room cheaply furnished and functional. It was a world away from anything Charles would ever have chosen. He would not have been able to stand the polished pine in the bar, the hectic carpet and the clashing green of the furniture. The dado rail and striped wallpaper would have offended him. The Christmas decorations and the easy-listening carols would have irritated him beyond words.

Who cares what he thinks? Not me.

She ate dinner in the restaurant, managing to make inroads into a salmon salad, despite a complete lack of appetite. She hadn't eaten since the previous day but the food was tasteless in her mouth and she pushed most of it away.

Her phone was off in her bag. No one knew where she was, and there was no way she could be traced. She was free. From here, she could go anywhere, she could start afresh if she wanted. Her passport was in her bag – why, she couldn't remember – so she could drive to the airport, leave the car and take a flight somewhere, to a new life, if she felt like it.

There's no hurry. I don't have to do anything at all.

Buttercup slept long and late, and then lay in bed in her room until almost lunchtime. After a bath, she got dressed and walked into Cambridge, cutting through a shopping centre and emerging in the heart of the town, where she wandered for an hour before finding her way to the Backs. It was even colder by the river and she wished she had warmer things with her. Her phone was in her pocket but still switched off. She knew that people would be calling her: Charles, Rose, Elaine, maybe Carol. *Where are you? Why don't we know where you are? How dare you go off radar like this? Come back at once.*

A naughty child, slipping out of school. Going AWOL. Scarpering.

She laughed grimly to herself.

They can fuck off. All of them. Every last one of them who knew and let me go on like this without telling me.

Eventually, freezing to the core, she went back to the hotel. 'I'm going to stay another night,' she told the receptionist. 'Is that okay?'

'That's absolutely fine. Would you like to book a table in the restaurant?'

Buttercup thought of the empty tables the night before. 'No. I'll just rock up if I need to. Thanks.' Then she went to her room, curled up in bed and watched a movie until she dozed.

My lost weekend, she thought as she hovered on the brink of sleep. *My run for the border. My escape.*

In the morning, when she woke, she realised that she'd been having a happy dream. Her father was alive again, her mother back to her old self, and they had surrounded her with love and care. At first, awake in her hotel bed, she felt the stab of loss when she remembered that she was alone, but then she recalled the delicious warmth she had felt in their company, and the joy of being in their arms. She remembered her mother's smile in that dining room of the nursing home, a tiny flicker of connection, if that were possible. Whatever it was, it was all that was left.

I think she saw me, properly. I believe it.

It gave her a strength she hadn't felt in a long time.

I owe it to them to be happy. It's all they wanted for me. But I can't slink out of my own life. I have to go back and face this. Face him.

Chapter Thirty-Eight

The next morning, Buttercup checked out of the hotel. In the car, she switched on her phone for the first time in over forty-eight hours and immediately a torrent of notifications flooded in. Texts flashed up, dozens from Charles:

Where are you? Call me at once.

And there were messages and emails from the house and office, asking where she was. She skipped the voicemails and flicked through the emails. Sometimes they said that Charles was ill and needed her; sometimes that Charles was well and needed to talk to her.

Well, which is it?

She turned the phone off again, and started for home. It was a long drive back to the south-west and she stopped often to sip coffee in service stations and steel herself for the return to the house.

As she turned into Corten Lacy, it seemed as if nothing had changed. Then she saw the lights on in the pub, lights twinkling outside, Christmas trees projecting out at angles all along the roof and sparkling with fairy lights. It was comforting, somehow, to see it alive and welcoming, speaking enticingly of hot food and good drink. It seemed busy, too.

Happy people. Normal lives.

A little further along the lane she saw the gates of Charcombe Park, the stone greyhounds standing on their pillars on either side, impervious to the dark winter weather.

I'm back, she thought, trying to stifle the sense of dread that was growing inside her. She had likened it to a prison last time she entered these gates. Now it seemed like a dungeon, a repository for rotting dreams.

I think I actually hate this place. I wish I'd never seen it, never come here. I wish it didn't exist.

She drove through the gates, went slowly up the drive to the garages at the back, and brought the car to a halt there. She got out and went to the stables, where Milky was standing patiently in her stall. Going to her, Buttercup rubbed her nose and patted her, inhaling the comforting smell of straw and warm animal.

'There, there, old girl. Have you missed me? Shall we go out for a ride, huh? It's cold but you won't mind that if you can have a good gallop and then some hot mash, will you, sweetie?'

'BC? Is that you?' Phil had come quietly into the stables and was standing just inside the doors, a bulky dark shape against the light of the doorway.

She looked round. 'Hi, Phil. Yes, it's me.'

'You're back then?'

'Yup.'

There was a pause as Phil frowned at the stable floor. Then he said, 'Everyone's been going bloody frantic since your disappearing act. They thought it was the same thing all over again, like when Ingrid left. And nobody wanted that.'

'No, I can well believe it.' Buttercup rubbed Milky's velvet nose. 'I almost left myself.'

'I almost wish you had.'

'Why?'

Phil shifted uncomfortably. 'None of us liked the way Ingrid was treated. We all saw it. But sometimes relationships are toxic and they'll never work, no matter what. Something about the chemistry just doesn't play. We all need our jobs, so we gave Mr R the benefit of the doubt. I suppose I can tell you now that we were all on Ingrid's side because we saw how hard she tried, how much she put into bringing up those kids, and what frustration she felt, trying to live with someone like the boss. It was best for her to go, and we all knew it.'

Buttercup had gone quite still, listening hard. 'I shouldn't be surprised that you saw it all. Everyone here knows more than they say, I understand that now.'

'When you came, we thought you might be the answer. Maybe you'd got his number and had made a bargain: I'll live the way you want in exchange for . . .' Phil hesitated, then gestured with his arm at the stable and towards the house. 'Well, I have to be blunt – for all this.'

'For the money.'

'The security, maybe.' Phil shrugged. 'It's a tough world out there. No one's saying you didn't love him, but it crossed

373

my mind that you knew what kind of man you were taking on, and that was a price you were willing to pay.'

'Then you found out that I didn't.'

Phil nodded, his eyes sad. 'It was the same thing all over again. I could hardly bear to watch.'

Buttercup nodded, not trusting herself to speak.

Phil sighed and said, 'I can see you're in a state, but I'm glad you're back.'

'For the moment.' She looked at him beseechingly. 'Don't say anything to anyone, will you, Phil?' Milky shifted and stamped in her stall. 'This party tomorrow night. It's going to be noisy. Lots of children. Would you mind taking Milky and the others in the boxes down to the Herberts' yard? I think it might disturb them to be here.'

Phil looked surprised. 'All right. If you're sure.'

'Yes,' Buttercup said firmly. 'Take them all there.'

'Okay.'

Buttercup smiled weakly. 'You've been a good friend to me, Phil. Thanks.'

'You're welcome.' He gave her a solemn look. 'We do understand, you know. If you have to go.'

'Yes. That helps. I'd better go in and face the music.'

'All right. Good luck.'

Carol was coming out of the kitchen in a rush as Buttercup walked back from the stables towards the back door.

'You're home!' she cried. 'You're all right!'

'Yes, I'm fine.' Buttercup raised her eyebrows. 'Why shouldn't I be?'

'You haven't answered your phone! No one's heard of you or seen you for three days! We've been worried sick.'

'I'm a grown-up and I'm perfectly okay. I needed some time to myself.' Buttercup walked past her and into the kitchen. 'How's Charles?'

'His health is all right, if that's what you mean. He's over his flu or whatever it was, but he's been going out of his mind with worry.'

'Where is he?' She went to the fruit bowl on the table, picked up an apple and inspected it. Then she took a bite.

'He's in the study, where he's been most of the time when he hasn't been pacing about, worrying.'

Buttercup leaned against the table, chewing her apple insouciantly, while she stared at Carol, who gazed back at her, puzzled. 'I suppose he's had the team out looking for me. No doubt he's been pulling strings with his important friends, trying to get me traced.'

'He was worried about you,' Carol said firmly. She picked up a tea towel and folded it in an agitated way. 'I don't understand. What's got into you? Aren't you bothered about all the worry? If you'd seen him, the state he's been in ... He's on the brink of cancelling the party tomorrow!'

'Oh dear. I'm sure he's worked himself up good and proper.' Buttercup took another bite of apple and, when she'd eaten it, she said, 'I think it's time for you to decide whose side are you on.'

'Excuse me?'

'You heard. Are you on Charles's side, or mine?'

Carol laughed nervously, refolding the tea towel, hanging

it over the rail of the cooker, and taking it off again to fold once more. 'I don't know what you mean. I don't take sides. I'm here to support you both, equally. So is Steve.'

'I don't know your husband. He keeps himself to himself. He's outside, you're inside. You know about what goes on in here.'

'What I know, Steve knows,' Carol said shortly. 'We're a team.'

'Yes, but are you Team Charles, or Team Buttercup? It's that simple. I know you spy on me, I've seen your reports. That's surprised you, hasn't it? Oh yes, I know all about those reports, telling the Hub what I had for breakfast and if I'm feeling a bit off colour and whether I'm pregnant or not.'

Buttercup watched a flush spread over Carol's face as her mouth fell open. The other woman looked astonished and shamefaced, unable to form a reply.

Buttercup said, 'Obviously that's all going to stop. But are you going to turn informant? Double agent, perhaps?' She took another bite of the apple and chewed it slowly, staring at Carol, who had now gone pale, her eyes wide. 'Here's something that might help you decide. Imagine you have a dream, a huge desire in life. And someone decides to deprive you of that thing. To take your dream and smash it up and destroy it forever. But here's the thing – they don't tell you what they've done. They pretend you still have a chance, when the reality is that you have nothing to hope for. That way, they get to keep you on *their* terms, and you're completely in the dark. Imagine that, Carol. Doesn't it sound pretty bad?'

Carol had gone still and quiet. 'Yes,' she said at last, her soft Scottish brogue grave instead chirpily cheerful as it usually was. 'Yes, it's pretty bad.'

'What should happen to that person, do you think? What punishment is bad enough? Do you think that maybe having *their* hopes and dreams destroyed is only fair?'

'I don't know. I'm sorry. I can't answer that.'

'I don't know either,' Buttercup said. She tossed her half-eaten apple into the compost bin. 'I thought that was good, but it turned out to taste bad after all.' She went towards the door. 'I'm trying to work it all out. But in the meantime, I guess we should all start concentrating on the lovely party we're going to have tomorrow night.' She turned back to stare at Carol. 'So give it some thought, Carol, and maybe let me know what team you decide on.'

In the hallway, she almost bumped into Elaine, who was coming downstairs talking frantically into a mobile phone but stopped short when she saw Buttercup. The phone dropped from her ear and she gaped at her, then gathered herself together and said, 'Look, the situation has changed. Mrs Redmain is here. I'll call you later.' As she clicked off the call, her lips stretched into a huge smile. 'What a relief to see you! Are you all right?'

'I'm perfectly fine, thank you, Elaine,' Buttercup said coldly. She knew which team Elaine was on and always would be. *Perhaps she's the only person in the world Charles can truly trust. But then again, she doesn't have to be married to him.* 'I'm a grown woman, you know. If I want to go away for a few days, I can.'

'Of course you can.' Elaine took a step towards her as if approaching a wild animal that she intended to capture. 'But you ought to have let someone know your plans. We've been worried about you.'

'I know. I've heard,' Buttercup said pleasantly. She gestured at the mobile phone. 'You've been marshalling your forces to track me down before Charles goes off his rocker, I expect. What kind of state is he in?'

'He's terribly upset,' Elaine said, her expression cooler. 'He's been concerned about your safety.'

'Concerned about my whereabouts, you mean. In case I've done a runner, like his first wife. What would that look like for Charles? One, misfortune, two, carelessness, and all that. And we all know what disloyalty does to Charles. It makes him *angry*.' Buttercup took a step towards Elaine, who stood stock-still. 'Have you ever been on the receiving end of his anger, Elaine? Has he ever turned those cold eyes on you, judged you and found you wanting?'

Elaine cleared her throat. 'No,' she said slowly. 'No.'

'I bet you've seen it though. You saw the boiling hatred that spewed out of him when Ingrid dared to rebel against being controlled and coerced and forbidden from making her own choices. Right? You saw what he did to her.' Buttercup's voice grew icy. 'But you didn't just watch him, did you? No – you helped him do it!' Buttercup's eyes flashed with indignation. 'How could you do that, Elaine? How could you help him try and destroy her?'

'She behaved outrageously. She cheated on him.' Elaine's voice rose defensively. 'She deserved some comeback for that. What was he supposed to do, smile and pat her on the back?'

'No, of course not. But he didn't need to torment her and punish her. Where are her things, Elaine? The belongings he won't give back to her?'

An angry shadow passed over Elaine's face and her eyes turned cold. 'I'm not in the dock, Mrs Redmain. If you have issues with your husband, I suggest you take it up with him.'

'Oh, I will. Don't worry about that.'

Just then a voice on the landing made them both look up.

'Darling? Is that you?' Charles's voice, raspier than ever, called down to her.

She looked up. He was there on the landing, his face gaunt and drawn, his sandy hair standing on end as if he'd been constantly running his hand through it. 'Hello. I was just coming to see you.'

He was smiling but his expression was bewildered, teetering on the edge of angry. 'Where have you been? Why the hell haven't you returned my calls, darling?'

'I needed to get away. I needed to think. I turned off my phone.'

Charles started to come down the stairs towards her but she stopped him, holding up her hand and saying, 'Stop!' He paused on the step, looking down at her and frowning. Buttercup did not usually issue orders. She was the one who obeyed. That was how it worked. 'I'm coming up,' she said. 'We need to talk privately. Let's go to the bedroom.'

He laughed awkwardly. 'All right,' he said after a moment.

'Elaine, would you wait for us down here, please. And let everyone know that Mrs Redmain is back.'

'Certainly,' Elaine said, and she walked off towards the drawing room, already tapping into her phone.

'Well then,' said Charles. He smiled, but it didn't reach his eyes, turning his mouth into a thin curved line. The dark shadows around the eyes made his face resemble a skull. 'Come on, then. I'm eager to hear exactly what you've got to say for yourself.'

Buttercup began to walk slowly up the stairs towards him.

Chapter Thirty-Nine

Xenia tied a jaunty red bow around the present she had just wrapped and put it with the others. The gifts looked wonderful, exactly like the best presents: enticing, mysterious and full of promise. She was sure Agnieska's little boys would love them, the woman in the toyshop had assured her that all the children were mad for these things. It had been fun hiding the bag from Agnieska on the way back home; Xenia had enjoyed the sensation of a lovely secret that would bring so much happiness.

She went to the window and pulled the curtain back to look at the road outside. Her porch light illuminated the white motes spinning through the air.

'Snow before Christmas,' she muttered. 'Unusual.'

The sight of it made her shudder. The snow settling on the backs of the greyhounds on the gate pillars and over the parkland reminded her too much of the terrible winter when Mama had her operation. She preferred to think of the house as it had been in summer, when life had been easier to bear.

And how strange it is that the little boy I remember from those years came back to see me, a grown man.

It had been impossible to resist the lure of the memories Gawain had set tumbling into her mind. And why should she? What harm did it do to remember? The pain was almost negligible now, so why not allow them back and take what pleasure she could from them?

That summer, Mama had been calm. Her mind was fixed on flowers. All day she would be out, tending to flowers, picking them, arranging them, drifting about with armfuls of blooms. There had been a stretch of warm, golden days, and many of the younger students had gone away on their travels. The house was quiet, the chill inside it welcome for once when the sun burned hard and the day was at its hottest. The little boy, Gawain, was occupied in building a fort with offcuts from his father's carpentry, and his sister drifted about, learning Tennyson off by heart and making pre-Raphaelite gowns from old kaftans.

Xenia watched Mama kneeling by the old flowerbeds, as she had years before, and patted the soil around the flowers, carefully pulling out weeds and removing pests. Despite everything, she retained enough of her old self to know what to do.

This is my life now, Xenia told herself. It was something she had learned to accept: that she would care for Mama until Mama no longer needed her. Her expectations for her own life had been closed down; fantasies became a powerful means of escape, and she found meaning for her existence in the memories of the past: her own and her family's. She was Princess Xenia Arkadyoff, and that counted for something. She had a beautiful house, even while it crumbled around her and she struggled to find money for heat and light. Her mother had once been a famous film star and a gifted actress, even if she was only a shadow of that woman now. Most of their furniture and possessions had been sold off one by one to keep them in food and clothes, to keep the car running and debt collectors at bay, but Xenia had not parted with the things that mattered most: mementoes of the family, relics from the Arkadyoff past. The residual payments for Mama's films provided an occasional boost that covered the cost of winter coats or essential repairs.

But even while she suffered, and sometimes wondered how she would survive the loneliness, Xenia would stand straight, set her shoulders and tell herself that she was the descendant of emperors and would take her misfortune with dignity.

It was just easier when the meadows were full of wild grasses and bright flowers, humming with insects, and the air was warm and fragrant.

'Xenia, are you there?'

'I'm here,' she said, a little stiffly. She got used to Luke's casual use of her name, and didn't mind it from him, but it still irritated her a little. She was in the washroom at the back of the kitchen, taking wet towels out of the washing machine to hang up in the sunshine. She was in a faded summer dress, one of Mama's old things, and open-toed flat sandals, her hair unbrushed, and she was about to say that she didn't want to see him, when Luke came in with an open-faced, friendly looking man: not tall or well built, rather short and stocky, his brownish hair thin on top, and certainly not handsome, but with a kind look in his eyes.

'Xenia, this is Harry. He's come to stay with us for the summer and learn the noble craft of furniture making.'

Xenia looked up, cross at being seen dealing with wet washing. 'How do you do,' she said stiffly.

'Hello.' Harry nodded his head in a small bow and smiled. 'We'll leave you in peace while you're busy and perhaps I can introduce myself properly later.'

Xenia nodded in return, grateful for his sensitivity, and they left her to her chores. She'd seen him later at dinner, one of Gwen's stews of beans and rice with exotic spices and unusual additions, in this case blobs of goat's curd on top, and she had listened with a distant kind of interest while he explained more about himself to Luke and Gwen.

Harry was a lawyer, and he'd taken a whole summer away from his job in London to learn a new skill. 'I've been slaving away since I was twenty-one and I was on the brink of burning out, so I negotiated a sabbatical from the company and I'm going to decide this summer if I'll go back at all. That all depends.'

'You'll never go back!' Gwen declared, spooning out more of her stew over the mound of brown rice she'd put on Harry's plate. 'You mustn't. Once you've discovered a place like this and a life like ours, you'll not be able to.'

'Perhaps that's true.' Harry accepted the plate from her. 'Thank you, Gwen, it looks delicious. We'll see.'

He hadn't addressed Xenia directly, and seemed to know instinctively how protective she was about herself, as though he sensed that it was the wound in her pride caused by her circumstances that made her so prickly and quick to anger. He understood she wanted her privacy and never invaded her territory, and she was grateful for that. She learned to accept his peaceful, unobtrusive presence in the house, mainly keeping to his workshop in the stables where Luke was teaching him how to cut, chisel and plane, how to make dovetailed joints and how to use a dowel, sand smooth and polish.

The day that Gawain hurt himself and Harry brought him to be bandaged up was the first time they had properly spoken and after that, Harry took to saying hello each morning, and coming into the kitchen at coffee time to see if she wanted anything. Her general coolness didn't seem to put him off, as if he could see beyond the stiff shoulders, haughty chin and the tendency to snap. He stayed unflappable, patient and cheerful. He said little and listened a lot, when Xenia railed at him for infractions of her house rules, or for the noise of his saw, or the wood dust fluttering round the courtyard.

'And look at the mess the boy is making!' she cried, waving her arms at the haphazard collection of planks and poles that Gawain called his fort.

'He's doing no harm,' Harry said, smiling. 'It keeps him out of the house. And your mother likes to watch him play.'

Xenia was silent. He was right. When she wasn't collecting flowers, Mama spent many happy hours sitting in the sun at the back of the house, watching the boy building his construction. As Xenia grew used to Harry, he started to ask her questions about herself, and how she had come to this house, and why she had stayed.

'I'd have sold it years ago,' he said quietly, shaving long strips of wooden curls from a plank, smoothing it down. 'It's got a strange atmosphere. Did you know it was under siege in the civil war?'

Xenia shook her head. 'I never heard of that.'

'There was a very terrible incident. The Roundheads killed the lady of the house while her husband was away and she was trying to defend the place on her own. And they killed at least one of the children too.'

'That's horrible.'

'I know. Barbaric.' Harry shaved another long golden ringlet of wood from the plank. 'Maybe that's the reason I don't think it's a very happy place.'

Xenia had stared, speechless. The house was simply itself. The happiness came from the people within it, surely. How could unhappiness live on in stones and wood? But then, they themselves had never been really happy in the house. From the time Papa had bought it, things had gone wrong and got worse. 'There may be something in what you say. But it would be impossible to sell the place. It's my father's house. He has asked me to maintain it for him until he returns.'

Harry looked about. He didn't need to say anything, as his gaze landed on the crumbling stables, the moss-covered roofs missing their slates, the loose bricks, the drainpipes hanging from the walls. Eventually he said, 'And where is your father? Does he know about this?'

Xenia pulled herself up tall and lifted her chin. *I am Princess Xenia Arkadyoff and it doesn't matter that my house is falling apart.* 'That is none of your business,' she said haughtily. 'But when he does return, we will be here waiting for him.'

After that, she noticed that Harry was spending less time on his carpentry and more time on little repairs around the house and the outbuildings. Slowly but surely, the slates were replaced, the roof cleaned. Weak timbers were bolstered or replaced. The hanging drainpipe was bolted back in place. His generosity, silently offered, touched her. The kindness in his eyes, the strength in his capable hands, the solidity of his body began to draw her to him. Her stiff carapace softened and melted away, almost without her noticing. As summer came on, she would go to him every morning with fresh coffee and small things she had baked for him, and spend hours watching him work, talking to him and telling him about her life. He was fascinated by Mama's time in Hollywood, but he wanted to know it from Xenia's perspective and what it had meant to her. No one had ever wanted to know that before.

They were sitting together in the garden, drinking some of Xenia's homemade lemonade, sheltered by the old sycamore tree. Harry had only been at the house for six weeks, but it seemed longer, as though he had always been there. He was, Xenia realised, her friend. The first proper friend she had had for many years.

Harry said, 'You've given your life to your mother, haven't you?'

Xenia nodded. 'Of course.'

'Not everybody would have done such a thing.'

'I had no choice.'

Harry looked perplexed. 'But why? Your own life – would she really have wanted you to sacrifice it like this?'

'You don't understand.'

He looked at her intently. 'But I want to understand, Xenia. I want to understand how someone like you – intelligent, cultured, beautiful – and yes, you are, don't look at me like that – how you ended up living like this.' He reached out and took her hand. 'Xenia, where is your father? What happened here?'

She stared down at his hand on hers, feeling the warmth of his touch like a healing light on her skin, as though his life force was crackling, travelling through his fingertips and into her. It set pulses thudding all over her and a whirling motion through her core. No one had touched her in years, not counting Mama. Not one friendly, sympathetic hand on hers in decades. She had given up on such things for herself and here, suddenly, unexpectedly, a man's hand on her skin, a voice telling her she was beautiful, asking her what had become of her.

Someone can see me! Someone wants to know me.

It was like being shut in a cupboard for an age and the door being opened to allow in the light. But it carried with it fear. Would the light be too blinding? Would stepping out be more dangerous than staying in? What now?

'Xenia? Are you all right?'

Not handsome but so kind. Not noble or vital, like Papa,

but honest and steady. That voice, with its tenderness and compassion . . . I could listen to it forever.

'Yes,' she said with difficulty. 'I'm all right. It's so hard to talk about – what happened to us.'

Harry said gently, 'If it's too hard, please, don't—'

'No. I want to. I've never talked to anyone about it but you've seen Mama, you know what's she's like.'

'What is her condition?' he asked quietly.

'Mania. Manic depression. She drank and took pills to escape it, but it only grew worse, then suffered at the hands of doctors for years afterwards. She had various treatments – she had many applications of electric convulsive therapy. Nothing cured her.'

'Your poor mother. An awful thing to happen to such a great lady, with so much to live for.'

'She suffered very much, mostly from the indignity her illness forced upon her. Somehow it was worse because in her real self, she was beautiful, elegant and refined. She was gentle and kind, but the condition made her coarse, slatternly and vicious. It broke my heart,' Xenia said, her voice trembling. 'My greatest wish was to make her better and stop her suffering. Papa wanted the same as well. The winter that I was twenty-one, my mother had an operation on her brain to cure her severe manic depression. Papa arranged it, he promised it would be the answer to Mama's illness, but it was a disastrous failure. It destroyed her personality completely, robbing her of any chance of living any kind of normal life. She became what you see today. Before it, we had periods at least when she was herself. After it – nothing.'

'That's appalling.' Harry shook his head, his expression grave. 'I'm so sorry, what a tragedy for you all. And your father left you here alone?'

Xenia felt an urge to defend Papa and to make excuses for what he'd done. But she had to tell the truth as well. He had gone. Deserted them forever. 'I believe Papa was eaten up by guilt about what he'd done to my mother. He was determined to do what he could to make amends.'

Harry looked dubious. 'I think a lobotomy is irreversible, even today.'

'Of course. But he had to *hope*. Or else, he was pretending. Simply lying to make his escape.' Xenia looked out over the garden, watching cabbage whites fluttering around the purple pom-pom heads of the alliums in the flowerbeds. 'She repulsed him, you see. After the operation, Mama was a shell of her former self, her beauty gone and only her bodily functions intact. He couldn't bear to look at her. The gorgeous Natalie Rowe was gone forever, we all knew it. Even so, he said that he was going to America to find some famous surgeons who would make Mama better. He needed money to pay them to come here and operate. So I gave him something precious I owned.'

The empress's jewel in its little velvet box. I pressed it into Papa's hand and he smiled. 'I'll come back, Xenia,' he said. 'As soon as I have the doctors' agreement to treat Mama. You must look after her and the house until I return.' And I said I would. I promised I would.

Harry thought for a while. At last he said, 'Have you ever heard from him?'

'No. Nothing.'

He never wrote to me, or to Mama. Not once.

'So you don't know if he's alive or dead.'

Xenia shook her head. 'I haven't heard from him for twenty years. Perhaps he is dead, but someone would have let me know, I suppose, and there's been nothing.'

Harry turned to look at her, concern in his soft eyes. 'Why don't you leave here? Why don't you both go?'

'I couldn't do that to Mama. It is all that's left to her – the hope that one day he'll come back. She still weeps and cries for him – you've seen her.'

'And you, what about you?'

She said quietly, 'I've waited for so long, I don't know what else to do with myself. Besides, I owe it to my mother to keep her here.'

'But why? She doesn't seem to know where she is.'

'I can't explain. I'm sorry.'

He tightened his hand over hers and she returned the grasp, grateful for the solidarity it imparted.

Because I told her it would be all right. And it wasn't. I can never undo it or make it right. We can only wait and wait, for the day when Papa finally comes home.

'There's still time, Xenia. There's still time for you.' Harry lifted her hand to his mouth and gently pressed his lips to it. 'If you want. There is still time.'

Chapter Forty

They stood facing one another in the bedroom, the great bay window like their own stage set, the stretch of carpet between them, the lamp on the dressing table glowing.

This is it, Buttercup thought, her insides giving a lurch of fear. Then she remembered the smile on her mother's face, and her utter determination to face him down and bring all the secrets out into the open.

'Well?' Charles said. He looked thinner after his illness but the determination in his eyes showed her that he still thought he could talk her into doing whatever he wanted.

He's going to fight me. He's not prepared to give any ground.

That realisation stiffened her resolve. She tried to remember how dear and beloved that face had been, what it looked like when it was open and merry, the blue eyes sparkling with vitality. But what did it matter now, when all that was over for good?

He frowned impatiently. 'I'm waiting. Are you going to explain this disappearing act of yours? I have to say, it's not easy to understand it. What the hell were you playing at? Your phone was switched off. No answer to anything. You must have known how worried I'd be.'

Buttercup said quietly, 'I went to London. Afterwards, I was terribly upset. I needed some time to get my head together. I drove to the coast and had some long walks to think everything over. Then I made a decision. Then I came home to you.'

There was a long pause while Charles absorbed this, his hooded eyes glittering in the lamplight. He was clearly pondering which of her statements to question. At last he said, 'Why were you upset?'

'Because I know for certain that you've been lying to me.'

He tensed a little, like an animal who has sensed danger. 'Lying?' he said silkily. 'What on earth are you talking about, darling?'

'Stop it, Charles,' she said in a low voice. 'I mean it. It's time to stop.'

He stared at her.

Buttercup straightened her shoulders, not prepared to quail under his stare. 'Let's begin by assuming that I know *everything*. So. What have you got to say about the parcel of lies you've told me?'

She stared back at him, refusing to drop her gaze, meeting his blue eyes, which were now icy. He stood there, his hands in his pockets, the stretch of carpet between them like the ground between two opposing armies preparing for battle. He was, suddenly, a stranger.

'This is a serious accusation,' he said in a cool tone. 'What lies have I told you?'

Part of Buttercup felt removed from the whole thing, like an observer of the angry, deceived wife and the slippery, evasive husband, both intending to fight for each version of the truth.

Here we are, batting the questions back and forth. He wants to know what I know before he admits to anything, and then he'll only admit what he thinks I already know. All right then, let's cut to the chase.

'Why don't you tell me the truth about you and Ingrid, for starters?' she demanded.

Charles seemed to relax just a little, as though he had worked out what she must have discovered and was now confident that he could manage the problem. 'Has someone been talking to you about Ingrid? Or perhaps Ingrid herself has decided to put her irritating little oar in? Darling, don't believe what jealous women tell you, or envious trouble-makers who want to stir things up.'

She stared at him and said again, 'Why don't you tell me the truth about you and Ingrid?'

His eyes narrowed. 'What do you want to know?'

'Just tell me the *truth*!' she yelled, her ability to stay calm deserting her.

He took a step towards her. 'Don't get hysterical with me. I have no idea what you mean. The truth about what?'

Buttercup took a deep breath and forced herself to let go of her anger for the moment. 'All right. If you insist on playing these games – why not? It won't make any difference in the end. Here's an example. You told me that you were not in touch with Ingrid. You told me she was the one who insisted on living in Fitzroy House. That wasn't the truth, wasn't it?'

Charles laughed, the sound making her feel sick and revolted: a patronising, mirthless noise that told her clearly in what regard he held her feelings. 'So that's it,' he said, his tone with the edge of a sneer in it. 'Rose let you into all the secrets, did she? I expect she's the one who thought you ought to know, probably now she's engaged and in some romantic haze of idealism, full of the wonder of pure honesty. You know very well that how I feel about Ingrid has nothing to do with you. How can it possibly matter to you? What concern is it of yours what was hammered out in our divorce before you were on the scene? That's my business.'

'It's my business if you lie about seeing her and speaking to her!'

'Why?' Charles's voice was cold now. 'It doesn't threaten you. I'm not going to leave you for Ingrid, I can assure you. It has nothing whatsoever to do with you.'

'Of course it does, trust is part of the fabric of our relationship. You didn't need to lie, I would have understood if you'd explained it to me. And now I don't trust you. Not one little bit.'

He blinked at her, expressionless. 'You didn't need to know. It's not a question of lying. Omission is not the same as outright lying.'

'I see.' She stared at the carpet, her fists clenched, trying to keep control of the emotions surging through her. She could see how it would be: he'd blank and block her at every opportunity, beat her back with cold logic and refusal to move an inch. And the more he did that, the more she could feel her own version of events slipping, as though facts were uncertain things that could change according to who said them and why. *Hold on, Buttercup, hold on to what you know to be true. You're strong. Don't let him beat you down. Let's see how much he's prepared to admit.*

'It *is* a question of lying,' she said firmly. 'Because you did lie, outright, many times. You've lied to me since the day I was unfortunate enough to meet you; you lied about Ingrid and the fact that you still see her and phone her often, and make her life hell with constant legal letters and quarrels. And you've kept her property, haven't you?'

'It's obvious Rose let you see things that were not your concern,' Charles said sharply. 'Elaine was right, I shouldn't have trusted her.'

'Rose inadvertently helped me.' Buttercup unclenched her fists and relaxed her shoulders. 'But this is between you and me. Don't take your anger out on her.'

There was a long, loaded pause as they stared at each other. She sensed a shift in him. He was prepared to give some ground.

Considering he's been found out, he's going to have to. He thinks this is all I know. Will he ever confess what he thinks I don't?

'All right,' Charles said, at last. 'You're right. I haven't been straight with you. I didn't want to involve you in the morass of my divorce and what it did to me.' He paused, went to the window and stared out, thinking hard. When he turned back, it was with the air of someone who'd come to a decision. 'It's hard for me to say I've been in the wrong, but perhaps I have. I'm a proud man and I find it hard to admit what Ingrid did, and how badly I took it. It was easier for me to pretend I'd thrown her out, and that I didn't care any more. But I do care. I know it's not mature, and that it's unattractive. That's why I didn't want you to know – because I love you, darling, and I was too vain to want you to see that side of me. But I do love you. You must believe that.' He held out his hands to her in supplication. 'I'll be honest with you from now on, I swear.'

She gazed at him, not moving towards him. He seemed so sincere. 'Good,' she said simply. 'I'm looking forward to that. It will certainly save a lot of time.'

'I agree with everything you say,' he said quickly, as if sensing weakness. 'I mustn't blame Rose, she's not involved with this. You have every right to know what's going on. I've been stupid over Ingrid, I can see that. I'll make arrangements and she can leave whenever she wants. I selfishly wanted to keep the children near me.' He smiled winsomely. 'But they're practically grown up. It's right that things move on.'

Trying to put a decent gloss on indecent behaviour.

'Where are Ingrid's things?' she asked. 'What are they?'

He shrugged. 'Her family photograph albums. They have photographs of her grandparents, her father who died ... that sort of thing. I meant to give them back. I ...' He blinked hard and looked away. 'Her affair hurt me so much.

I wanted to hurt her in the only way I could. As long as I had them, I could still have some power over her.'

'You had plenty of power over her without that,' Buttercup said softly. 'Don't you think?'

He nodded quickly. 'I'll return them to her. They're in my study.'

'So . . .' She fixed him with a strong look. *I want him to admit it of his own accord. I want him to prove he means what he says, even if it's too late to make a difference.* 'Your honesty. Your new-found honesty. I'm interested. Can I really trust you?'

'Yes,' he said at once, and smiled. 'You absolutely can.'

'That's good. Because now we've cleared up the issue of your lies about Ingrid, what about what you've done to me?'

His smile faded, his eyes unreadable. 'What?'

'The lies you've surrounded me with since the day of our wedding, probably before that. The watching eyes, the reports, the internet history, the roundups of my activities, the way you've cut me off from my friends and stopped me getting my old job back – controlling me and limiting me. Spying on me.'

Charles stared at her and said nothing while he absorbed her words. Then he said, 'I have no idea what you mean.'

She shook her head, incredulous. 'I think you do. You did exactly the same thing to Ingrid and she told you so, in no uncertain terms. What you don't seem to realise, Charles,' she said in a quiet but fierce voice, 'is that when you create a culture of secrets and a culture of watching and a culture of lying, you're not the only one who will watch, and lie, and have secrets. Others are watching *you*. They know your secrets. And you can't always guarantee that they won't tell.'

'I have no idea what you're talking about.'

'Other people know!' Buttercup shouted. A strange mixture of power and despair filled her. 'They will always know! You will be found out, eventually! And I know *all about you*. I know what you've done.'

He stared at her, implacable. He would admit nothing, she could see that. Fine. It only strengthened her resolve. 'Tomorrow,' she said calmly, 'I'm leaving here. I'm leaving you.'

'What?' He looked shocked, outraged. 'What are you talking about? You can't leave! This is ridiculous. Why? You're overreacting.'

'It's far from ridiculous. It's what's going to happen.'

'Why?' He moved out of the lamplight into the shadows, so that his face became gaunt again, his lips in a thin line, the hollows under his cheeks like caves.

'Because of what you've done to me.' *You know what it is. You know and won't say.*

He sighed impatiently. 'You're getting this wrong. Don't you see how hopelessly naive you're being? It's true that my life is monitored. Everything is. You knew that before you married me. I'm a very rich man with a certain value to people who might wish me harm, and by extension, you. I'm sorry if you don't like the fact that your privacy is invaded, I do my level bloody best to make sure you're not inconvenienced, so that life is as normal for you as possible. And for that, I'm being punished. You want to leave me? Why?

Because I care for you, protect you and make your life wonderfully safe and comfortable? Because I love you deeply and give you all I can? That makes absolutely no sense!'

She stared at him, unable to find the words to reply. Everything in her was revolted by the way he turned things around so that she was the mad one, the unhinged one, behaving irrationally, when in fact, he was the one who had destroyed it all. She felt a wash of grief drench her: for all her hopes and dreams, the love she'd had for him, the life they might have had.

He took her silence for wavering and stepped forward towards her, suddenly confident again. 'Don't leave me. You know you don't really want to. I love you, darling, and we can put everything right. We can talk all this through properly. I can see that you're deeply upset and that's understandable after the mix-ups and confusions we've had between us. We'll sort it out. I promise.'

'Don't even try, Charles,' she said dully. 'It's too late.'

'No.' He moved towards her, reaching out towards her but she flinched away. 'I don't want that to be the case.'

'You heard me.' Her shoulders slumped a little under the weight of misery. She realised that Charles was never going to tell the truth: he'd fight her with lies and half-truths and persuasion, she could see that. 'I told you, I know everything. It's too late. I'm going.'

He drew in a breath and, to her surprise, said, 'All right. Maybe it's good for us to have a break, a period of reflection, so we can try to sort all this out. But don't leave tomorrow. Please. It's our Christmas party, the whole village is coming. I want you to be there. Stay for that, and you can leave the following day if you want to. Please – will you do that? Not for me but for all our guests who want to see you there?'

She stared at him, feeling numb. What did it matter, if it was tomorrow or the next day? He wasn't going to talk her out of it.

'Fine,' she said. 'I'll stay till after the party. Then I'm going.' She turned on her heel and went to the door, then looked back at him. 'I'll sleep in one of the guest rooms tonight.'

Then she went out, shutting the door behind her, unable to bear looking at him for a moment longer.

Chapter Forty-One

Xenia looked at the snow, which had settled in a soft, powdery blanket over everything. She'd been worried about Agnieska cycling in this, because the car was at the garage having its road test, but Agnieska had arrived in a different car, driven by a man.

'Who was that?' Xenia asked her.

'My friend from the big house,' Agnieska said, and took off her coat to start work. Now Xenia wondered if the snow would have an effect on the party at Charcombe this evening. It was still fairly light and might well melt during the day. All morning, vans and trucks bringing all the equipment for the party had been making their way through the gates, but another snowfall would make the roads more dangerous and prevent people from venturing out. She stared up at the grey sky and wondered what was in store for them.

Just then, she saw a tall figure huddled in a dark jacket turn in through her garden gate, and after squinting at him for a moment she recognised Gawain Ashley. She hurried to open the front door.

'Come in!' she called, beckoning him. 'It's freezing out there.'

He quickened his pace obediently and hurried in, the end of his nose pink from the cold. 'Brrr,' he said, pulling off his scarf. 'It's a bit parky.'

'How was your journey?' she asked, pleased to see him again. It felt quite normal now, having people visit her. Gawain seemed like an old friend, even though it was only his second time in the house. 'I'll make you some tea.'

'Thank you. My hands are cold, the heater in my car is hardly working. A cup of tea is just what I need.' He smiled at her. 'Lovely to see you again. Are you well?'

'I don't like this snow,' she grumbled. 'I hate the winter.' He followed her to the kitchen as she bustled about making the tea. 'I hate the snow even more.'

'Careful, you sound a bit like Scrooge-like. You'll be telling me you hate Christmas next.'

Xenia shrugged. 'I don't care about Christmas much. It's snow I hate. Cold and ice. Christmas is just a way of trying to lighten the darkness of the cruellest part of the year, when we suffer most.'

'That's rather gloomy,' he said. 'Some people like the cosiness, shutting out the darkness with firelight and warmth.'

'Lucky them,' Xenia said shortly as the kettle boiled and she filled the teapot. 'That's not my experience.'

They took the tea back to the sitting room and settled down to drink it.

'So you came back,' Xenia said. 'You're still interested in

the house, are you? I could see that when I told you it was cursed, you were more interested than ever.'

'I'd had no idea of the civil war history of the place, so when you told me about that, I was even more fascinated. No one seems to have had a particularly happy time living in that house.'

'My life is better now I've gone,' Xenia said flatly. 'I wish I'd left years ago. And I don't much care what happens to that awful little man.'

'You don't like Charles Redmain?'

'No. From the moment I met him, I disliked him. If he hadn't offered me so much money for the house, I would have refused to sell it to him. But I liked his wife. She was different. It was no wonder that she finally left him.'

Gawain raised his eyebrows. 'So you mean the ex-wife? I assume you're not referring to the very nice lady up at the house?'

'No, no, she is the *second* wife. The first one lives over the road.' She turned to gesture in the direction of Fitzroy House.

'That's an unusual arrangement,' Gawain said with a laugh. 'They must all get on well.'

'Not at all. I don't believe they have ever met. And the husband sneaks in to see the ex-wife without the present lady knowing – or he used to.'

'You seem to know a lot about it,' Gawain said, glancing over at her.

Xenia felt a faint flush rise to her cheeks. 'Well, one finds out a lot without meaning to, given that we all live so close to one another. If he parks his car in the lane and I see it, I can hardly help it. But ...' She hesitated and took another sip of her tea.

'What?' asked Gawain.

'I feel somewhat guilty about my part in things.'

'What things?'

'The break-up of the marriage. You see, I knew that Mrs Redmain had fallen in love with another man. I saw them walking in the park, thinking they were out of sight, and they were kissing and carrying on. It was clear as day she was having an affair with him. And you see ...' The flush deepened. Lately she had lost that overriding sense of anger and frustration that used to make her feel she was going insane, but she still remembered clearly how it had felt. When the fever gripped her, she would feel not only the rocket fuel of rage push her out of herself into behaviour she could not control, but she would also feel fear – that this was a sign she was like Mama and would end up the same way. That potent mixture of fear and anger had made her do things she regretted.

'What happened, Princess?'

'For the first few years after they first moved in, every summer they would hold these frightful events in the park. They set up lists – real jousting lists! There were tents, a kind of medieval fairground and during the day, they held jousts with huge horses thundering up and down, the crashing of lances ...'

'Goodness,' Gawain said, 'it sounds brilliant. And they don't do this any more?'

Xenia felt a spark of anger. 'It was *not* brilliant, it was torture. I complained very strongly. Eventually the Redmain man came to see me, with his haughty airs and his conviction that he can make everyone do what he wants. He's a jumped-up little bully, I know his type, I tell you!' She drew herself up tall, straightening her shoulders and assuming her most regal air. 'He thought he could tell me, a descendant of emperors, what to do. He said it was an important historical event. I told him what I thought of that. He must stop it. And when he said that he wouldn't, I . . . I told him what I knew.'

Gawain frowned, his cup of tea held halfway to his mouth. 'You mean, you told him about seeing his wife and the other man together?'

Xenia nodded and said quickly, 'I was so angry, I didn't know what I was saying. I've regretted it ever since.'

'Oh dear.' Gawain put his cup down, his expression grave. 'Oh dear me.'

'I wish I hadn't done it.' She looked away, ashamed. 'I know what you're thinking, and you're right – it was a terrible thing to do.'

'And so – no more tournaments. No more fairs. No more cars and people.'

'That's right.' Xenia lifted her chin obstinately. 'No more noise. Just peace and quiet, like it's supposed to be.'

'And they divorced.'

'Yes. They did.'

Gawain shook his head. 'Well, well. The stories of misery and misfortune go on. The house is beautiful, so beautiful. Why is it so sad?'

Xenia felt mournful. 'I don't know,' she said in a quiet voice. 'But that was not the house. It was my fault.'

'Perhaps, perhaps not. You can't possibly know.' Gawain's gaze went to the fireplace, where a stiff white card sat propped up on the chimney piece. 'And yet, you've still been invited to their Christmas party.'

Xenia looked over at the invitation. 'That's only politeness. In any case, the second wife probably knows nothing of the past. I shan't go, though.'

'I've been invited myself,' Gawain said casually.

'You have?'

'Yes. My invitation arrived at the pub. It was nice of Mrs Redmain to ask me.'

'You liked her?'

'I did. She was charming. I'm hoping to meet the husband you despise so much at the party tonight.'

'I'll be surprised if you like him.'

Gawain drained his teacup and put it down. 'Funny you should say that. I'm planning to go up early to the party tonight and I wondered if you'd like to come with me. I think you'll find it interesting.'

Xenia stood in front of her mirror doing something she had never dreamed she would do again: she was getting ready for a party. She clipped earrings to her lobes, brushed out her silver hair into smooth curls around her pink scalp, and put on a small smear of red lipstick. She blinked at her reflection.

You silly old woman. Fancy trying to make yourself look presentable, as if anyone would care what you look like.

All her life, she had wanted to look like Mama – as ravishing and elegant as she had been. And now, ironically, she did look like her, as she had at the end, with her silver hair and softly wrinkled face.

She felt afraid of returning to Charcombe, but Gawain had persuaded her, and promised to be at her side throughout. Going back to the house in the snow was the stuff of Xenia's nightmares, but she knew it was simply fanciful. The bad times were over. There were a few good years left to her, and she intended to enjoy them. The house had lost its power over her, she was certain of it. *I've done my suffering. It's finished with me.*

A flash of memory came into her mind: a loving couple walking through the parkland, hand in hand, stopping to kiss tenderly before walking on. But it wasn't her and Harry. No. It was Ingrid Redmain and her handsome jouster. The sight of them had made her so bitter, so sad and angry that she not been able to control it.

It should have been me. Harry and me. But I couldn't take my one chance of freedom. That was my real inheritance: when happiness finally came to me, I couldn't accept it. And that was why, when I saw those two in their idyll, wandering in the summer meadow together, I wanted to destroy it.

She went to the window of her upstairs hall and looked out at the house across the lane. A light was burning downstairs. Mrs Redmain was back. Perhaps, all this time, she had been in some warm land, where the knight in his shining armour was waiting for her.

I hope so. I don't want to live possessed by anger any more. It can destroy lives so easily and nothing can put back what was ruined.

Chapter Forty-Two

The beautiful summer was ripening to autumn when Harry told her he was leaving Charcombe Park.

'I have to go back to my law work,' he said. 'But as soon as I get back, I'm going to hand in my notice and give it all up. This summer has made me realise that life's too short to waste doing something you hate, even if it makes money. I want to start living. I have a cottage in Cornwall, halfway up a hill overlooking the sea. I've learned everything that Luke and Gwen can teach me, so I'm going to live there and start my carpentry business.'

She was in the kitchen making soup for Mama, who was sick with a chill, and she'd stirred it slowly without saying anything. She'd closed her mind to the possibility of Harry leaving. She'd hoped he might simply decide to stay indefinitely.

'Xenia?'

She turned around to look at him, hoping he wouldn't notice the tears in her eyes, but his expression was too much for her, and two hot rivulets ran down her face. She sniffed hard and wiped them away. 'I don't want you to go. You're my friend. My only real friend.'

'You're my friend too.' He smiled at her and took her hand, his roughened by woodwork and sawdust. 'You know that. I want us to be closer.' He stared into her eyes intently. 'I've been meaning to ask you something for some time. I know that nothing has really happened between us, not romantically, but I feel something and I think you do too. I just don't think it can ever happen here, in this place. So I want you to come with me to Cornwall.'

'What? *Cornwall*?' She gazed back, taking in his words, a flower of happiness unfurling within her.

He nodded. 'My cottage is big enough for two. I want to get you away from here, so you see what life might be like without the mighty burdens you've got. They're crushing you but you can't see it.'

Xenia felt as though someone had switched on a light and banished darkness. What a wonderful, marvellous idea. A new life. Freedom. Companionship. Perhaps love ... Her happiness wilted almost as soon as she imagined it. She said blankly, 'I can't.'

'Why not?' Harry looked exasperated and miserable at the same time, but he wasn't going to let it go. 'This house ... it's no good, Xenia. I want to get away from it, and you should too. Come for a short while. Give me six months, just six months.'

'Harry, I can't leave, you know that, not for any length of time. What about Mama? She'd never go. She'd be so unhappy anywhere else.'

'She's ill, Xenia. You can't look after her for the rest of your life, she wouldn't want that from you. We'll find a wonderful place for her to live nearby where she can be cared for properly, and you can begin to live for yourself.'

As he said it, she wanted it more than anything. But she knew that it wasn't possible. She couldn't rip Mama away from Charcombe, it would kill her. If Harry left, he would go without her.

'We have to stay,' she said, turning back to her soup. 'That's all there is to it.'

'Xenia, please. I want to look after you.'

'I don't need looking after,' she said haughtily, taking refuge from her pain in her pride. 'We're never leaving here. How would my father find us if we go?'

'You can't still believe that he's coming back.' Harry looked at her sadly. 'You know he never will.'

She burst into tears and shouted, 'How dare you talk to me like that! How can you say such awful things! Go away.'

So he had.

I knew he was right.

Xenia was ready for the party now, wrapped up in Mama's fur coat. She went to her bedroom window with its view over the park towards the big house, a view she almost always blocked with a drawn blind, so that she didn't have to see it. But now she stared at the squares of light that showed the windows of the house through the dark, frigid air.

I wonder what's happening in the house. They'll be getting ready for their party, making it beautiful with decorations and lights, trying to mask the truth about that place.

It had been the sadness that soaked into its stones that drove Harry away.

'You'll always know where I am,' he said to her, pressing a paper with the cottage's address on it. 'If you're ever free, come and find me.'

'I will,' she'd said, but she'd known then that she would never be free, not while there was still time for her, at least.

The spikes of rooftops and chimneys stood out against the night sky, the whole facade turned golden from the floodlights, ready to welcome people in.

It's a terrible house and always has been. Why does it draw badness and corruption to it? Like the wicked surgeon who cut through the fibres of Mama's brain and destroyed her forever.

Only a few years later, he had been implicated in a huge scandal of illegal operations and jailed for his activities. But it was too late for Mama, and for all the other poor souls he condemned to a living death.

Harry had written to her too, begging her to change her mind.

'Please, Xenia – your mother would want you to live your life, not exist in the shadow of hers.'

She had not written back. He wouldn't understand. Xenia had a debt to Mama that she could never repay. Mama had agreed to the procedure because Xenia and Papa had told her to. Papa had promised he would love her and stay with her, and he had failed her. She, Xenia, could not also fail. Not when she carried the burden of guilt that tormented her.

But perhaps it was the house that did it, after all. Perhaps it arranged all of it: the madness and the failed cures and the terrible operation. It brought me Harry and then sent him away. It punished Luke and Gwen with illness. It banished Papa.

Or had it? Had Papa chosen to inflict the final, awful blow of abandonment on them himself? Had he been, at heart, selfish and deceitful to the last?

She thought of her mother's last days, before the pneumonia came and finally killed her. Natalie had appeared at the top of the staircase in a long white nightdress, her face bizarrely made up, her hair gathered into curls around old hair rollers and bits of twig. 'You've all come here today to find out one thing,' she said in that perfect American accent. Her voice was creaky now, but she still sounded like her most famous creation. 'You want to know who killed Delilah.' She walked down the stairs to Xenia and said, 'Do you want to know who killed Delilah? It's very simple. *I* killed her. And I'm glad I did. I'd do it again tomorrow – and so would you!'

That was the last thing her mother ever said to her.

The pain of loss hit Xenia with such force she thought she might fall down. Tears stung her eyes. *Where did you go, Papa? Why did you leave us?*

She turned to face the ancient old house.

If I had my way, every last stone of you would be torn down.

Chapter Forty-Three

So here we are. The final secret still unsaid. Perhaps it never will be. In a funny way, that makes it easier to go, knowing he'd let that happen.

Buttercup sat in front of her dressing table mirror, slipping the rods of her earrings through her lobes: glittering hoops that sparkled by her cheeks. Her fair hair was pulled up into a high coil, and her make-up was bold: dark smoky lids, spiked lashes enhanced with dozens of little false ones, and red lips. Her dress was red too, tight and slit at the side and worn with silver platform trainers.

So I don't look too dressed up.

It was a Christmas party and a lavish one at that, but there were children there, and she'd no doubt be running around all over the place. Heels were out of the question.

Downstairs had been a bustle of activity all day as the staff, organised by Carol, got the party ready. Dozens of canapés were cooking in the kitchen, glasses were being polished and placed on tables next to jugs of soft drinks and tureens of mulled wine. Throughout the house fires were blazing and carols played from all the hidden speakers on the ground floor. There were decorations everywhere: holly wreaths, fronds of ivy, tartan bows and tinsel, with nativity scenes, lights, angels and snowflakes. Glass baubles hung from trees and garlands, and there was a tree in every room, besides the huge one in the hall hung with candy canes and hundreds of sparkling decorations. In the dining room, a model train chuffed around a snowy track through miniature Alpine villages, delivering a cargo of jellybeans and Smarties.

It couldn't be any more Christmassy, Buttercup thought as she came downstairs. She knew that somewhere nearby Father Christmas was having his beard applied while he drank a mulled cider and practised his ho-ho-hos, and the real reindeer was in the empty stables eating hay.

'Charles!' she called up the stairs. 'You'd better come down. The first guests will be here soon.'

His voice floated down from above. 'Coming.'

She had wondered what the day would hold after their confrontation last night, and expected him to demand another interview so that he could try to change her mind, but he'd driven out early and been gone most of the day. Now that he was back, he was oddly distracted and distant, hardly seeming to notice that Buttercup had packed a small bag and begun to gather her things together from around the house, leaving everything in a neat pile in the guest room for her to take away the next day.

Charles's relative calm had made her suspicious. What was going through his mind? Surely, after all this time monitoring her, watching and observing to make sure she wasn't about

415

to leave him, he wouldn't simply give in, now that she had actually said that she would. Would he simply sit back and watch her go?

It doesn't matter what he does. I'm going, and that's that.

She'd stayed for the party only to make sure it went ahead. She knew it was a highlight for the village, particularly the children, and she didn't want Charles to cancel it on account of her.

Carol came out of the kitchen, looking pink-cheeked but calm, her Christmas tree earrings dangling over her shoulders. 'Can I have a wee word?' she asked, coming up to Buttercup.

'Of course.' She gestured to the small morning room near the kitchen. 'Let's go in there, I think it's empty.'

Inside, Carol looked serious. 'I've made my decision. I'm on *your* team. I want you to know that I did write reports about you, because I had to. But I never gave them the really private stuff, I tried to protect you as much as I could. I know it's cold comfort and you might not believe me, but it's the truth. And I'm sorry for it. Honestly.'

Buttercup smiled. 'I do believe you, Carol, and I'm glad. I always hoped we were friends.' A thought occurred to her. 'Did you tell Charles that I'd emailed my old boss?'

She shook her head. 'No. I never knew that. I didn't snoop in your phone or computer, I refused to do that.'

'I see. Then he was reading my emails, even my draft emails.' She shook her head. 'He really would do anything to know what I was up to. And I would have told him any of it, any time he asked me.'

Carol said, 'I just want you to know that Steve and I are going to hand in our notice.'

'What?' Buttercup exclaimed, astonished. 'You don't have to do that.'

'We do. We've talked it over. We've not been happy here. Ever since we arrived, things have been going wrong, in hundreds of tiny ways. The boss is not the right person for us to work for. So we're going back to Scotland to be close to the kids. Steve knows a place in the Highlands where they're looking for a housekeeper and maintenance man. It sounds perfect for us.' Carol smiled, her eyes warm. 'We want you to get away from here, Mrs R. What we've witnessed – it isn't right. And what I saw – well . . . you know how I feel about it.'

Buttercup grasped Carol by the arm. 'Thank you!' she said. 'That means a lot.'

'Promise me you'll leave.'

'Yes. I will. I can't stay. I know that now. I'll go tomorrow, after the party.'

'It's the right thing.' Carol nodded, though her eyes were sad. 'I always thought it might turn out this way. It isn't possible for people to be happy in cages, even golden ones.' She smiled. 'I'd better get back to the caterers, they're going crazy in the kitchen. I'll see you later.'

Buttercup came out into the hall, a riot of Christmas all around her, and saw Charles examining the decorations on the central table, smartly dressed in a dark suit, ready to play lord of the manor. She regarded him with a kind of detached interest, wondering for a moment in an almost clinical way exactly what she felt towards him; her grief at the end of their love and the pain of betrayal had come out of her on that beach in Norfolk. Ever since, she found that she could bear it. If anything, she felt superbly strong, confident in herself and absolutely sure that she was going to be free in a matter of hours. For Charles, she felt a number of complex emotions – but none of them were love. His lies had set her free from that.

She walked towards him and he turned to look at her, his eyes cool and remote. The sound of the old front doorbell suddenly jangled through the hall, and they both jumped.

Charles looked at his watch. 'We have an early bird. No one's supposed to be here for at least half an hour.'

Buttercup went over to the door and pulled it open, finding herself staring into the smiling face of Gawain Ashley, his coppery hair bright in the light from the lantern above. He was dressed in a well-cut jacket over a jumper and jeans, and his polished chestnut-coloured lace-up boots. Behind him was a small, silver-haired old woman with misty blue eyes and a strange, almost fearful expression on her face as she looked past Buttercup into the hall beyond her.

As if she's seeing things I can't.

'Hi,' Gawain said almost shyly. 'I hope you don't mind. Xenia and I have come up a bit early. I particularly wanted to meet your husband, and I had a feeling he'd be pretty busy once everyone started arriving.'

Buttercup stepped back. 'It's absolutely fine, we're ready as it happens. Please come in, Charles is right here.'

Charles was coming towards them, a broad smile on his face. 'Princess, how wonderful to see you again. Thank you so much for coming. And you must be . . .'

'Gawain Ashley.' He bowed courteously. 'I've already had the pleasure of meeting Mrs Redmain.'

'Yes, she told me. How do you do.' Charles shook his hand and leaned to kiss the air on either side of the old woman's face. 'Princess, I don't believe you've met my wife . . .'

'Buttercup Redmain,' Buttercup said politely, wondering if she should curtsey, but the old lady simply raised her eyebrows at the unusual name, bowed her head and murmured a quiet hello.

'Please come in.' Charles summoned a waitress from the corner of the room with an imperious snap of his fingers. 'Drinks for our guests, please. What would you like?'

'You're most kind,' Gawain said politely, 'but we might wait and have a drink shortly. I wondered if you might be kind enough to show us the wonderful little shrine you have upstairs to the memory of Captain Redmain. Such an unusual thing to have, quite a curiosity.'

'I'd be delighted,' beamed Charles.

Buttercup looked quizzically at Gawain but he avoided her gaze.

Charles was already heading across the hall towards the stairs. 'Follow me. The house must look quite different to you, Princess, we've done such a lot to it.'

'You certainly have,' said the old lady. Buttercup heard her add under her breath: 'Though you won't have changed anything at all.'

419

Charles led them up the stairs, talking eagerly about his quest to acquire memorabilia for his collection. Gawain, following close behind, was nodding with interest. As they went up, he turned and looked over his shoulder straight at Buttercup and his eyes contained an expression she was not expecting.

Apology? What's he got to be sorry to me for?

She brought up the rear, behind the old lady, apprehensive to be so close to her. So far, her knowledge of the princess was limited to the unpleasant outbursts, the shouting and fist waving, the fit of temper on Bonfire Night. She was half afraid she would turn round and start yelling, upbraiding Charles and her for what they'd done to her old home. But she seemed quite calm.

And Gawain told me those sad things about her – her mother being so ill.

She felt a sudden sympathy for the old woman in front of her. It was so easy to judge people without knowing anything of their story.

But everyone has their sadness, disappointments and burdens, she reminded herself. Even those who appear to have the world at their feet and their heart's desire can be horribly miserable underneath.

I'm proof of that.

'Fascinating,' Gawain said, walking around the Redmain room and looking at all the exhibits again as if for the first time. 'Really ... *interesting*. What a man he was.'

'Yes, I'm always keen to find out whatever I can about

him.' Charles smiled. 'It's a great honour to have such a distinguished ancestor.'

'I bet,' Gawain said. He stared at the marble bust with its tricorn hat and tasselled epaulettes, and turned to look at Charles. 'I expect you could give me a blow-by-blow account of his actions at Trafalgar.'

'I probably could!' Charles laughed.

'And of what happened after the battle? What do you know about that?'

'I know he bought this house and remodelled it extensively. I know he married a Mademoiselle Thierry and had five children, and died of a fever in his late fifties.'

Gawain was staring at the ornate blade mounted on the wall. 'Wow, what a fine sword that is! You must be so proud of Captain Redmain.'

'Yes,' Charles said, his eyes narrowing. 'Of course. I would have thought that goes without saying.'

Gawain put his hands in his pockets and took a deep breath. 'I don't want to rain on your parade, Mr Redmain, but you might need to prepare for a bit of a shock. I've done some investigating down in Portsmouth at the naval museum and at the British Library, and I'm afraid it's not quite as straightforward as it seems.'

Charles's eyebrows lifted and he said coldly, 'Oh? What do you mean?'

Gawain looked about, scanning the whole room. 'Redmain bought this house with his prize money, that's true. But he also bought something else with his loot: a sugar plantation, in Antigua, in the Colonies. And for his valuable cash crop, he needed lots and lots of workers. According to my research, he had at least two hundred and fifty slaves, imported from South Africa.'

The princess raised her eyebrows, her expression grim. She hadn't looked at the collection but had been watching Gawain intently. She sighed softly and shook her head.

Buttercup gasped. 'Slaves? Oh no . . .'

Gawain looked at her, sombre now. 'Yes. Slaves. And they made him a fortune. That money paid for the rebuilding of this house.'

Buttercup felt sick. *This beautiful house, built on such misery. This is terrible.*

Gawain continued:

'Then slavery was abolished. No more lovely free labour to sweat and toil to make Captain Redmain rich!' His voice took on a lightly sarcastic tone, one Buttercup knew would infuriate Charles, whose face was stony with a vein throbbing dangerously in his temple. Gawain went on: 'But all was not lost. The British government paid him compensation for the loss of his unpaid labour. He got a great deal of money – hundreds of thousands in today's money. His slaves, however, got nothing but their freedom.' Gawain paused. He looked serious as he turned back to Charles. 'I'm sorry, Mr Redmain, but your house – lovely though it is – has an unfortunate history that includes the civil war slaughter of women and children, and the blood and sweat of slave labour. The princess has told me it's an unhappy place – she thinks it's cursed, actually – and perhaps she has a point.'

Buttercup looked at Charles, who had now gone red in the

face. He seemed lost for words, spluttering as he reached for something to say.

'What an awful story,' she said in a low voice. 'I'm shocked. We had no idea.'

Charles found his voice, his tone indignant. 'How dare you come here and say such a thing, and so rudely?' he demanded, furious. 'I'm no apologist for slavery – it was terrible, inhuman and wrong. But plenty of institutions and buildings that we treasure, revere even, were built on the proceeds of it. It's hardly the fault of the building! *Cursed*?' He laughed contemptuously. 'What bloody nonsense. I won't have you spouting such superstitious nonsense, upsetting my wife in the process.'

'I'm not upset,' Buttercup said coolly. 'But I am appalled. Maybe the princess is right.' She glanced at the old lady, who sighed softly, her face slack with sadness. 'I've felt it too. The chill here. The sadness. No one seems to have found what they wanted here.'

Charles shot her a scornful look and said dismissively, 'Rubbish.'

Gawain was moving slowly around the displays in the room. 'It's not just that slave money built – or rebuilt, if you'd rather – this house. I'm afraid it's much worse. Redmain himself was a tyrant, both to the sailors under his command in the navy, and to those poor souls unfortunate enough to work for him in the Caribbean. He was harsh, cruel, unfair, an inflictor of violent and inhumane punishments. A man who fathered many children on his unwilling female slaves.' He turned to look apologetically at Charles. 'You may not like to hear it, Mr Redmain, but I'm afraid it's a matter of record. I'm surprised you haven't discovered for yourself what a thoroughly unpleasant man Redmain was.'

Charles could only stare, speechless and utterly taken aback.

'Or,' Gawain said thoughtfully, 'perhaps you did know, but decided that the likelihood of others finding out was pretty slim, when you had all these lovely things to show off.'

Buttercup looked at Charles and instantly knew that Gawain was right. Charles had known. He knew full well what a monster his ancestor was, but revered him anyway.

Charles would have made it his business to know everything there was to know about Redmain. But it didn't suit him that his hero was a beast, so he decided to ignore it and focus on building this shrine to him instead. And Charles is his descendant. No wonder he's capable of such things. Maybe this place helped him channel his own brand of ruthlessness.

Charles stiffened, his hands tense, and said in a low voice, 'Get out of my house, you shit. How dare you come here with your baseless rumours and unfounded gossip? I'm appalled and offended.'

Gawain turned and stared at him, his warm brown eyes suddenly hard and his expression contemptuous. 'Hardly unfounded, I'm afraid. Read the records in the naval archives and the British Library. And you know what? This nasty little exhibition offends me and it should offend you too. I'm happy to leave. In fact, I can't wait to shake the dust of this place off my shoes.'

He strode past the outraged Charles and out into the corridor.

The princess spoke for the first time in a clear, precise voice. 'Madness and misery and death. That's all this wretched house has ever brought anyone.' She turned and followed Gawain out into the hall and Buttercup heard them descending the stairs.

Charles was glaring at her, his face suffused with anger. 'You brought that disgusting man into my house!' he hissed.

'I had no idea what he was going to say, any more than you did.' She took a step towards him, her shoulders straight. 'Don't blame me for this. You knew all along about Redmain, didn't you? But you thought you could keep it to yourself. Because nasty little secrets don't matter if only you know about them, right?'

Charles took a step towards her. 'I've had enough of this nonsense. Your little tantrum has gone on for long enough. If you have something to say, then say it.'

'Little tantrum?' Fury boiled up inside her. How dare he dismiss her so easily? '*What*?'

'You heard me. Let's stop pretending that you're going to leave me. You know you won't. The luckiest day of your life was when Lazlo introduced us, and you know it. So why don't you be a good girl and stop this silliness? Things are done my way, and that's how it is.'

She stared at him, speechless and disgusted.

'Come on.' He took a step towards her, his eyes glittering. 'Marriage is a bargain, you knew what you were getting when you married me. I would give you this life, this smooth and comfortable life, give you my love and my adoration, but it would be on my terms. That's what we agreed.'

'We never agreed any such thing!'

'You agreed every day, in many little ways. Don't pretend you didn't. What have you got without me? You'll find out what Ingrid discovered – that life is difficult, unpleasant and grim if you cross me. So.' He put his hand towards her and smiled. 'Why don't you agree that we'll put this behind us and pretend it never happened? I'll forgive and forget. You start behaving. Do we have a deal?'

She stared at him for a moment, disgusted. 'No, we don't have a deal.' She spoke clearly and carefully. 'I never wanted this, and I never agreed to it. You don't seem to understand that I'm leaving you, and I never want to see you again. There's no bargain. No deal. I won't be behaving. And I won't be keeping quiet either – about any of this.'

Charles was suddenly still. 'Are you sure? Because there's time to save this unfortunate situation.' Unexpectedly, he smiled, his eyes softening and suddenly tender. 'I still love you, darling.'

'*Darling.* You never call me by my name!' she cried. 'I can't remember when you last called me by my name. Do you even know who I am? Do you?'

'Calm down, dar—' He caught himself and amended it to: 'Buttercup.'

The name sounded awkward in his mouth.

Buttercup shuddered. 'I can't stand it in this room. I can't stand being surrounded by this awful ancestor of yours. I've got to get out.'

She turned and headed for the door.

426

Chapter Forty-Four

Buttercup dashed out into the hall, feeling as if she was suffocating. The noise coming from downstairs told her that some of the guests had arrived and more were coming. She stopped on the landing, gulping for air, as though the atmosphere in the Redmain room had been fetid and rotten. Charles came up swiftly behind her.

'This isn't going to happen,' he said ominously. 'You're not leaving me.'

'Yes, it is. I'm going.'

He reached out swiftly and took her hand. She whisked it away as if she had touched something red hot.

'No!' she cried. 'Not any more. Never again.'

Suddenly, to her surprise, his cold expression changed. His eyes were full of pain. 'Why? *Why?* You have to tell me.'

She closed her eyes, her breath coming out in shaky exhalations. It all led to this, she could see it now. This moment had to come. Her time in the house and with Charles was almost up. Downstairs, she could hear laughter and children shouting, and the clinking of glasses. The front door was open and a stream of people were coming in. They would be looking for her and Charles soon.

I need to go. Now. I just don't know where.

She opened her eyes. 'All right, Charles. If you insist. Just so you know that there's no coming back.' She took a breath, still rocked with pain when she thought about it. *It needs to be said. The last secret between us has to be dragged out into the open.* 'There's the little matter of the operation you had, that you decided not to tell me about. The month after I got pregnant, you booked yourself into a private hospital in London for a vasectomy. It's in your medical file, there's no point in denying it. I never had a hope of conceiving with you. You didn't want any more children, and the strange thing is that somehow I guessed that you didn't. But it never occurred to me that you might do such an awful thing – string me along, letting me go through it all, month after month, hoping and waiting and having the crashing disappointment when it didn't happen ... when all along you knew that I wouldn't get pregnant. No wonder you refused to go to the fertility clinic. It would have taken them about five minutes to work out that you weren't producing anything.'

Charles's face was closed, his eyes cool. He'd been caught, but she could see that with one easy leap, he discarded the old state of affairs and moved on, only thinking of how he could make the best of the current situation.

He's not sorry, she realised with a horrible stab of pain. *He's not remorseful at all. Oh my God. He's not sorry.*

Charles took a deep breath and put his hands up. 'Okay. Yes. You're right. I know – it's inexcusable.'

'I agree,' she said simply. *I don't even sound angry.* Any last, small vestige of her old love for him withered and died. *He's not sorry. At least he's making this easy for me. He's killed my love like he killed our chance of a family together.*

'It was madness. I don't know why I did it. I can have the operation reversed, if that's what you want.'

'And that will make it all better, will it?' She smiled bitterly. 'I don't think so, Charles. Can't you see? You deceived me. Our life together is at an end. You can stay here with your beloved Captain Redmain. The pair of you make a perfect partnership.'

She turned and began to walk away down the hall. Charles strode after her and grabbed her arm, pulling her round to face him.

'You don't do that,' he hissed, his eyes blazing. 'You don't just walk away from me. You do as I say. I've given you everything you ever wanted. You've lived a life of luxury, thanks to me. You'd better think hard about what a cold world it is out there without my protection and how tough I can make things. And you know what? I'm still willing to forgive this madness, if you agree to stay. I let you have your little scene last night – you got to scream and cry and make your ugly accusations. That's out of your system. Now it's time to grow up and accept reality. But if you walk out the door, you'll never come back here. I can promise you that.'

His fingers dug hard into her arm. She tried to shake him free but his grip got tighter. 'Let go of me! I'd rather die than stay with you!' She glared at him, her eyes full of agony. 'You didn't give me everything I ever wanted – you took it away!

You can't understand that even now.' She stopped, her face contorting with the torment of it, pain twisting in her gut so hard she thought she might fall if Charles hadn't been holding her.

'You little fool,' he rapped out. 'You're a stupid child. I won't allow this. You're not going.' He grabbed her other arm and she stared at him, shocked and afraid. 'If you do, you'll regret it forever.'

'Let me go right now! You're hurting me!'

He was staring at her, his blue eyes hard and glassy as though he was partly listening to a voice in his head. He was breathing hard, his jaw set, his grip tighter than ever.

'I mean it!' she exclaimed, but he didn't seem to be listening. 'You're hurting me. Stop it, let me go.'

'Hello, here you are!' said a cheerful voice behind them.

Charles loosened his grip on her arms and Buttercup turned to see Cathy Tranter coming up the stairs, followed by Wilf. She tried to pull herself together, but she felt numbed and disconnected from the world going on just below them, still feeling Charles's fingers digging painfully into her skin even though he had released his hold. 'Oh – hello, Cathy . . . Wilf . . . We were just coming down, weren't we, Charles?'

He didn't seem to hear anything, but stared at Buttercup with a fierce, implacable gaze.

'Charles, are you all right?' asked Cathy, concerned, reaching them. She put her hand on his arm. He jumped violently, letting go of Buttercup completely. He looked dazed as he focused on Cathy, stuttered and found his voice.

'Ah – yes! I ... I'm perfectly fine. Let's go down and join the others. Have you got a drink? Oh good. Good.'

Charles began to walk uncertainly across the landing then turned back, looking at Buttercup, his face set in a strange, stricken expression. 'I'll see you later, darling.'

She stared back at him. 'Later,' she said.

He walked away.

Downstairs, the party was in full swing. Children raced around or stuffed themselves with goodies; adults loitered, eating the plentiful canapés and sipping drinks; the hall was full of noise, heat and ...

Eyes. Everybody's looking at me, everybody's watching me.

Cathy Tranter was talking to her as they moved through the crowd, pointing out Olly with a mince pie in each hand, and laughing, telling her about Bethany asleep at home, the Christmas rush at the pub and how well it was going.

Buttercup could hear her only vaguely, the voice coming in and out of her consciousness like a radio with the volume being turned up and down. She was aware of the many faces turning to her, the dozens of people who wanted an acknowledgement of their presence, a moment to talk to her and be polite. She saw Agnieska across the room, taking her two boys to look at the Christmas tree, and felt as though she remembered her only vaguely, from a long time ago. She walked on with Cathy, feeling as though she was drowning in the hubbub.

I don't belong here. This isn't my house. I have to get out of here.

431

But it was more than that. Charles had been a different man, in the grip of forces she didn't understand.

I'm afraid. I have to get out while I still can.

She thought wildly of grabbing Cathy and asking her to take her to the pub.

I can't. She wouldn't understand. Besides, they have a new baby.

From the corner of her eye, she could see Charles. His public face was back on, he was moving about, chatting and shaking hands, greeting friends loudly and seeming carefree and full of the bonhomie of the season. But she'd seen behind that mask, and it frightened her. She could still feel the pressure of his fingers on her arm, and hear the threat in his voice. Fear prickled over her skin.

This is my chance to get away, while he's not watching me. She thought of her bag packed upstairs. *I can't get it, he'll see. I'll leave it and get Carol to send it on.*

She turned to Cathy. 'I'm so sorry, will you excuse me? I must check on things in the kitchen. Let's catch up soon, okay?'

'Oh – yeah, sure,' Cathy said. 'Great party! Everyone's having a fab time.'

'Father Christmas is coming in a minute, make sure Olly gets a present. See you later.'

Buttercup turned and hurried in the direction of the kitchen, where the catering staff had taken over and were loading plates with fresh canapés and refilling jugs with mulled wine. She made her way through, muttering 'excuse me, please, thanks so much' until she reached the boot room, where she grabbed a coat, scarf and beanie hat and put them on over her red dress. She kicked off her silver trainers and stuffed her feet into wellington boots, then opened the back door and dashed outside, closing it on Tippi who had jumped up from her bed, eager for a walk.

In the courtyard at the back of the house, it was cold and dark, the snow whirling lightly in tissuey flakes where the light caught it. She began to march out of the courtyard towards the side of the house and the driveway. Suddenly she felt someone grab her arm and she gasped, turning around with blazing eyes.

'It's me,' Phil said. He was wrapped up against the freezing weather, only the pale circle of his face visible between the dark bulk of his coat and woolly hat. 'Where are you going?'

'I have to get out of here,' Buttercup said desperately. 'I'm sorry—'

'Don't be sorry, you have nothing to apologise for. I'm the one who's sorry. I should have talked to you a long time ago.'

'What do you mean?'

'I could have told you what you wanted to know: about Ingrid. All of the boss's nasty little ways. The fact he was going down there to see her. I should have done that.'

'It's fine. You thought you were doing the right thing. It's okay. Really.' The wind was buffeting her, chilling her beneath her coat.

'I'm sorry. That's all.' Phil looked up over the house's towering brick chimneys, soaring up into the sky to be lost in the darkness. 'It's a beautiful place, no mistake, but there's more to life than that. The heart is all wrong.'

'Yes, that's it. The heart is wrong.' Buttercup smiled at him through the freezing air. 'Thanks, Phil. See you later. One more thing . . .'

'Yes?'

'Look after Milky for me. Make sure she gets lots of exercise.'

'Don't you worry. I'll look after everything. Can I give you a lift somewhere?'

She hesitated, tempted. *I don't want him to know where I'm going.* 'No, thanks. I've got someone meeting me.'

'Okay. If you're sure.'

'I am. Bye.'

She turned and started to head out into the darkness, where the drive was illuminated by lanterns along its length, to guide the visitors in.

Buttercup went along the side of the drive, half jogging, half stumbling in the dark. Cars went past her at intervals: guests for the party, heading up to the house, driving slowly through the snow. She pressed on through the cutting wind, intent on reaching the wrought-iron gates where upturned lights bathed the stone pillars in an orange glow and made the greyhounds on the top look like strange, otherworldly beasts poised to come alive, spring down and rampage along the lane. The gates were open for the visiting cars, and she slipped through unnoticed. As soon as she was outside the purlieus of the house, she felt a wild elation and broke into a run, sprinting as fast as she could in her wellington boots until she reached the gate she was looking for. It swung open under her hand, and she went up the path towards the front door, where the fanlight glowed above.

Oh, thank God. She's back.

At the door, she looked about for a bell or knocker, and then saw an old dangling pull with an iron handle. She yanked on it and heard the rocking chime of a bell inside. Panting, she waited anxiously and then, after a minute or two, the door opened.

A woman stood just inside, disconcertingly normal, with dark hair loose around her face, wearing jeans and a long polo-necked jumper. She looked at Buttercup, raising a quizzical eyebrow.

'Well, well,' she said drily. 'I wondered how long it would take you to get here.'

Chapter Forty-Five

Ingrid stepped back to allow Buttercup to step inside out of the cold. The hallway was warm and lit by a lamp on the console table. Buttercup, shivering, unwound her scarf and looked anxiously at Ingrid. 'I'm so glad you're home.'

'I've just got back,' Ingrid replied. 'Are you all right? You look terrible.'

Buttercup took off her coat, revealing her red party dress.

'Here, you'll need this shawl,' Ingrid said, passing her one from the coat hooks. 'It's your Christmas party tonight, and you've run away?'

'That's the size of it.' Buttercup shivered again, not just from cold. 'I had to get out of there.'

'Then you must be desperate. Come through to the kitchen.' Ingrid led the way down the hall to a large flagstoned kitchen, cosy with the heat of a range cooker. Everywhere was colour: bright Mediterranean pottery, family photographs in red wooden frames, paintings in hot tones of yellow and orange, reds and green. The kitchen cupboards were painted bright blue and the range was a shiny post-box red, with a row of hand-decorated jugs on the shelf above it.

'Do you want some tea or coffee?' Ingrid asked as Buttercup sank down into a chair at the kitchen table.

'Yes, please.' She was still shaking hard. 'Tea would be lovely, thank you.' She pulled the shawl tight against her flimsy red dress, trying to get the warmth into her cold bones, but her teeth were chattering now. *This is ridiculous. I'm colder now than I was outside.*

Ingrid looked over from where she was switching on the kettle and came over at once, her expression concerned. She sat down next to Buttercup and took her hand.

'S ... s-s-s ... soh ... sorry.' Her teeth were juddering uncontrollably together and she grimaced with frustration. 'S-s-s ... sorry ...'

'Stop apologising. It's fine. You're in a state.' Ingrid squeezed her hand.

Buttercup was shaking harder, her shoulders wracked with the movement, her hands uncontrollable. 'I ... d-d-don't know what's h-h-h-happening to me.' She gazed up at Ingrid pleadingly.

The other woman leaned forward, her eyes serious. 'You're terrified. Has Charles hurt you? Are you in danger?'

'N ... n ... no.' As soon as she said that, the shivering began to scale down, as though the one word had released something. 'He hasn't hurt me.'

'But you're afraid he might?'

'I don't know.' Her trembling eased off. Ingrid's blue-grey eyes were scanning her anxiously. 'I thought he only engaged in psychological warfare.' She managed a weak grin. 'But suddenly, tonight, I thought . . . I thought perhaps—'

'You were afraid that he would maybe get physical . . . ?'

Buttercup gazed at her, beseeching. 'Did he ever hurt you?'

Ingrid blinked slowly and said evenly, 'Let's say . . . it only happened once or twice, and it wasn't as serious as it could have been. Not that that excuses him. It was the beginning of the end, though.'

Buttercup's eyes filled with tears, she bit her lip and gave a sudden, sharp nod, unable to trust herself to speak for a moment. Then she said in a quavering voice, 'I realised tonight it was a possibility. He seemed so different, as though he was possessed by something, listening to a voice I couldn't hear.'

Ingrid nodded sadly, her eyes full of compassion. 'Yes. That's how it is. And I know what you mean. That voice of his.' She got up and went over to the bench to make the tea, dropping teabags into a teapot, filling it with hot water and collecting mugs. 'I've sometimes wondered what the voice in Charles's head would sound like if you could bring it out and listen to it. I think it would be one of the nastiest, mean-spirited bullies you could imagine. We're all victims of it, and its cowardly paranoia and extraordinary narcissism. But at least we don't have to listen to it day and night.'

Buttercup's adrenaline rush had subsided and she was cold again. She huddled tighter into the shawl.

Ingrid took a moment while she poured out the tea, added milk and brought the mugs over to the table. As she sat back down next to Buttercup, putting a steaming cup in front of her, she smiled. She had thick straight dark brows, a rosy complexion with a small scatter of freckles over her snub nose, and wide, friendly mouth. 'Charles is a driven man, always pushed on by that voice. That's its upside – it gives him verve and intensity, it's made him the success he is. I just don't think it's worth the awful downside of what it does to him and everyone who loves him. On the one hand it puffs him up, tells him he's the greatest thing in the world, that he can do anything and be anyone, and on the other, it beats him down, telling him he's worthless, alone, unlovable, being betrayed at every turn. It makes him angry, miserable, afraid and it tells him to trust nobody.'

Buttercup stared at her, speechless. She found her voice. 'That's it – that's exactly how it is. That's what I can't understand. Why didn't he trust me?'

'He trusts no one.' Ingrid lifted the mug to her lips and blew at the drifting steam. 'The voice in his head is the most powerful thing in his life, it governs everything he is and does and thinks. My frustration was that I could never drown it out. No matter how much love I gave him and how much I stood by him and proved my loyalty over and over ... he never believed in me. He couldn't stop listening to that voice. And in the end, he brings about what he fears the most – being abandoned.'

Buttercup wrapped her fingers around the hot cup, shrinking down into the softness of Ingrid's shawl. 'Yes,' she whispered. It felt as though Ingrid had taken a confusing mass of jigsaw pieces and calmly laid them together to make the picture complete.

'We're victims,' Ingrid said quietly. 'But Charles is the biggest victim of all. In the end, we have to save ourselves because we can't change it and we can't fix it, no matter how much we want to.'

'Where does the voice come from?'

'It's the voice of his past.' Ingrid shrugged lightly. 'That's my theory, anyway. His father left him, his mother loved his brother best and married an unlovely stepfather who banished Charles to boarding school. That little boy got the message loud and clear – *people I need and love will always let me down and leave me.*'

Buttercup nodded. 'That makes sense.' She sipped some tea; the hot liquid trail down her throat comforted her and warmed her insides. 'I felt so angry that he could destroy what we had – all that love and happiness and the promise of our future together. I can't understand why he'd deny himself that, deny *both* of us.'

'He can't help it. I'm not excusing it. I suffered plenty, and sometimes he's just pig-headed, obstinate, childish and selfish. But, like I said, in the end, he's the one who suffers most.' Ingrid was thoughtful as she drank her tea. 'I meant what I said – I've been expecting you. I didn't know exactly when, but I guessed that one day you'd want to talk to me. We are probably the only people in the world who know what we've been through.'

Buttercup nodded. Her lips trembled and she felt as though she might be on the brink of tears, but fought to hold them back. The peace and cosiness of this house was so different from what she had just left: the chaos of the party, the unpleasantness of the Redmain room, and the horrible encounter with her husband. She took a deep breath and got control of the tears.

Ingrid said, 'Since you've turned up like this, I'm assuming you've got to the end of your rope.' She shrugged with a wry smile. 'It took me much longer. Maybe Charles is getting better at driving his wives mad. What happened? Do you want to tell me?'

Buttercup managed a weak smile in return. 'I found out that he's been lying to me. I wanted a baby, you see, but after a miscarriage, I couldn't get pregnant again – just couldn't. There was no obvious problem. And then . . . I got access to Charles's private records.'

Ingrid raised her eyebrows. 'Well done you. I never managed that, I'm afraid. Elaine was like a lioness whenever I was around, padding about ready to strike me if I seemed to threaten her boss.'

'She was quite nice to me,' Buttercup said, almost apologetically. 'But I think that might have been because she thinks I'm stupid.'

Ingrid laughed, then her smile faded. 'I'm sorry. This is serious, I know. You found out that Charles had had a vasectomy, didn't you?'

Buttercup nodded, astonished. 'How do you know?'

'He told me. But I had no idea he hadn't told *you*. He said you were quite happy, because you didn't want any children.'

Buttercup gasped with shock. 'Why does he say these awful things?' she whispered numbly. 'He lies and lies.'

Ingrid nodded sympathetically. 'It's a compulsion, part of

the way he protects himself but – like the rest of it – completely counterproductive. For years, I've taken everything he says with a massive pinch of salt. Generally, I ask myself "How does it benefit Charles if I believe what he says?" and there's usually a reason. So I have no truck with anything.'

'Why would he want you to believe that about me?' Buttercup asked, wretchedly. 'When the thing I wanted most in the world was a family.'

'I suspect he liked to sow the seeds of dislike between us, and make sure we wanted as little as possible to do with each other.' Ingrid put her mug back on the table and began to trace the pattern with her fingertip. She sighed. 'Divide and rule is his motto, and he does it even when it's completely unnecessary. In his head, he would have wanted to keep us apart, for some unspecified reason, or simply because it makes sense to him. You see, he has so many secrets that he finds it hard to keep track of them all.'

Buttercup felt strange, as if she were about to float free of her body. Dizziness flooded her brain and her vision blurred, cleared, then blurred again.

'Are you all right?' Ingrid's voice sounded far away and fuzzy.

Buttercup closed her eyes: they were stinging, prickling as though hundreds of tiny hot needles were punishing them. The grief came spiralling out of her inner self and engulfed her, the way it had in Norfolk on that windy beach. Her head drooped and she felt exhausted, soiled by all the lies, beaten. She put her hands to her face and wept.

*

It was some time before she could speak, and when she stopped sobbing, she found that Ingrid's arm was around her shoulders, and she was comforting her with murmured comments and soothing sounds.

When Buttercup was calmer, Ingrid said quietly, 'I'm so sorry. Are you feeling better?'

'Yes, thank you,' Buttercup said, sniffing. Ingrid handed her a tissue. 'I was destroyed when I found out about the vasectomy. That's when I realised that everything was over.'

Ingrid gazed at her solemnly. 'I knew Charles didn't want more children. He told me himself after we had Charlotte. Right from the start he was determined. Luckily, I agreed with him, but if I hadn't, I wouldn't have given much for my chances of having another baby. I didn't know how ruthless he's prepared to be. Except . . .'

She got up and went to the dresser, with its load of coloured china, postcards, and odds and ends, and opened a drawer. She took out a folder and came back to the table. Opening it, Ingrid poured out a shower of stiff confetti, the haphazardly cut-up remains of photographs.

Buttercup looked up, questioning, but she already knew what she was looking at.

'Whenever I've displeased him over the last few years, I've received another through the post. One of my family photographs, taken from my album and cut to pieces. They're usually of me, but there's always the threat that it will be my father, or my grandparents. The pictures that are irreplaceable.' Ingrid smiled grimly. 'I'm expecting one any day, actually.

443

I always get one after I've been to visit Joachim. He always knows when I've gone, and when I get back.'

Buttercup ran her fingers through the chopped-up photographs; they looked like a difficult jigsaw puzzle of hundreds of tiny pieces. 'I'm so sorry. Joachim was the man you left Charles for?'

Ingrid nodded. 'I had to stay here, you see. Joachim couldn't stay, his life and work are all over Europe. He's a jouster.' She laughed. 'It sounds so ridiculous, but he is. My actual knight in shining armour. He attends events across the world, takes part in competitions. One day, perhaps, I'll join him.'

'It sounds extraordinary. Completely different to life in Charcombe.' Buttercup smiled and picked up some of the photograph pieces, letting them fall in a spiky shower to the table. 'But this is awful. I can't believe he'd be so cruel.'

Ingrid shrugged. 'What you have to understand is that Charles carries his grudges to extremes. He'd almost rather hurt himself than give quarter to anyone who's crossed him. He's always threatened to destroy something I love – and do you know, sometimes I even worried about the children. I knew it would hurt him just as desperately if anything happened to them, and yet I also knew that the thought of condemning me to a lifetime of pain might prove sufficient enticement to make it worth condemning himself to the same.'

Buttercup gasped. 'But that's terrible. It's wicked!'

'He didn't do it. Chopping up photographs isn't quite as bad.'

'It all comes from the same place.' Buttercup looked up at

Ingrid, calm and serious. 'Ingrid, can I stay here tonight? I'm going to get my things from the house and then I'll make my plans for where I'll go and what I'll do. I'm afraid that I don't have a knight in shining armour to escape with, but I'll think of something.'

'You're more than welcome to stay here, I can lend you a nightdress and you can help yourself to any toiletries you need. There's no need to go back to the house. I don't think that's a good idea.'

'I'll be fine. Carol and Steve are there, for now. But there are personal things I must get, especially if there's any likelihood Charles might take it into his head to destroy them.'

'If what you say is right, he'll be in an extremely strange place. I wouldn't risk a confrontation with him, if I were you. Stay here tonight, then we'll go up tomorrow once it's all calmed down. We could even ask a policeman to come with us if you think there'll be trouble.' Ingrid put her hand on Buttercup's arm, her expression earnest. 'Seriously – don't go. I mean it.'

Buttercup gazed back at her for a moment, and said, 'All right. I won't go. We'll go tomorrow instead.'

'Good. I'll make up the spare room for you.'

Chapter Forty-Six

Gawain and Xenia sat facing one another over her kitchen table, a pot of tea cooling between them.

'What really brought you back to Charcombe, Gawain?' Xenia asked. He was a fuzzy shape in front of her, spiked with starry lights and surrounded by a golden halo. *My sight is getting worse.* 'I feel as though you had more of a motive to go up to the house tonight than you've confessed. Is it just this book you're planning, or something else?'

Gawain shrugged and smiled.

'You took a particular pleasure in passing on your knowledge about Captain Redmain,' Xenia said drily.

'I did, it's true,' Gawain said a little sheepishly. 'Perhaps that wasn't very nice of me. But he's exactly the kind of puffed-up pleased-with-himself individual it's impossible not to enjoy deflating. And ... I couldn't bear his wife believing in him, or believing the tripe about the horrible captain.'

'Oh ...' Xenia gave him a meaningful look. 'Is that your real motive, making the scales drop from her eyes?'

She couldn't make out Gawain's features with clarity but

446

she could hear the embarrassment in his voice and imagined a pink blush on his cheeks. 'I wouldn't go that far. It's true that she's far too good for a man like that. But I doubt I'll see her again. I won't be welcome in Charcombe Park after this. She kindly invites me to her party, and I repay that by giving her husband's favourite fantasy a good kicking.' He reached out and Xenia felt the smooth warmth of his fingers on her hand. 'I came back because I owe you something, Xenia. I've been thinking about it: I'm sure we can try to find out what happened to your father. We might be able to track him down, locate him, wherever he is.'

'He must be long dead,' Xenia said mournfully. 'You'll never find him, I'm sure of it. I would have known years ago if he wanted to be found.'

'There must be records somewhere. You can tell me everything you remember about his departure and his plans, and we'll take it from there. If he sailed or flew, there'll be passenger lists. Immigration records. There has to be a trace of him, and it's much easier to find out now with so many records being put online.'

'I appreciate it.' Xenia shook her head. 'It's too late. I don't even know if I want to find out what happened. It would break my heart if I discovered things I'd be better off not knowing.'

There was a pause. Gawain squeezed her hand lightly and removed his own. He sighed again. 'I'm sorry. I will try, but you're probably right.'

After a moment, Xenia said, 'I imagine you must need to get home now.'

Gawain nodded. 'I'll head off tomorrow. I ought to get back, I've got some work commissions to finish. I'll come back and visit you soon, though. I'm worried about leaving you alone.'

Xenia laughed suddenly, loudly enough to make Petrova, snoozing on a chair, wake up startled. 'Alone! I was alone for years, even when my mother was alive. Don't worry about me.'

'But you're older. You shouldn't be by yourself.'

'I've got Agnieska. She's helping me more and more. One day, perhaps, I'll suggest that she comes and lives closer. I can help her with that. She's a good girl and I think she'll look after me for as long as I need her. I have no family, no one to leave my possessions to. Perhaps she and her boys can be my family.'

Gawain's voice sounded suddenly tender. 'That's a lovely idea, Xenia.'

Looking at him, she could see odd waving lights around him, like pointed little flames dancing over his shoulder. Xenia hesitated and leaned forward, blinking heavily. 'May I ask you a favour? Will you stay here this evening? The guest room is always ready. My eyes are bad tonight, and recently I've started to get some odd changes in my vision – strange things happening on the edges of what I can see. I find it happens less if someone else is around.'

'Of course I'll stay. I'll pop down to the pub and get my things, and then I'll be right back.'

'Thank you. I'm grateful.'

*

448

Gawain was back half an hour after he left, shuddering with the cold blast of the wind outside. 'That weather is nasty. I don't remember it ever being so bad this early in December.'

'A Christmas present from Russia,' Xenia said with a smile. 'In the old tradition.'

Gawain looked back towards the front door, closed against the freeze outside. 'The lights were on in the house over the way.'

'Fitzroy House? Ingrid Redmain must be back.' Xenia looked away. 'Shall we have something to eat?'

'You should make your peace with her,' Gawain said as he took off his coat. 'Apologise. It would make you feel better about her. I can tell you don't like thinking about her.'

'I don't do apologies,' Xenia said stiffly. She began to walk through to the kitchen, keeping an eye on Petrova at the edge of her vision to avoid tripping over her.

'Why not?' Gawain said, coming up behind her. 'A good apology is a noble thing. Nothing to be embarrassed by. Besides, you might discover that your guilt is completely out of proportion to your responsibility. Now that I've met Mr Redmain, I think that his first wife may even have been grateful to you for breaking the news. Perhaps you gave her an out.'

'It is certainly a possibility,' Xenia said with finality, determined not to talk about it. But Gawain's words stayed with her as she spooned out the casserole they were having for supper.

'Perhaps,' she said afterwards, as Gawain was washing up and she was boiling the kettle for her hot-water bottle, 'I will

449

see the lady tomorrow. Mrs Redmain. You're right. It's something I need to be free of.'

'Good idea,' Gawain said heartily, as though it was entirely Xenia's suggestion. 'Excellent plan.' He looked suddenly thoughtful. 'I wondered about taking another look at the old house, going around the grounds perhaps, but I don't think I will. To be honest, I'll be glad never to set eyes on it again, especially now we know its unsavoury past. I'm not an iconoclast but for once, I wouldn't be sorry if that house disappeared forever.'

'Perhaps,' Xenia said, 'we would all be better off. Good night. Sleep well!'

'I will. Good night, Xenia.'

Xenia found it hard to settle. She wandered about her bedroom, picking up family photographs, squinting through her blurred vision and trying to make out the faces of her parents. It was easier, she realised, to remember them in her mind's eye than to trust to her eyesight any longer.

She went over to the bed and lay down, closing her eyes and conjuring them up from long ago. She saw Papa, his case packed. They were all standing in front of the house, the car ready on the gravel. It was icy cold, the sky a brittle blue as if ready to crack wide open. 'I will bring back the Americans, I promise,' he'd declared. 'They'll cure Mama. They'll make everything better.'

Xenia felt a spark of hope even through the dull certainty that no one could make Mama better. *Maybe, just maybe there's a way* ... But how could there be a cure for a brain irrevocably sliced by a blade, the fibres severed forever?

'Trust me,' Papa had said, as if reading her mind. His blue eyes gazed into hers. 'I'm going to do my best.'

Even though she knew so little, Mama had realised what was happening, from the sight of the suitcase and the car on the driveway.

'No, Paul, don't go, don't leave us!' she cried, tears running down her pale face, pudgy and ill formed since her operation. She put her arms around Papa and clung to him, snivelling wretchedly.

'Natalie,' Papa said firmly, unpeeling her arms from around his coat, 'you must be brave. I won't be long. I'll be home before you know it.'

'Come back soon, won't you, Papa?' Xenia had said, pulling Mama gently away to stop her from hanging on to Papa. 'We need you here.'

'I'll be back as soon as I can.' He kissed her distractedly on the cheek. 'Promise you'll look after Mama. And stay here until I get back, do you understand?'

'Yes, yes, I promise.'

She could tell he was eager to be off, excited to be away from Charcombe Park, heading to America for goodness knows what adventures.

'Goodbye!' she cried. 'Goodbye!'

Her last sight of him was of a hand waving from the window as the little car raced off down the drive.

And we never heard from him again. He left us.

She thought of the woman on the boat so many years ago,

the one Papa had kissed that night after dinner, and how she'd realised then that his heart might one day leave them, her and Mama. He had the capacity to chase adventure, the desire to live his life to the full, and the need to be free of anything ugly and onerous.

Mama and I became a burden. When Natalie Rowe was no longer beautiful, intelligent, desirable and able to earn a small fortune, he didn't want her, or me. And that is the bitter truth.

She knew, for sure, that the heart of all her troubles was Papa leaving them.

Perhaps he felt it too. Maybe it was the house he couldn't bear. Or maybe he simply didn't love us enough.

Chapter Forty-Seven

Buttercup lay awake in the comfortable spare room in Fitzroy House. Like the rest of Ingrid's home, it was cosy and colourful, with turquoise walls covered in paintings and thick red curtains shutting out the night.

It was tempting simply to close her eyes, forget all the torment and pain of the world outside this room, and sleep. Tomorrow, perhaps, things would be better.

No. They'll never be the same again.

She had left the house, and left Charles. She hadn't switched on her telephone but it might already be jammed with texts and calls demanding to know her whereabouts and insisting she return.

I don't think he'll guess where I've gone.

How strange it was to have been so suspicious of Ingrid for so long – to have hated her in some ways – and to be in her house, sleeping in one of her bedrooms.

They had talked until late, sharing stories of what it was like to be married to the same man. They shook their heads over the similarities of what they had experienced.

'Except that maybe you had it worse than I did,' mused Ingrid. 'I think perhaps he was trying to ensure that you'd never leave him in the way that I did.'

'But the irony is that the more he tried to lock me in, the more he brought about what he most feared.' Buttercup shook her head. 'I loved him. I would have given up so much for him – but I couldn't give up my dream of becoming a mother. That was too big a price to pay.'

'Do you know what? I don't even know why Charles had such a bee in his bonnet about it. He would probably have enjoyed fatherhood much more this time round, with his career so established and more time to spend at home.' Ingrid smiled ruefully. 'But we'll never know.'

Buttercup wondered what Charles was doing at this moment. She had fresh and vivid knowledge of how vicious he could be when he felt crossed, and she thought of the shards of photographs falling through her fingers.

There are pictures of my father up at the house. Some precious things that belonged to Mum. Charles knows what they mean to me.

She had visions of him smashing her mother's watch with a hammer, along with the pieces of jewellery given to mark special occasions: her twenty-first birthday and her graduation. Perhaps at this moment he was ripping the treasured photograph of her father out of its silver frame and tearing it to shreds.

I know he's capable of it. He would know just how much it would hurt me.

She had been tossing and turning for what felt like hours

when she suddenly sat up in bed. She had told Ingrid she would wait but she had the strongest feeling that she couldn't and must not wait to get up to the house.

I'm so stupid. I should have taken my things when I had the chance. I didn't think of it then, but I can't risk losing them.

Besides, she'd thought of something else she wanted to do there.

It was easy enough to let herself out of Ingrid's house, leaving the back door unlocked so she could get in on her return. Ingrid had lent her clothes for the morning – jeans and a jumper – and Buttercup was muffled up in her coat and scarf but the icy air was enough to take her breath away and set her fingers tingling on the first stage to numbness.

She trudged as quietly as she could along the path, her boots crackling on the frosted snowy gravel. The light from the fanlight over the door illuminated the clouds of her breath and for a moment she wondered if she should give this all up and go back to where she was safe and warm, far from Charles's rage.

No. I've started. I'll be fine. I'm not going to be beaten.

She got to the gates at the end of the lane and stopped. It was silent. The darkened houses were still with no signs of life. No cars were on the road. The gates were closed, the party over. Buttercup thought about all the times she had driven carelessly through these gates, never thinking about their real purpose. They were merely decorative; and they might shut other people out, but they were always open to her, whenever she chose. They loomed above her, forbidding and grand. The world behind here is exclusive and special, they seemed to say. And it is no longer your world.

She tapped her code into the keypad, her fingers clumsy with cold, and for a moment she thought they were not going to open. Had Charles changed the code already? But then they began their silent swing inwards, opening in that eerie way as if by themselves, and she walked on through. Ahead was the house, as silent as the rest, and dark too. She realised she had never seen the house this way, all its windows unlit so that the glass reflected the moonlight like hundreds of little diamonds. It had never looked so uninhabited before.

Charles must be in there all alone. Carol and Steve will be in their cottage.

For a moment, she felt sorry for him and then sad. All their hope and love had come to this, in the end: alone in a huge, deserted house, without the family it needed, without anything but the memories of all the pain and suffering that had taken place within its walls.

It's not going to get me. I'm not going to be a victim too.

She walked up the driveway, keeping to the shadows. No doubt the security cameras were on, the alarms might be set as well. She would deal with that as she came across it. As it was, she still had her door keys and she still knew the codes. No one would be watching the cameras' footage and if they saw her at some point in the future, what did it matter?

I'm not going to think about the future.

Dark things lay ahead, she knew that. Confrontations, battles, divorce. But for the time being she was going to con-

centrate on rescuing her treasures, then she would happily . . .
what did Gawain say? *Shake the dust of the place from my
feet.* Yes. That was it.

On reaching the house, she skirted the turning circle at the
front, making sure to keep away from the lights that were
triggered by motion sensors. She didn't need them tonight –
the moon was shining hard and bright above, making the
windows glow with pearly grey adularescence. Everything
was quiet.

Tippi, she thought suddenly. *How could I have forgotten
her? I hope she doesn't bark when I come in. And I'll take
her with me. Charles can never look after her on his own,
not if Carol and Steve are leaving.*

That thought made her look instinctively in the direction
of Carol and Steve's cottage. It, too, was in darkness, though
grey smoke rose wispily from the chimney showing the fire
was still lit. But it was half past one at night. They would
probably be asleep.

Buttercup made her way around the side of the house and
in through the courtyard gate, the cobbles slippery with
frozen snow. She was glad that Milky was safely at the Herberts' yard. The back door was locked but the bolts were not
shot into place and her key opened it. She expected the
alarms – usually set at night when everyone had retired – to
start beeping and was all ready to tap in her code before they
went off, but there was nothing. Tippi woke from her bed in
the boot room as Buttercup came in, clambered to her feet
and was nuzzling her, tail wagging furiously.

'Good girl, Tippi, good girl. Lovely to see you too,'

whispered Buttercup, rubbing Tippi's ears. 'Where's your master, eh? Has he gone to sleep?'

As her eyes grew accustomed to the gloom in the kitchen, she saw that it was pristine. The caterers had cleared away all signs of the Christmas party. Everything looked completely normal and, for a moment, she wondered if it had all been a dream.

The normality of the scene soothed her nerves and renewed her courage.

'Wait here, good girl,' she said to Tippi and slipped off her wellington boots. In her socks, she moved quietly across to the door and let herself out into the hall. The marble busts looked eerie in the moonlight that fell in grey beams through the windows, more alive than they ever looked in the day. Two Christmas trees stood on opposite sides, dangling with ornaments, their lights off, and swathes of holly and ivy were still festooned about. Buttercup walked carefully across the marble floor, skidding slightly in her socks on the slippery surface, and stood at the bottom of the staircase that rose into the shadows above.

Where is Charles?

That was the question. If he was asleep in the bedroom, she would have to tiptoe past him to get her things. If he was awake, he could be anywhere. The thought made her insides flutter nervously and the tips of her fingers prickle.

Come on. What's the worst that can happen? A bit of shouting, that's all. He won't hurt me, I won't let him.

She went quickly up the stairs, soundless on the carpet, and along the corridor to their bedroom. Outside, she stopped and listened, trying to keep her breathing calm although her heart was racing. There was no sound from inside, and slowly, she opened the door as quietly as she could. The room, she saw at once, was empty: the curtains weren't closed but hung open so that the park lay in dark beauty before her, lit by the frosty moon. To her surprise, a window was open, which explained the chill in the air. The bed was empty, still perfectly made from that morning. Buttercup went swiftly to the window and shut it, closing out the frigid breeze.

Letting out a sigh of relief, she went to her side of the bed and switched on her reading light. The golden glow was comforting, and she opened her bedside drawer to take out some of her things: bits of jewellery, notebooks, a keepsake or two. She was glad they were still safely there, gathered them quickly up and put them on the bed along with the family photographs in their silver frames that stood on the shelf near the bed. Then she went to the dressing table and opened her jewellery box, taking out her favourite pieces and the sentimental items, leaving the showy gifts that Charles had given her but she hadn't particularly liked, such as the flashy necklace of diamonds and emeralds that had made her think of trophy wives and slave collars, because it was the sort of present a rich man gave to display his wealth around his woman's neck.

She added her bits and pieces to the pile on the bed, then opened up the small bag she'd packed earlier and put in all her keepsakes. She grabbed her wash-bag from the bathroom and filled it with her toothbrush and face creams.

When she'd collected everything she thought she might need in the next few days, she stuffed it into the bag, then looked around at the room. So much still remained but she couldn't carry much.

I'll get it all later. Carol will pack it up for me, I'm sure.

Then she stepped quietly out into the hall, dark after the moonlit bedroom, looking up and down for any signs of Charles. It was silent apart from the tick of the grandfather clock, and she wondered where he was. Had he made a sudden trip to London, perhaps? Maybe he and Elaine were deep in conference somewhere to work out their next move.

Never mind them. Best get on with the other thing I came here to do.

She walked lightly down the hall, her bag strap over her shoulder, and as she passed the Redmain room, she noticed that the door was ajar and a light was on inside. Gasping, she pressed herself against the wall, thinking that Charles must be in there, but as she waited, frozen, her heart pounding with fear, she could hear nothing from inside and eventually she dared to edge to the door and peep through the gap.

There was no one in the room, but someone had been in there. The carefully curated display cases were smashed; the contents, along with shards of glass, were scattered all over the room. The commemorative chair had been knocked off its dais and lay on its side on the floor. The plates and everything else mounted on the wall had been ripped off, broken or discarded. The bust of Captain Redmain was on the floor, its nose broken off and the edges of his tricorn hat shattered. Charles's private museum had been comprehensively wrecked.

'Oh my goodness,' breathed Buttercup, taking it all in. 'Oh, Charles.'

She felt a rush of real fear. If Charles had destroyed this, his most precious collection, what else might he be in the mood to destroy?

Maybe he feels as though Captain Redmain has betrayed him, after everything he's done for him – rebuilding his house, taking his name, tending to his possessions . . .

She shivered with fear. *Where is he?*

Buttercup turned and headed back down the corridor to the next door, Charles's study. Listening hard at the door and seeing no light around it, she opened it slowly and found it also empty, also with a window open, letting in the icy air from outside. She went over and closed it, before turning to Charles's desk. He had told her that he had Ingrid's family albums in his study, and the desk was the most obvious place. Would he have locked the drawers? She stood behind it, in front of the chair, and realised that she had never been on this side of the desk before. In fact, she had hardly ever come into this room. Here was where Charles worked, and she had no knowledge of that side of his life. He kept it private. He assumed she had no interest.

She switched on the lamp, bent down and pulled at a drawer. It opened smoothly. Inside it was neatly arranged: pens, pencils, a stapler, a charger . . . everything perfectly laid out.

Typical Charles.

It was his obsession with order and tidiness that made what had happened in the Redmain room so disturbing. It was hard to believe that anyone who loathed chaos and mess the way Charles did could have left the room in that state.

Pulling open a few more drawers, she inspected the contents as well as she could without moving anything. In the bottom right-hand drawer she found what she was looking for: a small pile of three albums, one extremely old, another less so and a modern one. She knew what they were as soon as she saw them, but she opened one anyway to check. The first thing she saw was a wedding photo and she realised to her surprise that it was Charles, young and fair, smiling broadly with a young Ingrid on his arm in her long white dress and long trailing veil. They looked so happy and certain of themselves as they gazed into the camera, unaware of the rancour and grief ahead.

Buttercup snapped it shut, pushed the albums into her bag and switched off the lamp, blinking in the sudden darkness.

I'll go back downstairs, get Tippi and we'll be off.

The end of all this was finally in sight.

She heard a distant bang, like a muffled explosion, and instantly froze, listening for more. Nothing came. The house was silent, except for the ticking of clocks and a faint buzz – the electrical system, probably. Wondering if she'd imagined the bang, she headed back into the hallway. She was hurrying down the stairs when she heard another sound, similar to the first but much closer. It was a menacing sound: the pop of an explosion but somehow soft. Not like a firework but like the whoosh of a hot-air balloon or something igniting . . .

Buttercup felt a sudden, instinctive certainty that something was very wrong. Why were the windows open and the alarms off? Why was Charles not here?

The sound had come from near the kitchen, where a doorway led down stone steps to the cellar. She padded towards it, her eyes wide with apprehension. The door was open and she could hear a sinister sound from below, like a threatening whisper with accompanying cracks and creaks. The cellar was where the boilers were housed, so it always gave off a musty warmth, but the heat coming from below was more intense than usual.

Is there something wrong with the boiler?

She dropped her bag at the entrance and went cautiously down the stairs, turning on the light in the first underground room as she went past the switch. It looked quite normal. She moved on into the next room. The temperature was rising, the blowing whisper growing louder. As she turned the corner to the next room, she saw it in the room beyond that, registering the implications in one appalled instant.

She could see a curtain of bright, burning yellow and sheets of jagged, rolling flame whipping up the walls of the furthest cellar.

'Oh my God!' she shouted. Her eyes fell on a saucer with a candle in it, sitting right in front of her in the middle of the room. The candle was almost burned out, the flame feeding on the wick gyrating wildly as it reached the end. Around the candle was a strangely reflective substance, like dark, rainbowed glass, shining in the candlelight. Buttercup pulled in a horrified gasp as she realised that she was looking at a plateful of petrol and a flame about to meet it. Just as she understood what it was, the last bit of wax collapsed and the burning wick fell into the liquid. A massive sheet of flame whoomped upwards and outwards all at the same time, filling half the room with fire.

Buttercup turned and ran as fast as she could, full of the energy of panic. She put everything she had into reaching the stairs and running up, and yet time seemed to be moving painfully slowly, her legs going at half speed while the ravening flame chased her up and out of the cellar. Panting, her chest burning, she reached the top, pushed herself up and out of the door, and slammed it behind her. The house, she realised, was full of open windows, draughts to feed flames and draw them upwards. The air of the hall was icy and moving, the ornaments on the Christmas trees swaying eerily in the breeze.

I have to get out, get help, the house is going to burn down! The alarms must be off! I bet the whole thing has been disabled – the sprinklers, the alert to the fire service. Oh my God, it's going to burn! I have to dial 999.

Her hands went to her pocket. The mobile phone wasn't there and she had an instant picture of it lying by the bedside in Ingrid's house.

Shit.

She picked up her bag, slung the strap over her head and headed for the landline in the drawing room, running as fast as she could across the marble floor. Then to her horror, the floor seemed to disappear from under her as her slippery socks lost their grip. She felt everything turn the wrong way, her head went down, crashed on the marble floor and she sensed the world vanishing as she disappeared into darkness.

Chapter Forty-Eight

Xenia woke with a start, gasping suddenly as if for air after a period under water. She blinked into the darkness, feeling her shock subside. Something had disturbed her.

She had, she realised, fallen asleep on top of the covers of her bed, in her clothes. She groaned slightly as she moved herself, feeling the stiffness in her limbs as she tried to swing her legs over the side of the bed. As she sat on the bedside, waiting for the feeling to return to her shoulders, she became aware of a strange light in the room. Turning, she saw to her horror the awful sight of flames in the corner of her bedroom, sharp and crisp as they flickered upwards, licking the walls and the curtains.

She went to scream, a trembling croak coming out of her dry throat, but then realised that the flames were not actually burning anything. The wall and the curtains were untouched even though the red and yellow fire was burning hard against them. No heat emanated from them.

It's a hallucination. I don't need to be afraid. It's a mirage.

And yet, they looked so real, so terrifyingly present – a fire, in her room.

I must stay calm, she thought. Lately she had begun to notice strange lights in her vision: sparks, flashes, waving lights. This must be an extension of that; another marker of her age and the degeneration of her body, something else to torment her, another challenge to deal with. *You're only imagining them. They will disappear*, she told herself, fighting to keep control of her fear.

The hallucination grew stronger, the flame wall larger and more menacing. Though she knew that the fire wasn't real, she couldn't keep the panic from building in her chest. She got off the bed and stumbled to the window, not wanting to look at the false fire any longer. There, far away, over the wall and across the park, was Charcombe, its dark chimneys reaching up into the air, its many windows reflecting the white of the moon.

Except . . .

She squinted. There was something strange about the house.

Oh, my eyes. I don't know what I'm seeing any more.

There was more light at the upper windows than the reflection of the moon, and it was gold and orange, coming from deep within the house.

What on earth is it?

She felt a clammy sensation of fear creeping over her. She knew that something was wrong.

No. It's a mirage. More illusory fire. Nothing.

She turned her back on it and walked away.

*

Downstairs in the kitchen, she decided to make a cup of tea to calm her nerves and give her something ordinary and everyday to do. When she returned to her bedroom, she was sure that the hallucination would be gone. The fire would have disappeared.

The kettle on the stove began to hiss as the water within started to heat. She couldn't shake the morbid feeling that the fire had brought to her. She wasn't sure if she could stand tormenting visions like these. She would have to talk to the doctor about them. *The strangeness of the house, though*. The problems with her sight were always in her immediate vision, not far away like that. She could still focus quite well on the remote distance.

Impelled by a need she couldn't identify, Xenia walked out of the kitchen, along the hall and to the front door. Picking up her coat and scarf and slipping on her boots, she opened the door and went out into the bitterly cold darkness. It was slippery and she went carefully, placing one foot slowly ahead of the other until she'd reached the end of the path. On the lane, she walked in the middle where it was least icy, making her way up towards the gates of the house. They were shut, high and forbidding, barring the way to Charcombe Park.

Xenia stood outside them, screwing up her eyes to try and see more clearly. Then, squinting, she made out a dark cloud of smoke in the distance, a red slash across the top of the house. It was not a vision after all.

She gasped and turned, trying to hurry on the lane but fearful of tripping over the potholes and stones on the surface of the road. She couldn't go fast. Her heart pounded and her breath came in short, urgent pants.

It's burning! Burning! Charcombe is alight! I have to get help.

Just then, Gawain came running out, a coat thrown on over his pyjamas. 'Xenia!' he called, horror over his face.

'The house is on fire!' she cried. 'We must call for help!'

He was with her in a moment, holding her steady as she stumbled on the icy lane, his eyes drawn to the ominous glow over the great house, the awful black smoke sitting above in the inky sky, puffing upwards as the fire grew.

Ingrid Redmain came out into the road in a dressing gown and wellington boots, her dark hair askew, panic all over her face. 'Oh my God!' she shouted. 'The house! I've called for help. But Buttercup was in my spare room, and now she's gone!'

'What?' Gawain's gaze flew back to the big house and the inferno within it. 'Could she be up there?'

'She must be.' Ingrid was pale and panicked.

Gawain started running toward the gates. 'I'm going up there.' He shouted to Ingrid, 'What's the code for the gates?'

'1805 – the Battle of Trafalgar!' Ingrid started running back to her house. 'I'll get my keys and drive us there, it'll be quicker.'

Gawain hadn't waited, he was already at the gates, tapping in the code. Xenia watched him sprint through them and disappear into the darkness. A moment later, Ingrid's car roared out of the driveway and through the open gates towards the house.

The old woman stared shakily at the awful sight: an ancient house in flames, being consumed by fire as they watched. 'The house, the house is burning.'

She felt filled by wildness, but it was hard to tell if it was elation or despair.

Chapter Forty-Nine

Buttercup groaned and blinked on the floor of the marble hall. She could hear the sound of crackling and roaring all around, the splintering of wood and the pop of exploding glass. And she could feel heat: intense and terrible heat, not far away.

But she was moving, being pulled across the floor, her bag thumping into her and then sliding away. Someone was dragging her towards the front of the hall. She looked behind her and saw vicious flames emerging from the cellar door, now a blazing rectangle. As she watched, they climbed higher, rolling out across the ceiling and into the hall.

Oh no, she thought in a daze. Her head was thudding with a crashing pain, her nose, mouth and throat were full of an acrid, bitter taste and the thick smell of smoke. The house was being eaten by the fire, devoured, releasing this foul odour as it was consumed. *I didn't get help, I didn't phone.*

She looked forward to the dark shape at her feet, holding her, dragging her along.

Who is it? Where are we going?

It was, at least, away from the fire. She closed her eyes, unutterably weak and tired, desiring only to be asleep. Then she felt a prickly roughness under her neck, unpleasant enough to jolt her back to wakefulness.

I'm lying on the doormat.

A huge stretch of rough matting, spiky as a field of small thorns, lay in front of the door and she was on it. She heard the great bolts being thrown back, the large key being turned, and slowly the door was opened.

Icy air gushed over her but at the same moment there was a mighty whoosh as the flames inside were drawn outwards to the open door. Buttercup opened her eyes and saw a wave of flame cruising rapidly outwards across the ornate plaster-work of the hall ceiling, engulfing the ceiling rose and the top of the lamp.

The house will be destroyed, she thought dimly. *Perhaps it will take me with it.*

She was alone, she knew that. Whoever had pulled her to the front door had gone, leaving her to make her own way out of the building.

Get up, she told herself. *Get up and get out!*

But she couldn't move. There was no strength in her to allow the movement of her limbs. She felt as if every ounce of power had been drained out of her, leaving her body just a heavy object, of no use at all.

Perhaps the house doesn't want me to leave, she thought, and almost laughed grimly to herself. *It knew I was going forever. It pulled me back and decided to keep me here.* She closed her eyes. *There's something poetic in that, I think.*

A voice seemed to pierce her consciousness, distant but getting closer.

'Buttercup! Buttercup – where are you?'

Was that Charles's voice? It must be – who else could it be?

'Buttercup? Buttercup!'

'I'm here,' she said but her voice came out croaky, barely audible. The mixture of cold air and acrid smoke had stifled it. 'Help me. Charles! I'm here.'

'Buttercup.' The voice was closer. A presence was beside her, panting and panicked. 'I'm here.'

'Charles?' she said, confused.

'No. Gawain. Come on, you have to stand up.' Strong hands grabbed her arms and started to lift her up. 'What's this bloody bag you're wearing? Let's get it off you. Christ, it's hot.' He choked and coughed as he tried to pull her bag over her head.

'No, no!' she protested weakly, trying to push the hands away. 'I have to keep it.' She winced. 'My head!'

'You're hurt. Come on, we have to get out of here, the fire . . .' He didn't need to say more, she could feel the intense heat around her, and the brightness as it took hold on the ceiling. The beams were creaking loudly. She knew that it would not be long before things began to collapse. 'Come on,' Gawain urged, fearful. He coughed again, his eyes streaming with the acrid smoke. 'We have to get out of here.'

'Hurry up!' cried a terrified voice outside. 'It's going to cave!'

'Stay there, Ingrid!' yelled Gawain. 'We're coming!'

He was lifting her to her feet. Her weight shifted, she was

upright. One strong arm was round her waist, the other holding the hand of the arm across his shoulders.

'Let's go,' he said, his voice hoarse with the smoke. 'Off we go, one, two, three. Hop along with me.'

They began to move away from the heat and light, out into the darkness through the front door. Never had cold seemed so welcoming.

Suddenly, a warm presence was beside her, nuzzling her hand, whining.

'Tippi,' she said. 'Thank God you're all right. Someone must have let you out.'

'Let's keep going,' said Gawain in a coaxing tone. 'I don't think we've gone far enough yet.'

They went forward, Buttercup limping, Tippi beside them, her tail down as she stuck close.

The house was fully alight around them, turning the night sky around it to velvety blue tinged with orange, like an opal. There was a huge crash as something collapsed into the interior.

Ingrid came rushing up, relief all over her face. 'Thank God you're all right! What happened? What on earth were you doing up here?'

Buttercup looked back over her shoulder at the house. 'It's going,' she said.

'Where's your husband?' Gawain asked urgently. 'Could he still be inside?'

'Maybe. He dragged me to the front door, I think. Then he vanished.'

'Listen!' cried Ingrid. Sirens sounded distantly on the night air.

'They're coming,' Gawain said, his voice full of relief.

Ingrid started to run across the gravel to her car, which stood haphazardly, the doors still open. 'I'm going down to make sure the gates are open!'

Gawain tightened his grip on Buttercup. 'We'll tell them to look for your husband.'

'Stop,' Buttercup said, as he pulled her further away from the house. 'I want to look.'

They both looked at the awful yet majestic sight of the old house in flames. It seemed that all that remained was a facade, the front silhouetted against the orange and gold glow within, the smoke billowing up and turned pink and yellow by the fire, like some kind of extraordinary sunset.

'It's all over,' Buttercup said, almost awed.

'Purged by the flames,' Gawain said quietly.

The sirens grew louder and a moment later two red fire appliances, lights flashing, came racing up the drive. Gawain pulled Buttercup off the drive and out of their way so that the huge vehicles could rush past. They came to a halt in front of the house and at once the fire crews were out, releasing hoses and setting the ladders to tower over the house.

'Wait here,' Gawain said, letting go of her. 'Can you stand on your own?'

'Yes.' Buttercup put her weight on her uninjured foot. 'I'm fine.'

'I'm going to tell them that Charles may be inside. I'll be back in a moment.'

Buttercup stood, Tippi nestling close alongside her, and watched as Gawain went back up the drive towards the house.

The firemen were already valiantly fighting the flames.

It's no good, Buttercup thought. *It's all over. It's gone.*

Chapter Fifty

Buttercup sat shivering in Ingrid's kitchen. The old lady was there too, and Ingrid was constantly on the move, pouring cups of tea or making phone calls, trying to see what was happening at the house. Everyone was pale and drawn, the mood one of disbelieving shock.

'It's so awful,' Ingrid was saying. 'That beautiful house, it's a historic building! It's just dreadful. Think what will be lost! It's irreplaceable – and your things, Buttercup!'

'That doesn't matter,' Buttercup said, her voice flat. 'Clothes and things – they don't matter. I got my treasures.' She extended a shaking hand towards her bag and pulled the zip open. Reaching inside, she grasped the albums and put them onto the kitchen table. 'And I got these too.'

Ingrid gasped and turned startled eyes on her. 'My photo albums! You found them!'

Buttercup nodded. 'In Charles's study. I got them before the fire started.'

Ingrid's eyes filled with tears. 'Just as I was thinking that they were gone forever – here they are. Safe.' She came over,

477

put a hand on them and closed her eyes. 'I thought I'd never see them again,' she murmured. Then she bent down and flung her arms around Buttercup. 'Thank you so much. I can't believe you did that for me.'

Buttercup smiled weakly. 'There are some things you can't replace.'

Ingrid sobbed, but when she pulled away, she was smiling. 'I don't know how I can ever thank you.'

'Well . . .' Buttercup shrugged. 'I might have to occupy your spare room for a while longer, if that's all right.'

'It's yours as long as you need it.'

Buttercup looked down at the table and bit her lip. 'I just need to find out where Charles is.'

Ingrid said, 'We all do. I'm not sure what to tell the children yet. I don't want to worry them unnecessarily.'

'Let them sleep till morning before you phone them,' Xenia agreed. 'There's nothing they can do.'

Ingrid turned back to Buttercup. 'Did you see Charles there, at the house?'

Buttercup shook her head. 'I didn't see him, but I think he was there. I can only think he set the fire deliberately. In the cellar, there were saucers of paraffin or petrol or something.'

'Arson,' Ingrid said, her voice despairing. 'I can't believe he would do this, not after everything he went through with the house. He's put so much into it, not just money but his life. It's his pride and joy, I can't imagine him destroying it. And yet, it's also exactly what he would do, in a broken state of mind.'

'The Redmain room was completely destroyed,' Buttercup

told her. 'It was done with so much hatred and anger – he must have had enough in him to destroy the house as well.' She sighed. 'At least he decided to save me and to let Tippi out. Someone pulled me to safety; it must have been him.'

Ingrid frowned. 'Are you sure? If you leaving him sparked this rage, why wouldn't he want you to burn inside the house? And he has never been bothered about animals before.'

'It's a big leap from arson to murder. I don't think he's capable of that, no matter how ruthless he might have seemed at times,' Buttercup said.

'Is there anyone else who could have done it?' Xenia asked.

There was a pause and then Buttercup said softly, 'When you stop to think, there are plenty of people who had a motive to destroy Charles's most treasured possessions.'

There was a ring at the doorbell and Ingrid disappeared to answer it, returning with Gawain, still in his pyjamas and coat, his face smoke-stained and his coppery hair wild. Next to him was a policeman.

'I'm afraid it's not looking good for the house,' Gawain said, his face solemn. 'They've been battling it for over an hour, but the fire is as strong as ever. There's so much to feed it and not enough water to fight it. It's going to be completely destroyed.'

They looked at each other in quiet solemnity. All of it gone – the history, the art, and craftsmanship, the possessions, the furniture – reduced to ash in a few hours and vanished forever.

Buttercup looked over at Xenia, sudden sorrow on her

face. 'I'm so sorry. Your mother's portrait. It will have burned with all the rest.'

Xenia shrugged. 'What can we do? So much has gone. It will live on in the film and photographs, and in my mind.'

The policeman said, 'I'm sorry to disturb you all but, Mrs Redmain, I'll need to take a statement from you about what you witnessed at the house this evening. In fact' – he looked around – 'we'll need statements from all of you. I've got reinforcements on the way, so I hope it won't take too long, I realise it's late.' He looked at Buttercup. 'Mrs Redmain, if we could start with you? Let's go somewhere private.'

In the sitting room, Buttercup told the policeman everything she could remember about the events of the evening, from arriving at the house to being hoisted up and out by Gawain.

'My husband,' she said anxiously. 'Do you know where he is? Has he been found? I've called his mobile phone but it's going straight to voicemail.'

The policeman shook his head. 'There's no news. Everyone knows he has to be located so we're working on it. But can I just check again, Mrs Redmain – there was definitely someone in the house with you, but you can't be absolutely certain it was your husband?'

Buttercup shook her head. 'I never saw whoever it was. Just a back. It could have been anyone. I just assumed it was Charles.'

'You knew that the couple who worked for you . . .'

'Carol and Steve Croft.'

'Yes, the Crofts. You knew they'd gone?'

'No.' Buttercup was surprised. 'I knew they were going to hand in their notice, but not that they'd actually left.'

'Had they fallen out with your husband?'

Buttercup stared at him, not sure what to say. She didn't know where to begin. Suddenly she understood that the fire was not simply about the burning up of the house, but about everything that had gone before, right back to the miscarriage.

No, even before that.

It was about all of them, and their various links to the same place, a beautiful house where they had all, in their different ways, belonged at one time or another.

'No,' she said slowly. 'They hadn't exactly fallen out with him. But I knew that they'd had enough and intended to go.'

'But you were staying here last night, with Mr Redmain's ex-wife.'

'Yes, that's true. I was. My husband and I had had a row, during our party.' She looked at the policeman. 'I'm afraid it very much looks as if my husband set the fire. I still find it very hard to believe he'd destroy the house he loved so much, but what other explanation is there?'

He looked at her meaningfully. 'There was plenty of time for anyone to have set it up.'

'I don't know who else would have wanted to do such a thing.'

'We're keeping our minds open at this point,' the policeman said portentously.

She was filled with terrible frustration that the police might waste their time looking for other suspects. 'Just find my husband!' she said with a trembling voice. 'I'm worried to death about him – he might have been trapped in that awful inferno! We have to know where he is and what's happened to him. Then we can worry about the blessed house.'

They all gave statements and at last, as dawn was breaking, the police left. The smell of smoke was thick in the air, but the flames were dying down with the arrival of the morning and the efforts of the fire service. The village was waking up to the news; the shock was almost palpable.

Gawain had taken Xenia home, helping her gently out across the icy road to her own house. 'I'll come back later,' he said to Buttercup before he went. 'Get some rest if you can.'

Ingrid urged Buttercup to go to bed but she refused. 'I can't,' she said flatly. She didn't even want to shower: the smoke in her clothes and hair somehow kept her connected to the house. It wasn't over yet and she didn't it want it to be, because that might mean she had to accept something awful and final that she didn't want to think about.

At 6 a.m., sitting in Ingrid's kitchen, she called Elaine from the landline.

'Mrs R?' Elaine sounded wary, obviously recalling the recent spikiness between them. 'Is everything okay?'

'Elaine, I've got bad news.' She explained briefly. 'Do you have any idea where Charles is?' Ideas and theories had been whirling round her head all night, and she'd come up with various scenarios for where Charles might be, which included him fleeing to London or abroad.

'Sorry, what?' Elaine sounded dazed, disbelieving.

'I know it's a lot to take in, but the important thing right now is finding Charles. No one has seen him since about one thirty this morning. Has he arrived in London or made any travel arrangements? I didn't see his car last night, but it might have been in the garage.'

Elaine's voice was croaky. 'I have no idea where he is. I thought he was at the house, what with the party and everything. I wasn't expecting to hear any different. He hasn't been in touch at all. He might be at the flat – I'll check, but he'd usually let me know, and he hasn't asked me to make any travel arrangements. He always has his passport on him, though.' She sounded fearful. 'Do they think he didn't get out?'

'No one knows. We're all worried sick. Please ring at once if you hear anything – and the police might be in touch as well.'

Buttercup finished the call. She turned anxious eyes to Ingrid, who was making strong coffee.

'That's not a good sign,' Ingrid said. They both knew that Elaine was the walking encyclopaedia of information about Charles. What she didn't know, only Charles himself would know. The two women exchanged sorrowful looks.

'Whatever he did to us,' Buttercup said quietly, 'I would never wish harm on him.'

'Nor me.' Ingrid shook her head sadly.

They stared at each other, reading in one another's eyes what they were both thinking.

'He destroyed the house and . . . *killed himself*?' Buttercup hadn't considered this before. She'd assumed he must have got out, gone somewhere – or else been caught inadvertently in the flames. Horror washed over her. 'No!'

'It looks like the only possible answer if he doesn't turn up soon. If he were going to destroy Charcombe, then I think he would have destroyed himself too. It was like some kind of final act – wrecking the Redmain room, then razing the house. He loves it so much, I don't think he could stand destroying it and carrying on.'

Buttercup stared, numb with shock. It seemed the only answer and yet it was still impossible to accept it. Yesterday, Charles had been full of energy, anger, spite and a seemingly implacable desire either to force Buttercup to stay with him, or to punish her for going. How could he have moved to the decision to kill himself? She had a flash of memory: Charles's face, frozen, his eyes blank and glassy. *Listening to that voice. What if it told him to make that final, extraordinary statement of rejection? If it said, better dead than disgraced?* 'Maybe you're right,' she said in a small voice. 'He was losing me, he'd lost the hero he revered. Maybe there's more to it we don't even know about, things that contributed to pushing him over the edge.'

Ingrid nodded, solemn. 'But at least he saved you rather than let you burn too. That's something.'

Buttercup looked at the window. It was still dark outside but there was a grey quality to it, as though full daylight was not too far off.

'I don't know if it's worth going to bed,' Ingrid said, gazing outside. 'I'll need to phone the children soon and let them know. Lots of their things were in the house. They'll all be gone. I just wish I knew what to tell them about Charles. I'm afraid I'm going to have to prepare them for the worst.'

Buttercup sighed, overwhelmed and utterly exhausted. 'I still feel so bewildered. I'm expecting my phone to ring at any moment, and Charles to be on the other end, saying, "Don't be so stupid, darling, I'm fine." But I also know realistically it's not going to happen.' She turned anguished eyes to Ingrid. 'Do you think we'll ever know the truth?'

Ingrid said thoughtfully, 'If we find Charles, maybe. If not . . . I don't believe we'll ever find out what happened. It's where we go from here that counts.'

Chapter Fifty-One

Ingrid managed to persuade Buttercup to lie down, and as soon as she started climbing the stairs, she was bleary with tiredness. She stayed awake only long enough to take off her smoky clothes and climb under the covers, then she was fast asleep in one of those absolute and dreamless slumbers which pass in what seems like an instant.

She woke in the early afternoon, still groggy and wondering where she was, until the memory of everything that had happened came flooding back to her. She picked up her phone and switched it on.

A text sat in front of her eyes, and she blinked rapidly, hardly able to take it in. It was from Charles.

Come up here. I need you. Please, darling, come now.
Cx

Buttercup leapt out bed, grabbing a bathrobe from the bedroom door hook, and pulled it on, panting with shock as she ran downstairs. Ingrid was in the kitchen as Buttercup came racing in. 'Look!' she shouted. 'A text from Charles! I have to get to him right now.'

'What?' Ingrid grabbed the phone from her, and read the message. 'Good God! You're right.'

Buttercup was turning in a confused circle, trying to decide what to do, whether to get dressed or simply pull on a coat as she was, and go.

'Wait!' Ingrid held up a hand. 'Look – this text was sent last night, just after midnight. Was that before you went to the house?'

'What?' Buttercup took back the phone. The time the text was sent was clear: 12.17 a.m. 'No, I was still here then. I didn't leave until almost one.' She gazed at Ingrid. 'What does it mean?'

Ingrid looked baffled. 'He wanted you back at the house.' She frowned at Buttercup. 'You saw no sign of the fire when you went in?'

'Nothing. I heard a noise from the cellar as I came downstairs later, at about two a.m. But the fire must have been burning before then, and the candles I saw much longer.' She looked at Ingrid, frightened. 'Does this mean he wanted me there after all, and it just so happened that I went up of my own accord? Was it to talk to me, or to lure me into the fire? But then why not show himself when I arrived? And if he wanted to kill me, why go to the effort of saving me, after all that?'

Ingrid bit her lip. 'I have absolutely no idea, but you'll have to show this to the police. They need to know.'

'Yes.' She felt deflated, almost defeated. 'I'll go and get dressed.'

When she came downstairs later, fresher after a rapid shower, she found Ingrid putting on her coat in the hall.

'What's the news?' she asked quickly.

Ingrid looked up, her eyes sad. 'Nothing. The fire is out but the house is a shell. No one will be able to assess it properly for days. Still no sign of Charles, either.' Her eyes suddenly filled with tears. 'I've had to talk to the children. They're both devastated. I'm going to pick up Charlotte from school now. James is on his way back from university.' She buried her face in her hands. 'Charles might have been many things, but he was still their father and they loved him.'

'This is terrible,' Buttercup said. 'I'm so sorry.'

'We have to prepare for Charles being dead. Every hour that goes by when we don't hear from him makes it more likely that he's not coming back at all.'

They stood in solemn silence for a moment, thinking of Charles.

Ingrid shifted, picking up her car keys. 'I have to get a move on if I'm going to collect Charlotte from school and get home at a decent hour.'

'I'll look after things here,' offered Buttercup. 'Shall I get some dinner on for you both when you get back?'

'I can't pretend that won't be welcome. Just have a rootle round and see what you can come up with. I'll let you know when we're on the way home.'

*

It was comforting to explore the fridge and cupboards and make plans to cook. Buttercup realised it had been a long time since she'd been allowed such freedom; Carol had always done the cooking. She was at the stove, stirring her creation, when the front doorbell went, and she strode down the hall to answer it, wondering if it might be the police with news about Charles, but Gawain stood on the front step, muffled against the cold by his dark overcoat and scarf.

He smiled tentatively at her, his brown eyes warm. 'I've come to see if you're all right after last night.'

'Thanks, that's kind. Come in,' she said, 'it's freezing out here.'

Once they were in the warm sitting room, Gawain's heavy coat hanging in the hall, they both sat down, Gawain's expression concerned.

'Have you managed to get some sleep?'

She nodded. 'A bit.'

'Good. I wanted to say how sorry I am about all this. You've lost so much – your home, all your things . . .' His face was full of sympathy.

'Thank you.'

'I can't begin to understand what you're going through. Any news on your husband?'

'Not yet. But I found a text from him.'

'What?' Gawain exclaimed, astonished. 'He's texted you?'

'It's not what you think.' She explained the timings. 'So we still haven't heard from him since last night. I'm trying to take it in – that maybe, after all, he wanted me to be there when the house burned.' Anguish made her shoulders slump.

'It's just so hard to believe he would actually have wanted to go that far, maybe even kill us both.'

'But in the end, he couldn't go through with it. In the end, he saved you.'

'No.' Buttercup fixed him with a candid gaze, staring at his frank, open face with the clear brown eyes, the mess of thick coppery hair. He made her think of a red setter, or a soft bear – strokeable but strong. '*You* saved my life.'

'Well . . .' Gawain looked embarrassed, suddenly unable to meet her eyes. 'I did what anyone would do in the circumstances. I can't pretend it was particularly brave, I'm afraid.'

'That's not true,' Buttercup said firmly. 'Not everyone runs into a burning building. If you hadn't come in to see what was happening, there's no guarantee I would have made it out. So I mean it. Thank you.' She smiled at him.

'I would do it a hundred times out of a hundred,' he said sincerely.

Something in his brown eyes made her feel awkward and she dropped her gaze. She spoke quickly to cover her awkwardness. 'So . . . you're going back home?'

'That's right. Back to London. I've got a little flat in Bloomsbury, and a very small cottage on the coast in Hastings. The two places balance me out and keep me sane. But it's back to the city for now. I've got work to do.' He fixed her with a solemn gaze. 'I know it's early days, but do you have any idea what you're going to do?'

Buttercup shook her head. 'I'll stay here for now, I suppose. But I don't want to impose on Ingrid for too long. It all depends what happens with . . . everything here.'

He nodded, understanding.

'I could probably go to our London flat for a while.'

Gawain pulled out his wallet and fished out a business card. 'Here are my details. If you need me at any time, just call or email. I mean it.'

'You're very kind.'

He smiled at her, then stood up. 'Right, I'm off. Goodbye. And I hope to hear good news about your husband.'

Buttercup was expecting Ingrid home with Charlotte when the police arrived to go back over her statements with her. She went carefully back through everything she had said to the two officers, a man and a woman.

'That's all correct,' she said when they'd been through it all. 'The only thing to add is that my husband texted me last night – I only found it today.'

The officers examined the text with interest, noting down the new details. 'You say you didn't see this? It's coincidence that you decided to go up to the house at almost the same time as he asked you to go?'

'That's right. I wanted to get my things, like I said. I didn't see the text as my phone was switched off.'

The police officer nodded, his expression blank. After a moment, he said, 'And you requested to have your horses moved away from the house last night?'

'Yes, but I often did that,' Buttercup said quickly. 'I had them moved on Bonfire Night too, it's not unusual.'

The policeman nodded slowly. 'Right. What do you know

about all the alarm systems, sprinklers and cameras being disabled?'

'Nothing at all. I guessed they had been switched off.' Buttercup began to feel anxious. 'What are you trying to say? That I did it?'

'Elaine Richards, your husband's PA, says you've disabled the systems before. In fact, she says you switched off the entire wireless network, including the cameras, earlier this month.'

Buttercup blinked, remembering the day she had turned off the cameras, the day Gawain appeared for the first time. 'Yes, but I can explain that. And I switched it all back on again.'

'Except the cameras.' The policeman consulted his notes. 'You didn't switch them back on.'

'They were on, though, I'm sure of it. They can't have been off all that time. Someone must have put them back on again before they were switched off last night.'

'Very well.' The officers exchanged glances. 'We'll be examining all the available footage. You'd fallen out badly with your husband, hadn't you? We've had a few accounts of what went on between you, and the extremely bad terms you were on. You were going to leave him, in fact?'

'Yes, I was.'

'And he was angry about that. His assistant says he intended to cut you out of his life, restricting your access to your home and his money. You relied entirely on your husband, didn't you?'

Buttercup felt anger rising to the surface. 'This is ridiculous, I didn't set the house on fire and try to murder my husband!'

They stared at her, implacably calm. The policewoman said, 'You're the one suggesting that, Mrs Redmain. Not us.'

'You are suggesting it!' she protested. 'I went back to the house to get my personal items because my husband is a very vengeful man and might destroy them. But I certainly wouldn't have hurt him or the house, not even his horrible Redmain room.' She gazed at them, beseeching. 'You have to believe me. What about the text?'

'We'll be looking carefully at all the evidence,' the officer said, as unreadable as ever. 'But this is very serious. Your husband has been missing for almost twenty-four hours, with no contact and no evidence of travel or spending. It's looking very grave indeed.'

'I know that,' Buttercup said, her voice rising in a mixture of grief and outrage. 'But I had nothing to do with it. I swear that!'

Oh my God – did Charles set me up? Was that his final revenge – to get me punished for what he did?

The police officers had left and it was dark outside when Buttercup checked her emails. There was one from Carol Croft, a long outpouring of sadness and sympathy at the loss of the house and the disappearance of Charles.

We just can't believe it. We must have been the last people to see the boss after the party. We stayed to clear up and see the caterers and staff off the

premises, then we told him about handing in our notice. He took it very well, said he'd been expecting it and it was fine. He seemed completely calm. The only thing was that he said he'd like us to go that evening. We had holiday booked for Christmas in any case, and he said he wanted us to go immediately and we could come back for the rest of our things after the break. So that's what we did. Steve was glad to get away while the boss got used to the idea of us leaving. That's all we know. I just can't believe the whole house is gone, and the boss missing too . . . let me know if I can do anything at all. We've given the police our statements but we're due back for more interviews tomorrow. Maybe see you then.

Carol x

Chapter Fifty-Two

Ingrid returned late with a white-faced and teary Charlotte, and James arrived even later. Buttercup went to bed early to leave them together and not impose her presence on the family. In the morning she went out early for a long walk. The smell of smoke and ash still hung heavy in the cold air, with no rain to wash them away, and plumes of grey cloud still made their way upwards from the last of the embers inside the burned, sodden mess that was once Charcombe Park. Buttercup turned away from it and walked out over the hills, Tippi trotting beside her, not looking at the terrible mess behind the gates. She felt Charles's absence almost like a presence in itself: she was constantly aware of him, thinking about him, wondering about where he was and what had gone through his mind that last night.

What was likely was that he had set fire to the house. Whether he intended to kill himself and hurt or kill Buttercup too, or ever frame her – that was unknowable, unless Charles appeared to explain. But each hour with no contact, 'no trace of him, and it became more likely that he was dead, by accident or design.

She took a circular route around the village, skirting it across the fields, up the hill and along the woods, then back down to return from the other side. She had reached the pub and had decided to go in for a coffee before going back to Ingrid's when she saw a familiar beaten up car. As she noticed it, the door opened and Phil got out. He waved to her as he walked towards her, and she nodded back, as she snapped on Tippi's lead.

'Hi, BC. I came down to look for you.' He was his usual gruff self, his jaw thick with gingery stubble, his small blue eyes staring out from under beetling brows. 'I wanted to say how bloody sorry I am for all this. Are you okay?'

'Thanks, Phil.' To her surprise, he put out his arms and pulled her into a tight hug, before releasing her and scanning her face carefully.

'It's a bloody bad state of affairs, that's all,' he said.

Buttercup nodded. 'I'm going in for a coffee. Want to join me?'

'Sure. Why not?'

Inside, the fires were blazing and there was the comforting smell of breakfast: toast, bacon and coffee. Guests were eating over their newspapers or chatting as Buttercup and Phil found a table and ordered their drinks.

Phil stirred three sachets of sugar into his coffee and said, 'I wanted to let you know that Milky and the others are fine at the Herberts' yard. They can stay as long as you want.'

'That's good. I should think the stables are gone.'

'I'd be very surprised if they weren't, but I can't go near them right now with the police around.'

'Thank God I thought to move the horses. I can't bear to imagine what might have happened if I hadn't.' Buttercup became aware of people looking over and murmuring. 'What is everyone saying about it?'

Phil shrugged and sipped his coffee. 'The usual mad gossip and rumour after something like this. There's talk that Charles was seen in town the day of the party, and he was buying petrol in a jerry can.'

'The police didn't say anything about that!'

'They'll say nothing until there's evidence.'

'They asked me about moving the horses, and why I was up there at the house. They seemed to think I might have set the fire.' She laughed mirthlessly. 'I suppose they have to explore every possibility. Have they talked to you?'

Phil nodded. 'Yep. I told them that you usually got me to move the horses if you thought they might be disturbed, that was nothing out of the ordinary. I said I saw you leaving that night, and that the boss told me to put his car in the garage because he wasn't going anywhere. Then I went home.'

Buttercup went still, her coffee cup halfway to her mouth, and stared. Somewhere, she realised, she'd been hoping that Charles had gone – she'd imagined him driving off into some other mysterious life and a new existence. But if he'd left his car, surely now a pile of molten metal – *that beloved red car of his* – then how could he be anywhere but in the remains of the house? It was hard to envisage him setting off on foot, and surely someone would have seen him leaving the village.

'That's it then.' Her voice came out thick and tearful. 'He's gone.'

'I'm sorry, BC, I really am. I guess you can live the rest of your life now, though, right? You're okay, you got out. You don't have to worry about him treating you like he did Ingrid. You'll get his money and whatnot.'

'Phil!' she said, appalled. 'It's too soon to talk like that!'

Phil nodded, a little shame-faced. 'Sorry if I spoke out of turn. I didn't mean to offend. I'm just realistic, that's all. No one wished the boss dead, but he's gone – well, it's not all bad. That's all I'm saying.'

The conversation with Phil left a bitter taste in Buttercup's mouth. She could guess that, from the outside, it all looked convenient for her. Her marriage had been on the rocks, a bitter divorce ahead. Now she had no husband and no need for a fight.

No wonder the police want to make very sure about me.

But there's no evidence, she told herself firmly as she walked back to Fitzroy House with Tippi. Because I didn't do it.

She replayed the events of the night before last in her head, going over everything as carefully as she could. She remembered being pulled over the marble floor of the hall, carefully placed by the door and then abandoned.

Ingrid said Charles wanted to save me by putting me by the front door. But what if he was actually setting me up, making it more likely that I'd look like the fire starter. Perhaps

498

he wanted me to asphyxiate right there, looking like I'd been caught by the flames before I could escape.

No, she told herself. She didn't want to believe that. Charles had wanted to save her. Maybe he wanted her to come to the house so that he could have one last try at reconciling and when he got no reply, decided on his frightful course. He'd not expected her. She'd turned up, fallen over and he'd found her unconscious. His last act had been to get her out of the building before he'd dived back inside to burn with all that was precious to him.

Except he didn't get me out.

He must have known I'd be saved, perhaps he'd seen that help was coming, she countered herself.

That's what I want to believe. It's what I will believe.

The following day, the police told Buttercup she was free to go for the time being. The business of sifting through the remains of the house would take a long time.

Signs of Christmas were everywhere, trees glowing through windows, lights sparkling on hedges and over gables. The pub was festooned in decorations, with festive pop playing, but Buttercup hardly noticed it when she went in to say goodbye to Cathy and Wilf.

'We're all so sorry,' Cathy said, as they sat in the flat upstairs, Cathy nursing Bethany and Buttercup curled up on the sofa nearby. 'We've had lots of journalists and press people round. They're all tremendously interested in the whole thing, but we're not talking.'

'Thanks. It's pretty awful. I know people are gossiping like crazy, but if they could see Charlotte and James and what a state they're in . . . It's so rough on them.'

'Poor things.' Cathy looked down at Bethany's head and stroked the sprinkling of downy hair.

'So, now that the police don't want another statement, I'll leave them in peace. I have to let them know where I am, but they don't seem to think I was involved. I'll go to London and get some of my things from there. I need to talk to Elaine about how the business is doing without Charles and visit the lawyers too about what we can do without a body, or . . . well, you get the idea.'

'Complicated. Horrible. I'm so sorry.' Cathy put out her hand and squeezed Buttercup's, her face full of sympathy. 'Come and talk any time you like.'

There was no sign of Christmas at Ingrid's house, where there was a pile of cards not put up, no tree or decorations. They didn't have the heart to celebrate with Charles still unaccounted for.

Buttercup thanked Ingrid for everything she'd done for her, and said she was going to be on her way.

'I'm going to London for a while. Would you mind keeping Tippi for me?'

'Not at all. I love her.'

She hugged Ingrid. 'Thank you so much. I will be back.'

'You won't have a choice,' Ingrid said wryly. 'Like it or not, you'll have to come back. If Charles is dead, we're going to have an almighty mess to work out if we don't find his body. I have no idea what we do in that situation. I don't even know what it means for this house.'

'Let's think about it after Christmas,' Buttercup said. 'We all need a rest.' She smiled at Ingrid. 'Thanks for taking me in, and being so understanding.'

'Don't be silly. It was the least I could do. Thanks for returning my things to me.'

They gazed at each other, smiling. They'd only known one another a couple of days and yet it felt as though they'd been bound together for years, invisibly in each other's lives, and now they'd shared this intense and emotional experience. Their futures were intertwined as well, as they both faced a life without Charles, the one who had held all the power, pulled the strings and manipulated them both.

'We'll be all right,' Buttercup said quietly. 'It'll be tough, but we can do it. I'll make sure things are worked out fairly, if that's what has to be done. Don't worry about that.'

'I trust you. And thanks – I need to deal with the kids right now, I'm glad to be spared some worry as well.'

'Get in touch any time.'

'You too.'

'Thanks, Buttercup.'

'Thanks, Ingrid. With all my heart.'

Before she left, Buttercup walked up the drive to the house. It was a blackened ruin without a roof, its empty walls standing around mountains of charred and smoky mess. The insurance assessors would be coming soon to start sifting through it, and the police had already been looking for evidence, though it was hard to imagine what might be found in the piles of filthy ash and rubbish and half-burned timbers. Plastic crime scene tape showed where they had cordoned off areas already searched, and around the whole building were signs warning people to keep away.

It was hard to believe that this wreck had been her beautiful home. The garage and stables were reduced to a charred wreck but most of the outbuildings survived, and the Crofts' cottage was unharmed. Everything else had gone, except the beautiful bushes at the front of the house, though their strands of fairy lights had melted in the heat.

'Goodbye, Charcombe Park.' She couldn't imagine how it would ever be rebuilt. Surely it was beyond saving. And who would want to? She said more softly, 'Goodbye, Charles.'

She was sure he was here. In her heart, she was certain that he had laid the fire, and let himself perish in it too. But he had saved her first, and Tippi. For some reason, the mix of events that had come to pass had proved too toxic for him, and in his wild desire to escape it all, he had taken the house and everything in it with him.

And he as good as expunged Captain Redmain too. The chair, the sword, everything – gone forever.

'Goodbye, Charles,' she said once more. 'I hope you've found your peace.'

Then she turned and walked away.

Chapter Fifty-Three

The police knocked at Xenia's door in the cold and miserable days between Christmas and New Year. She had spent a quiet festive season, mostly alone, though Agnieska had come to drive her back to Galston to have a traditional Polish meal at her house with her and her two sons, and her mother.

'Where is your husband?' Xenia had asked.

'He's gone,' Agnieska replied. 'Back to Poland.' She shrugged. 'He was angry man and now we are divorced.'

'I see. Well, that sounds as though it was for the best then. Here, help me hand out the gifts I've brought you all.'

It was the highlight of Xenia's Christmas. It had been lovely to be in the heart of a family again, and she was more certain than ever that she wanted Agnieska to move closer to her. She began to look around for likely cottages and houses that might suit the family.

Agnieska was not there when she opened the door to the police officers, the same man and woman as before, though she had to squint to make them out. Flashes and whirls of light rushed around her vision, obscuring them. 'Yes? What is it this time?'

She had already grown more than tired of the visits to go through her statement once again, or to ask her about the history of the house – who had lived there and when and for how long. They wanted to know what she had witnessed of the behaviour of the others who lived nearby, and when she had spotted fire and smoke up at the house. She tried to tell them about her bad sight but they didn't seem to pay much attention.

'Can we please come in, Princess Arkadyoff?' the policeman asked politely.

'More questions?' Xenia sighed. 'I've told you everything I know at least twice.'

'Well, it's not quite like that this time. If you let us in, we can explain.'

They sat in the warm sitting room and the policewoman said, 'What we have to tell you, Princess, is that we've found a body.'

Xenia gasped, her hands flew to her face. 'Mr Redmain! That poor man. Where did you find it?'

The policewoman shook her head. 'No, it isn't Mr Redmain we found. The body is much older than that. Let me explain. We've been searching the grounds for any clues about the fire at the house. In the woods at the side of the property, where the undergrowth is extremely thick, past the wall, where there's a stretch of old fence, we found a car. It's been in there for a long time, many years, in fact. It looks as though the car came off the road at speed heading away from the house, broke through the fence and sped into the undergrowth where it crashed into a tree, out of sight of the road or the house. It's in a state – the roof is gone, the wheels are rotted, and it was almost completely obscured by brambles and weeds.'

She had felt the colour drain from her face as the policewoman spoke. 'It's been there a long time?'

'We estimate more than fifty years, from the make of the car.' The police officers glanced at each other. 'That's why we've come to you. The body we've found was in that car.'

Xenia was trembling. She couldn't speak.

The policeman cleared his throat. 'We removed the body yesterday for examination by forensic pathologists. That will tell us a great deal more about what happened to this person. But we wondered if you might know anything about who this is – you were living at the house around the time this car crashed, weren't you?'

Xenia nodded, hardly trusting herself to say anything even if she could. The thoughts were racing around her mind. But the one that spoke the loudest in her mind was saying: *So he never left us after all.* The officers waited while she found her voice.

'I believe it was . . . is . . . my father,' she said clearly, fighting to stay calm and controlled. 'Prince Paul Arkadyoff.'

The policewoman wrote down the name carefully. 'Your father went missing?'

Xenia nodded. 'He left us to go to America many years ago and we never heard from him again. It was winter, the road was icy, he was full of excitement to be on his way. He was always impervious to risk.'

'He must have skidded clean off the road and into the undergrowth,' supplied the policeman solemnly. 'And no one noticed the break in the fence.' He shook his head. 'Terrible.'

Xenia had closed her eyes and was remembering. 'I assumed he had taken the boat to America and then vanished. But it seems that he never caught the boat at all, or even left the village. And he's been here all this time.' Her voice caught. 'All this time, he was with us! He never left us. The house never let him leave. Another of its acts of vengeance. It caught him and kept him hidden away until it was finally destroyed.'

The police officers exchanged bemused glances, then the woman said gently, 'We wondered if you might recognise this.'

She held out a box, rotting and almost black but still recognisable as having once been velvet.

Xenia stared at it, able to see it quite clearly, though for a moment she wondered if she was hallucinating it. But she knew she wasn't, and she knew what it was. *So it is him. For sure.* She said, 'I'll tell you what should be inside. A beautiful jewel. An exquisite sapphire rimmed with diamonds and beneath it a large tear-drop pearl.'

'That's absolutely correct,' the policewoman said, surprised. 'Then you know whose it is?'

'Oh yes.' Xenia took the box and opened it carefully. The jewel lay within, the white satin filthy and speckled with mould. It glowed in the lamplight, as beautiful as ever. 'I know. It was once the property of an empress. Then it belonged to my grandmother, who gave it to me. So, yes, I know whose it is. It's mine.'

The jewel had come back to her.

I never thought I'd see it again.

It glowed in its rotting box, unchanged from the day she had last seen it.

Almost the only thing in my life that hasn't altered.

Xenia sat in her sitting room, Petrova beside her, the television playing unheeded, gazing at the jewel and remembering. She had imagined it sold by Papa for ready money to finance his life in America; money she'd assumed would have been spent on hotel and restaurant bills, in casinos and on fur coats for unscrupulous mistresses, with never a thought for Xenia and her mother and their terrible struggles at home alone.

If he hadn't taken it, I would probably have sold it years ago. Now I have it still.

And yet . . . wouldn't it have made her life easier if she had been able to afford better food and better care for Mama? Wouldn't they have been more comfortable with the money this jewel would have brought them?

What's done cannot be undone.

What made her feel peace at last was the knowledge that Papa had not left them after all. She didn't want to speculate on what might have happened to him; if he had died quickly in the accident, or if he had lingered on, alone and injured in the car, waiting for help that never came. Whatever happened, it was a long time ago and nothing could be done about it.

All those years of waiting, and waiting, and hoping . . . All the anger, resentment and despair . . . and it had been pointless. He was there all the time. He could never come back to us because he'd never gone away.

It was a strange kind of peace that she had, but it was still peace, and she was grateful for it.

Xenia was still staring at her imperial brooch, holding it close to her face to see it, when there was a knock at the door. She got up and felt her way to the front door. Opening it, she said, 'Yes?' to the blurry dark shape on the step.

'Princess,' said a soft voice, 'can you see me?'

'Is that you, Mrs Redmain?'

'That's right.'

'My eyes are bad. My sight is going, you know.'

'I know. I just came to say that I've heard about your father – that he was found on the estate. I'm so sorry.'

Xenia could hear the sympathy in her voice, and could imagine the tenderness in her face. 'You shouldn't be apologising to me, Mrs Redmain.'

'Please, call me Ingrid. And why not?'

'Because of what I did to you. I told your husband about your liaison with the jouster.' Xenia heard her voice quavering and wished she didn't sound quite so much like an old woman. 'I've regretted it ever since.'

There was a silence and then a surprisingly jolly laugh. 'Did you? I had no idea.'

'He never said . . . ?'

'Oh no, not a word. When did you tell him?'

'The week of the joust, that last summer that you held the festival.'

'My goodness! But I didn't tell Charles about Joachim until a month or so after that.' Another pause while she thought and then she said, 'So he knew all along. That would explain why he was suddenly so charming towards me in the weeks before I told him I was going. Almost a different man. I had second thoughts about leaving and if Joachim hadn't used all his powers of persuasion, I would have stayed with him. So if anything, you gave Charles and me a second chance. When it ended, it was my choice. He didn't throw me out.'

'I see.' Xenia frowned. 'Things have worked out quite oddly lately. As if nothing has been the way I thought it was.'

'It must have been a horrible shock, to find out your father had been on the property all the time.'

'Yes. It was. But also – a relief. To know at last what happened to him.'

'Yes. I understand that. I hope we will find out what happened to Charles as well.'

'Thank you for coming by, Mrs Redmain. I hope we can be friends.'

'I hope so too.'

'How is the other Mrs Redmain? Have you heard from her?'

'She's all right, I think. Staying in London for the time being. I'm sure she'll be back. Don't forget you can call on me whenever you need any help. Goodbye, Princess.'

'Goodbye, Mrs Redmain.'

*

When Xenia went up to bed that evening, she realised that it had been some time since she had been plagued with the visions of fire that had afflicted her since the night of conflagration at Charcombe. As her sight got worse, the mirages of flickering flames and shimmering lights were disappearing. They seemed to occupy the halfway house between good sight and blindness, an odd stage where the mind wasn't exactly sure what it could see and what it had imagined.

Not so different to normal life, then. And I'm changed too.

She no longer had the burden of rage and bitterness she'd carried for so much of her life. The urge to run out and attack people as they passed had entirely gone.

For the first time she had hope for the future, or at least as much of a future as she had left.

Chapter Fifty-Four

It was five months later, with London bursting into spring bloom, when Buttercup received the visit from the police that she had been both wanting and dreading. When it was over, there was only one person she wanted to talk to.

'Can you come over? Now?'

'Of course I can. I'll be right there.'

Buttercup paced around the penthouse flat, looking out over the roofs of Westminster. She was longing to be free of this place, but it was impossible to do anything with Charles's assets frozen and everything up in the air. Elaine was still working downstairs, though Rose had gone, moving on to a better job as assistant to a glamorous fashion editor. Elaine's presence made things awkward, but she was the best person to remain in charge of the day-to-day running of Charles's very complicated affairs.

Maybe I'll be free of it all soon. I can get out of this place, get somewhere that only belongs to me.

Gawain arrived half an hour later, having made the

journey down from Bloomsbury as quickly as he could. 'Are you okay?' he asked, after kissing Buttercup on the cheek.

She nodded, white-faced. 'It's Charles. They've found him.'

He hugged her. 'Oh God. I'm sorry.' He let her go and stood back to scan her face anxiously. 'How are you?'

'I'm okay. Better than I thought. Relieved. It means we can start to move on.'

'Is it definitely him?'

'They're very sure. But there will be some final checks to be certain. There's just no one else it can be. And there's been no sign of Charles since the fire. So.' She gazed at him, baffled. 'But here's the weird thing. He was in his car. In the garage. That's why it's taken so long – they were sifting the house first. The whole thing was burned to ash but they're sure that's how it was, although there's more to investigate.'

'In his car?' Gawain frowned. 'So he decided to . . . what? Set light to the house, lure you in, then gas himself in the car rather than burn in the fire?'

'I suppose that's what it looks like.' Buttercup shook her head.

Gawain thought for a moment and said, 'Maybe he didn't want to die in a fire, and who can blame him. So he hitched it up so he'd lose consciousness in the car instead. The forensics will probably show it all in time.'

'Yes.' Buttercup sighed. 'In any case, that's the end of it. It'll resolve the outstanding legal issues. He'll be declared dead, we can have an inquest, and start clearing up the mess. We'll be able to move on.' She sat down, shaking her head again. 'But I will always wonder – what did he intend to happen that night? Did he want me to die as well? Or did he want to frame me? I can't work out the answer. Both are awful.'

Gawain said softly, 'We'll never know. But you're still here, that's the important thing.'

'Yes.' Her head fell onto his shoulder. She had got in touch with Gawain just before that terrible Christmas on her own in the London flat and they had met for a drink. When he heard she was planning to drive herself to see her mother for Christmas Day, he'd said, 'Well, that's handy. Because I'm going to spend it with my folks in Norfolk. My sister has a big house there and we all descend for the festivities. So I'll drive you, and you can spend the day with your mother and then come to us. We'd love to have you.'

Buttercup had protested but she had quickly let herself be persuaded. It had been just what she had needed: a family untouched by the grief and tragedy of the last few weeks, a rambling house, nieces and nephews running about shrieking with excitement, Gawain's sister and her partner and various in-laws, none of whom seemed to mind the chaos. Gawain had worried it would be too much, but she'd loved it all, from the endless parlour games to the late-night singsongs around the piano. If she needed time alone, she simply disappeared and no one asked questions or demanded to know what she was doing and when she'd be back. It was a relief to be part of something, not its sole focus, but part of a merry, rambunctious family.

'Tell me if you want to go home,' Gawain had said, 'and I'll get you back right away.'

But she'd stayed three days and loved every minute. It had been balm for her lonely soul.

Two months later, in London, Gawain had taken her hand and said, 'I know it's soon. But I'm here for you, if you need me.'

She had gazed at him, letting him hold her hand. 'Slowly. That's all. It has to be slow.'

'Yes. I understand.'

And he'd been true to his word, not rushing her but letting things settle into an affectionate friendship as her wounds healed and she came to terms with what had happened. Now she stared at him. 'I need to see my mother,' she said. 'Will you come too?'

'Of course.'

'But I want you to meet her this time.'

'I'd be honoured.'

In the small private room in the nursing home, Buttercup's mother lay on the daybed, her leg moving restlessly as usual.

'Hello, Mum, it's me.' Buttercup kissed her and sat down next to her, Gawain joining her on the adjacent chair. 'I need to let you know that they've found Charles. It's all over. It's finished. And I want you to meet someone.' She took Gawain's hand and placed it on her mother's cool one. 'This is Gawain. He's my friend.'

Gawain leaned in and said quietly, 'Hello, Buttercup's mum.'

'Wendy,' she supplied.

He smiled at her. 'Wendy. Good to meet you. I want you

to know I'm going to look out for Buttercup. I mean, she's very good at looking after herself and everything' – he grinned at Buttercup – 'but I hope it helps to know I'm here for her as well.'

Her mother let out a small bubbling sigh and her leg moved a little faster.

'Is that the seal of approval?' he asked.

Buttercup laughed lightly. 'Well, it might be. She'll need to get to know you a bit better.'

'I'm glad she'll get the chance,' he said, staring at her meaningfully.

'So am I.' She tightened her hold on his hand. 'So am I.'

She kissed him softly and happily.

Xenia sat in a wicker chair on the terrace, listening to the sound of Agnieska's children playing in the garden. They were kicking a football about, laughing and shrieking, shouting to each other in Polish. They were equally fluent in English but they often spoke Polish when they were together. Agnieska, who was pegging out washing in the weak spring sunshine in the hope that it might dry a little, sometimes called to them in her language, and though she didn't understand a word, Xenia smiled with pleasure at the sound of their chatter.

I like listening to them talk Polish to each other. I can pretend it's Russian.

She had never learned Russian. The language of her family had been English and French in any case, and her father had never spoken Russian to her.

I'm Princess Xenia Arkadyoff, descendent of Tsars, and I can't speak a word of Russian.

It made her laugh at the way life turned out.

Since Agnieska had moved into a comfortable three-bedroom brick house just down the lane, life had become a great deal easier. Xenia's sight was almost entirely gone, so she didn't know what she'd have done without Agnieska to look after her, and the house, coming up every day to assist her in all the things she couldn't manage on her own and do the housework. When the children weren't at school, they came too, to play in the large garden or eat freshly baked cakes in the kitchen, or watch the television with Xenia, though she only listened to it these days. Her hearing, in fact, had become a great deal better since she had lost the rest of her sight, or so she thought anyway. Perhaps she was simply more tuned into sound then she had been when there was vision as well to rely on.

Now that it was spring, she looked forward to the time when the flowers would bloom so she could smell their perfume. She would ask Agnieska to take her to the graveyard to lay some on the grave where her mother's body lay and where Papa's ashes had recently been interred. It was a pleasure to be with them, even if for a short time. The joy was in knowing that at last they were together and her mother's spirit was finally at peace. The mournful cry of 'Paul, Paul . . .' had echoed around the house so many times, and now Paul was here, with her.

And I shall join them before too long.

The house that had brought them so much unhappiness

was still a ruin, but at least the discovery of human remains meant that things would be able soon to move forward. Until identification was confirmed, Charles Redmain was, officially, still alive, so Charcombe Park would remain as it was until the legal issues had been resolved. Xenia recalled how it had looked the last time she saw it: a blackened, roofless and jagged ruin with empty windows and broken walls. People often came to stare at it, drawn by its tragic air and the sense of what might have been.

'Such a shame,' they would sigh as they stood by the gates, gazing up the drive at the shell of Charcombe. 'Such a pity! What a beautiful house it must have been.'

You don't know the half of it, Xenia would think grimly. *We're better off with that house gone. I wish they would knock down what's left.*

There had been rumours that developers were interested in the plot for a new village-style retirement complex: a yoga centre and vegan organic café, gym and an art house cinema, with supported one-level apartments in tasteful shades of off-white and grey. It was the future, apparently.

We shall see. It should remain a ruin, as a warning.

But a warning of what, she never could quite decide.

'Afternoon, Princess,' said a cheerful gruff voice, and she turned in its direction.

'Oh – good afternoon,' she said politely. 'Agnieska is hanging out washing, on the other side of the hedge.'

'Okay, thanks. I'm going to surprise her. Everything all right with you?'

'Yes, thank you.'

Xenia heard the man clamber over the terrace and make his way down onto the lawn. From there he crept in silence along the small stone path that ran parallel to the hedge until he came to the gap that allowed access to the side garden where the washing line was.

'Hello, gorgeous!' She heard a squeal of delight from Agnieska and then a smacking kiss as he took her into his arms. 'How are you?'

Agnieska answered in her sing-song broken English and soon they were talking as she carried on hanging out the washing.

Xenia leaned back, the sun on her face, enjoying its warmth.

I truly am old. I never thought it would happen to me, but it has. Fancy that. I'm an old creature who likes quiet and sunshine and snoozing, like Petrova.

The voices on the other side of the hedge began to resolve themselves from a shapeless murmur into words that she could snatch and weave into sense.

'What do you mean?' she heard. It was Agnieska's voice. 'Tell me simple.'

'They found the boss at the house – up there. They know he was in the car.' The man was talking in a low tone, obviously gesturing and using sign language to enhance his spoken communication.

'*How*? You said they never find—'

'Well, don't worry, Aggie, they can't do anything. It's fine.'

'Everything else burned?'

'Yes, everything else. No evidence, no proof, no fingerprints . . .' A sigh of frustration at her incomprehension. 'You need to learn more English, love.' He spoke slowly and clearly: 'All gone. All burned.'

'But . . . what if they find garage locked from outside?'

'Stay calm. Wait and see, that's all. The lock's probably melted. I made sure the jerry can was by the door. The day he fired you, that's when he signed his own bloody warrant. And he was going to let that poor girl burn while he drove off. If I hadn't been there, she wouldn't have made it. He started the damn fire, if he burned in it, that's justice. I just made sure he didn't get away with it. Right? Understand? Justice.'

'Yes, he was bad man.' She had gone to him, Xenia could tell, as her voice grew tender. 'You were very kind, to do that for me.'

'I wasn't going to let him get away with it.' His voice was gentle, muffled as if he were nuzzling her neck. 'He wasn't going to treat you like that, and not get what he deserved. So when I saw the chance to reset the balance – I took it.'

'You made it all better,' Agnieska said. 'All better. My brave man. Thank you, thank you, Phil, you did that for me.'

'Yes, darling, I did, and I know you're going to repay me good and proper.'

Xenia, cold suddenly, could hear them kissing.

Oh, she thought. *I understand. Now I know.* Afraid, she got slowly to her feet, and felt her way inside. Suddenly she felt it was important that Agnieska and her boyfriend – Phil, was it? – did not know what she had heard.

The Redmain man wanted to burn his house with his wife

519

in it, and get away somehow. But Phil put a stop to that. What must Charles Redmain have thought when he realised he was trapped in his garage with no way out, sitting in his car and understanding it was all over?

The two cars, sixty years apart, unable to escape the boundaries of the house. The house holding them, not letting them go. Only a few were allowed to leave.

I'm safe now. I'm free and at peace. I'll forget it too. What good can it do? What's done is done.